PUBLIC COMMENT
A DEBRA WOLFSON MYSTERY

PUBLIC COMMENT
A DEBRA WOLFSON MYSTERY

S. L. JACOBS

TUCKER
DS
PRESS

Public Comment ©2026 S. L. Jacobs
All Rights Reserved.
Reproduction in whole or in part without the author's permission is strictly forbidden. This is a work of fiction. Names, characters, business, events, and incidents are the products of the author's imagination. Any resemblance to actual persons, living or dead, or actual events is purely coincidental.

Cover and Book design by Scott Ryan
Edited by David Bushman

Published in the USA by Tucker DS Press
Columbus, Ohio

Contact Information
Email: TuckerDSPress@gmail.com
Website: TuckerDSPress.com
Twitter: @FMPBooks
Instagram: @Fayettevillemafiapress

For Stephen

Now and Always

One never quite allows for the moron in our midst.
-Agatha Christie, *The Mirror Crack'd from Side to Side*

—CHAPTER 1—

Wendell's first murder was just a rehearsal.
    He would come to regard it as a perfect rehearsal, but the preparation was erratic.

He made notes and annotated the margins. He usually saved and hid his notes, or arbitrarily tore them up. He had no idea who, or on his more grammatically observant days whom, he might kill for practice purposes, which all too often mucked things up, but he was patient. And when luck teed up, he swung.

It was an evening like any other, late in the golf season and chilly, but Wendell had a good feeling about the rehearsal. Just that morning, he had been told to begin digging a new sand trap on the eleventh fairway. A new sand trap and digging were both mentioned in one of the concepts for his plans, so he was feeling pretty chipper as he pondered whether to go to one of his usual drinking spots near the university in Elmstown or to try an untested local bar in any one of a half dozen neighboring towns. Randomly, he drove toward the Triple B in nearby Rockmore. He was happy to get out of his mother's house for a few hours, and a search for the right kind of girl and the very real probability of a body-disposal dress rehearsal made him prickle.

The young woman he met was already tipsy, drunk more likely, and he was none too sober either, but she had quietly smiled at him. Wendell assessed her height and heft and deemed them useful. He motioned her to sit next to him, farther down the bar and away from the kid working the cash register. He bought them both more than a few drinks. He easily steered the conversation, hoping to hear the right answers. He did.

No, I have no family here, she said. No, I moved here from the Midwest. Yes, I don't stay anywhere too long, just make a buck along the way. Yes, I just started at that dress shop here in town. I'll probably move along in a few months. No, I don't know anyone here. No,

I've never been in Connecticut before. "Funny, huh?" she said. If she had mentioned her name, he didn't hear it, or didn't care if he had heard it. He said his name was Tony, but his name was not the point. He twinkled and feigned interest, then signaled that his car was just outside. She got up from the barstool and headed into the ladies' room. He waited a moment, left cash on the bar, and walked outside, hoping he had made it clear to anyone watching that they had not left together.

Wendell loped over to the barely off-the-lot car he was driving, a brand-new 1989 Lincoln Continental, purchased by his father right before he dropped dead just six months earlier. Wendell's mother went on and on about selling it, but in the meantime, it was at Wendell's disposal. It wasn't as cool as Wendell's used Camaro, but it was huge. He opened the passenger-side door and moved the front passenger seat forward to maximize room in the back. He slipped in behind the steering wheel and waited.

He saw the young woman poke her head through the Triple B door, and he flashed his headlights. She smiled as she slid into the front seat. Wendell was briefly distracted, but he kept his mind on task as he drove to the deserted and distant end of the nearby shopping center. He parked and used the driver's-side power control to thrust his seat forward. A moment later they were both in the cushy back seat, now as big as a sofa. Wendell pushed the ever-present pile of damp pool towels from The Club onto the roomy rear floor of the car.

Zippers, buttons, hooks, one, two, three, boom, the frolic was over.

But the serious business, well, that took a bit longer. And contrary to his plans, it was inelegant in every way. Her hair clip banged against the closed back-door window as he throttled her head against the glass, and the pounding noise gave him force and a beat. Even as he slowed the tempo and stopped, his hands remained clinched around her small neck, still crushing. In the sudden silence, he could not let go, and then still he could not let go. His fingers began to cramp. He felt a rising, surprising, and breathless panic. He finally unwound his hands, flexing them, and breathlessly gathered the used towels off the floor of the car to make room for her dead body. The back seat was suddenly very crowded with the unwieldy towels, his own long and lanky legs, and a slumped, very fresh corpse. It was a squeeze, and he would remember that, avoiding a car for the important murder he was planning. Her arm got caught in the dangly seat belt, and he had to lean over her and yank at the strap to get her fully released. Although most of her body quickly ended up on the floor of the car, her feet and arms only reluctantly followed. She landed in an unattractive squashed heap, her arms akimbo, her mouth and eyes agape.

Bare hands, seething brio, plans or no plans, whatever. However Wendell got there, he got there. He was wholly focused on getting a body, and indeed he had.

The sex was a bonus.

•••

He could not look directly at her. He would later make a note to remind himself to keep his eyes open so he could see what he was doing. He scrambled back into the far-forward front seat, only to discover that he barely fit. His knees were up against the steering column, and the steering wheel was pressed against his chest. He tried moving the seat back, but her body was jammed up against it. There they both were, impossibly wedged in a huge, well-appointed, four-door American luxury car. He was suddenly very drunk and more agitated than he would have thought. He got the door open just in time, leaned out as far as he could, and barfed all over the pavement. He hated that he was dripping with sweat and barfing. It felt like a failure, somehow.

The opened door had triggered the car's interior lights. *Not good*, he thought. *Shit.* Wendell slammed the door shut and quieted himself. He rested his head on top of the too-close steering wheel. He knew he had better get out of there and not waste time throwing up.

His rehearsal plans were proving inadequate, in no small part because he had not made provision for driving around with a dead body. He did not know what to do. He felt like he might throw up again, so he sat, wishing he had a thermos of cold water. He flexed his hands, his fingers unpleasantly recalling the crush of her neck. Wendell was shocked that he was shocked. He had not anticipated the jolt to his own mind and body from the horrific act of murdering this poor young woman in cold blood. He had watched countless murders on television and in the movies, and the murderer never threw up afterward.

I should remove my license plate, he thought. *That's what they do on TV*. He filtered through any number of license plate scenarios—girl in the trunk with no license plate, license plate in the window with dead girl in the front, ditch the license plate and ditch the girl—and in the end, he couldn't be sure he was even asking himself the right questions or thinking about the right TV show. He had led a fairly dull and conventional life so far, and four years of college, even with a double major in accounting and agriculture, had not prepared him for the level of critical thinking needed at this moment.

He realized his pants were unzipped. He got the door open just in time to throw up again.

He finished throwing up. He closed the car door. He zipped up his pants. He calmed himself.

Wendell pulled his tiny tool set from the glove compartment and retrieved a tiny screwdriver. He awkwardly unbolted the license plate from the rear bumper, bending it as he did so, and tossed the bolts and nuts into the nearby bushes, realizing, too late, that he had created an auto parts errand for himself. *Shit*, he thought. *But at least no one can ID the car*. He glanced through the car's back window, but all he saw were towels, no hand poking an accusing, lifeless finger at him.

He waited a few minutes, obsessively checking the rearview and side mirrors. Then, engine and lights on, he pulled out slowly. He was on the road.

He headed toward Somerville, driving just at the speed limit, the beat-up body in the back of the roomy car and the slightly bent license plate up front with him. The long country roads from the valley town to his town were so poorly lit that he would have seen a cop car's flashing lights from any distance, but he was more wary about a deer running across the road or any number of wild turkeys ambling about. He did not want to stop short. He did not want to stop at all.

If he could have avoided Somerville, he might have, but in every iteration of every plan, he reasoned that if he someday did score a dead body, he would have to end up somewhere, and somewhere he knew was marginally better than somewhere he did not know. Once he hit upon the ultimate body-disposal answer, it was a no-brainer. *Tremendous breakthrough*, thought Wendell. *Absolutely tremendous.*

He was within fifteen minutes of his house. Without a doubt, his mother would be home, because there was no golf or bridge game in the middle of the night. His mother, born and married to wealth, loudly complained to nearly everyone about nearly everything, but to Wendell's ear, even more so. Wendell hated her.

He drove past the driveway of the house he shared with his mother, the house right across the road from the golf course some people in Somerville still called the "new" golf course even though it had been there for more than thirty years. His parents and all the neighbors had opposed the development of the "new" country club from the very start, but no one could tell Old Farmer Appleby or his family what to do with their own property, and if the Appleby scions came back from the war and chose to sell all one hundred fifty acres of farmland to a Jewish country club, there wasn't much Wendell's parents or their neighbors could do about it. "No," said Wendell's father, "nothing to be done, at least not anymore, not since all our land-use regulations have been invalidated by some liberal court somewhere." His parents stayed loyal to the "real" country club in town, the one that had excluded Jews from the beginning. "Appropriately so," said his father. They had grumbled plenty and made sure that the first selectman and all the selectmen knew how they felt, as did all the neighbors whose property abutted the boundaries of the Appleby Farm. After all, this was Somerville, and change, for many, was a slow and unwelcome journey, like death.

But over the course of decades, convenience lubricated much of their resistance, and eventually Wendell's parents could be seen driving their golf cart right across the street onto the "new" golf course, up the cart paths to the clubhouse, and right on to the first tee. His father concluded that "It might be Jewish, but it's a damned nice course, and the Grille Room is excellent." Still, Cecil and Stella Williams could not let go of their social life, the dances, the bridge games, or women's events at the "real" club, and so they belonged to both, alternating rounds of golf between the two but firmly entrenched socially at the "real" club, where the people were more "like us."

Wendell did not understand his parents or their marriage, and his father's death had not awakened in Wendell any reflective impulse. All he knew was that his father had happily retired at an early age, that they wanted for nothing, and whether they wintered in Florida or summered in Connecticut, they played golf or bridge all day, and during the week, wherever they were, they were parked in front of the television by seven thirty watching *Columbo* or *Hill Street Blues* or some other cop show, all the while frittering away his inheritance. They played golf, ate at one Grille Room or the other, and came home to watch cop shows. And news. They loved golf and the news. They were Republicans.

As luck would have it, proximity to and membership at The Club made it easy for Wendell to be employed. He was the third guy down on the golf course maintenance staff. It drove his mother crazy, which is partly why he liked it so much, but he was happy to be able to drive a golf cart to work, or hop the porous fence, or just walk up the edge of the rough along the back nine. And he loved the big machines. Now, as he maneuvered the Lincoln Continental toward the maintenance gate to the short driveway just off the road, he felt the course's big arms hold him in a familiar hug. The gate was locked, of course, but he had a key to the padlock. He had a key to everything. *This makes so much sense*, thought Wendell. *Tremendous sense, unbelievable sense.* He scurried to unlock the gate, move the car, relock the gate, and move the car inside the course, well in and hidden. He turned the car off, flexing his fingers. He hunched over the steering wheel and took in the golf course and its familiar topography and foliage. He felt manly, making manly decisions about burying a dead girl on a golf course.

For just the briefest of moments, he pictured a cowboy hat on his head.

He stared out through the windshield. The dark night and dense verdure were not a hindrance. He could clearly see the outlines of The Turn, the little snack bar at the far edge of the course where the players finished the ninth hole, turned, and headed up the back nine. It was an abbreviated structure, slightly raised on posts, erected for the purpose of emptying and refilling the exhausted bladders of old men. He had considered its little dirt parking lot a possible burial choice, but there was always talk about knocking the building down to create a much nicer lunch-and-beverage spot, and knocking the building down would likely expose anything buried underneath. He did not concern himself with the ongoing neighbor angst that an upgraded sandwich place for the golfers might become a commercial establishment, but commercial or not, private club or not, that building had plumbing for toilets, sinks, and irrigation. Plumbing, even plumbing serviced by public water, is never a good bet when one is looking for undisturbed continuity. A burst pipe is only one winter away.

So, he kept it simple, and his rehearsal plans had long ago coalesced around any deep and permanent burial opportunity the course might provide, in the hope that the opportunity intersected with procuring a bloodless body.

Oh, happy day for Wendell! "Wendell," the general manager had said only the day before, "here are the specs for the eleventh fairway hazards work. Get to work on this." Wendell got to work, maneuvering his backhoe to dig out the slope on the eleventh fairway, well after the turn of the course but completely out of sight from the snack bar, the main clubhouse, or the houses that sat well back and buffered along the road. The specs directed him to dig, smooth, stabilize, and fill a new sand trap closer to the rough. Perfect.

Oh, happy night for Wendell! It was late enough that any adult or teen trysters were likely long gone, leaving their used condoms strewn about for him to clean up the next morning, but he hung back for a while with the car window open, listening. "Spooky," he muttered to himself. He drove slowly and without headlights toward the eleventh fairway, staying close to the edge where the turf met the rough, neatly following the perimeter of the course. It was dry and hadn't rained for several days, but even if it had, he and the other maintenance guys traversed the course on this outer edge all the time, so as not to disturb the golfers. His car tracks would not be noticed. The new bunker was close to the exterior edge, and even in the dark he could make out the hulk and bulk of the parked backhoe, which he had used all that day, as per the GM's directive to dig a new bunker, moving dirt from here to there.

Wendell parked and, using the small flashlight on his key chain, squatted baseball-catcher style to get the lay of the land at the gaze level of the average golfer, looking for the lie, the slope, the uncooperative tuft of turf. He had already spent considerable time worrying about footprints from future golfers and about cleats and golf clubs, but he paused, as any murderer would, and worried about it all again. He was particularly concerned about his fellow maintenance guys, who, like him, carried around trimmers, relentlessly plucking errant blades of grass, as if the edges of a bunker were the brows on the face of the course and needed to be shaped to give the course just the right expression.

He stood up, checked that the body was still on the back floor of his car under the towels, and shook his head at his own folly. He tried to picture the irrigation system, because he needed to stay away from it. True, the piping was horizontally consistent, but the surface was not, and even after all this time as a grounds guy, he still wasn't certain where the secondary pump was located. And although he needed to avoid the wet areas, the leaky areas, and the highly maintained areas, he had set himself an elusive quest, given that he and all the maintenance guys were paid to hover over every square inch of the severely tended acreage.

But those challenges would have to wait. He had a body to bury.

Wendell returned to the car, poked the young woman again, and with lights off, nosed his car up to the backhoe. Both the bucket and the loader were resting on the ground with the stabilizer bars in place, just as he had left them at the end of his workday. The bunker was already at the specified depth, but he wanted an additional three feet down.

Maybe four feet more. Or even five.

Whatever, he told himself. *The Club will always be The Club. This bunker will always be this bunker.*

He had heard the rumors, of course. Everyone had. The rumors are fake, he told himself and anyone who would listen. Golf was seemingly golden, and this club, the Somerville Country Club, referred to by everyone as simply The Club, was seemingly successful, with a robust membership, a great clubhouse and pool, a full calendar of golf outings every summer, and banquet facilities that had to be booked two years in advance for weddings or bar mitzvahs. It wasn't a championship course, or even as good as the university course just down the road in Elmstown, but it was, as his father said, a "damn good neighborhood course for both Jews and Gentiles." It would never be shut down, and it would never be *completely* redesigned. If a bunker failed for any reason, it was just filled with earth, leveled off, seeded, turfed, and abandoned, and a new one was created, just as he had been doing this week. Abandoning one bunker and creating another. *My plan is perfect*, he told himself.

Perfect plan or not, Wendell was a bit nervous as he climbed into the cab of the backhoe and faced the shovel end of the machine. He thought about the people sleeping in the houses on the skinny two-lane road on the other side of the course boundary, but Somerville's minimum two-acre zoning and setback rules ensured that while the houses might enjoy the grassy views offered by the golf course, they were largely buffered against any noise or intrusion. He turned on the engine. The shovel woke up and seemed to turn its long, hinged neck to get a look at who had disturbed its sleep. Wendell cranked up the gears and, with thunderous commotion, commanded the shovel to dig, dig down, in a small dry spot.

With each bucketful of excavated dirt, he nodded in triumph, and when it looked about right, he casually maneuvered the equipment around so the front-end loader attachment flatly faced the dig. He took a few moments to smooth his hair. *I got this*, he thought.

He hopped out, just the way he did every day, easily, landing with his feet already moving to the task. He walked quickly to his car, just on the other side of the backhoe. He still didn't want to look. His fingers tingled as he opened the car door. He threw the towels that had covered her from the back floor onto the front seat, and there she was, her tumbled, teased brown hair, her mouth open and sloppy, her neck red and bruised. An hour ago, she had been cute enough to hustle in a bar, but now she was just a mess, her eyes wide, terrified, and smeared with black makeup and only one of her earrings still hanging. He briefly wondered whether dead people leak, and if so . . . well, he couldn't complete the thought, he was so grossed out.

Wendell pulled the single earring dangling from her pretty earlobe and shoved it in his pocket.

He hoisted, twisted, and yanked to dislodge her, using his considerable height to advantage, but as her body nearly cleared the car, her shoe got caught on the deep edge of the door frame. He jerked hard and her foot came free of the shoe, but the momentum forced him backward onto his ass, her limp body following and landing on top of him, his arms still crooked beneath her shoulders. He struggled out from under her, stood up, smoothed his hair again, and got ahold of her, half dragging and half carrying her over to where the equipment was still chugging. He unceremoniously rolled her into the front-end loader bucket, and she landed in a fetching pose, her miniskirt bunched up and her blouse awry, one arm draped dramatically over her head.

Wendell flexed his hands as he got back behind the controls. He positioned the front-end loader as close to the edge as possible without tipping in or over. He poised the bucket high over the deepest point, proudly telling himself that not every backhoe operator could do this, that his backhoe skills were enormous, that he was the best backhoe guy, ever. He tilted the loader just a smidge, confident her weight would nudge her forward when a bit of momentum was established. He was right. She spilled out all at once, tumbled a full spin in the air, and dropped from the extended height of the loader with a thud on the soft earth. Her position mattered to him not at all.

Starting tomorrow, he thought, he could stop going to bars for murderous purposes and just go to bars to get blow jobs, like a normal guy. He could stop thinking about a rehearsal burial, and if he succeeded tonight, he could focus on his eventual target. Then he would be done, finished, sitting pretty. He wouldn't have to think about murder ever again.

In ten minutes, her body was covered with backhoe buckets of soil, and using the curved shovel teeth like knuckles flattening a cookie crumb crust, he compacted the earth. He thought he heard crunching, causing his fingers to burn, but he would never be sure on that point. She was undetectable and, to his eye, fully compacted. He threw considerably more dirt on the spot so that it looked messy rather than deliberate.

By the time he finished digging, dumping, and distributing dirt, he was thinking about a cheeseburger. He returned to the car, searched under the massive back seat, and found her other earring. He added it to the mate in his pocket. He found the hair clip that had once held her hair up to dizzying heights wedged between the back seat and the door. He gathered up her single shoe, the towels in the front seat, and her purse.

He hesitated. Her name was still a mystery to him, but whatever she said it was, he chose to believe it was a fake name anyway. He considered looking inside her purse but decided that wouldn't be nice. *Whatever.*

Wendell stood there, her shoe in one hand and her purse in the other. *Maybe I should have cut her up*, he thought. But he didn't think his miniature tool set would be up to the job. *And besides*, he told himself, *what a mess.*

He threw all that was left of her life and her death into the front seat next to him and drove the perimeter to the gated drive at the back of The Turn. He kept the headlights off, unlocked the gate, pulled out, stepped out to relock the gate, and, if it were possible to ask a car to tiptoe, he did just that, silently pulling away, having committed an unspeakable crime, depriving her family, if any, of knowledge, closure, or justice. He considered fries to go with the cheeseburger.

He drove toward the nearest small town, not the one where he met the girl, but the other one. He worried that he had no license plate on the car, and he really regretted throwing those screws into the bushes. He headed toward a little strip mall where he knew there were two or three dumpsters behind the liquor store. He drove around back and pulled one of the dangly earrings out of his pocket. He smudged it against his jeans to obliterate fingerprints. He had seen that on *NYPD Blue*, so he was pretty sure it was the right thing to do. He got out of the car and quietly popped open one of the dumpsters, fully intending to throw one of the earrings in, but he hesitated, not wanting to commit to the disposal. He put the earring back in his pocket with its mate and then, instead, wiped down the single shoe and tossed it into the dumpster.

Wendell drove back to Somerville and pulled into his driveway. He closed his eyes, flexed his hands, opened his eyes, tapped his fingers. He was jumpy, anxious for the sun to come up. At first light, he eased his way out of the car and quickly walked back to the bunker.

He was impressed. It looked like a bunker under construction. Dirt and fill everywhere, a few shovels lying around, samples of sand on pallets just off to the side. It did not look any different from when he had left it the day before. Yes, there were new tire tracks, and yes, there were new piles of dirt here and there, but tracks and dirt would be suspicious to no one. He picked up the shovels and leaned them neatly up against the side of the front-end loader. The engine was still warm to the touch, but it would cool off by the time the GM and the landscape architect showed up.

He climbed back up into the backhoe cab and sat, wakeful, finally closing his eyes for a rumpled doze. He startled awake when the GM pounded on the panel window. "Wendell, wake up, it's 7:45. We have to take a look at how this trap turned out. Let's get going." The landscape architect, the agronomist, and the general manager all walked around the site, mumbling and pointing.

"It's too deep here," grumbled the landscape architect. "It will slope too much when it's filled. I think we should reshape this side to offer more elevation and less of an angle." He pointed to the low end, where the dead girl was crumpled in a hidden heap.

The GM turned to Wendell. "Wendell, why is this side out of spec?" Wendell had rehearsed a just-in-case lie. "Well," he said, "I was hitting up against a bunch of tree roots, so I used the chainsaw and cleared it out, which changed the shape, I guess, so I, uh, had to adjust a bit."

The GM gave Wendell a skeptical look, but Wendell had long ago inured himself to the GM's doubts. Wendell's mother was still a member of The Club, and although she was mostly a pain in the ass, she played golf on a fairly regular basis, so the GM and the rest of the staff mostly shrugged in the face of Wendell's casual lies and shortcuts. Wendell's chainsaw account was sketchy, as there was neither a chainsaw, nor sawdust, nor a tree with interfering roots nearby, but Wendell was confident the GM would not make an issue of it, particularly since he was under pressure to get the bunker finished, sanded, and seeded. There was more pointing and squatting, but no one clambered down into the depression. After several painful moments, the architect told the GM that he could live with it and that the change was not as radical as he had at first thought. "Okay, Wendell," shouted the GM, "let's go."

By the end of the morning, Wendell had filled, coifed, sanded, and raked. He was humming a celebratory tune as he finished. *A job well done, a hole in one*, thought Wendell. On his lunch break, he walked the edge of the back nine to the perimeter, hopped the fence, and loped the short distance to his house. He easily ignored his mother and her questions.

He went in, showered, and shaved off his mustache.

—CHAPTER 2—

Debra Wolfson discovered that she had lost a glove. She had likely lost it months earlier when the weather was still cold, and of course it was the right-hand glove because that is the one that gets pulled off with one's teeth while looking for keys or a pen in one's purse in the dark, holding bags of groceries while it is snowing or raining. The loss rendered the remaining glove useless, which was too bad because she really liked the pair, pliant leather, warm lining, and in that cozy shade of reddish-brown that works with all color jackets.

The glove was nowhere to be found in the half hour she dedicated to a search, and although she had multiple other pairs of gloves and needed to be at a Somerville Zoning Board meeting by 6:00 p.m., she drove the fifteen minutes to the little dress shop in Rockmore where she had originally bought the gloves.

The tiny shop was near to bursting with four seasons' worth of merchandise. Winter scarves, summer hats, spring rain jackets, and fall sweaters were all on display, well segregated and poised to be moved around according to seasonal inevitability. Debra headed toward the far side of the shop where the fall merchandise was ascendant. She found a pair of gloves to replace the missing-piece pair, and then found another pair, pitched perhaps for a younger buyer, as it had a furry pom-pom garnish. She decided to purchase both.

The owner of the shop, whom Debra knew only as Florence, was seemingly on her own in the shop, with no assistant to work the register or help customers with sizes and colors. Florence held her own, to be sure, but with several people lined up waiting for the owner's attention, Debra wandered back to the fall section, where a sophisticated poncho had caught her eye. *Very Princess Leia*, thought Debra, *but with the right kind of boots, very possible.* With gloves and poncho in hand, she returned to the register.

"Oh," said Florence, "Mrs. Wolfson, so nice to see you again. Are you all set? I can ring you up. So sorry you had to wait. I'm a little shorthanded at the moment."

"Not a problem, Florence. Please, call me Debra. Glad to see you're busy."

"Yes, uh, Debra, lovely, busy, yes, but not staffed as I should be. So much for my fall sale." She laughed, trying to be casual about the whole thing, but she was flustered and a little sweaty. "Here, let me just get these gloves priced for you. Oh, the poncho too?" Florence gave Debra a nearly imperceptible head-to-toe. "Yes, very nice, yes. Ponchos are very forgiving and never too small."

Debra paid and asked when the fall sale would happen. "Well, it's in flux at the moment," answered Florence. "I had a new girl here for a couple of weeks. I was training her, and she seemed to be getting the hang of it, so I was just about to schedule the sale dates when she just disappears. Never shows up for work. No phone call, nothing. I need extra hands if I have a sale, so now, well, I'm interviewing a few girls this week, so I'll have a better idea then."

Debra had stopped listening, but she managed a supportive mumble. "Oh, yes, uh-huh, that's unfortunate and so rude. Not even a phone call. Uh-huh."

"I called the place where the girl was boarding," Florence babbled, "but the landlady there had the same problem. The girl just disappeared, leaving her suitcase. There was hardly anything in it according to the police, but still."

"Yes, the police. The police? Still, yes, still. Okay, now, thank you, Florence. I'll check back about the sale."

"Yes, thank you, uh, Debra."

Debra drove back through Rockmore toward Somerville, happy with her new gloves but nursing a perpetual peeve that Rockmore, smaller than Somerville, had sidewalks on its tiny main street and Somerville barely even had a main street. There were muffler shops, a bowling alley, oh, and of course the little food shop that did its best to hold the commercial end of town together, but for all that, not much to boast about. Public clamor for sidewalks was generally met with public resistance to sidewalks because there was nowhere to walk to in the first place.

In the midst of these municipal musings, Debra wondered if she had heard Florence correctly. Did Florence say she called the police because she had to delay her fall sale? *That can't be right*, thought Debra.

Debra arrived at the Zoning Board meeting a little early and took her place at the big table where her name placard had been placed. "Debra," said the new guy on the board, "how come you know so much about zoning?"

The new guy had been to only three meetings. He wanted to chat. Debra did not want to chat. Debra wanted to ask him why it was that he seemed to know absolutely nothing about zoning, but she refrained, as one does, and instead answered his question.

"I used to be a land use and zoning lawyer."

"Really? Wow. Sounds kind of boring."

"Really? I loved it. I still love it."

"What kind of lawyer are you now?"

"I'm a divorce mediator."

"Wow, I'll bet that's not boring. All the sex and stuff."

Good grief, thought Debra, *this guy is an idiot.*

"You want to hear a joke my wife told me?" She was trapped. She took the youthful gloves out of the bag she had brought into the meeting room and removed the tag.

"If you put ten random people in a room and talk about zoning, four of them will die right on the spot and the other six will pass out. They are zoning out. Too funny, right?"

It was not funny, but it was probably true.

"Why did you agree to sit on the Zoning Board if you think it's so boring?" Debra was smiling, but she wanted to smack this guy and whatever Republican had nominated him to occupy the Republican slot on the Zoning Board.

"Well, I got asked, so I said yes. Why not? One less night I have to help put the kids to bed, right?"

It was a very short agenda. No one was present for Public Comment, and there was only one site plan review, which was quickly addressed. The chair suggested they meet for the balance of fall and winter only if there was actually something on the agenda that required their attention. Following a robust discussion, his common sense suggestion met with approval. It could have gone either way, given that everyone on the board had strong opinions on all issues, including sidewalks, signage, and public sewer and water for anything other than fire safety and green turf at the golf courses. Thankfully, no one seemed to feel that a couple centuries of zoning regulation would be toppled if the Zoning Board skipped a few winter meetings.

The Zoning Board adjourned. Debra wouldn't have to see or sit next to the new guy for at least a few months. She went home to her husband and her big house, which met the two-acre-minimum zoning requirement and all the setback rules and, although on a main road, lacked any indicia of public water, sewer, gas, or trash removal and had not even a suggestion of a sidewalk, whatsoever.

•••

Somerville did, however, have a police department, a very nice, itsy-bitsy police department. Rockmore had a police department also, even tinier than Somerville's, so small, in fact, that when Florence called the police about her missing shopgirl, no steps were taken to dispatch a detective because they weren't entirely sure any crime had been committed, and besides, the department technically did not have a detective. It used state police investigators if there were any reason to think genuine criminal activity was afoot, and even then, it had to compete with two other, even smaller towns to get anyone assigned. No one was going to bust a budget to dispatch a detective to ask a few routine questions, so a beat officer would have to suffice. The Rockmore chief knew who was on duty because the department had only three officers to begin with, so the chief sent Vinnie to make inquiries and report back.

Vinnie was a shiny new cop. He had just completed the last of his course and fieldwork and was now a sworn and certified law enforcement officer in his very own hometown. He was pretty sure he was happy. He had been on the job full time for about three weeks.

The Rockmore chief called Vinnie in and handed him a color photo of a cute teenage girl wearing a brown sweater and a green hair ribbon. It was one of those high school photos taken for the yearbook, the ones your mother orders sheets of in all sizes, and while one finds its way to a frame on a wall in the stairwell, the rest sit in packets in some cabinet in the basement, uncut and surreally connected forever to the multiples on the sheet.

It was date stamped on the back "June 1983."

"Vinnie," said the chief, "run over to the Triple B."

"Oh, we know whoever this is was at the Triple B?" asked Vinnie.

"No. But I got a five-year-old photo of a pretty girl and a name. That's it. Pretty girl? Doesn't know anybody in town? Around twenty-two or so? Trust me, start with the Triple B."

The Triple B was the only bar in Rockmore. Vinnie walked over. It was four in the afternoon, and the Triple B was open, but empty.

Vinnie sat down. "Bob, have you seen this girl in here?" Bob was the owner and bartender.

Everyone knew Bob.

"I think so." Bob took a closer look. "I'd say yes, but this must be an old photo. She was in here about a week ago. I don't know who she is, but yeah, I'd say it's her." The usual conversation followed, but no, Bob hadn't seen her come in with anyone, didn't see her leave with anyone, but did see her talking to some young guy for a while. "Yeah, he bought her a drink, a couple of drinks as I recall. We got busy that evening because it was a Friday, but it seems to me she started with a glass of wine and he had a beer. White wine, with ice. Him? Beer, I think. Quite a few. Maybe a Coke at some point. No question, they had a few."

"A few too many?"

"Probably."

"Did anyone card her?"

"I doubt it. She certainly looked to be old enough to drink."

"Any reason you remember her? Or him? Or what they drank? Did something happen that stood out?"

"No, not at all," answered Bob. "But Vinnie, we're not a big place, you know that. I know my regulars, and on most nights in this place, that's who's here. My regulars. A new face always stands out, and I can't help it if I remember what people drink. It's an occupational thing, I guess."

"Did you see whether they left together?" asked Vinnie.

"Nope."

"Do you know if anyone else saw him? Or her?" asked Vinnie.

"Vinnie, jeez," said Bob, suddenly uncomfortable. "Look, I had my youngest, you know him, Patrick, working here that night. He's underage, only seventeen. Don't get me in trouble on this." Vinnie had no intention of busting Bob for putting his underage kid to work in the family business. As it was, Vinnie had gone to high school with Bob's older son, and the families all attended the same Rockmore church.

"No, of course not, Bob. Patrick is seventeen already? Well, any chance he saw this guy? Or the young woman?"

"He must have. He was working the cash register on that end of the bar, and I made sure he didn't move from that spot. He didn't serve anybody, I know that, because my wife would have killed me. No, she and I were running around serving and taking care of the customers at the bar and the tables. You know the crowd, the same just about every Friday night. Patrick's at school, but he'll be around later. You can ask him directly."

"Could you describe him, Bob?"

"Patrick?"

"No, the guy with the girl." Vinnie leaned in, just a little bit hopeful.

"Oh, yeah, of course. Absolutely. Late twenties or so, tall, brown shirt, stupid mustache like they all have now."

"That's it?"

"That's it."

Bob told Vinnie that the guy paid in cash and that he hadn't seen a car or any other ID.

"Could you pick him out of a lineup?" asked Vinnie.

"Lineup? Why're you asking about a lineup? What did this guy do? What happened to the girl?"

"Nothing that we know of at the moment," said Vinnie. He told Bob the little he knew, that Florence Nuffield, the owner of the dress shop at the end of Main Street, had reported that the girl hadn't shown up for work. "According to Mrs. Nuffield, the girl seemed a little squirrely, but Mrs. Nuffield hired her on a temporary basis to help with her fall sale, whatever that means. Cash basis, no payroll. All Mrs. Nuffield knew was that the girl was boarding over at the Duncan place."

Vinnie reported back to his chief. The chief had no choice but to stare meaningfully out the window.

"What now, Chief?" Vinnie stared at the chief as the chief stared out the window.

"We got a young woman, early twenties, I guess, with no connections to the town, no parents or family here, no record of a Connecticut driver's license, or any driver's license for that matter, nothing, just a couple of weeks working on a cash basis in a dress shop." The chief turned from the window to stare meaningfully at the large filing cabinet on the other side of his small office. "In fact," he continued, "we can't be sure that the name she gave Florence Nuffield is even her real name."

Vinnie waited, knowing the chief would, as he always did, turn his meaningful gaze toward the small filing cabinet on the opposite wall. There were only so many things to meaningfully gaze at in the chief's little office. Finally, he turned back to Vinnie. "Vinnie, you said Bob said she was at the bar Friday night? She doesn't show up for work Saturday. Mrs. Nuffield is ticked off, so she calls Mrs. Duncan. Mrs. Duncan has no idea where the girl is, went, or was supposed to be. Mrs. Duncan said the girl was paying board by the week, in cash, and that she seemed a little drifty, but other than the mostly empty little suitcase still up in the room, Mrs. Duncan knows nothing about her. The shop is closed Sunday and Monday. Tuesday, Mrs. Nuffield opens her shop and the girl never shows to work. Not Tuesday, and not the rest of the week. That's the whole story."

"Nothing in the suitcase?" asked Vinnie.

"No," grunted the chief. "No letters, no address book, nothing valuable. Just some clothing, a few toiletries, or whatever girls call that stuff. And the photo, but Mrs. Duncan wasn't even sure the photo is of the girl who was boarding. I mean, who knows? Teenage girls grow up and change, and old ladies can't see. Either way, it's not going to help us find her. Even if she really is lost. Or gone. Which we're not even sure of."

"What should I do, Chief?"

"Write it up, Vinnie," said the chief. "Check with the state police to see if anyone reported a missing person and keep it as an open file."

"What about the suitcase, Chief?"

"Get prints, I guess, bag up and keep the contents. Give it a month or so and then tell Mrs. Duncan it's abandoned property and she can do what she wants with it. It's not evidence of anything, so we don't need it here taking up room." The chief's gaze now took in all of his minuscule workspace. "Oh, and follow up with the kid, Patrick."

Vinnie did all that he was told. In the way of teenage boys, Patrick was not helpful. "But look," added Patrick, with more enthusiasm than was actually called for, "I would recognize the guy if I ever saw him again, definitely. I would definitely recognize him if I ever saw him again. No question."

That kid watches way too much TV, thought Vinnie.

•••

Wendell was certain he had matters well in hand, and he wrote a note to himself confirming that everything was under control. He now knew the challenges of body disposal, and his questions about bulk, heft, timing, and method had mostly been answered. As he had done for most of his life, he wrote it all down and hid what he wrote, assuring himself that the rehearsal was perfect, that it was an incredible rehearsal.

But he couldn't help himself. All during those first days, his thoughts turned to the bunker, the sand, whether it was smooth and looked good. He drove or walked by the bunker every chance he got. He wasn't obvious about it, he was sure, but that sand trap had his full attention, even when he wasn't paying attention. Over the course of the week, the sound of the mowers reminded him of the rattle of her hair clip against the car window, and every time he saw the bartender in the Grille Room, he thought of the white wine with ice she ordered at the Triple B. He was unsettled, and as cars with golf clubs pulled into the parking lot, he paced, rubbing his aching hands. He was preoccupied and more than a little tense.

The guys on TV aren't tense, he told himself. *Damn.*

Still, he mentally patted himself on the back for not using his recently acquired gun. It had been a relaxed purchase, and no one at the camping store had even asked Wendell a single question about possible murderous intent or whether he even liked camping. When he got the gun home, he realized he didn't know how to load it, hold it, or shoot it. He considered that it was a dangerous weapon. *I could get hurt*, he thought. He stashed the gun and box of bullets way up high in his bedroom closet.

He wrote a congratulatory note to himself on being an excellent hider.

But even though Wendell had not shot the young woman, he had nonetheless weaponized the Lincoln Continental. If he could have torched the car without involving his mother and an insurance company, he would have. Instead, he scrubbed the doors, the carpet, and the seats with every solvent he could find in The Club maintenance garage. He comforted himself with new floor mats for the front and back.

A few days after he killed the girl, and while his mother was at her regular bridge game at the "real" club, Wendell lit his parents' old Weber grill, a grill his father had used every night of every summer but that his mother had abandoned since Cecil's death. If vermin were attracted to the smell or the warm cabinet beneath the unused grill surface, no one was the wiser. Wendell waited for the coals to get sear-a-steak hot and put the girl's little purse right on the embers. He then spritzed ignition fuel all over it. The purse mostly melted. Wendell had a beer, and then another, waiting impatiently while the blob cooled. He then scooped and bagged the blob and the ash in three separate plastic bags, using those bags to collect the trash from The Turn's trash bins, ultimately tossing the bags in three separate dumpsters on three separate days. He had not looked inside the purse, preferring the blurry version of her he had concocted. It was only later that he thought there might have been money in the purse, but, *Jeez*, he told himself, *I'm not a thief.*

Over the next week, he disposed of the murder detritus at multiple locations employing various receptacles and was delighted at his newfound skill at spreading garbage all over the place. But he could not bring himself to get rid of the earrings. They always found their way back into his front pocket. *Maybe later*, he thought.

Golfers were still on the course, fewer than just a couple of weeks ago, but still showing up and playing eighteen holes. No one had yet gotten caught in his bunker, surely an impossibility given the skill set of these duffers, and he was riveted by the trap's purity. He couldn't wait for the course to shut down for the season and really empty out so that he could get a little peace.

Doubts crept in and out of a small mental loft.

He had no idea what he would have done with her body if he hadn't had access to the golf course and its equipment, and he failed to consider that he might not have murdered her in the first place. He thought about turning himself in. He told himself that he wasn't a criminal, just a bright, good-looking guy with good hair and a very good brain who worked at a golf course and might have made a mistake. He could not come up with a version of events that would, somehow, make the whole thing her fault. Even if he could convince a cop that he hadn't meant to strangle her, he was certain no one would believe that she accidentally got buried in a bunker.

But over time, the doubts moved to a secure and teeny mental closet. He continued to flex his still-tingly hands, but he calmed down a little more each day. No one came asking questions. No cops knocked at his door. He was just a grounds guy cleaning up fallen leaves across one hundred fifty acres of coiffed land.

Finally, the course shut down for the season and the seasonal staff left, leaving him, one of only two full-time staffers, free to work without the distraction of actual golfers on the course. His confidence returned. When his work called for a backhoe, he made sure to use the one he had used for the rehearsal, and he relived all the thrilling moments. He wrote and reviewed multiple notes to himself, each confirming he was an excellent backhoe guy.

As the months progressed, rain, then snow made traversing the course a messy, muddy, and, ultimately, impossible effort. But if he drove along the skinny two-lane road that bordered the property on the far side of the course, he could just see through the trees to where the bunker sat, not far from the rough on that nearly hidden side of the property. He thought about how cold she must be, buried under the snow.

The events of that murderous evening seemed hardly to have caused a ripple. There was nothing in the local newspapers or on TV about a youthful female who had gone missing. Now, with a clear head and the jitters fully behind him, he assessed the ongoing perils. There just didn't seem to be any. He expected the police to call, come by, ask questions, arrest him, something, but it was as if he didn't exist and she had never existed. He was enormously relieved and a little bit insulted. And this was only the rehearsal.

He could just walk away, move to Arizona or somewhere his mother would be unlikely to follow or harass him, but he had his reasons for staying, several million reasons, all soon to be in his control, so he was committed to the full project. He would bide his time. There was no real rush. He might have to wait as long as a year before he could execute the full plan, but the second and final murder would give him all he wanted or would ever need.

He had learned an important lesson. He could get away with it.

—CHAPTER 3—

From the moment Cecil Williams dropped dead on the sixteenth fairway at The Club, Stella and Wendell quarreled. Wendell screamed that he should be in charge of the funeral arrangements because he worked at The Club. Stella shouted that she wanted the post-funeral reception at the banquet facility of the "real" course because that is where she and Cecil maintained their social connections. They squabbled over the tradition that a golf course death should be honored at the golf course where the death occurred, who could violate or honor that tradition, and whether the tradition was made-up bullshit, but Wendell hollered that he worked at the golf course, so he knew more than she did. Stella shrieked that she, and she alone, would decide who would speak, toast, and eulogize.

In the end, the arguments didn't matter because the banquet facility at the "real" course was, in fact, fully booked with a wedding gala to which Stella and a good many of Cecil's mourners had been invited. Stella was funereally stuck with The Club, and to top it off, she would have to miss the glitzy wedding. She told Wendell to just shut up and show up.

The church service was a blur to Wendell, with the exception that the eulogies were inexplicably peppy. Yes, Cecil died doing what he loved, yes, yes, he went out on a long drive, yes, the sixteenth fairway will never be the same, yes, we are all proud and happy to have known Cecil Williams, a fine upstanding citizen of Somerville and congregant of this church. Yes, a golf course death is a good death.

But the post-funeral reception at The Club brought clarity. Wendell watched Stella lap up the attention of The Club membership as she performed her role as the grieving widow. He stood off to the side, not willing to costar in her grief extravaganza. He wanted his own extravaganza, a grieving-Wendell extravaganza, but Stella wasn't having it. By the time the reception line tapered off and the final condolence was paid, Wendell had made a decision.

He would kill Stella, carefully, on his terms, and at just the right moment.

And, he told himself, *I'll take my time. And rehearse.*

Having to wait for the right moment was not easy. Living with the newly widowed Stella was another level of hell, and she wore her martyrdom front and center. No one would have been the least bit surprised to learn that mother and son each regarded the other as unbuffered, strident, disdainful, demanding, all day, all the time. Stella complained that she had no one to complain to, as there were no cousins, aunts, siblings—no one. And without Cecil, her efforts to keep Wendell on the emotional back burner of the family hob were now fully hobbled.

Of course, she had the money to comfort her. She was a very wealthy martyr. But Wendell wanted the money. She threatened him on a near-daily basis with disinheritance, so Wendell told himself he really had no choice. No way was he going to wait to cash in on his parentage.

Wendell assured himself that killing his mother was an absolute last resort, but it was, really, a first choice. After all, she scolded him for failing to study for the boards to become a CPA, chastising him all the while for continuing to work as a grounds guy at the golf course, not even the "real" course, but the "other" course, the one they joined only because it was across the road and incredibly convenient. She criticized him for his food choices. She found fault with both of his college majors and was certain, absolutely certain, that one of them was really just a minor. She thought he should really learn how to play golf. The maternal-appropriate nagging about laundry and taking out garbage was heavily annotated with criticisms about his attitude and his smart-ass mouth.

At least that's what Wendell heard. Stella had the money, and no matter what he did, said, drank, ate, cleaned, folded, studied, or conceded, she was going to cut him off. Period. No money for Wendell.

He could have walked away from the money, but as far as he was concerned, it was his money. He wrote a multitude of notes to himself on that very subject. To Wendell's eye and felt-tip marker, Stella kneaded that pile of dough the way she kneaded Wendell, shaping both to suit her needs. *I'm entitled to that money,* he noted, *all of it, right now.*

If Wendell was honest with himself, which was nearly impossible because he was fundamentally dishonest in all things, he would have to admit that even if there was no money, he would kill his mother. But the money gave him an excuse. He wanted the money, and he wanted to get rid of Stella.

He had no idea that all of this was cliché in the extreme, but even had he realized it, it would not have made a difference.

He used the monthslong intermission between the rehearsal and the ultimate performance to don his good-son costume to accomplish three things. First, he went out of his way to make sure the GM noticed an artful change in Wendell's attitude. Shortcuts and bullshit were off the table. He purposefully became a sort-of adult, cooperative, polite, and eager to please. Wendell might have been surprised to learn that the GM told the agronomist that he doubted that Wendell shaving off his mustache was the cause of the attitude adjustment, but the correlation was impossible to ignore.

Second, he paired the GM charade with an on-purpose chance encounter with his parents' estate lawyer in the parking lot of The Club, where the lawyer was a regular and die-hard golfer. Oh, Wendell, said the lawyer, in response to Wendell's seemingly sincere questions, yes, you're correct, yes, now that your mother got everything in your father's estate, of course, that's how it was, uh, set up, and, yes, we should ensure that her affairs are now in order. Sure enough, within a short time, Stella's updated estate documents were signed by Stella and hidden where she hid everything, in the little cabinet between the two club chairs in the living room. It was a hiding place unworthy of the name. Still, Wendell considered the updated estate documents a nice, really very nice, even perfect touch.

Third, he affected compliance with Stella's demands just enough so that she would back off from the worst of the disinheritance threats. It likely didn't matter, but to Wendell it was a matter of misplaced and wholly ironic principle.

So, with the rehearsal well behind him and his next steps at the ready, he considered all that he had accomplished. He credited the success of the rehearsal, in part, to his handwritten alternative plans and both his random and purposeful notes. *Good thing I kept my rehearsal notes*, he wrote, *because they are coming in very handy*. "Don't kill in a car" was particularly helpful.

He knew he should have destroyed the rehearsal memos, knew it was dangerous to commit any of his thoughts to writing, but the notes and the earrings were all he had left of his Bunker Girl, and he couldn't, just couldn't, get rid of them. The earrings were with him all the time, and he kept the notes hidden in a shoebox next to the shoebox containing his unused gun, high up in the closet, well out of Stella's sight or reach. He referred to his rehearsal notes, wrote more notes, hid them, and told himself he had a very good brain. He doodled, drank, and planned. His rehearsal had been a huge success, huge, commensurate with his expectations, and even though nearly a year had elapsed, now here he was on the precipice of the big step. He took great satisfaction that there had never been a news story or anything on TV about a murdered young woman. No cop, no bartender, no one came forward to ask him anything. Of course, he never returned to the Triple B, and if his mother wanted to shop at the little dress shop on Rockmore's Main Street, she could drive herself. Even Wendell wondered how it was that someone could just vanish.

He was now certain the moment was upon him. *After all*, he thought, *it's not as if I'll ever get caught.*

•••

The Club was winding down the summer season.

All of the course maintenance, remodeling, and redesign plans that were supposed to be implemented throughout the fall and early winter were postponed, and rumors were flying around that The Club was in financial trouble. But Wendell needed to create or remodel a bunker. Otherwise, he might have to improvise.

Otherwise, indeed. He had no choice but to come up with an alternative plan. He did his best thinking, he thought, when he was close to Bunker Girl, and even more so now that he had christened her as such, so he visited her as often as he could. She was no longer a bunker virgin. He was nearby when Mr. Balliol, a club regular, got hung up one day in the bunker, thwacking and hacking to liberate his ball from the trap, sending sand soaring. Wendell was riveted. But all was raked and tended to, as per etiquette, and virgin or not, Bunker Girl was his inspiration.

He could, he would, improvise.

It was a cold and breezy fall afternoon. Wendell pulled his truck up to the swinging gate, turning hard to maneuver into the little dirt parking lot next to The Turn. He off-loaded a few supplies for the still-open snack bar and, hugging the outside boundary of the property, drove the truck up to a large copse of trees not more than two hundred yards from The Turn. He pulled a tank out of the back of his truck, the kind exterminators use, and began spritzing the area where the grass met the edge of the copse. No one would have thought anything about it if they had seen him doing this. He was a golf course maintenance guy spraying pesticide, or weed killer, or a grub poison, or an herbicide. An observant or curious person might have wondered why he was doing it in that area, at the end of the golf season and well away from a cart path, fairway, or tee box. An observant or curious person might also have wondered why he was wearing dangly earrings while spraying whatever it was he was spraying. But no observant or curious person was nearby, so no one wondered what might have been wondered.

Over the next week, he sprayed in that spot every chance he got, often after dark or before the sun came up. As long as he was out of sight of anyone, he clipped the earrings to his ears, or his belt, or his hat. He was careful to always return them to his pocket.

Finally, the GM said something, as Wendell knew he would.

"Wendell," said the GM, "what the hell is going on over on that spot near that bunch of trees by The Turn? It looks terrible."

"No idea. I know what you mean, though. It's all brown. Very brown."

"I'm going to send the agronomist up there when he gets a chance. We've got to take care of that. It's visible from the road, and I can already hear the neighbors along that stretch complaining. It looks like hell. And it looks like it's getting bigger."

The agronomist reported back. "We better get a handle on this before it spreads even more. Scrape off at least a foot of the dead grass and the dirt underneath. Let it breathe for a few days, and I'll go back out and take a look at it. We're going to have to get fresh dirt in there and sod. Yes, I know it's pricey, but seed will take forever, and if there's a problem, seed won't take anyway. It has to be sod."

The GM was not happy with this expensive recommendation, but it was a cheaper option than watching the entire grassed area die off and having to deal with it on a much larger scale. He pulled funds from the dwindling contingency column and directed Wendell to create a buffer and start removing dirt and dead grass. "Dig about a foot down. Be careful of all those tree roots there. That's a decorative clump of trees, and I do not want to spend money replacing those. Just scrape off a layer."

"I'm on it," said Wendell.

Wendell's beloved backhoe was old and filthy, but he was at his happiest when he sat in the creaky cab and swiveled the seat around to face first the shovel end and then the loader end. He had begun this backhoe pirouette only a day or two after he buried Bunker Girl, and he imagined that she loved the new name he had given her.

Wendell's connection to the backhoe only deepened when he lost one of Bunker Girl's earrings. He had been digging away astride his backhoe on the edge of a water hazard and singing a tune he was sure

Bunker Girl would have liked when he jostled the gears, and the earring that was clipped to his belt slipped off. He lurched for it, but instead of catching it, he flicked it, knocking it even farther from where he sat. He heard the earring tinkle against metal somewhere in the backhoe cab and land, possibly, in or near the turret housing the gears. He stopped mid-dig and searched in and around the turret, on the floor, under the foot pedals, but it was nowhere to be found. If it had fallen through the narrow channel of the gear turret, it would be irretrievable, and the earring itself might compromise the gear mechanism. He could have panicked, but he was now a seasoned murderer. It would take more than a lost earring for him to lose his cool. *Besides*, he reasoned, *if I'm looking for it and can't find it, it will never be found by someone who is not looking for it, and no one is ever going to be in this backhoe looking for an earring that they don't know is in here.* When he shifted gears, he girded himself for mechanical calamity, but the gears worked. The machine moved forward, backward, up, down, around, and all the digging and loading that needed to happen happened. He was enormously relieved and would make a number of notes about the incident that evening.

He pledged to himself that the remaining earring would always have a safe place in his front pants pocket.

Now, with the sod project at hand, Wendell gazed lovingly at his backhoe. He made sure he was the only one who used it, and his fellow maintenance guys were only too amused to regard it as *Wendell's* backhoe. The Club owned three other backhoes, and so, it was said, if Wendell, the wanker, wants to claim the oldest one, who gives a shit.

He gave the rear hinge an affectionate pat and mounted his backhoe like a knight mounting his steed. He performed his seat-bound spin and got the backhoe up and running. The scraping would have thwarted a lesser backhoe guy because it was a tricky area bounded by the low post-and-rail fence and further impeded by the low-hanging branches and shallow roots of the scraggly cedar in the center of the copse. But he was an excellent backhoe guy.

The fence slowed him down, and he had to leverage and maneuver a dozen scattered boulders, but he didn't care. The later in the day he finished, the better. It was getting near evening, and there would be golfers walking around for another couple of hours, so he took his time, letting dusk settle in, digging a little deeper, much deeper, much, much deeper, in the spot he had chosen, the spot with the fewest roots, and as the course cleared out, he dug even deeper, not worried the neighbors might hear the little backhoe, because, well, he had to finish this area as directed by the GM.

He isolated the poisoned grass and dirt and carefully piled the clean, fresh dirt where he would need it, close to the edge of the copse, directly next to the deep and narrow hole he had created. He would have to backfill by hand and shovel. His hands hurt just at the thought of it.

He left the backhoe parked next to the spot where he had scraped, covering an area about as large as half a tennis court. He had done a pretty good job of poisoning only the grassy area. It was just getting dark, but he didn't want to go back to his house just yet. He walked to The Turn, now locked up for the evening, let himself in, helped himself to a beer and a sandwich, used the bathroom, had another beer, then left, locking the door behind him. No one would know or care. He was careful to sweep the floor on his way out because, well, he was a maintenance guy. He had purposefully left his own car parked way up top at the big clubhouse, so he hopped the fence to walk home, just down the road. He walked up the driveway of his house, past his parents' golf cart, parked beneath the little carport his father had constructed for that purpose. He pulled one of his mother's golf clubs out of the huge and clunky case that sat up in the back of the cart. It didn't matter which club. As he entered the back door to the kitchen, he could hear the TV blaring from the den. Wendell poured himself a Coke, loudly clinked lots of ice in the glass, as if in summons, and waited for his mother to get up from the easy chair in the family room, where he knew she was sitting, watching television, alone. Sure enough, she answered the summons.

Stella came into the kitchen and stood at the sink railing at Wendell about his late arrival, the state of his career, and some out-of-nowhere Arkansas governor who was about to run for president. Her back was to him, and she didn't notice when Wendell slithered into the dining room. He silently watched her wipe the kitchen counter in cadence to her complaints. He reached into his pocket and fondled his beloved earring, briefly congratulating himself on the close approximation of his mother's stature to Bunker Girl's height and heft. He knew just how tall and looming he needed to be, because he had rehearsed. Later, he would tell himself that he was the best approximator ever, but he stayed in the moment. He quickly came up behind Stella, holding the club with two hands, flat in front of him, and easily and quickly cleared her head and face, using most of his strength to jam the horizontal shaft against her windpipe, pulling it toward himself. He braced to get adequate leverage against her shorter, older body. Stella struggled against Wendell and the golf club, making a considerable amount of noise, dreadful gagging and retching sounds, and knocking the entire dish drainer full of dishes onto the kitchen floor, flinging a kitchen chair against the refrigerator and kicking over the trash bin, all the while crashing and thrashing about. The minimum lot size required by zoning ensured that the neighbors were too far away to hear any of this, and Wendell, well in possession of the upper hand, took his time, making sure Stella struggled. Her strength was no surprise. She had been thwacking a little ball around miles of well-kept grounds three times a week for forty years, but in the end, of course, he was stronger and taller and younger, and when he had had enough of her noise, her tussle, and her fight, he simply brought all his strength and height to bear with one final, lethal tug. She collapsed and, finally, shut up.

Wendell let her slide to the floor. Her neck was a mess under the best of circumstances, saggy and wrinkled with that jowly wattle gravity imposes on women in their sixties and leathery from all those hours out in the sun hitting a defenseless dimpled ball all over the place. Now it was even worse, black and red and not at all attractive.

Her eyes were wide and gaping. He needed to catch his breath, and he took the moment to commend himself for not using the gun in his bedroom closet, which would have created a huge cleanup job and dozens of clues, and, as well, for having had the good sense to rehearse all of this so he knew exactly what to expect. The breathlessness, the shaking, the trembles—he waited for it all to abate. No barfing this time.

Twenty, maybe twenty-five minutes, and she hadn't blinked.

If he could have hired someone to drag her out the back door, he would have. After all, this was his mother, and if touching her when she was alive was problematic for him, touching her when she was dead was even more so. But needs must, so he lugged her toward the back door, her height and dead heft familiar and anticipated, but *yuck*, he thought, *so gross*. He pulled her into the golf cart and sat her up, leaving her to slump like an untethered marionette. There was no point in bagging her up, and even if there were, there were no dead-human-sized bags in the garage, the carport, or his parents' toolshed. He would have liked to cover her head, but all he could find was a large paper bag from the supermarket, and with her sitting as she was in the cart, the paper bag made only a comical contribution. He left her in the cart, completely obscured from the view of any neighbor, and then covered the entire front of the cart with a furniture blanket he found in the garage. He got another Coke and waited for his heart to stop pounding.

When his body calmed, he waited another hour before he drove the cart all the way down to the swinging gate, nearly at the corner. It was dark, but he managed without incident to unlock the gate, pull in, and relock it, just as he had done so many months ago with Bunker Girl. He drove the golf cart to the spot where he had been scraping all afternoon and waited another hour or so, just staring out over the course. It was so beautiful. He heard an animal, and it so startled him that he was sure it was a wolf. It was a squirrel on a branch overhead.

The more he listened, the quieter it got.

Finally, he pulled his mother off the cart and let her body sink into the deep, narrow hole he had dug, just up against the edge of the clump of trees. He wished he could have rolled a couple of boulders into the hole to offset what would likely be a depression in the ground at some point, but it was the middle of the night, and this time he was close to the road. He could not afford the noise the backhoe would make. Instead, he piled a bunch of branches in the hole, using all of the limbs he had stockpiled over the past week beneath the scraggly cedar. He shoveled clean dirt back into the hole, compacting it as best he could, making it a solid mass, letting the branches do some of the work of filling the hole, and brought the dirt up to the level he had scraped, about a foot below grade. She was five or six feet down in a crumpled heap, as there was no way he could have fully laid her out. It took him a long time to fill up the hole by hand, and he was exhausted.

He drove the cart back, parked it in the carport, and cleaned up the house and himself, scrubbing the kitchen table and floor until his arms ached. He doubted Stella would have appreciated the irony of his momentary commitment to household cleanliness.

The next morning, more tired than he would have thought, Wendell met the agronomist at the site. The agronomist poked around the dirt, looking for fungus or grubs or anything that would explain the sudden demise of the grassy area. He examined the pile of excavated grass, ignorant of the purposeful death of each and every blade. He mumbled about a weed killer but went no further than the mumble. Wendell, the agronomist, and the GM discussed and fussed, but there was never any real question what the next step would be, so by the end of the next day the entire area had been covered with clean dirt and lovely sod. Wendell had mentally marked the spot where he had placed his mother, where he had dug the deepest. Using his backhoe, he clumsily moved several of the boulders back from the edge of the work area and piled them up against each other on top of his mother's ersatz grave, leaving the remaining boulders off at the edge of the copse of trees, away from the new sod.

It looked as lovely and natural as anything ever did on a golf course.

— CHAPTER 4 —

Initially, Wendell had to jump a lot of hurdles in order to kill his mother and keep her alive, all at the same time.

He had to immediately get on top of the paperwork. Two days after he buried Stella, he called the Florida club where his parents golfed in the winter as well as the property manager for the course-adjacent high-rise apartment. Yes, my mother fell and broke her hip. No, no snowbird sojourn this year or—who knows?—possibly any other year. It being Florida, both the golf manager and the property manager were accustomed to adult children managing the affairs of aging parents, so neither questioned what might have been questioned, but both offered the obligatory and rote wishes for Stella's full recovery.

Stella's now-derailed plans for Florida had included leaving her brand-new Cadillac in Somerville. She was not about to drive down all by herself, all alone, she had told Wendell, so she would have to fly, repeatedly pointing out over and over and over and over that a grateful son would have driven her down, left the car for her use, and made his own way back. As it was now, Wendell drove her car a few times to The Club, where the GM asked if he had gotten a new car, and to the town refuse facility, where the Public Works guys who saw him every week on Garbage Saturdays asked him the same thing, so he could reply to all of them that it was his mother's car and she had left it at the house while she was in Florida for the season.

He drove his own car to the local travel agent and told her that his mother had broken her hip and needed to cancel the winter flight arrangements. The travel agent hesitated. She had every reason to believe her business was about to radically change, as self-booking on something called "online" was in the offing, and every cancellation augured only the worst. She didn't know Wendell, and she was not accustomed to adult children acting on behalf of aging parents. She told Wendell she would need to hear from his mother directly. Wendell smiled his best smile and twinkled and said, of course, that makes sense, absolutely, he would have his mother call just as soon as the painkillers wear off, no problem. He went home, called the airline directly, and easily canceled the ticket.

But Wendell now had to face the fact that even with his extraordinary brain, he could lose track of what he had told this one or that one. Was Stella in Florida or was she in Connecticut? Had she broken a hip or was dementia on the horizon? Juggling multiple versions of events and lies was proving unnerving. He decided to ramp up writing his notes, and he committed himself to a full-on regulated note-making schedule. *There could be charts*, he thought, *or even graphs*.

And the more notes he made, the happier he was. He loved seeing his thoughts reflected back at him, his unique cursive coursing all over the index cards, the Post-it stickies, and the scratch paper on his father's old desk. The notes were a huge help, and he enjoyed being an audience of one. He fully intended to destroy the notes on a weekly basis, but weekly extended to monthly, and monthly seemingly extended to never. As the weather turned brisk, Wendell would drive his parents' old golf cart up to Bunker Girl and read his notes to her, out loud, so Bunker Girl could hear him talk about himself. He loved his notes and notebooks even more than he loved obituaries.

And it helped him keep track of everything too.

Throughout that fall, Wendell sorted through every drawer in his father's old desk, finding ancient bank statements, account information, and piles of tax returns on top of the filing cabinet. Wendell meddled with every cubby and opened every folder. He purged decades of useless paperwork and streamlined the filing system.

He found Stella's everyday checkbook, and to his surprise, his name was on her checking account, no doubt in case something ever happened, which it clearly had. She obviously did not want him to know, as she had signed his name on the signature card and provided his Social Security number to the bank, but there it was. It did not surprise him that she was as sneaky as he was turning out to be. He discovered that her Social Security check based on his father's earnings came each month in the mail, as did statements for her savings accounts, her brokerage accounts, two healthy dividend checks from some stock, and a check from some kind of retirement account in his father's name, made out to her as beneficiary.

He did what needed to be done to ensure direct deposit of the Social Security check, and as to the other checks, he used the drive-through window at the bank, where the teller was sure he was doing his mother a favor. No, no identification needed when you're putting money in the bank, only when you take it out.

It took a few weeks, but then it dawned on Wendell that he might have really screwed it up. He drank himself sick at the thought. Florida thought she was alive in Connecticut, nursing a broken hip. Connecticut thought she was in Florida, playing golf, playing snowbird. That was well and good, and according to plan. But no one thought she was dead, even though she was dead, so he could inherit nothing. He had no idea whether a murderer could benefit under his victim's estate plan, but that was beside the point because there was no estate, no estate to speak at death, so to speak.

I have the money, he told himself. *I just don't **have** the money.*

But when he sobered up, he read through the packet of estate documents he found stuffed into a bulging folder in the cabinet between the club chairs. He discovered that his mother had not disinherited him. It was a useless point, because the world thought she was still alive, but for Wendell, it was immensely satisfying. He wrote himself several notes to that effect. In addition, she had conferred powers on him under a durable power of attorney. He had only a vague idea of what that was, but it sounded great, and he was captivated by it. *I have durable power*, he marveled. *My power is durable*. He had no idea what, if anything, he had power over, but he thought it might be the key to the carrot or even the whole produce aisle that formed the basis of Stella's estate planning torment. *Whatever.*

He spent his winter evenings in front of *Hill Street Blues* reruns, drinking whiskey and practicing his mother's signature.

He considered that even with all the extended family dead, he still had to worry about his mother's friends, all of whom were nearly as annoying as she had been. Hopefully, and more likely than not, they were caught up in their own lives, planning a daughter's wedding, traveling to Seattle to see new grandchildren, or healing, themselves, from broken hips and knee replacement surgeries. The golfers, whether in Florida or Connecticut, believed Wendell when he told them that Stella was still in Florida or had just briefly returned to Somerville or was on her way back to Florida or was still recovering from some malady or was increasingly hobbled with dementia or whatever he needed to say to ensure she was unavailable to speak on the phone because, oh, you *just* missed her. Her answering machine still had her voice asking people to leave a message, and although beepers and pagers were becoming fairly popular, there was no way in hell Stella would have ever had a beeper.

He grew so adept at moving his mother around, shifting the

geography as needed, nimbly and quick, that it wasn't long before her Connecticut friends accepted that she had moved to Florida full time and her Florida friends, who had seen her only infrequently anyway, accepted that she had stayed in Connecticut and no longer traveled to Florida. Yes, he told the occasional bridge lady, she's been confused since my dad died, and I fear we are looking at some serious senility, and yes, he told the occasional golf lady, she's getting more muddled by the day. He listened to these ladies, inflating his good-son cred, playing out the role he had cast for himself. He was affirmed. When these old biddies decided to chat, they invariably let on that Stella was always a difficult person, a great golfer, not as good at bridge as she thought she was, devoted to Cecil, but not an easy person to be with, always hard-edged, fractious, but they had gotten used to her ways. For Wendell, it was a bonus. With her pretend dementia well established and her friends relieved, it seemed, not to have to keep up, the calls tapered off.

And bit by bit, he gained mastery over his mother's wealth. When Stella, dead though she was, transferred title of the house to Wendell, he signed Stella's name with a flourish and happily took advantage of the no-notary-required status of Connecticut property-conveyance rules, affixing instead a phony signature of a phony lawyer and made-up witnesses. Recordation on the land records was a cinch, and he committed to Cecil's tradition of paying real property taxes in person, because it looked sincere.

His accounting major/minor ensured that he was capable of preparing, filing, and forging her income tax returns, and he did so in a timely fashion.

In due course, technology provided the decisive power, rendering the conferred and somewhat mysterious durable power of attorney wholly superfluous. When Wendell killed Stella, it was all paper all the time, and he rarely touched the wealth contained in these accounts in the interest of avoiding any ruffles, but Stella soon began receiving bulky envelopes from her brokerage firm and the issuers of the couple of stocks she owned, urging her to sign up for access to her accounts online. She could check her balances! She could transfer money around! She could transact, sell, exchange! She could save trees! Just log on now and create your account, using the exclusive PIN we will send to you at your home address! Give us your email! Give us your external bank accounts! Give us everything and you never have to interact with another human ever again!

He stole her life, and then he durably stole her identity.

•••

Wendell continued to work at The Club. He was near the top of the maintenance hierarchy.

And when anyone asked why Stella wasn't present at Wendell's wedding, the excuses were at the ready: dementia, geography, whatever.

As it turned out, Wendell's marriage holds the record as the shortest marriage ever in Connecticut. It was a disaster. A full golf year had come and gone since Wendell interred Stella, and on the cusp of the upcoming second season, The Club had hired a new part-time lifeguard. She was hot and he was horny, having dipped that particular toe in the water only on occasion since the second murder, but he was pretty sure they really liked each other. He felt like his old self, or at least the way he saw his old self, the easygoing Wendell, the Wendell who was charming, conversational, glib, and quick, the good-looking Wendell with a future. Their courtship went on for two weeks before they impulsively obtained a marriage license, and with no further thought they stood before a Somerville justice of the peace on the huge wraparound terrace at The Club. There were no guests. The GM and the on-duty bartender served as official witnesses, and anyone who happened to be on the driving range, or in the cocktail lounge, or coming in from the Pro Shop—essentially any member of The Club who happened to be at The Club on that day—served as unofficial witnesses. The intimate turn of events surprised everyone, and smiles abounded.

After the wedding, Wendell and the bride went back to work, grinning and laughing, finishing their shifts, accepting the toasts and smiles of The Club membership, having surprised everyone with a splendid story to tell. Wendell practically shimmered in the brief spotlight. They spent that night and the next few days at a nearby hotel, calling it a honeymoon, and Wendell, to his joy and surprise, could even tolerate being away from Bunker Girl. They went straight to his bride's depressing apartment in Elmstown, where, in the course of packing up all her stuff to move to Wendell's house in Somerville, he found it all in a drawer in the kitchenette—department store accounts, two bank credit cards, a gas credit card, someone's wallet with cash still in it, bills in her name totaling more than $50,000, and two questionable drivers' licenses, one from Connecticut and one from Michigan, each with a different name and birthdate. Her lifeguard certificate had a third name and might have been sham as well. He shuddered at the life-and-death pool-safety implications. She was a grifter, looking for an easy payout with a rich guy, and she had latched on to Wendell.

He had no idea how she knew he was a wealthy maintenance guy, but he thought it was possible he had let it slip right before she agreed to sleep with him. Now he was horrified, aghast that he had married a common thief, that her love for him was just a hoax. It was so shabby, he thought, no finesse, no care. He could never respect or share his life with someone who gave so little attention to important details, like where and how to hide stuff that needs to be hidden.

He had no choice but to just walk out. He wanted his gun, which he still did not know how to use, but he could not act on his anger. He would not harm her, or kill her, or do anything to her that would involve hospitals or morgues or cops, because, well, he had his reasons. He had spent too long successfully hiding in plain sight, and he intended to keep hiding.

He left, drove home, and called the GM, who made a confidential call to Frank Ellis, who had golfed at The Club for years and practiced family law. Annulments require proof, Frank told Wendell. No-fault divorce is easier, no truth or proof required. Wendell wanted nothing to do with truth or proof. "Let's see what we can do," said Frank, wondering how a seemingly bright guy like Wendell had gotten himself into such a pickle.

•••

Frank Ellis called Debra Wolfson and asked her if she would represent a guy in court for a quickie divorce. "What do you mean 'quickie divorce,' Frank? It's Connecticut."

"I know, Debra, but look, there's this young guy at The Club. He's one of the maintenance guys. I knew his father, who's been dead a few years now, and from what I can gather his mother has advanced dementia of some sort and didn't even attend the wedding. Anyway, he manages to get himself married after knowing this girl only for a couple of days, and no surprise, she turns out to be a fraud, or something. I'm not really sure. I just know he wants out. And fast. Look, I already filed the papers, and she left the state as soon as she got served, so she won't bother to show up. I have a conflict on the court date, which is the day after tomorrow, and I know you're in court that day as a special master because I saw it on the docket. Can you just say that I'm not available and you're there to hold the guy's hand?"

"Is this the grounds guy at The Club that everyone was talking about? I heard about it at the little food shop. Crazy story, no?"

"Crazy story, yes."

"Frank, I am not filing a formal appearance. I don't want that responsibility."

"No, no, that's fine. Just get him through it. The marriage lasted only six or seven days, there's no property disposition, obviously, just the formality and paperwork. Annulment would take too long and require proof. Quicker to go for the divorce."

"Can you just call the court ahead of time and let them know?"

"I can try, but it's August. Everyone is on vacation, and the judges are just covering for each other. They're even pulling civil and criminal judges out to cover family matters and vice versa."

"Frank, you know I'm converting my practice to mediation. I've had it with the family litigation circus."

"Good for you, Debra, but please, can you do this?"

"Fine," said Debra. "I'll hold the guy's hand, but that's it."

Frank arranged for her to meet with his client in the courthouse atrium.

He was easy to spot, crumpled against a wall, as far from the security marshals as he could get.

"Hello. I'm Debra Wolfson. Are you Wendell Williams?"

"Yes. I mean, yes. I guess. You're the person who, uh, Frank sent?"

He stood up to his full, considerable height, wobbling as he did, shoulders sagging, sandy hair drifting over his forehead. He did not look directly at Debra, alternatively glancing instead at the floor, or the wall behind her, or the ceiling. The smell of minty mouthwash and alcohol nearly knocked her over. He was completely intoxicated. Debra had no idea what a judge might do in these circumstances. She was not happy.

"I want this over with as fast, or as fast, or as quick or fast as possible," babbled Wendell. "I can't believe what she did to me . . ."

Debra had heard more he-did/she-did stories and tales of woe than she had lost gloves. Wendell was not her client, and she didn't want to get involved or even hear it. She was not nor had ever been a member at The Club and had no connection to or sympathy for this guy. She was doing a colleague a favor, no more.

". . . I know she must have liked me a little bit, but no standards, no standards at all. If you're a thief, at least be an excellent thief. What a bitch. I hate her. I really hate her and . . ."

He was man crying and blathering, his words becoming increasingly slurred. His hand was in his pocket and moving around a lot. Debra resolved that Frank would owe her a lunch to make up for this.

One of the security marshals gave Debra the eyebrow, subtly asking if she needed help with this puddle of a person. She shook her head. This was not her first fall-apart-in-the-atrium-on-divorce-day experience, but she was determined it would be her last. "Wendell," she said, a little too loudly, trying to get him to focus, "pull yourself together. You have to get through this, but no stories. This judge, no judge, cares what happened or how you feel at this moment. The judge doesn't care."

They entered the nearly empty courtroom, and Debra directed Wendell to sit in the front row so that he would have a shorter walk up to the client table when the judge called his case. As it was, he was swaying. Debra explained the circumstances to the clerk, leaving out any mention of alcohol or mental impediments.

"Debra," said the clerk, not even bothering to look up, "you know the judge is not going to let you speak for this guy if you don't have a formal appearance in the file." The clerk and Debra had disliked each other for years. Debra would not miss her as she segued away from courtroom brawls.

"I am not going to file a formal appearance. I do not want to be attorney of record. I'm just doing Frank a favor. The judge can speak to this guy directly. Who is the judge today, anyway?"

"It's Judge Hamlin, Marlene Hamlin. She sits in criminal court."

Twenty minutes later, the whole thing was over and done with. Wendell had preserved a scintilla of coherence, and Debra had preserved her boundary and did not have any connection to the file. The judge saw a six-day marriage and either a drunk guy or a good act, but it mattered not at all. All legal requirements were in order. Wendell sloppily left the courtroom single and unmarried. As far as Debra was concerned, Frank Ellis now owed her lunch with cocktails.

"Okay, Wendell, you're set. Frank will be in touch with you next week. I'll let him know what happened." They were outside on the wide sidewalk in front of the courthouse exit, and it was hot and sticky. To his credit, Wendell had worn a tie, but he was otherwise a mess, his face streaked and his shirt sweaty. He tried to smooth his hair, but he made it worse. He flexed his fingers, like a pianist about to strike a three-octave run.

His rambling had ramped up, and to Debra's horror he swigged from a small flask he had pulled out of his pocket. Security would not have let him in if they had found the flask, which begged the question why hadn't they found the flask. *So much for security*, thought Debra. She was more than a little annoyed.

". . . jus' a thief, a so-so thief, bad, sad, thief, and a big hoax . . ." He paused and took a swig. "Am I divorced?"

"Yes, you're divorced. You can't drive. You're drunk."

"Jus' a liddle." He burped and, again, ran his hand through his hair. He pulled something from his other pocket. He quickly lost hold of it. It fell with a tinkle on the sidewalk, and as he reached for it, he stumbled and tumbled, lurching and grasping, landing on his side, pathetically curling his knees up to his chest. He clutched whatever it was he had dropped and lovingly looked at it before quickly shoving it back in his pocket.

Good grief, thought Debra, *this guy is pathetic.*

He was mumbling. Debra didn't bother to listen because it was an incoherent and choppy babble.

". . . I dint dirt hurt, or a thing, bottom sex element banjo guy. Bitch. Best tobacco buy. Too drunk to hurl, hurl, my reversal fling . . ."

Debra had no idea what "bottom sex element banjo guy" meant, but she thought she heard that he was too drunk to hurl and that he'd had a reversal fling, which she assumed was a new term for a rebound booty call. *Whatever,* she thought. *Yuck, and get me out of here.*

Debra looked back at the door leading to the courthouse, but there were no raised-eyebrowed security guards. She had four choices. Leave Frank's client drunk in front of the courthouse. Let Frank's client drive home drunk. Drive Frank's client home. Call Frank's client a cab.

She pulled out her flip phone and managed to call a cab, but by this time, Frank's client had thrown up on the sidewalk, just barfed right there on the pavement in front of the courthouse. He clearly was not too drunk to hurl, she thought, whatever that meant in his soggy mind at that moment. It was revolting. The cab pulled up, saw what was going on, and waved off. *Shit.*

Debra now had three choices. She dragged Wendell over to her car, which was just across the street, and pushed him into the back seat. She looked up his address on the papers Frank had faxed over to her and was only a little surprised that he lived on Appleby Road, just a mile and a half from her own house. She knew this character lived near The Club, where this marriage nonsense had started, but she was not happy to discover that this guy was her neighbor.

Debra drove through the Dunkin' Donuts on the way back to Somerville and got Wendell a bottle of water, a large black coffee, and two bagels with cream cheese. In the fifteen minutes it took to get to Appleby Road, Wendell's scrambled ramble about being either the best van Gogh guy or best banjo guy was unrelenting. Debra could hear him all too well because he was loud, but his sad story, whatever he was dribbling on about, was unintelligible. *God, I wish he would shut up,* thought Debra. She put the beverages and bagels on the front porch and, with some difficulty, pulled him out of the back seat.

"Okay, Wendell, back home. Go inside. Drink the water and have a good cry. Bye now."

"G'bye, Frank," he said, already drifting up his driveway toward the door. "Thanks, Frank. S'long, Frank."

Debra drove the short Somerville distance to her house, more determined than ever to never set foot in family court again.

—CHAPTER 5—

Somerville's bureaucratic intensity was utterly out of proportion to the size of its municipal campus, an oversell in and of itself. There was a single parking lot surrounded by Town Hall, the library, the Congregational Church on the Green, and the old elementary school, converted to a multiuse town center called The Center, which housed, among other things, the Senior Center, which had recently changed its name to The Center at The Center, all of which were on a road called Meetinghouse Lane, but there was no meetinghouse. The Annual Town Meeting, in fact all the large public meetings with an anticipated attendance of more than twenty people, convened in The Center gym, the gym that had served the old elementary school.

While wholly suitable for basketball and marginally suitable for Boy Scout meetings, the gym was entirely unsuitable for any presentation involving sound or visual technology, and every meeting held in the gym was punctuated with a good many "can't hear you" shouts from the folks midway down the cavernous room, generating the annual budget joke that the budget should include money for a sound system for the gym. It got a laugh, every year, but not a dollar. The old stage hadn't seen a children's performance in decades, but overflow tables for deputy registrars who administered elections and voting were set up several times a year amidst dusty old curtains, and whatever had been stored behind the stage was forgotten with the deaths of successive custodial crews. Unknown sums were dedicated to the purchase of thousands of folding chairs with a useful life of five years, which were set up, taken down, and set up again, multiple times a day, to accommodate students and parents and, decades later, townspeople attending innumerable meetings. It was one of those unavoidable Somerville inefficiencies. There was, simply, nothing to be done about it.

As it happens, there was nothing to be done about a whole host of issues in the little town, but that did not stop Debra Wolfson from agreeing to join the Democratic slate for a seat on the Board of Selectmen. She initially thought her easy election victory was a reward for her many years of community service, not only on the Zoning Board, but on the education, police, and library boards. But she had to ultimately recognize that it was a punishment. She went from one meeting a month on the Zoning Board to countless board, committee, and liaison meetings per week, just for the privilege of serving in an elected volunteer position on the Board of Selectmen.

To make matters worse, she joined the Board of Selectmen just as the details and decimal points of Somerville got morbidly complicated.

The Club went out of business. Kaput, done. To those who paid attention, its demise was a long painful slide toward extinction. The old-white-men-in-plaid-pants-and-white-shoes era had run its course, and a financial crisis coupled with multiple bad business decisions cinched the knockout. Course improvements had long been deferred, amenities had been curtailed, and with each passing season, memberships and outings were cancelled, signaling only the worst.

To the vast majority of those in Somerville who did not pay attention, it seemed to fall apart quickly and all at once. The Club was suddenly on the brink of bankruptcy and a developer was sniffing around, intending to build god-knows-how-many two-acre single-family houses on the entire one hundred and fifty-acre golf course, in prime Upper Somerville, all of which would be connected to public water and sewer, as if Somerville were a big town, or a real city. All of those newly built houses, with their huge kitchens and en suite bathrooms, would be purchased by families, each with 2.2 children, guaranteeing that the school system would be overwhelmed.

But whether The Club had slid or leapt off the cliff's edge, Somerville, suddenly, had an issue.

On the one hand, there was resistance and fear. We cannot, it was said by any one of the antidevelopment cohorts, let this property be sold to an opportunistic and unscrupulous developer who knows nothing about the unique character and pristine beauty of our town and who will shabbily build cookie-cutter open-concept houses served by public water and public sewer.

On the other hand, there was resistance and fear coupled with rumor and hysteria. There were whispers of what an opportunistic and unscrupulous developer might build on the property if, God forbid, someone took it into their head to effectuate a zone change. Phantom zoning-prohibited multiple-residency dwellings of all kinds haunted the imaginations of more than a few folks in town. If the zoning were changed to allow for any kind of housing other than a single-family house on two acres, then the availability of public utilities could trigger a whole set of state requirements for affordable housing.

It was a perfect Somerville housing storm—a huge piece of developable land, access off a state road, and, of all things, public water and sewer, not to mention an aging and creaky population tired of two-acre maintenance.

It was said by some that piety, privilege, and prejudice were also in the mix.

First Selectman John Weston gauged the town's mood. If the town purchased the property, it could well prove either perpetually divisive or wholly unifying. He assiduously tested the municipal waters for a sign of what was best to do, but he had to act fast lest the golf course property get sold on the open market. And no matter how deftly he might pull the municipal levers, there were processes to be followed, all as dictated by The Charter.

Ah, The Charter, older than time, just a clunky old dear of a thing, fussy, always desperate for attention and devotion to its needs, a pile of provisions and procedures for public notice, transparency, and categories of meetings, all framed within the core norm that old is better than new and the same is better than change. It held out rules for a civilized society, even if that society was a small and entitled town in a small and insignificant state. The Charter was much like a cranky grandmother—needlessly complex, rigid, and demanding—and like a cranky grandmother, it was not to be ignored.

But First Selectman Weston was an old hand. He thought the town should purchase the property to control and determine the future of the vast acreage, period. There were a thousand reasons why that was a good idea. There were also a thousand reasons why that was a bad idea.

So, even though he succeeded in getting the entire five-member Board of Selectmen, both Democrats and Republicans, to vote in favor of the purchase of the property, and even though that vote occurred at a Regular Meeting where anyone could enjoy Public Comment on just about any topic, Granny Charter had other ideas. She regarded that vote as, at best, Step One, insisting that the Board of Selectmen convene, as Step Two, a Special Town Meeting, where the townspeople themselves, with or without large black colonial hats, would have the power to vote up and empower the Board of Selectmen to complete the purchase transaction, or vote down, which would force the issue to an at-large referendum.

Granny Charter had a hundred more steps up her sleeve.

If and when the town took title to the property and became the owner, a whole new slew of decisions would have to be made and votes taken on whether and to what extent the property should be owned by the town going forward, or sold in whole or in part to one or more developers, or conserved, or dedicated to municipal purposes, all of which would involve developers, lawyers, real estate people, appraisers, more developers, planners, and controversy. And, every decision and vote, whether convened pursuant to the rules of a Regular Meeting, Special Meeting, Emergency Meeting, or a half dozen other characterizations as set forth by Granny Charter, would all be subject to Public Comment.

It had been ever thus.

The 'The-Club-is-bust' hubbub added a challenging layer to everyday municipal governance, and the Board of Selectmen meetings increased accordingly. Debra, along with some of her fellow selectmen, often found herself in Town Hall several times a week. The little Lego-like structure housed a dozen municipal functions, all on top of each other, squeezed into small offices, tangents off a comparatively wide central hallway. On one particular but otherwise unremarkable visit, she ambled down the big hallway to leave, stopping at the tax collector's small office, getting no farther than the doorway. Even though it was the end of the day, there were three or four people in the tiny space, jammed together and all present to pay taxes, right before closing time.

She peered over the taxpaying heads and waved goodbye to the tax collector and her assistant. "Bye, Sylvia. Bye, Maureen. Be careful out there. It's icy."

"Bye, Debra."

She turned to walk down the long hallway and there he was, the barfing divorced guy, perusing official and community notices on the large bulletin board. She had not seen him since that day in court, nor heard any more about him, even though Frank Ellis had, indeed, bought her lunch with cocktails. Wendell barely glanced at Debra as she passed him, but he had turned his head, so she nodded, by way of greeting. Whether because of passage of time, consumption of alcohol, or the emotional punch of the day, he did not seem to recognize her, and Debra was perfectly happy with that. She saw no reason to remind him.

She scooted out of the building, leaving him standing there, smoothing his hair, just a barfy guy with poor judgment reading notices on the town bulletin board. Debra had no idea why he was in Town Hall, but she had an odd and vague feeling that he didn't belong there.

Debra was back in Town Hall early the next morning to attend a personnel committee meeting and to pop into the tax collector's office to pay her own property taxes ahead of the upcoming December deadline. The line of six people spilled out into the hallway. Debra didn't mind. The bulletin board was right there, and she could let her eye drift over the messy community side of the board, which displayed announcements for private yoga, church yoga, recreation department yoga, tennis court yoga, indoor yoga, sweaty yoga, and goat yoga. *Good heavens*, thought Debra, *those poor goats*.

On the tidier side was the Notice for the upcoming Special Town Meeting, setting forth in Charter-mandated legalese all that would be required for the townspeople to vote up or down the purchase of The Club property by the Town of Somerville. She was shocked. Across the top of the Notice, someone had wielded a thick black felt-tip marker and in distinctive and spiky handwriting written "Fuck You Somerville."

•••

Wendell was not sure how to vote, or, for that matter, if he should even attend the Special Town Meeting.

He was not a voting kind of guy. But a sale of the golf course to the town—*his* golf course, *his* Bunker Girl and, oh, yeah, fucking Stella—well, he could see that he needed to pay attention to that.

He showed up. Even with 250 folding chairs set up, there was standing room only. The mood in the gym was upbeat and joyful.

The presentation could not have been duller, but glitz was not the goal. Everyone—the old-timers, the residents whose property abutted the golf course, the university klatch, the other university klatch, the garden club, the golfers, the politically active citizens in Somerville, all the stakeholders, and then some—listened as the first selectman, the town attorney, the town finance director, and bond counsel all droned on about the particulars, including emphasis on the one and only presentation slide, which provided that "The Purpose of the Purchase is to enable the Town to Control the Development and Use of the Property and Some Development would be needed to Offset the Debt Service that would be incurred to make the Purchase." Not a single soul paid any attention to the single slide.

There was Public Comment, sweeping and robust, all in favor of the purchase, and when the first selectman asked the folks to vote, consensus lifted the room with applause and jubilant whoops and cheers. The pro-purchase majority mightily carried the day, allowing for just a smidgen of "no" votes and hushed opposition. Yes! We must purchase the golf course!

Wendell was riveted. *His* golf course! *His* backhoe! *His* beloved Bunker Girl! *His* fucking mother! He was genuinely concerned, so much so that he went home and wrote several notes about it.

Someone might start digging on fairways and bunkers and find BG. Very sad and bad.

I like the Public Commenting part with the microphone attention.

Just spin plates.

Town approval set the wheels in legal slow motion and a full six months passed before the town actually took title and possession. Wendell, along with the GM and the entire staff, had been laid off well before that. Wendell had simply put his grounds guy skills to work and had set up a relaxed residential maintenance business. He easily picked up a dozen customers because word spread amongst the old golfers, and some of his mother's former bridge ladies and Club families, that Wendell, the grounds guy with the wedding debacle on the patio who took such good care of the bunkers, was now in business. He didn't need the money, but he was the only one who knew that, and he thought it might be suspicious if he didn't at least appear to work at something, so he kept careful books and records, and purposely did nothing to expand his business. His choice would have driven Stella crazy, and he took great pleasure in that. He wrote an extensive note about it.

I am a grounds guy who becomes a landscape guy who is a disappointment to his mother. Totally normal. I am an excellent disappointment.

He worried about and missed his backhoe, which, along with the other three backhoe/front-end loaders, as well as pallets, mowers, and trucks, was now securely padlocked in The Club maintenance garage. He did not have a key to that padlock, and even though he still had a key to the backhoe itself, he could hardly break in, steal, and conceal a medium-sized backhoe. He occasionally worried because toward the end of his maintenance guy tenure, he had gotten sloppy, using the backhoe cab on rainy days to drink heavily and nap, sometimes leaving notes in the visor telling Bunker Girl how much he loved her, or using a steak knife from the Grille Room to carve "BG" into the hidden metal of the door panel. The earring that was long gone was still long gone, but he shuddered at the memory of a particularly sodden nap when he discovered that the remaining earring that had been clipped to his ear was no longer on his ear when he woke up. He had been briefly terrified, but he found the earring wedged in the seat. He revowed never to clip the earring on his ear and newly vowed to never again take a nap in the cab, ever. He would not keep the re-vow or the new vow.

But even with those glitches and concerns, as long as the property remained a golf course and the boundaries porous, he could keep his secrets. But the backhoe, his backhoe, his Bunker Girl, made his heart ache.

He meandered. Sometimes he wore his old fluorescent vest and hard hat, looking to anyone who paid attention like he was part of the town's Public Works Department. Sometimes he carried a long walking stick or even a golf club. He often spotted walkers, joggers, and strollers following the routes of the crumbled cart paths, but other than a wave hello he did not speak with any of these folks, nor they to him. He had long ago lost touch with the few friends he had, and the handful of people he dealt with on a daily basis over the last decade were all former maintenance guys from The Club, all of whom had secured other gigs at the end of the final season. His meanderings always took him to Bunker Girl, where he would sit and fondle his/her earring, reveling in the depth of his obsession for her. Wendell had no choice but to drive by the stack of boulders on top of Stella because her grave was practically across the street from his house, but he only occasionally sat at the boulders, and even then, he never stayed long. In all the ways that matter, and even in all the ways that don't matter, Wendell was alone. Except for Bunker Girl. He would do anything to protect her.

Wendell decided to pay his property taxes. He wanted to see if the bulletin board had any updates.

"Wendell, it's only December 12," said Sylvia Purdue, the tax collector. "You're welcome to pay, of course, but you know it's not due until the end of the month, and, well, I shouldn't be pointing it out, but you never pay the first installment until well after February 15 or so. Are you all right?" He was a little surprised. It was a small town, true, and everyone did seem to know everyone, but still, he had no idea that she actually took note of him or of when he paid his property taxes.

"Yes, I'm fine, thank you," Wendell replied. "I thought I would just get a jump, big jump, on this, you know." He paid the tax installment and stepped across the hallway to the bulletin board, skipping the glut of updated yoga posters and scanning the tidy side for any new or updated notice about the town-owned golf course property. He was rewarded. There it was, a Request for Proposal for a golf course operator to come in and "open the course for the upcoming season, on a management basis, to be determined . . . according to the attached proposal parameters . . ."

He read the notice again, from the beginning. He could go back to work, he thought. He'd have a real reason to be there, so he could look after Bunker Girl. He could be a grounds guy again. Of course, a manager would likely have his own staff and maybe even equipment, brought in from other courses that he managed on a contract basis. But still, the town purchased a lot of the maintenance equipment when it took on the property, and who knew that equipment better than he did? *No one, I am still the best backhoe guy.*

Mrs. Purdue lingered at the doorway to her office and watched Wendell staring at the board. She waved to him when he finally moved off and left the building.

"He is such a nice guy," said Mrs. Purdue's assistant, Maureen. "So good-looking in a scruffy kind of way, don't you think?"

"Yes," said Mrs. Purdue, "but he seems so lonely. I haven't seen his mother in years. Not that I knew her all that well, but she would come into Town Hall every so often and, you know, how you just run into people. She was kind of a pain, though, as I recall."

And as Wendell wended his way out the front door and down the one little step toward the parking area in front of the Congregational Church, the tax collector saw the first selectman come out from his office.

"Good morning, Sylvia. How's the tax collection business?"

First Selectman John Weston was invariably courteous and, most would say, a nice guy, but he was only occasionally chatty. When he was first elected as first selectman, he set about consolidating his popularity with voters by avoiding all controversy. It was a winning strategy, and he remained an innocent, certain that people would always rise to their best levels. He cared not a whit that his comfortable reelection margins had more to do with his pragmatism than with his obscure charisma.

"Good, John, good. By the way, I love the wreath on the door. Who got it this year?" And Sylvia the tax collector, Maureen, her assistant, and John, the first selectman, nattered on for a few minutes about Town Hall Christmas decorations and who ordered what to put where, John pointing out how important it was to recognize the Jewish holiday Hanukkah, along with Christmas, although the rabbi at the synagogue called him and told him that they were not parallel holidays at all, but he did what he thought the community would want and kept the menorah up on the Town Green as long as the Christmas tree was up. "Yes, I'm going to have Father Charles reach out to the rabbi and arrange a coffee so that we can all get on the same page for next year, maybe think about Kwanzaa, too, not that I know what that is, so complicated in a small town, just trying to look out for the whole community."

The natter ended of its own accord as John stepped over to the bulletin board. "Oh, good, glad that the Request for Proposal is out there now. No one ever sees it posted here, I mean, it's online, not that I know what that means, exactly, and marketed to all the possible vendors, but we still have to follow this paper-and-pen rule in a digital world. 'Post it in the hallway!' Well, it's progress, for sure. Of course, we never did find out who vandalized that Notice from last year, did we, the one for the Special Town Meeting. Well, at least this one hasn't been vandalized. Thank God for that!"

John ambled off to the men's room, where he had been headed in the first place, before the church-and-state conversation with the tax collectors and the review of the untouched bulletin board notice.

—CHAPTER 6—

Nothing is easy.
To start, everyone—selectmen, commissioners, staff, residents, gadflies, everyone—was simply exhausted from saying "The One Hundred Fifty-Acre Parcel, formerly known as the Somerville Country Club or The Club, golf course and country club property." Debra came up with Somerville Woods, a clever play, she thought, on "woods" and "woods"—the former what one played golf with, and the latter what one tried to avoid while using the former. It stuck, however, not because it was clever, but because it was short.

And all and sundry had to say it a lot. Somerville Woods, the opportunity, Somerville Woods, the burden. As thrilled as the townsfolk were with the purchase of the property, that is how grumbly they were about the management, use, and future of that acreage. The reasons to be unhappy were exponential. No manager ran the course correctly. The course costs too much. Golf is more important than schools. Golf is a waste of town resources. Do not sell or develop the property. Sell the property immediately. Never raise taxes.

Debra could not have cared less about golf. She didn't play golf. She played tennis, or at least an older, plumper version of tennis. But the town of Somerville had not purchased a complicated tennis court property, it had purchased a complicated golf course property, so as a responsible municipal leader she had to be knowledgeable of and attentive to the game and business of golf and all the controversy that enveloped Somerville Woods. There was no avoiding it.

As a result, she could not avoid Wendell.

He had become a Public Comment presence.

Debra secretly flinched every time Wendell showed up at Public Comment, and she told herself she would give up rugelach for a month if she could unremember Wendell and the vomit on his divorce-day tie. But her wish for selective amnesia only intensified the recollection.

She had to be content with the fact that Wendell still did not seem to remember her.

And, indeed, when Wendell would sit down at the little Public Comment table, he would look right past and through Debra, and every other member of the Board of Selectmen, keeping his focus and gaze on the cable access camera suspended from the far wall. His spiel never varied.

"Hello. My name is Wendell Williams on Appleby Road. I am against any changes to the golf course property. Leave it alone. Golf should stay golf, in perpetuity." And then, like every other Public Commenter, he would leave the meeting.

But it wasn't long before Debra sensed an impending Public Comment transformation. It started with as many as four or five people showing up for Public Comment, more than the BOS was used to in a nonelection cycle, all vaguely miserable over Somerville Woods. It was not long before there were six or seven people at a time, and Public Comment began to track the low discernable hum in town about a developer coming in and buying all the acreage for creation of something called active-adult-over-fifty-five-age-restricted-high-end housing.

Thanks to Wendell, the low, barely discernable hum rose to a shriek.

It might have been a Board of Selectmen meeting like any other, but it was destined to be otherwise. Debra had managed to plop into the wheeled executive chair at the big table just as the first selectman called the BOS meeting to order. As she settled in, she saw that Wendell was part of a minyan that had gathered in the back of the room for Public Comment. With the cable access camera rolling, the first selectman called for Public Comment. Members of the gaggle each took a turn, collectively making the case that the Board of Selectmen was to blame for much of the unhappiness in the world. Mr. Haggarty complained about his neighbors' trash cans and Dr. Holzer, a dermatologist, was there to push for shade at the playground, but everyone else who rose for Public Comment had something nasty to say about potential active-adult-over-fifty-five-age-restricted-high-end housing in Somerville.

Nods and thank yous. The first selectman asked, "Anyone else for Public Comment?"

Wendell dramatically rose. This time, he took his time as he walked up to the little Public Comment table and sat, adjusting the chair, the mic, his hair, and affect. He was carrying a poster. There was a quiet gasp because no one had ever brought a poster before. The poster, no more than a homemade sign, read "No Upsetting Development Ever" in big red letters. As he held the sign up for the BOS and the cable access camera, he read from his big index card. "I am Wendell Williams on Appleby Road. Let me repeat my comment of last month, and all the months, best comment, incredible comment, that I want the golf course to be a golf course. Forever. Only golf. Tremendous golf. Just leave it alone. Don't touch it, in perpetuity. Thank you."

The Board of Selectmen slogged along for another ninety minutes before the first selectman gaveled in a ten-minute break. Debra turned her microphone off and leaned over to Liza Beecham, who had been a Democratic selectman for the past five cycles. She knew everyone and was in the loop on just about everything that had a loop.

"Do you think that Wendell guy did that on purpose?" Debra whispered.

"Did what on purpose?"

"The acronym. No way was that an accident."

"Debra, what acronym?"

"No Upsetting Development Ever. His sign. NUDE."

"Oh my god." Debra could see Liza moving the words around in her head. "Oh, my god."

"Is it funny or is it offensive? I can't tell," smirked Debra.

"Can it be both?"

"Well, if it's an accident," said Debra, "it's hilarious. If that Wendell guy did it on purpose, it's obnoxious. How could you not see it?" But there was no time for Liza to answer that question, even if she could have, as John called the meeting back to order, and the BOS plowed through for another hour.

By the next morning, it was out there. There was chatter at the little food shop and over the next day or two, lawn signs appeared, with a singular message. NUDE.

But First Selectman John Weston's controversy-avoidance skills were on full display. The Charter was trudging up the procedural hill and no silly acronym was going to put a stop to forward progress. "This is a great plan," John told anyone who would listen. "Older folks can dump their four-bedroom colonials for maintenance-free cluster living and we can diversify Somerville housing for the first time in decades."

Granny Charter was in her full glory. Public notice, pre-votes, scheduling votes, documents, resolution language, and a thousand other things were already in the works, and what had to happen pursuant to The Charter would, indeed, happen to get this project to the voters for approval. But NUDE had seduced more than a few, so much so that the next BOS meeting started an hour early so they could get some work done before the agenda called for Public Comment.

But when John Weston did call for Public Comment, Wendell was there, along with a swell of members of the public. Wendell now sat with the Regulars, signaling only the worst. Nearly all of them had posters with NUDE written across the signage. A few had been illustrated, but no one could say the illustrations were tasteless or vulgar.

Small favors, surely, thought Debra.

"What are we, in the seventh grade?" said Town Counsel David Silver, during the break. "So what? It says NUDE. Who cares? We have a town to run."

"David," said Debra, "it's catchy. People like it because it's catchy. It sums it up. No thought required."

"I don't even get it," said John. "No Upsetting Development Ever? Upsetting to who? Whoever holds the sign?" John was frustrated. "I just don't get it."

When the break was over and the meeting reconvened, it was clear that a good number of the Public Commenters, not including Wendell, had every intention of hanging around for the entire meeting. This was new. No one ever hung around for the whole meeting except during the municipal election season, but clearly folks wanted to be the first to know what the Board of Selectmen would do with Agenda Item No. 14.

"Okay," said John, "we are on Agenda Item No. 14. I'll entertain a motion to schedule, in accordance with The Charter, a Special Town Meeting to put the Active Adult development proposal before the town, either by acclamation or referendum . . ." John went on for a while and ultimately made the motion himself. "Good, is there a second? Discussion?" It passed unanimously, Democrats and Republicans all in favor. Debra was already exhausted from saying active-adult-over-fifty-five-age-restricted-high-end housing, telling Liza that "we badly need an acronym."

•••

On the night of the Public Hearing at the Special Town Meeting, the gymnasium was packed. The custodial staff had been told to provide two hundred and fifty chairs to facilitate a public quorum count, and with ten minutes to go, each chair was occupied, and people were starting to gather along the back and side walls of the gym. It was November, chilly against the growing crowd. Debra, along with everyone else, easily recognized the half dozen Republican and Democratic Town Committee operatives who were sprinkled about, gauging what their neighbors were thinking, calculating the political cost or benefit. One of the Republican Town Committee operatives had Wendell by the shoulder and was gesturing expansively. Debra did not like the look of that at all.

The Board of Selectmen sat in the front, squashed together along the length of a too-small table, and First Selectman Weston called the meeting to order. The first and only agenda item was the development of Somerville Woods.

The developer was a huge, deep-pocketed corporation with a battalion of people who made presentations all over the country, trying to get a foothold in this town or that city, to build traditional housing developments, apartment complexes, mixed-use development, retirement and nursing homes, retail, or, as on this evening, active-adult-over-fifty-five-age-restricted-high-end housing. Neither the faceless developer nor its sales force was a stranger to public outcry, resistance, and displays of support or anger, and, indeed, the presenter proved unflappable. He wielded his laser pointer like an artist, painting his presentation slides with highlights about housing models and upgrades, proposed roads, age-restricted housing around the country, census graphs, and aesthetics. He was a dervish. By the time he got to amenities, he was Darth Vader in full lightsaber battle mode, alternating his red laser pointer with his green laser pointer for maximum effect.

Peter Reilly, the Town Finance Director, did not have a laser pointer. He made a presentation on the impact on town finances.

David Silver, Town Counsel, then made a presentation about zoning. David confirmed that a zone change would be required for the parcel. If he said it once, he said it a hundred times, and he said it a hundred different ways. A zone change will be required for this development.

No applause, no booing, only silence.

John Weston let it all sink in for a moment. He returned to the lectern. First one, then three, then a slew of signs appeared, scattered throughout the crowd, all homemade and all saying NUDE. It was clear where this was going. John let out a loud sigh and asked if there was any Public Comment. "If so, please line up behind the microphone in the center of the gym and state your name and address." People rustled and exchanged glum looks, everyone ready but reluctant to engage. The line gathered behind the microphone, extended to the back of the gym, and snaked up the far side wall.

"Desmond Boxer, Maple Hill Road. This is going to require a zone change, right? Our zoning doesn't permit this kind of development, right?"

It went downhill from there. Each person who rose to speak repeated what the person who had just sat down said, agreeing with the points made, then stating their own objections or complaints. The BOS learned that too much had changed since 1870 when so-and-so's family came to Somerville, that big national corporations are the antichrist, that the experience of a friend in a different state in wholly different circumstances had not gone well, that old people don't want to be forced to move into elder prisons, that Somerville should only have golf courses and no schools, that Somerville needs another park and more open space, that everyone knew the Board of Selectmen were secretly making deals with Walmart, that public water and sewer would mean rentals in, god forbid, Upper Somerville, and that the selectmen were all idiots, morons, corrupt and shady.

"It's getting nasty out there," whispered Liza to Debra.

"I know." Debra paged through her meeting binder. "Remember this?" She subtly showed Liza an old article she had written for the local paper years prior in which she sang the praises of Public Comment, writing that "It embodies all that is fundamentally correct and right, and it belongs to all of us, whether positive, negative, substantive, indulgent, political, personal, irrational, or irascible."

"God, I used to love Public Comment," said Debra.

"Ancient history. Now hush up. We should look like we're listening."

"Okay," said Debra. She put on her attentive face, mentally adding to the article "hostile" and "uncivil," tuning in just as Mrs. Cherwell, Park Town Road, insisted that the tax returns of all the selectmen should be immediately produced for public inspection and scrutiny for payoffs.

Liza whispered to Debra, "I'm pretty sure that if I ever got a payoff, I wouldn't report it on my tax return."

"Of course not," Debra deadpanned, looking to all the public as if she were paying attention as she continued to page through her meeting binder. "Remember this one?" She showed Liza a meeting notice from a year or two earlier, which inadvertently announced a "Pubic Meeting."

"Debra, cut it out."

There were a few very reasonable concerns and objections, but they were lost in the noise.

The number of people in line ebbed and surged but overall did not diminish. Debra began to seriously question her love for Public Comment.

Wendell was fidgety and anxious to have his turn, but he had been advised to try to be the last to speak. He basked in the glow of a gymnasium full of NUDE signs. Everyone had congratulated him all evening on the coinage. He warmed to the praise and, as someone said, the naked adulation.

It had been close to two hours and although some people left, no doubt to go home, have dinner, and resume their lives, there was still a line of citizens waiting for their turn. Debra had spent the better part of the civic exercise coming up with an acronym they were unlikely to ever need.

"How about RALLYS?" Debra scrawled on the back of her agenda.

"What's RALLYS?" Liza wrote back.

"Restricted Age Luxury Living for Youthful Seniors," Debra wrote back.

"Really?"

"No, not 'Really.' RALLYS." Liza tore up the agenda and shushed Debra.

Dr. Holzer got to the mic to emphasize that senior living facilities should have shade. Debra took it as a blessed sign that Public Comment was winding down.

Wendell had followed the advice from the intrusive Republican operative and, sure enough, he was last in line to speak.

He stood at the microphone in the middle of the gym and the room went silent. For gratuitous dramatic effect, he moved his gaze from one selectman to the next. Debra had no idea what he was playing at, and she was pretty sure Wendell didn't either.

"Wendell Williams, Appleby Road. I want the golf course to be a golf—"

He stopped midsentence. Debra had looked up at just the wrong moment, and he caught her eye. He stared at her in surprise. She could practically smell the mental tinder catch flame. He made the connection. He knew that Debra had been with him on divorce day. *Shit*, thought Debra. ". . . a, uh, golf course. Yes, of course, a golf course. Forever. Only golf. Tremendous golf. Just leave it alone. Don't touch it. Perpetuity . . ." He trailed off. Debra thought he had finished, and everyone must have thought so as well, because jackets and papers rustled but, no, he threw his head back and bayed like a wolf at the moon ". . . or remain open space, no matter what, forever."

The room erupted in applause.

It was ridiculous.

—CHAPTER 7—

Wendell left the meeting, went home, and opened a bottle of whiskey. He was shaken. He downed a full glass of alcohol before he moved to his closet to gather his most recent notebook full of notes. He caught sight of the shoebox with the gun and cursed the fact that he still didn't know how to use it. *Things were going so well*, he thought, *I was NUDE. But, maybe, possible, could be, I said something about Bunker Girl on divorce day and horrible Debra Wolfson might have heard it.*

He lovingly looked over the notes he had made the night before.

Oh, Bunker Girl, I am now a Regular.

I love Public Comment everyone has to listen when I talk.

No one will ever know about you. About us.

I am going to really Special, Very Special Town Meeting to protect you, and me. Very Special Town Meeting.

He poured and drank another glass of whiskey and, with his head in his aching hand, wrote several new entries.

Big change since yesterday, the big bad Wolfson on divorce day. Did I mention you Bunker Girl? Does she know about you and divorce rhymes with golf course. Sort of. In a way. Best way. Good poet, me.

Still a Regular, better than all the other Regulars. Good posters, good applause.

Divorce day, not nice.

But No police, so probably no problem. Probably, very very not sure.

No matter what, protect golf course and Bunker Girl.

Think about killing that Debra person.

By the next morning, Wendell had compartmentalized the Debra Wolfson worry and thoughts about how to get rid of her at least enough so that he could go all in on his Public Comment performance. He blossomed. He had grown from Public Comment new-nervous-guy into go-to Public Comment Regular-repeat-guy. His script now varied with the disinformation he freely sprinkled about, and the act got traction.

He honed and extended his Public Comment, finding voice at nearly every board and commission meeting. His NUDE sign morphed into a NUDE baseball cap, red, with black Sharpie lettering.

Someone had the bright idea for a bunch of folks to each chip in twenty bucks and order a bunch of NUDE hats. Sure enough, it wasn't long before NUDE hats seemed to be everywhere, worn by everyone, particularly since the controversy did not cleave to a partisan divide. The bipartisan Golf Commission saw Wendell as a natural ally, the guy who was steadfast in his insistence that golf is golf. The incipient open space stalwarts, whether Democrats or Republicans, also saw Wendell as a natural ally, because if it wasn't going to be a golf course, then, of course, the rationale went, it should be open space. The bored people were entertained. The gadflies had something to gad about and got a hat in the bargain. NUDE was supple and bendy, so it meant whatever anyone wanted it to mean.

Once NUDE took hold, there was never any doubt that the sale of the golf course property for active adult housing would be forced to referendum, thereby shifting decision making, aka power, responsible or otherwise, from those who govern to those who are governed.

To Debra's disappointment, RALLYS had not caught on.

But to Debra's relief, the long-standing perimeter rule hadn't budged an inch. As with every election that anyone could remember, the all-purpose gym in The Center building was converted into the single and sole Somerville polling place, and the election officials marked out the seventy-five-foot boundary around the entrance. Within that boundary, campaigning or any indicia of partisanship, pro-ship, or con-ship was strictly prohibited, encasing the voting space under a dome of imposed neutrality. Debra loved that perimeter. In her imagination it was a childhood game of make-believe, the boldly marked boundary magically transforming partisan fervor to public-good nonalignment.

But at the seventy-sixth foot around the bulk of the perimeter, it was an opinionated ruckus. Folks on their way into the building stopped at the boundary and chatted with the folks who had just voted, and folks who had just voted never quite made it back to their cars as they stepped over the imaginary line to pick a little, complain, or arm-twist a neighbor or two. NUDE baseball caps were dutifully removed at the inbound boundary and immediately redonned on the other side. Coffee and doughnuts appeared early on, pizza and sandwiches followed, and even as the day waned, there was a steady stream of citizens turning from beige to rage as they crossed and returned over the perimeter of neutrality.

The usual dribble of voters became a controversial gush.

All the selectmen were present, of course, on and off, throughout the day, first casting their own votes and then, lingering on the other side of the perimeter amidst an awful lot of red hats, to shake hands and answer questions. There were no questions whatsoever, so it was a silly exercise, but de rigueur and all that. Wendell was present, very present, at the seventy-sixth-foot perimeter, and he was visible, tall, part of the scrum, his cap on his head, smoothing his mustache and rubbing his hands. Liza told Debra that she didn't think Wendell had voted, or that he was even registered to vote.

"Nothing about him would surprise me," replied Debra, who was annoyed just at the sight of him. "But, whatever. I have to go to work."

•••

Debra had a late-afternoon mediation session scheduled at her office with new clients, and while the back-and-forth commute between her volunteer and working commitments occasionally wore her out, on this day she was only too happy to get the hell away from Wendell and galvanized adults. She made her way down the long hill toward Elmstown, relieved that she could avoid Wendell and the politics of zoning for at least a couple of hours.

She got to her office and waved a quick hello to the paralegal who worked for other lawyers on her floor, signaling that she had no time for their usual chat. For the sake of first impressions, she moved a pile of papers on her disheveled desk to a different part of the disheveled desk. It did not help. Between the voting and the seventy-sixth-foot perimeter tumult, she was frazzled. *This is no way to start a new mediation with new people*, she thought. She took a breath and focused.

Vinnie and Marlene Hamlin arrived at Debra's office, together, and within ten minutes she knew what this divorce would look like. But it was not her role to predict, hurry, or decide.

"Tell me a bit about yourselves," she said.

They were efficient in the telling. Vinnie had been a cop for a very short time in Rockmore, didn't like it, and with the encouragement of his chief, who was going to cut his position anyway because funds were needed for a new radio system, he enrolled in law school. He graduated with honors, passed the bar, and as a former cop, easily got hired by the state prosecutor's office, where he focuses on gritty street crime. Marlene, a few years older than Vinnie, went from college directly to law school, then directly to the prosecution of white-collar crime. They met at work, dated for a few months, fell in love, and got married.

They were happy together. Vinnie was on the rise and Marlene got appointed to be a judge in criminal court. Shortly after their first anniversary, Marlene concluded that when all was said and done, she was a lesbian. They still love each other and are close. They want everything to be amicable.

Debra had no intention of making mention that she was the shadowy attorney once holding a drunk guy's metaphorical hand, but Marlene put it on the table. "Debra," she laughed, "I think you were in the courtroom on the one and only day ever that I sat on the family bench. Divorce karmic full circle, no?"

"He was not my client."

"I know, I know, but I've told that story a hundred times. My one and only turn on the family bench and I get a guy who is completely drunk."

"It was a nightmare. And he was NOT my client." Marlene chuckled again, but the last thing Debra wanted was to get lost in distracting memories of a certain barfy divorced guy. She was about to launch into her mediation spiel, but given that these two were steeped in the law, she first questioned why her services were even needed.

"It's good to have structure," said Marlene.

"Arm's length and all that," said Vinnie.

"Ah. Fair enough." Within an hour, Debra had covered all that needed to be covered and Vinnie and Marlene left. Debra watched them walk down the long hall toward the exit. They were holding hands.

Debra stalled as long as she could before she drove back to the voting site, where neither the cold weather nor the dinner hour had diminished the crowd. She spotted Wendell off in the herd and, to Debra's misfortune, he spotted her as she got out of her car. He strode toward her, carrying a stack of NUDE hats. He blocked her way.

"You're Debra."

"I know."

"No, I mean, you're Debra, right?"

"You know I'm Debra. Hello, Wendell."

He barely eased up, but he took a step back.

"You're Frank."

"I'm pretty sure I'm Debra."

"But you were Frank. On that day at the courthouse."

Debra hardly had any patience to begin with, so she decided to help him get to the point.

"Yes, Wendell," she said, as she maneuvered around him and walked toward The Center at The Center. "You know this, you knew it, but you were intoxicated. Frank Ellis asked me to be there with you in family court on the day you got divorced."

Wendell was now walking with her, shortening his pace to stay in sync with hers. But he didn't say anything. He reached into his jacket pocket and handed Debra an index card.

"What's this?"

"I just want to be clear about what I did not say in court that day. I wrote it down."

"You wrote down what you didn't say?" It sounded to Debra like the beginning of a mystical new-ager chant. *Write what you did not say. Search for what is not missing.* "Wendell, you answered the judge's questions and you threw up. I don't even think about that day," she lied, "let alone what you didn't say."

"Well, of course not, how could you think about what I did not say?"

Debra glanced down at the card and immediately recognized the distinctive spiky scrawl of "Fuck You Somerville" fame.

"Wendell, you wrote—"

He cut her off and grabbed the card out of her hand. "No, I didn't, I didn't write anything that I didn't write. Or say." He walked off.

Debra didn't know what he'd written on the card, but she now knew that Wendell had defaced the Notice posted on the bulletin board next to the Tax Collector's Office, oh so many Special Town Meetings ago. That handwriting was as idiosyncratic as Wendell was turning out to be.

His hostility was not a surprise, but it was now clear to Debra that throwing up at the courthouse was not an aberration. He had contempt for institutions like law and bulletin boards. She was angry.

She needed to find that Notice.

•••

By the next morning, two things had been confirmed.

First, the defaced Notice had been shredded long ago. "Don't be ridiculous, Debra," said the first selectman's executive assistant. "It's been ages. Why on earth would we have kept it?" No one even thought to call the FBI or file a report with the Police Department, which was just across the parking lot.

Second, the referendum on the Somerville-Woods-Sale-to-An-Active-Adult-Developer question got trounced.

The Somerville Golf Commission was thrilled.

The Board of Selectmen had no choice but to take a collective deep breath. At its next meeting, it voted, unanimously, to authorize the Golf

Commission to enter into a new one-season contract with a national golf operation in the hopes it might resurrect golf on a profitable basis. But the national golf group really knew the golf business, so between the municipal maelstrom that continued to swirl around the long-term fate of the property and the millions of dollars that would be required for much-needed improvements, the big national golf operation concluded that neither ownership nor operation of the golf course fit their model. All the negative feedback they offered was subject to public transparency rules, so there was no hiding the fact that lovely little Somerville was a golf reject and not a great place to do business.

The big national company pulled the plug, surely a merciful death.

It wasn't long before the grass grew to hay, the trees began to look like trees, and there were more birds, strolling wild turkeys, and migrating geese overhead. More people than ever walked the property along the crumbling cart paths.

The Board of Selectmen took another collective deep breath and unanimously voted to disband the Golf Commission, prompting Wendell to call for a march on Town Hall or even a coup d'état. The chair of the Golf Commission took to calling it the Great Abandonment. Former commissioners, dissatisfied on all fronts, briefly continued their public squabble over whether a "sand trap" is properly called a "bunker," or vice versa, but soon enough even they lost interest in that dispute. The Town of Somerville was out of the golf business, once and for all.

But Wendell continued performing at Public Comment and said whatever needed to be said to sow confusion and spread this-and-that rumor. He visited his beloved Bunker Girl every day, flexing his hands, noting still the feel of her crunched neck against his fingers, always pleased with the depth of the former sand trap and the depth of his commitment to his own preservation. His note-writing activity gave his day structure, jotting thoughts in the morning, then late in the day, and a "Goodnight Wendell" note before bed. The entries were now systematized, and he often wrote notes that said simply "I love to see my own thoughts. I write excellent notes and have huge thoughts" or "I have excellent handwriting." He wished everyone could see his thoughts and know what he was thinking, all day, whenever he thought the thoughts, but he knew that would be impossible because even though email was now pretty common, he didn't have the email addresses for the entire world and, oh, yeah, his thoughts confirmed his love for Bunker Girl, the girl he murdered.

Grass had started to take hold in his special bunker, and it was full of leaves, dirt, and debris from the surrounding woods. It had not shifted or moved in any way. It was barely distinguishable. Just a dip. Always, he stroked the earring in his pocket. And, always, he told whoever asked that his mother was in a memory care unit in Florida, that she had little or no coherence or recall, that she mixed up the phone and the TV remote control, so there is no point in calling her and that, yes, he visits when he can.

He had been forced to learn more about Somerville than he was ever interested in. *So complicated. No one's ever seen anything like it*, he wrote. But now, even with the Debra doubts, he was certain he would be left alone, free to deploy his ever-growing arsenal of lies.

Wendell still had a key to the swinging gate at The Turn ("No, I turned in all my keys, really"), but he didn't need to use it, as the fence was hoppable and the entire boundary was porous. Sometimes he walked about with one of his father's old clubs and sometimes he threw on the old fluorescent vest he used to wear whenever he did work on the fairways, using the big machines. Sometimes he wore his old hard hat, but mostly he wore his NUDE baseball cap.

Sometimes he had a big, bushy mustache, sometimes the mustache was trimmed and clipped, and sometimes he was clean-shaven.

He mixed up his daily visits, walking purposefully or strolling, massaging the tender ache in his hands, keeping to the cart paths or crisscrossing, so in his mind, at least, he was elusive, even while in plain sight. His pile of boulders was always an afterthought, but he walked by it often enough, particularly since it was much closer to his house on the swinging-gate side of the course. Always, whether he strolled or carted, he looked at the trees, the sod, the bunkers, his special bunker, the once gracious clubhouse, now closed due to its state of disrepair, and The Turn, the snack bar on stilts that was practically collapsing. He measured what he saw against the good years, when The Club was thriving, when revenues were up and it was tough to get a tee time. He gauged it against the last lean years when The Club could no longer ignore its upside-down books and its dwindling membership roster. *No question, he thought, this place is a mess.*

There were those who were sure that the first selectman could twitch his nose and turn the property into a nuclear energy plant, but the interregnum meant that Public Comment became mushier and less clamorous. There was nothing to clamor for or against.

But someday, bad future very sad digging or stuff.
Too many old people really in the way like that Debra Frank.
Oh, my Bunker Girl I will never stop protecting you.

∙∙∙

Sure enough, unburdened as it was by children, property, joint debt, or decades of marital turmoil, Vinnie and Marlene's divorce moved legal-quickly and, given Marlene's position on the bench, discreetly, through the family law court system. They were single and unmarried and, as far as Debra knew, no one barfed.

A few weeks after the entry of final judgment, Vinnie called Debra. "Is everything okay?" asked Debra.

"No, yes, I mean, yes. Marlene is fine, I'm fine, we talk a few times a week. No, I want to talk to you about politics, Somerville politics."

They met for coffee at the new Starbucks on the Elmstown Green.

"First," said Vinnie, "I guess you should know that the whole time you were mediating our divorce, I knew you were on the Somerville Board of Selectmen."

"I don't think I kept it a secret," Debra said. "In fact, I think I mentioned it once or twice."

"Yes, of course. Marlene knew it too, but we both figured you kept clear boundaries. You know, keep substantive politics separate from professional ethics and stuff. She has to do it that way and so do I, so we assumed—"

Debra interrupted. "You assumed correctly."

"Okay, good." Vinnie looked right at Debra. "Second, and the reason I wanted to talk with you, in fact, Marlene is the one who suggested I connect with you, the Democrats have asked me to run as State Representative for the 154th General Assembly Seat. In Hartford. In the next cycle. You might have heard."

Of course, Debra had heard. "Of course, I heard, yes, of course. Sounds great. Is it great?" She thought she should stay in the middle lane until she knew what Vinnie was asking, even though the rumors and gossip were all leaning in his direction.

"Well," started Vinnie, "it's an open seat and everyone who was gunning for the nomination got knocked out for one reason or another. I guess I check a lot of boxes for the Dems in all three towns that make up the district, except that I'm a white male, but there's not much I can do about that." Vinnie laughed. "I've never held elective office before, so I have, am, the proverbial clean slate. The caucus was largely in my favor, so any challengers looked in the baggage they were carrying and backed off."

He continued, enthused over fundraising, conflicts of interest, likely coalitions, his chances of getting elected, and how much and to what extent he should use his slight background as a cop in the campaign.

"Hmm. Uh-huh. I know. What do your people say? Hmmm," Debra replied. "Hmm."

Vinnie got quiet. He got up, placed an order with the barista, paid, and returned to the table with two chocolate chip and two oatmeal raisin cookies. "You know," he chomped, "I'm a Rockmore kid, and most of my support will come from Rockmore, but I need to know more about the issues in Somerville. What's with this golf course thing?"

"Now I know why you got me a cookie," Debra groaned. She took her time with the oatmeal raisin before using a broad brush to paint the Somerville Woods picture.

"Okay, I get it. But what's with this Wendell guy? You're telling me he loves the attention he gets. Is that all it is? It's sort of a limited platform, right?"

"I would not elevate it to a platform," said Debra. "He lives across the road from the former country club. He is not a golfer and I have no reason to think that he has any credibility on environmental issues. He's a total lightweight who wears a stupid hat. It might be about nothing more than the view from his living room window."

"Really?" Vinnie offered and she took the chocolate chip cookie.

"It's impossible to know, because he will say anything about anything. He lies. About everything," said Debra.

Vinnie raised an eyebrow. He was a good-looking young man, tall and lanky, not unlike Wendell, but more muscle-forward. His dark hair, slicked back and smooth, framed an angular face and its slightly crooked jaw. He lightly wore his suit and tie. *He has a smile made for politics*, thought Debra.

"His slogan has certainly caught on," said Vinnie, with a grin.

Debra was so aggravated she could have easily eaten a third cookie. Or, possibly, an entire layer cake. "It's galling at every level."

"It's such an odd coincidence that Marlene presided over his divorce, her one and only. Well, except for ours, but she didn't preside over that, well, you know what I mean." Vinnie briefly looked pained. It occurred to Debra that Vinnie missed Marlene and that he must have loved her very much. But he refocused. "I guess Wendell's behavior was, uh, quite memorable. Marlene said the marshal said that he saw him throwing up all over the sidewalk after he left the courtroom." He paused. "Does that happen a lot in family court?"

Debra said nothing, certain that Vinnie really had no interest in an answer to that question. She was correct, as Vinnie immediately asked a different question. "Do you think the Republicans might recruit Wendell to run for something?"

Debra was uncharacteristically flabbergasted. "Wendell? No way. He's a nut, a complete whack job. I don't think he gives a hoot for governance at any level. He's never impressed any of us as a serious person with anything to offer. He has certainly never expressed any interest in politics or municipal issues. No way. He is not worth the political risk. I don't think the Rs would chance it." She didn't mention the long-ago defaced Notice on the bulletin board.

"Well, we can speculate all day about what the Republicans would risk." Vinnie smiled, now getting to the point. "But, in the meantime, do you think I need to deal with this golf property thing as part of the race for the 154th district? I mean, it really only affects Somerville, not the portions of the other two towns in the 154th. What do you think?"

"Well, unless you can figure out how to put 'A Vote for Vinnie is a Vote for or against Possible active-adult-over-fifty-five-age-restricted-high-end housing in Somerville, Depending on the Proposal and Wendell's Lies' on a billboard, I would try and stay away from it."

"Maybe I should do an end run with the Republican Committee chair in Rockmore and see what he knows. He's a decent guy. He might be willing to tell me what the Rs in the other two towns are thinking."

"Good. No point fretting. Do something, anything. And raise money."

— CHAPTER 8 —

Vinnie won.

His contest to represent the 154th Assembly District was decided on the first Tuesday in November. Cities, states, the country, nearly everyone everywhere votes for stuff and people on the first Tuesday in November.

But not Somerville. Somerville had to be different. It held local elections on the first Monday in May. No one ever wanted November conformity in case it worked to the detriment of their own party or the advantage of the other party. It meant that immediately after a given two-year November election cycle, Somerville had to gear up for its two-year May election cycle, sending both Democrats and Republicans scrambling in the dead of winter to create slates and get the troops out. Once the slates were slated, February, March, and April of alternate years were a squall of meet and greets, fundraising efforts, and everyone from both sides showing up for everything, elbows out. On the first Monday in May, an impossible date for people to remember, the election took place. Historically, winners and losers went back to being neighbors, but the golf course had changed all that.

Wendell, previously oblivious to these municipal rhythms, was now attuned and practically vibrating. He continued to use every opportunity to speak at Public Comment, always sporting his red NUDE cap. He never bothered with eye contact, preferring to speak directly to the camera hookup on the ceiling beam that faced the public. "Hello, I'm Wendell Williams on Appleby Road," he read, "and as you know, I was once passionate about golf, but now I am passionate about open space. I have NUDE passion. Don't touch the property, period." If he had stopped there, it would have been more than enough. But Wendell never stopped there, adding something new, different, and untrue each and every time he spoke at Public Comment. "And, also . . ." he would go on, appending a glittery new falsehood to his commentary, "we can't ignore the talk around town that the Board of Selectmen are committing to . . ." any number of hotel chains, perhaps, or a maximum-security men's prison, or several and various religious cults, all and each to be built on Somerville Woods over the course of who-knows-how-many decades. "The only way," Wendell would conclude, "to prevent this municipal massacre is to keep the property as open space and never, ever build anything on it, ever."

No question, Wendell loved that cable access camera.

First Selectman John Weston would patiently wait for Public Comment to conclude before trying to deny, clarify, correct, or disclaim Wendell's creative disinformation. It didn't matter. Wendell just showed up at the next meeting with more made-up crap. Still, good form and all that, so thank you for coming.

It was exhausting for both the Rs and Ds on the Board of Selectmen. It would get much worse.

At the December BOS meeting, newly elected State Representative Vinnie Hamlin showed up so that, by prior arrangement, he could say something, on camera, about how much he was looking forward to representing Somerville in Hartford and so on and so forth. With a subtle wave to Debra, he made a quick escape, as there were as many as eight or nine people gathered about, all of whom wore NUDE hats. John called for Public Comment.

"Hello, you all know me, I'm Karen Falstaff on Rock Road. I'm against everything you idiots are discussing. Golf or open space. And you're idiots. All of you. You should all be arrested."

Thank you for coming.

Every comment was to the same effect and every comment generated applause from fellow commenters. Wendell went last and, of course, got the biggest round of applause. John didn't even try to correct the pile of lies. Finally, Public Comment concluded, and the group drifted out of the meeting en masse, noisily, slowly, not caring that it delayed the duly constituted-pursuant-to-The-Charter meeting, with its rules, process, and structure. As Wendell meandered out of the meeting room, he glared at Debra, aggressive and dark.

The commenters lingered in the huge hallway, visible to all who remained in the meeting room through the windowed wall, bonding over whatever they were for and whatever they were against. Wendell, taller and younger than all of them, loomed over the cluster, smoothing his on-and-off mustache and rubbing his aching hands, nodding and smiling, wearing his NUDE hat, and spreading lies.

As the group thinned out, Betty Halloran grabbed Wendell's arm.

"Wendell," she whispered, "hang on. Doreen and I need to talk to you."

"Okay." Wendell knew Betty, but only because she was one of the old ladies who showed up at the BOS meetings and spoke at Public Comment about Somerville Woods.

"No, not here." Betty linked arms with Wendell and tried to maneuver him away from the windowed wall, but Wendell didn't budge. Doreen sidled up next to him, all too aware that they were being watched by the selectmen who were pretending to listen to the human services director's presentation.

"Look, Wendell," said Doreen, "everyone understands what is really going on here. The Democrats have squandered the open space issue, at least for the time being. It's a great bridge issue for us, the Republicans, and it will appeal to a lot of independents. I don't want to get into too many details right now, but we need to ramp this up."

"Yes," interrupted Betty, "whatever that property was, as it were, we should now be more concerned with what it will be. Or won't be. And since it doesn't look like it's ever going to be a golf course again, we want to ensure that it remains, or reverts to, or gets reestablished as open space. The dedicated kind. The dedicated kind of open space that you can never build on, ever again, as it were."

"Yes, remain, revert, reestablish," repeated Wendell. "That's a good slogan, uh, Betty. The three Rs, yes, and I think it will fit on a hat." He looked at Betty. "As it were."

"See, Betty," said Doreen, "I told you. He gets it."

Wendell didn't get it, not really, because he had no idea what "revert" actually meant, but even as he glared and stared at Debra through the windowed wall, Betty kept going. "As Doreen said, we need to ramp up our collective efforts, as it were." She paused and Wendell smiled, with just a hint of condescension. "It seems silly to us," continued Betty, "that we show up individually and get little or no response during Public Comment when what we should be doing is organizing and shutting down this conversation once and for all."

"Which 'we' are we talking about? As it were," asked Wendell, turning toward Betty.

"'We,'" said Betty, "are the preservationists."

"And 'we,'" said Doreen, "as you know, are the Republican Town Committee."

Jam and logjam, thought Wendell. "Uh-huh. Okay."

"Bottom line, Wendell," said Doreen, "we think we should get political about this, and, well, we're bringing people into the conversation. We're developing a convergence with the preservationists."

"Convergence. Huh."

"And," continued Betty, "we think a chat, not in this hallway, of course, even though we're chatting in the hallway, but a different chat, somewhere better, would be productive. Do you have time during the day? Somebody told me you don't work, that you're retired or something." She covered her mouth with her hand. He was clearly not of retirement age, but she had been told something about his finances, or his mother in Florida, and she lost track of which part was secret, which part was well-known gossip, and which part was factual, so she stumbled.

"Uh, sure." He gave her a full pass.

"Wendell," said Doreen, "we want to talk about your future. Our future. There is a lot to talk about. But not here."

"No, of course not, not here," muttered Wendell, staring over the heads of the two busybodies and scowling at Debra Wolfson through the glass. He waited a moment before going on. "Look," he said, shifting his focus from Debra to Doreen. "I just want to talk to the camera at Public Comment. I think people are watching me talk. I didn't know it would be such a good thing, a great thing, but now I know. It's great, the cable access camera is great." And I love Bunker Girl, he thought. I love her.

"Yes, Wendell," said Doreen, guiding Wendell toward the exit. "Yes, whatever, the camera, but also other stuff. Come to my house tomorrow night, around six. We all want to talk with you."

•••

Early the next morning, Debra got a call from Howard, the chair of the Democratic Town Committee. Howard taught chemistry at one of the state college campuses near Hartford. He liked precision. He liked things he could measure. He measured and treasured his time commuting back and forth between Hartford and Somerville because he turned his flip phone off and didn't have to talk to anyone. Nevertheless, it was his burden to create slates, juggle candidates and elections, and keep the Dems on message, if they had a message.

"Hi Debra. The DTC needs to caucus. Tonight. At your house. Can we come to your house and caucus?"

"Who's 'we'?"

"I want the selectmen, just you, Liza, and George, and of course John."

"Not David?"

"No, no legal matters. No David."

"Are we talking about the golf course or fire trucks? Do we really need a caucus for that?"

"No. We need to pin down the slate. It has to be certified by the end of January."

Debra was puzzled. "Aren't we all running again? Why is the slate a mystery?"

"Yes or no, Debra. Your house, tonight, sevenish. Yes?"

"Yes." Debra would bake of course. She always baked.

By seven that evening, the homemade cookies were just cooling. Debra's husband grabbed a few and retreated to his study to write or rewrite a chapter for yet another one of his many books on American government, all very senior elite faculty stuff, very scholarly and much cited. Over the course of their long marriage, Debra could not remember a time when he wasn't writing or rewriting a chapter for an upcoming book on American government. It meant that while Debra had spent decades running for itty-bitty public office and mucking about in government trenches, her husband had spent those same decades with his arms folded telling her how the trenches have historically been structured and countering all of her political impulses. Debra needed no further proof that God traffics in irony.

Liza was the first to arrive.

"Debra, why was Wendell giving you those dirty looks last night?"

"I don't think he likes me," Debra said, grinning.

"No, it's got to be more than that. I mean, I, well, I assume all of us could see it through the windows in the wall in the hallway. The whole time he was talking to Betty. Why was he talking to Betty anyway? And Doreen, what was going on there? I can't even imagine what they're cooking up."

Debra took a cookie.

Liza took a cookie. A moment passed. "So why was he looking at you like that? It's like he was threatening you."

Debra cocked her head at that, but she had to face the fact that Liza might be right.

"Is he actually threatening you? Oh my god," said Liza, "we have to tell someone."

But before Debra could answer, the troops trooped in and sat down at the kitchen table. Liza let it drop. No one said yes to coffee, but everyone took a cookie.

"Why isn't the nominating committee of the DTC doing whatever it is we seem to be doing?" asked Debra.

"They will, Debra," said Howard. "They will but, well, John, go ahead."

John looked up. "I'm not running for reelection."

There was a flurry of "oh my Gods" and "why nots" and "what happeneds," but in the end, it could not have been more straightforward.

"My wife and I want to relocate to where our grandkids are, in Colorado. Last time around, I promised the family it would be my last election. I'm done. We're done."

The brief chatter included congratulations, questions about timing, choice of realtors, and whether people played golf in Colorado, but Howard raised his hand and said, "John wanted to preview this with all of you so that we could line up a first selectman candidate and get ahead of the curve." This was new. This group rarely got ahead of the curve. Half the time they didn't even know where the curve was.

John interrupted. "I think we all know who my successor should be, and yes, that person is sitting at this table." *Oh shit*, thought Debra.

"Debra, I want to go to the nominating committee with this, so we need to act fast," said Howard. "I assume you'll agree to run for first selectman. I think it's a great idea."

Liza had been passed over so many times that she no longer expected to be asked, and George had been trying to get off the slate for years because his frequent requests for pee breaks during the BOS meetings were recorded by the cable access camera, and it was becoming embarrassing. But there was nothing that required the first selectman candidate to be an incumbent selectman.

"Well," began Debra, "it remains to be seen whether it's a great idea. It doesn't have to be me. What about . . ." She trailed off. No names came to mind, and all she could think of was the partisan anguish that the Dems always seemed to have a shallow bench. "Look, I'm very flattered, but . . ."

Liza's concerns about Wendell's threatening countenance played no part in Debra's reluctant rumba, but that didn't stop all the back-and-forth. By the end of the hour all the cookies were gone, and Debra agreed to give Howard an answer in the morning. Her husband asked all the right questions. Yes, her mediation practice would have to be scaled back. Yes, she would have less control over her day. Yes, it would be incredibly aggravating and challenging. Yes, the punishment for decades of public service continues. Yes, she will have to figure out the fate of Somerville Woods.

Yes, she'll do it.

•••

At the very moment the Dems were consuming homemade cookies, Wendell was at Doreen's kitchen table, along with Betty, and Anthony Delgado, the chairman of the Republican Town Committee. Tim, the Republican operative guy who always had his arm around Wendell's shoulder, was there as well. There were neither homemade nor store-bought cookies, just a sad bowl of pretzels.

"We are all here just to have a chat," Anthony began, turning to Wendell. "We're mostly informal about these things, at least at the beginning, and whether you end up running for office or not, these are always productive conversations, and of course we've all known each other in one way or another for some time, right? I have to say you've been pretty low-key politically, but now you have a reputation as the 'open space guy.'"

Wendell let the air quotes slide. "Really?" he answered. "I thought I had a reputation as the NUDE guy."

Wendell wasn't sure why they all laughed. Doreen said, "Wendell, why don't you tell us about yourself."

It had been a long time since anyone had asked him about himself, but he had thought it likely it might come to that in this setting. He was so thoroughly unqualified to run for office, let alone serve if elected, that he considered he might as well tell the truth. Not about everything, of course, but as he had little interest in public service, he might as well sell himself realistically short. He launched into a version of his story, leaving out his marriage, which everyone at the table knew about anyway, and the two murders, which no one knew about, but generously peppering his autobiography with tales of high school football, an uncle, something about a Florida golf course, and an adult education creative writing stint, concluding with the success of his residential landscape business, which he had set up after The Club laid off all the grounds guys.

All of what he told them was true, except nearly most of it.

"You know, I *thought* you were Cecil Williams's son," said Anthony. "I think I remember your folks, well, your dad anyway, from a long time ago. Your mom is still with us, I take it, living here in Somerville?"

"Yes, my mother is still alive," he recited. "She's in a memory care unit in Florida. She's very far gone. She no longer knows me." *So true*, thought Wendell, *so true*.

Tim broke the momentary tension. "And you're, uh, commitment to open space? That grew out of your love of being outdoors while working that golf course in Florida, correct?"

Wendell paused. "Sure. Okay. The golf course. In Florida. And here of course."

Betty turned to face Wendell. "Look, Wendell, I'm not the most political person in the world. My husband, God rest his soul, was, but he's been dead ten years already. He loved this town and had a lot of respect for the Board of Selectmen . . ." She stopped and looked around the table. "Where was I going with this? Hmm, wait a minute. Oh yes." She picked up her lost thread. "It's no mystery that the Rs and the Ds, or whatever the initials are, I think I have it right, anyway, all the people on the Board of Selectmen all want to develop Somerville Woods. I'm pretty sure I'm right about that, but don't quote me. Anyway, that seems to be the case, I think it's all about money for them, and they can't see past the dollars."

Tim said, "So what we need are better Rs. And better Ds."

"Exactly," said Betty.

"Rs or Ds who will support open space, no matter what."

"Exactly," said Betty.

"No, not exactly at all," said Anthony. "This is not about getting rid of the Rs. I'm Chair of the Republican Town Committee, for chrissake. If open space is a crossover issue, then the Rs will embrace it if it means we can get the majority on the Board of Selectmen." Anthony had been chairman of the RTC for the better part of fifteen years, and he had a hammer of a personality. Anything that called for subtlety was beyond his remit. He was red in the face more often than he was not. "Don't start talking to me about better Rs. We have perfectly good Rs."

"Okay, yes, of course, yes," said Tim, "but we need to run somebody as an R for the BOS who is all about the open space issue. That's the way to get that bloc of votes."

"Okay, yes. Exactly," said Betty again.

"Let me make this clean and simple," said Doreen. "The RTC needs an issue with crossover appeal, and Betty's group, the nudists, or the preservationists, or whatever they call themselves, wants power. Strange bedfellows and all that. Hah."

Wendell blinked twice. He could almost hear the preparatory drum roll.

"We and they want you to run for first selectman," said Doreen.

Ah, thought Wendell, *convergence.*

Wendell looked around at the faces at the table. "I can see why you would want that, but how does this work exactly?"

Anthony did not want that. He was skeptical about Wendell and his antics, but he had been pressured by Doreen and Tim. Nevertheless, over the years he had explained the process to dozens of candidates, his explanation always sounding like a recitation of the Pledge of Allegiance. "Each party puts up a first selectman candidate and three at-large selectmen candidates. The first selectmen race is head-to-head. The at-large candidates get in if they are in the top-five vote count. The sixth person doesn't make it." For liberty and justice for all.

"So if I run against that John Weston guy for first selectman, it's just the two of us against each other."

It was a long moment before anyone spoke.

"Yes," sighed Anthony. "And in fairness, I have to tell you, you cannot win. John is a popular incumbent, and no matter who we put up, it will likely be a sacrificial candidacy. In a way, that's why it works. You create a lot of attention for this open space shit, and it gives a leg up to our three BOS candidates for a shot of knocking out Debra, Liza, or George. I think George is vulnerable. He's constantly leaving the meetings to pee. You'll still have to campaign like hell, but low expectations are all any of us need to have. But it gives you some, uh, credibility, so if you run for anything in the future, you'd sort of be ahead of the game."

Under his mustache, Wendell smiled his best smile. He didn't care if he ran, won, or lost. But this was a great opportunity to continue to sow confusion and spread disinformation. He'd have exposure for his NUDE movement. The bigger the platform, the bigger the lies, the more he could protect Bunker Girl. This was an open door, a bungee jump, a chance to glow and give speeches. He could stay openly hidden and be the center of attention. The more notice that came his way, the more he rationalized that it was worth the risk. He had committed two murders, so it might be said he didn't deserve the attention, but how terrific that the attention he wanted, craved, hoped for would be the very thing that would cloak the very thing that prevented him from getting attention in the first place.

He read the glances that were caroming around the table and saw affirmation. And possible glory.

He shoved his hand in his pocket and touched his earring. Bunker Girl, his Bunker Girl, he would do it for her.

Doreen wanted her kitchen table back. "So we're agreed then," said Doreen, starting to clear up the drinking glasses and pretzel crumbs, "that the preservationists, or whatever Betty calls them, and the Republicans will nominate and run Wendell as first selectman. Henry Dorchester and Caroline Hastings will run as incumbent selectmen, and we'll get someone from Betty's group to run in the third slot, for three seats, for the Board of Selectmen." Wendell did not nod or assent, but everyone else did it for him. "We will cross endorse and use each other's leverage to raise funds for the campaign," continued Doreen. "This is only a recommendation at the moment, because we have to follow the formal procedures of the caucus and whatnot, but I'm pretty sure we will have a really useful joint strategy to give us the edge on the BOS and the power we want. This is great."

Anthony was uncharacteristically quiet. Doreen had finished clearing, and although she still had a sponge in her hand, she sat down and looked directly at Wendell. "Wendell," she concluded, "meet me at Town Hall first thing tomorrow morning and we'll get you registered as a Republican."

•••

Wendell left Doreen's clean kitchen table, went home, and revisited all his brand-new online dating profiles. It was the latest trend, and it relieved him from the burden of going to sketchy bars far from Somerville. He agonized over the half dozen profiles he had set up. Did you go to college? Yes. What was your major and why did you choose it? Accounting and agriculture studies were the first two things listed in the catalogue. Ultimately, he made up a few profiles, several Wendell-ish persons with various names, doppelgängers for most purposes except truthful purposes, and only occasionally dated women at arm's-length, always in public, and sex only if she made the advance first. Never in a car, meet in neutral territory, her place, a motel, never anyone from or near Somerville or Rockmore or any nearby town. He had to be able to leave, get away quickly, not be confined, but he was polite and nimble about it so as not to offend. If he was honest with himself, which he was not, he didn't care whether he offended or not. Just an occasional, anonymous, and well-regulated sexual encounter and he was out of there. *After all*, he told himself, *I no longer have access to a backhoe.*

He now added to one of his profiles, under "Interests," "Local Politics."

He made the mental adjustment from isolated loner to partisan team player. He pictured himself standing aloof but leaning in, as if he were listening. He envisioned making eye contact while he looked past. He imagined he had a patter, like an easy-listening radio station.

He spent the evening with several whiskeys, his index cards, and his earring.

Connecting with Doreen the next morning and getting registered as a Republican was no big deal. He met her in the registrar's office in the basement of Town Hall. It was all of ten minutes. *God, that Doreen is so peppy*, thought Wendell.

On the way back, Wendell stopped over by the pile of boulders and wrote a note to Bunker Girl: "Dear Bunker Girl. I am about to be a hero and I will protect you forever. No adult old people housing, golf or freeway off-ramp or on-ramp. I will talk about stuff that I know nothing about and people will pay attention because I got elected to something. I don't have to care. I only have to pretend to care. Just like at Public Comment. I love you."

He knew he was a murderer, but he didn't think he was a criminal. It just didn't seem to matter either way. He had gotten away with murder. Twice.

•••

It took all of fifteen minutes for the news to get out.

Debra got a call from Liza. "Did you hear? Wendell, the Public Comment guy, registered as a Republican."

"Yes," she answered. "I already got a call from David."

"What do you think it means? What could it mean?"

"Liza, god help us, I think it means Wendell has graduated."

"Graduated?" she snorted. "What do you mean by that?"

"He's graduated from annoying Public Comment guy to annoying Republican something."

"Well, all I can say is we have an upcoming campaign season and Doreen had him in tow, from what I heard. I don't like the looks of this at all."

"Liza, don't even think it. There is no way. No way."

But there was a way. As much as Howard and Anthony wanted to control their respective political messages and flow of information, by the end of the next day everyone knew that the first selectman slot was an open seat and that it would be a head-to-head matchup between Debra Wolfson and Wendell Williams.

—CHAPTER 9—

Two weeks after he agreed to join the slate, Wendell got an email from Tim, the campaign chair, with a tentative schedule of candidate events. The first was a mandatory photo shoot for all the candidates. Wear a tie, location TBD.

"Hello everyone. You know me. I'm Tim Norton, and I got stuck running the campaign this year." Everyone laughed. At the last minute a location had, in fact, been determined, and they were gathered at Doreen's house. Tim quickly introduced the candidates for the various elected boards. "Today belongs to the photographer. Our preference was to have the photo shoot outside, but it's January and this is Connecticut." Everyone laughed, again. "Doreen and her husband were kind enough to offer their home, and we can photoshop any background we want so it looks like we're in front of town hall, right? Never believe anything you see!" More laughter. Everyone seemed to know this ritual, this political Kabuki performance. Talk, laugh, talk, laugh. Wendell didn't really get it. He thought he should have been the center of attention because, well, after all, he was the first selectman candidate, not this Tim guy.

"Okay," continued Tim, "the photographer will call us in as needed, and in the meantime, Doreen has kindly set up coffee and, uh, pretzels in the kitchen."

The next hour involved a good deal of traipsing between the kitchen and the living room, first individuals for headshots and then groups of candidates by board. Caroline Hastings and Henry Dorchester, the two Republican selectmen incumbents, were getting to know Kate Banbury, the third member of their convergence/slate.

"Welcome," said Caroline, "to the local political circus."

"Thank you," said Kate. "I'm really excited, but you know I've never run for office before. What should I know?" Kate laughed and Caroline laughed with her. Henry was not laughing.

"Hey, this is serious business. I know the Republican Town Committee endorsed your position on the slate, but you have no background in politics, and this guy Wendell who we've put up as first selectman, no less, has no background in politics either. I mean, I'm a little concerned that we've opted for the amateur hour."

"Henry," said Caroline. "Shut up."

"I'm just saying—"

But Caroline cut him off. "Look, Henry, we all had to start somewhere, and, yes, it's not like it used to be, what with the golf course misery. Kate, don't let him scare you. He's just ticked off that he's not the first selectman candidate."

That was true, and Henry admitted as much. "It's not as if I've been shy about this. Yes, I want to be first selectman."

"But you never wanted to run against John."

"Well, I didn't want to lose. We could never win against John. He had too much crossover support."

"Your commitment is, as always, underwhelming," said Caroline.

"No need to mock me, Caroline," said Henry. He looked at Kate. "I apologize. I didn't mean to be rude. Welcome, of course, welcome. New blood and all that. Yes, and you have support with the open space people. Sounds like NASA or something, but you know what I mean, the open space, preservationist people."

Caroline looked him in the eye. "Henry, be honest. Do you think you could beat Debra? She has a lot of crossover support too, you know."

Henry sighed. "Probably not. And there is no way this Wendell character can beat her. I can't believe we have to campaign with him. He's such a weirdo."

Kate was summoned to the other room for her headshot. Caroline lowered her voice. "Henry, Kate has a chance to knock George Goldsmith out. That would hamstring Debra enough to give us some heft. True?"

"True. But our top of the ticket is a one-note song. I can't tell if he's smarter than all of us or stupider than everybody." They could hear camera clicks from the other room and the photographer telling Wendell to raise his chin. "I don't know what he thinks is going on here," continued Henry, "but he keeps talking about his numbers. Doesn't he know we don't do numbers? But even if he has numbers, they can't be all that big. I mean, it's just Somerville. Betty's group, the preservationists, or whatever she calls them, are, what, maybe four or five households, maybe ten voters tops? But people who like him really, I mean, *really*, like him. It's like some kind of cult or something."

"More like a diffi-cult, if you ask me," said Caroline.

The Board of Selectmen candidates were summoned for their group shot. The photographer told them to smile wide and look serious at the same time.

The session finally broke up. Doreen was thanked, there were some brief scheduling remarks, and everyone wandered off to their cars, all parked and blocking one another in Doreen's driveway. "I just don't trust this Wendell guy," Henry whispered, as if they were still inside. "I think he just makes stuff up. At least he shaved off that stupid mustache."

"Well, buckle up," said Caroline.

A week later, having looked up "revert" in the dictionary, Wendell was sporting a T-shirt he had made. On one side it said "The Four Rs" and on the other side "Remain. Revert. Reestablish. Republican." He wore the T-shirt and his NUDE hat everywhere.

But Anthony was furious that he had not been consulted on either the T-shirt or the message, telling Doreen that "no one knew what the hell 'Remain. Revert. Reestablish' referred to, and whatever the hell it means, it should have come *after* 'Republican.'" Doreen tried to emphasize to Anthony that Wendell was a rugged individualist who was focused on his message and goals.

"The golf course is the biggest chunk of land we have left. We have to have it remain as open space, or have it revert to open space, or reestablish it as open space," Wendell repeated to anyone who approached him at a campaign event. He tailored his embroideries, and he turned on his version of charm. Some folks were sure he was committed to looking after their interests.

And he told anyone who would listen that he'd be happy to sell them a T-shirt.

The campaign was stripped bare of all traditional and ordinary Republican points. The campaign was NUDE, full and frontal.

•••

Debra's political life had become a nightmare.

"This is unbelievable," she told David at one of the all-too-many campaign meetings. "I mean, look, you know me. I'm a balance-and-compromise kind of person. I've given hundreds of hours to do-gooder commissions and ad hoc everything. I can cite The Charter by chapter and verse. I sing goddamn soprano in the community Thanksgiving interfaith choir, for crying out loud. And now," she huffed, "I have to justify myself every day against this nuisance candidate, this pesky, barfy, divorced guy."

"Why do you call him that?" asked David.

"It's a long story. Never mind."

"Whatever, less drama, for chrissake."

"Public Comment has become a soapbox. Wendell and the Rs use it as a soapbox," complained Debra.

"So do we," said David.

"It's not the same," countered Debra.

"No? How is it different?"

Debra changed tactics. "You're so dismissive. I'm telling you, David, it's one thing to hear the everyday 'praise-damn' shit that happens with Public Comment, but Wendell is just using it to make up stuff and tell lies. I have to behave. I'm on the BOS. I'm a responsible municipal whatever. But Wendell will say anything." She took a deep breath. "He's a chaos candidate."

"Well," said David, "chaos or not, we're going to be mighty unhappy if he wins. And he might."

"Why would you say that?" Debra asked. "He's a complete idiot."

"When has being a complete idiot ever prevented someone from getting elected?"

"Do we really have to have a debate this time around? I mean, what would be the point?" Debra was getting edgy.

"We're not going to have a debate about whether to have a debate. It's nonnegotiable. It's a tradition, and the voters expect it."

"But he'll just use the time to make up more lies," said Debra. "When is it scheduled?"

"Two weeks from tonight."

History told the debate organizers that only a small crowd would attend, so a multipurpose room at the elementary school was pulled into service. On the night of the debate, Debra wore a dark pantsuit. She fussed for a half hour about whether to wear heels or flats. She wanted, needed, to look taller standing next to Wendell, but she had to consider what it might feel like to stand for an hour in heels. She opted for flats, but she was not happy with the optics.

She was also not happy with the long walk through the endless maze of hallways at the elementary school, but she was silently relieved with her shoe choice. In the end, though, it didn't matter because the organizers had opted for a seated arrangement in the front of the room. Wendell had already plonked himself in his designated chair and did not even bother to look up when Debra took the chair next to him. The moderator was a volunteer from the League for Activism and Civic Engagement (LACE) who provided opening remarks of a sweeping and patriotic nature.

Cable access had been set up and would broadcast the debate live. The one and only reporter who worked at the local paper was there with her usual notepad at the ready and a camera around her neck.

But neither rules nor format nor common courtesy caged Wendell. Whatever the question, Wendell ranted. Whatever the topic, he found a way to blame Debra. He repeatedly insisted that Somerville Woods morph into Dedicated Open Space, in perpetuity. He stood up and loomed over Debra, forcing the LACE moderator to be less than moderate when he asked, then told Wendell to sit down. Whatever the question, Wendell couched his response in Open Space terms. But Debra, to the extent she got a word in edgewise, offered concrete and coherent responses on taxes, Somerville Woods, open space, education, and fire trucks.

The audience, which consisted almost entirely of partisan die-hards, pretended to be polite in support of the two candidates, but twice the LACE moderator had to shush Wendell's NUDE crowd for being disruptive.

Finally, closing statements. Debra went first, as per a coin toss earlier in the day between the moderator and campaign operatives. She stood and delivered a passionate, coherent, and convincing case for her candidacy. Only an idiot would have said otherwise.

Wendell rose for his closing statement. He pulled out from under the table a homemade poster. *Good grief*, thought Debra, *now what?* Wendell stood up to his full height and raised the poster over his head. In big block letters it read "No Useless Democrats Ever. NUDE. Say No to Debocracy." The NUDE cohort jumped to its collective feet, applauding and cheering, with NUDE hats flying. The reporter snapped a dozen photos of Wendell.

The front page of the local paper featured Wendell's photo launching his "Say No to Debocracy" poster.

The Rs were delighted that Wendell snagged all the attention but were, as well, vaguely mortified at his antics. The Dems were also delighted. No one will vote for Wendell, not after that disastrous performance, they all said. What a clown! What a buffoon! He's not a serious person. What a showboat!

Debra was more circumspect, mostly satisfied with the way she had handled an impossible forty-five minutes and all too mindful it was Wendell on the front page of the local paper, not her. *I should have worn heels*, she thought. But David was truly dubious, worried that Wendell's wackiness might appeal to voters at the very moment when the challenges of Somerville Woods were on the increase.

But even with the debate distraction, Debra still had every reason to believe she would win and that the Democratic majorities on all the boards and commissions would remain intact. She had every confidence that her soon-to-be-former spot on the Board of Selectman would be filled by the Dem new guy, Brendan ("the future of the party, no doubt," said John), young and techy, who had just finished a four-year term on the Somerville Board of Education. Debra had neither cause nor intel to suggest that Wendell would rack up an electoral victory.

Nevertheless, she stocked up on chardonnay.

And she dutifully stuck to the demands of the campaign. Be everywhere no matter what, and don't miss a meeting or an event. Wear your selectman hat, your liaison hat, your candidate hat, all the hats all the time. Debra was only too mindful that Wendell had only one hat, but still, heeding the broader point, she dragged herself to the library commission to show her liaison face. She was early, so she headed to the nearest shelving for a brief solo meander.

But there was Wendell, straddling, it seemed, the fiction and nonfiction sections, holding a half dozen hardcover books.

If she could have disappeared, she would have, but she was stuck. "Oh, Wendell. Oh, I, uh, I'm surprised to see you here."

"I'm here all the time. I take out a lot of books."

Without thinking, she asked, "Do you read them all?"

"What does that have to do with anything?"

Debra had hit a nerve. "Wendell." She gathered herself and summoned her best mediator voice. "I feel like we need to clear the air. We're political opponents, but I feel like you are angry with me for some reason, all the time."

"I don't know how to answer that." He stumbled around a bit, readjusting the books in the crook of his arm. "I'm not angry. I'm very nice, tremendously nice."

"Well, you seem angry. Is it about the golf course? I mean, I kind of agree with you, part of it could be open space, but part of it can be housing, or something, or—"

"No. Absolutely not. No Upsetting Development Ever."

"Why?"

"Why? You're asking me why?"

"Yes. Why?"

"Because, well, because. Open space. Nothing more important. No burrowing, uh, no digging."

"Yeah, yeah, I've had to listen to you say that a thousand times. But why? This is a golf course. It's not pristine land. It's full of chemicals and pavement. It's not pure and unspoiled. You can't make it untouched just by not touching it, you know."

With that, Wendell shoved his free hand in his front pocket and touched Bunker Girl's earring. Debra averted her eyes, but then swung back.

"And by the way, Wendell," said Debra, abandoning her best mediator voice and taking a step toward him, "I know you defaced the notice on the bulletin board, and even though it was a long time ago, you can hardly call yourself a good citizen—"

"Yeah, so what? I thought it was a bad idea, very bad idea, whatever that notice was, as it were. And you have no proof. It's a big lie, just a big lie. Even if it's true it's a big lie."

In a twinkling, he had confessed, denied, admitted, and retracted. It was both breathtaking and alarming, and Debra recognized that Wendell's chaotic edges were, in fact, his core. Whatever his fellow Republicans or supporters thought they were getting with candidate Wendell was amorphous, but if they had asked Debra, she would have happily told them they were getting a complete lunatic.

She took a step back. She had a meeting to go to, and there was no upside to escalating the exchange. Liza's comment about Wendell's threatening behavior hovered. "Okay, Wendell." She held up her hand. "Enough."

Wendell eyed Debra suspiciously. "What do you remember about my, you know, my, uh, divorce day?"

This was a trick question, no question. There was a dance going on here, in this random moment amid the library shelves, and Debra did not know the music or the steps. She decided to make up her own dance.

"Wendell, the question is what do *you* remember about that day?" He loomed over her, but she oozed authority. He looked away.

Debra was quickly calculating. She remembered too much and more than she wanted to about his divorce day, but Wendell seemed worried that she knew something he didn't want her to know. The public parts were public, and the private parts, the throwing-up part, took place in public. He dropped his lucky charm, the same one he was probably fondling right there in the library, and then he mumbled incoherently about being a van Gogh guy and being too drunk to hurl, but he hurled anyway, and then he, or maybe his blip of a wife, had a reversal fling. Debra remembered all of it, to her horror. *But so what?* she asked herself.

She took it down a notch. "Wendell, uh, look, I know it was a difficult day for you. Divorce is always difficult, particularly the day you spend in court. I remember that I did Frank Ellis a favor, and you were drunk, really drunk. That's about it. Okay, Wendell? We good? I have to go to the Library Commission."

She scooted away. As brief as the Library Commission meeting was, it was too long. Debra was antsy and unsettled. She got to her car. One of her tires had been slashed.

•••

All told, by the time Wendell was asked to run for the Board of Selectmen, he had mastered the art of the password, the PIN, security questions, online tax return filing, user IDs, two-step authentication codes, landline backup, and an email recovery system. Everyone had accepted Stella's absence from wherever she was not meant to be. He was mindful that there might be trouble spots here and there. After all, as he got older, Stella would get older too, and the Social Security Administration might be suspicious that Stella Williams was still getting checks at the age of one hundred and twenty. That dilemma, and the fact that he had no checks written to a memory care unit in Connecticut or Florida, occasionally kept him up at night.

But the money made it all worth it. He was in his early thirties, spent little, and even if he did not have his residential property maintenance business, he would be set for life.

And he *was* set for life, set in stone, or dirt, or bunker sand, set and immovable. The freedom he murdered his mother for was just out of reach because he could not, would not, ever leave Bunker Girl. He was, in fact, stuck for life and stuck for death. In all other ways, though, he felt he had achieved autonomy. *At least,* he told himself, *I make all my own decisions, I am the best decider, ever. No one makes better decisions than I do. No one.*

Wendell therefore decided that he did not need to write a campaign contribution check, telling himself that the Republicans were lucky to have him and he shouldn't have to pay for the so-called privilege of running for office.

"Wendell," shouted Anthony over the phone, "fuck you, man, fuck you. We give you a spot on the ticket, we take a huge risk giving you the prime ballot spot, and you won't write a check? Who do you think you are anyway? Fuck you."

"Jeez, Anthony, okay, fine. I thought it was a good decision, you know, because I decided it. I didn't know it would be such a big deal. I'll write a check. What's the least amount I can give?"

Campaigning was relentless, and Wendell sensed he might be losing track of which alternative facts he told to which Rs or which voters, so to keep up with his own fabrications, he ramped up his note making. He referred to his notes every morning so he could keep all the stories straight. He purchased notebook inserts, the kind that photographs, six to a page, could be slipped into to create a photo album, so each note was secure. As he eyed each page, it looked to him like six little screens, each with a momentous message to himself.

My devotion to open space crap is crap. They don't know that.
I am doing the R people a favor.
I am a master debater. Excellent new poster.
Look over here. Now look over there.
I don't want to write a check.

He grumpily wrote a small check from himself to the campaign and, upon inquiry, got Stella off the hook due to her ersatz dementia, all the while dutifully showing up at any event where he could be the center of attention. He smiled when he met new townspeople at fundraisers, and he applauded when state-level pols showed up to support the slate at meet-and-greet events.

Municipal mishmash so complicated, very, no one's ever seen anything like it.
Debra knows about BG or maybe not but maybe.
I alone can fix the town problems. Oh yeah, I don't give a shit.

He loved that the early part of the campaign was in the winter. The snow covered all that needed to be covered, and only the hardiest townsfolk walked or cross-country skied across the frigid golf course. He visited Bunker Girl as often as he could. Sometimes he brought a lawn chair and a blanket, looking like a too-young active adult permanently plopped at the vista the spot provided, penning notes to himself.

I love you BG.
I told a voter that I support dispatch reform.
No idea what dispatch reform means sounds like ironing.

Occasionally, he sat on the boulders where he had buried Stella.

The library should have snacks. Good campaign thing.
I should've killed Debra in the library. But I didn't rehearse a murder in the library.
Murder in the Library. Good title.
Good thing I shelved the idea. I'm so funny very, really, very funny.

The note writing intensified and morphed into an obsession. He loved the reflected love. By the end of the day, no matter how many notes he wrote, Wendell made sure they found their way into the next sequenced slot in the next ordered notebook.

Complicated destiny! My Bunker Girl! I have to go campaign now, so I can win and protect you! And me.

Door-to-door campaigning was always treacherous. No sidewalks meant walking significant stretches of frontage on icy roads in late winter and early spring temperatures, with gloves, scarves, hats, clipboards, and pencils. It never worked, because the houses were too far apart from each other, so spouses and politically inclined teens would be recruited to be drivers for the door-to-door attempts. By car or on foot, Wendell liked going door-to-door. He got to peek into houses he had driven by his entire life. He was chatty and spoke only about open space and NUDE, in perpetuity. When the candidates door knocked as slate mates, Henry and Caroline had all they could do to hold it together, and when Wendell wasn't around, they complained to Anthony, to each other, and to Tim, necessitating constant reminders that politics is a team sport, so suck it up. Twice Wendell went with a candidate who was on the Board of Education slate so he could meet younger families and hear about education issues and become even more practiced at pretending to care. He shook peoples' hands, he waved goodbye, he accepted tea, he handed out campaign information. Don't forget to vote! He had expected lots of envelope licking and stamp stamping, but he got introduced to direct mail companies, bulk postage rates, and email outreach.

But the billboard carried the day.

Somerville's proportions justified only one billboard per party, and because of zoning restrictions, the two billboards were practically on top of each other.

But Wendell was thrilled!

I love the billboard tremendous billboard hair looks great.
I'm OUT THERE on a BILLBOARD. EXCELLENT BILLBOARD.
I should have a billboard to myself. ME.
Horrible Henry not nice, very sad.
I should not have to share my billboard with those other people.
They are NOT the BOS of me. I'm funny.

There he was, Wendell, bigger than life, with his twinkle and his strut, standing just to the side of his slate mates, at the intersection where the dry cleaner sat kitty-corner from the gas station. Everyone saw it, absolutely everyone.

As both campaigns progressed, attendance by candidates at every sort of municipal meeting increased. John, still first selectman of course, still ran the BOS meetings, but with one foot out the door, he subtly deferred to Debra to respond when anything momentous, controversial, or prickly arose, giving her the chance to sound first selectman-ish in the context of an actual BOS meeting. She had no problem rising to the challenge, but it was wearing. First, she had to really pay attention. Second, she hated that her campaign manager was constantly gesturing to her from the back of the room, shaking or nodding his head, and third, no matter what she said, Wendell used it as fodder for the next day's lies.

And Wendell still rose and spoke at every Public Comment opportunity. As Election Day got closer, he got nastier. "Thank you, I'm Wendell Williams, as you all know, and I will be the best first selectman ever. Yes, I know I'm not supposed to campaign during Public Comment. Fine, but stupid rule. Let me say, I'm against the budget, just against it. Too much spending, not enough money. I'm against anything you're going to vote on tonight. Debocracy, very bad, carnage. Debra, nasty woman, very not good."

Fuck you, Anthony. I'll say what I want at Public Comment.

It might have been that he lacked skills, courtesy, or common sense, or it might have been that he was razor-sharp and blazing a trail. He either could not or chose not to constructively criticize the Democrats nor effectively campaign for the Republicans.

Wendell subtly, perhaps not even consciously, delinked himself from Anthony and the Republicans, running a rogue Wendell-centric campaign.

He wanted to be first selectman.

• • •

Debra treasured her mediation practice and office time for the bit of distance it provided. But as the campaign progressed, the breathing space collapsed, and even as she sat across from her new mediation clients, Debra was distracted.

"We have separate checking and savings accounts. We've sold our house and divided the proceeds. We have small and separate retirement accounts."

Debra managed a relevant response. "You've been married for ten years and you've never merged your finances? Who pays the household bills?"

"I pay some and she pays some. We split the cost of food. Oh, and we have no credit cards together. Or kids."

"Then what is it you want to mediate?"

"Well, we have a cockatoo."

This couple perched expectantly, waiting for Debra's response. "Well," she began slowly, "let me bring some, uh, perspective to this. I, um, charge $350 an hour. You want to spend an hour and a half talking about custody of a cockatoo?" Debra looked at them, expecting them to see her point.

"Yes. We want to do what's in the best interests of the cockatoo, and we can't seem to get there on our own."

Her eyes drifted over to her ancient law school diploma hanging on the wall. She sighed. "How old is the cockatoo?"

"She's twelve. And we both love her."

A thousand questions came to mind, but over the course of Debra's own long legal career and her own very long marriage, she had come to believe that it is often better not to ask any questions whatsoever.

"If she's twelve, that means one of you owned the cockatoo prior to the marriage."

"Yes," said the wife. "She was my cockatoo before we were married."

"Then," Debra pronounced, "she's your cockatoo after the divorce."

Debra could not have cared less whether that was correct or in the cockatoo's best interests. This couple just wanted someone to make a decision for them. They didn't know that when they walked into her office, but Debra could summon clarity to the table when all was a teary blur to others.

She left her office and drove straight to the Board of Selectmen meeting, where, inexplicably, her mind kept returning to the cockatoo. Even as John called the meeting to order and the school superintendent ran through the budget impacts of special education demographics, she pondered how many cockatoos could be bought or rescued for the cost of one hour of her professional time. How did they know the cockatoo was a she? Is there even such a thing as cockatoo rescue? How big is a cockatoo anyway? She mentally meandered from the cockatoo to the leftover roast chicken that was in her fridge at home, next to any number of bottles of white wine. What else was in the refrigerator to go with the chicken?

The superintendent finished, and John Weston went to Public Comment. The meeting room was full, and the comments were predictably partisan, and when Wendell spoke, he disparaged the Dems as well as the incumbent Rs, Henry and Caroline. Henry fumed.

How do you love a cockatoo? Does it reciprocate?

Finally, Public Comment ended. John declared a ten-minute break. Liza turned off the nonoperating microphones before her, just in case, and whispered to Debra, "So, I guess it's true. Wendell is running a rogue campaign."

"I know. I don't get it." She looked around to make sure no one could overhear them. "He doesn't give a shit about the Board of Selectmen or town government. He is such an odd duck." Debra was clearly in a fowl mood.

"I know. I heard he wouldn't even contribute to his own campaign." Liza looked around before continuing. "So weird. I hear they're calling it a 'convergence.'"

"I know. Anthony must be furious that the Rs are linked to crazy Wendell and his bucolic *mishegoss*."

"What's 'bucolic' mean?"

"Rural and sylvan. Really, you don't know 'bucolic'? Never mind."

"What's 'sylvan'?"

"Like bucolic. All I know is, these campaign alliances make no sense. The open space ladies should be with the Dems."

"I heard that Betty is pressuring her people like crazy to make sure they vote for Wendell. Brunches. Phone calls. NUDE meetings every morning." Liza shuddered. "Makes me crazy."

"Well, how do you think I feel?" said Debra. "I can't wait for this election to be over."

Postmeeting, the Dems convened in John's office and engaged in their usual postmeeting chatter, leading to nothing, ever, but the spectacle of Wendell speaking directly to the cable access camera always warranted an extra five minutes.

"Well, that was quite something," said Liza. "This new one is a whopper. Does anyone really believe that we are secretly creating a six-screen drive-in movie complex and a fast-food strip mall on the golf course property? Where does he come up with this stuff?"

"No one believes him," said John.

"If they believe him, that's one problem," said David, always ready to plot a negative narrative, "but if they don't believe him and they vote for him anyway because they think he is, I don't know, outrageous, then that's an even bigger problem. And," he continued, "he's not just going after the Democrats. He threw Henry and Caroline under the bus on that one. They're all on the ballot together, for crying out loud."

Debra went home and told her husband about the meeting. "I know," he said. "I watched some of it on cable access."

"Really? You never do that."

"I know, but there was nothing else on."

Debra was fussing, deciding whether she was still hungry. It was a decision in name only. She was always hungry.

She had a glass of wine, then another. It might have been the wine or the fate of the cockatoo, but she knew this was going to be a toss-and-turn night. She tried everything to get sleepy and turn her mind off. She named all fifty states, then all the US presidents, which agitated rather than soothed, then started in on the 169 separate towns in Connecticut, but she gave up after only seventy-three. She threw on her robe and went downstairs.

She poured another glass of wine, surely a stupid thing to do.

Debra turned on the TV and found cable access. It was replaying an old Board of Selectmen meeting. There she was on camera, eating a sandwich. *Damn*, thought Debra. And there was Wendell, stepping up for Public Comment. She turned the sound off and flipped through the channels, looking for something, anything, without car crashes, death, guns, or blood and finally landed on a nature program about cheetahs. She turned the sound back on. The cheetah show was followed by a show about baboons. She was still wide awake. Maybe a snack would help. She made toast. The baboon show was followed by an antelope show. Ah, antelope ear rhymes with cantaloupe. But her husband had finished the cantaloupe. Maybe more toast. She finished the toast, closed her eyes, sleepy, half listening, hoping that her new animal-food rhyme game would not grab hold and keep her awake, but all hope was lost when a show started called *Parrots and Their Cousins*. Parrots and carrots! An ear rhyme! An eye rhyme! And an entire segment on cousin crested cockatoo! Debra was now fully awake and riveted by cockatoo best interests and care requirements. She felt a bit guilty that she had been so cavalier about the custodial fate of the cockatoo, but who even knew that cockatoos had best interests? The narrator was forcefully pointing out that the first thing a cockatoo parent-owner needs to do is to think like a cockatoo. That assumed a great deal, it seemed to Debra.

But what a show! Debra learned that cockatoos are neurotic and suspicious. They can become depressed and aggressive if cornered. Their crested crowns express their moods. They need a lot of attention. A cockatoo will chirp, tweet, and whistle at itself in a mirror. Or a cable-access camera.

Shit. Wendell is a cockatoo.

•••

Over the next several respective campaign gatherings, the Republicans and Democrats reciprocally cursed each other, criticized the other for decades-long power grabs, and revisited campaign strategies only to capitulate to whatever strategy had been employed the last time around.

Wendell attended all the Republican get-togethers not because he cared about anything they talked about, but because he still had to conceal two murders.

"Wait a sec," he flumphed at one such meeting when the group had veered toward a conversation about resurrecting golf. "I thought the point was to keep it open space. That's my platform."

"Platform, shlatform," said Anthony. "First, we win. Then we figure the property out. So what if a golf operator has to rebuild it as a golf course? We just don't want any zone change or condos or senior housing or that stupid idea of active adult housing." He grimaced. "I'm still not sure I even know what active adult housing is anyway."

"It's for people who are older but who still have reasonably good bladders," said Doreen, ready to laugh at her own joke.

But no one laughed. It was an old joke by this time. Wendell spoke up. "It's my destiny to protect this property, in perpetuity."

Henry looked over at him. "Your destiny seems to depend on who's listening. You used to say that the property had to remain a golf course. Now you're an open space pundit?"

Wendell didn't know whether he was a pundit or not, but he didn't like the sound of it. "Fuck you, Henry."

"Fuck you, Wendell."

"Look, Wendell," said Anthony, unused to being the calming force at a meeting, "whatever happens with the property in the future is off in the, uh, future. Just keep talking about open space. It makes everyone nervous and unhappy. That works for us."

In the meantime, the Democrats had their own ongoing kerfuffle because George Goldsmith, the very senior member of the BOS incumbents, kept reminding his Democratic cohort that although he had agreed to be part of the slate, he had done his bit, he hated the evening meetings, life was short, he didn't care if he lost, and he still had to pee all too frequently.

"Besides," he said at one of these confabs, "I don't care about the golf course one way or the other. It sounds to me like it's going to be open space no matter what."

"Whoa," said Howard, "just remember, George, the Rs don't care about open space. They care about winning. Wendell is a misaligned partisan, so now it looks like the Rs care about open space."

"We care about winning too," Debra said.

"I know," sighed Howard. "But you know what I mean."

"I hate to say it, but now it's not just an open space platform. It's a Dedicated Open Space Platform," said David, using elaborate hand gestures and exaggerated sounds to signify the difference. "If Wendell wins and gets his way, it could well become Dedicated Open Space. It will be legally dedicated to *never* being developed, not even as a new golf course."

Debra loved these meetings because she loved these people, and she would line up for a robust discussion about zoning any day of the week, but she did not need a lecture on the meaning of open space or Open Space, particularly couched in Wendell-esque terms. As it was, she was still unnerved by the dream she had that featured Wendell crouching in a cage hiding behind an enormous campaign T-shirt, loudly chirping and flapping.

"All I know," said George, "is that this Wendell fellow is not going to make much of a selectman. I mean, we have to keep all the issues front and center, all the time. Caroline and Henry know that. Why don't they straighten him out? It makes them look kind of stupid, nodding and going along every time he opens his mouth about open space."

"Or Open Space."

"That's what I said, open space."

"No, I mean Open Space."

Don't even ask.

Whether the Republicans were screaming at Wendell or the Democrats were yelling at each other, each of their respective meetings ended the same, with shaky assurances that in Somerville, no one remembers what was said from one campaign to the next.

•••

The campaigns progressed through the wet early spring. Lawn signs sprouted and grew into fundraisers, mailboxes were filled with campaign pieces and personal postcards, and the Board of Selectmen meetings turned longer and more contentious as posturing replaced municipal governance.

Wendell campaigned like his life depended on it.

Finally, Election Day, the first Monday in May.

By 6:00 a.m., benches, coffee totes, muffins, and candidates appeared beneath the partisan tents, set up just outside the venerated seventy-five-foot neutral boundary that protected the entrance to the gym where everyone would vote. The tents were on the main path leading into the gym, purposefully within arm-twisting distance and only a scant ten feet apart, shielding candidates and partisans from the weather, but not from each other.

All the candidates and cohorts stood waving to the cars as they cruised into the parking lot, chatting with voters who had little choice but to walk past the tents. There was a lot of handshaking and air-kissing. Some knew to park behind the library and walk in from the other direction to avoid the partisan gauntlets. Those who didn't know or who were happy to join the last-minute hellos and I-hope-I-have-your-vote conversations surged and ebbed over the fourteen hours, following the patterns of on the way to work, dropping off the kids, picking up the kids, and on the way home.

Debra got to the voting center early of course, and there was Wendell already under the Republican tent, wearing his NUDE cap, leaning in to talk to voters. Debra was certain that Wendell had slashed her tire after their library encounter and was equally certain that he had defaced the Notice in Town Hall, but she had no way to prove either act. She was itching to confront him again, even at the risk of another tire, but given that it was Election Day, she settled for making him nervous. It was not unusual for the candidates and operatives to meander over to one another's tents to share a coffee or chat or return a confused partisan voter, so Debra made a big show out of crossing the ten-foot sidewalk boundary and waving to Wendell with a loud "good morning." Caroline waved back, but Wendell made an equally big show out of ignoring Debra. He just kept up his handshaking, removing his cap every so often to smooth his cockatoo crest *qua* hair.

Midmorning, Debra wandered over to the Republican tent again and offered Wendell a muffin from the Democratic tent. No response, but he took the muffin.

At lunchtime, she crossed under the Republican tent again and handed Wendell a bagel with cream cheese. He scowled.

"Debra, are you mocking me?" he hissed, a little too loudly.

"No, I'm offering you a bagel and cream cheese. How is that mocking you?"

"You know." He lowered his voice. "That Jewish divorce thing."

She should have been shaking hands with voters. "Wendell, what? I have no idea . . ."

"Yes, you do. When I got divorced, that day. I thought you were Frank, but it was you, and you were yelling that the, I don't know, the sludge doesn't care, or the judge doesn't care, or the fudge doesn't care, or something stupid like that. You left me in my driveway with two bagels on my chest. Nobody puts fudge on a bagel. That's ridiculous. I thought maybe it was a Jewish burial thing, so I worried that maybe I was dead, but then I wasn't, and I realized it was a Jewish divorce thing.

Don't do it again or—"

"Or what? You'll demand lox and sliced onion?" Debra waited for the laugh, but Wendell tensed up and took a step toward her. She took a step back. "Wendell, I really don't know about any indifferent fudge. I left the bagels on your front porch. I do not know how they got on your chest."

Wendell grabbed the bagel from her extended hand. His face was in a tight grimace, and his fist was clenched. Debra took another step back. "This bagel isn't even toasted," he growled. He gave Debra a dirty look and, with bagel in hand, went back to greeting voters.

Debra returned to the Democratic tent, but she was distracted. Jewish burial and bagels. The connection was obvious, thought Debra, at least if you're Jewish, because one has to serve something at a funeral, but Jewish divorce and bagels? The connection was only in Wendell's head, and Wendell wasn't Jewish. *Was his wisp of a wife Jewish?* she wondered. *A Jewish grifter who was hot and a lifeguard?* No, that didn't link up in Debra's worldview, so she thought perhaps Wendell was a confused anti-Semite who slashed tires and performed religious rituals that involved deli goods. It occurred to her that bagels and tires are the same shape, a circle surrounding a hole, a circle within a circle, but so what?

She was finding it increasingly difficult to concentrate on voters and handshaking. *It's something about his divorce day*, she mused. *He keeps referring to something he didn't say.* That solved nothing, and she still had to wave to people for another eight hours. *But maybe*, she thought, as the day dragged on, *he **did** say something.* She continued to wave and smile at voters, but as the dinner hour approached, she grasped the reason for Wendell's scary scowls in her direction. *He's trying to intimidate me*, she realized.

But irrespective of whatever fear Wendell was trying to engender, it occurred to Debra that Wendell was the one who was acting scared. Of bagels? Of fudge? Of Debra?

The day was endless and was further extended by the reliable crush of last-minute folks who wanted to vote and then hang around for the vote count, a strategy that inevitably slowed the closure of the polls. Finally, the doors shut. The election moderators, registrars, official personnel, and anyone wearing a badge went to work, certifying the machines, accounting for the count, truing up the numbers, unglitching the inevitable glitch, finally allowing in the crush of candidates, partisans, D and R committee officers, and families who had gathered in the way-too-small entryway to the gym. All NUDE caps and other campaign paraphernalia were dutifully removed. The herd of the politically committed was corralled by a long rope running the width of the gym, but it was discipline and adherence to standards that separated the voting officials, their machines, and all their paperwork from the anxious and cranky public, all craning toward the ultimate announcement. It was a thoroughly American moment and, in its small-town intimacy, completely tender and wholly ridiculous.

Debra loved these moments.

Debra spotted Wendell down at the other end of the political scrum looking, to her eye, a little worse for wear, anxious, unsure, his newly conferred feathers a bit ruffled.

Howard, standing next to Debra, had his own problems. He kept his eye on the Democratic registrar. "Debra, is she wiping her brow? I think she's wiping her brow. That's our signal. But the Republican registrar is wiping her brow. Do the Republicans have a signal? Shit, don't fucking tell me we have the same signal." He was very irritated, and he was wiping his brow. "I can't remember if the signal means that we're losing or we're winning. What did we agree on for our signal? Damn."

Several minutes passed as the officials continued to fuss and tabulate and glare at each other. It was freezing in the gym, but both registrars wiped their brows repeatedly.

Wendell had never been in this situation before, and though he loved the all-day attention he got standing beneath the Republican tent, every friendly handshake from voters about to cast a vote in his favor reminded him of the crunch of his fingers against Bunker Girl's fragile neck. Debra's presence, so proximate and hours long, made him crazy. Was she talking about him? Does she know about Bunker Girl? Were his notes really, really, very well hidden? Even as he stood there now, inside the gym, waiting as everyone else was, he flexed his hands.

Damn, he thought, *I forgot to vote.*

The elections moderator came forward and shushed the room. "We are going to retabulate the ballots," he announced. "This will take a while."

Everyone was pacing, speculating, and wiping their brows. Anthony stood off to the side, his face redder than usual. Howard had abandoned his signal clarification mission. Wendell told Tim that if he lost, they should complain that the voting machines were broken.

Forty-five minutes later, the moderator stood to announce the winners of the down-ballot races. "For the Board of Zoning Appeals, the winner is . . ."

"Howard," hissed Debra, "why is he starting at the bottom of the ballot? Why isn't he announcing first selectman? What the hell is happening?"

"I don't know. I don't know," said Howard.

The entire room was fidgeting, but all the down-ballot spots were going to the Dems, so applause emanated from at least one side of the cavernous gym. The moderator got to the Board of Selectmen. "The votes are as follows . . ." and everyone scrambled to account for the math. Liza, George, Brendan, Caroline, and Henry were in, and Kate, the Republican newcomer, was out. "This is good," said Howard, "very good."

Debra's husband took her right hand, and Liza grabbed her left.

"So, for first selectman," began the moderator, "the numbers are . . ."

Debra lost.

She lost by six votes.

Wendell got six more votes than Debra got. If he had voted, he would have had seven more votes than Debra. The convergence carried the day.

Dignity, Debra told herself. *Be dignified*.

She was. She shook hands and offered congratulations to everyone who had won except Wendell, but she could not get out of there fast enough. Debra and her husband briefly stopped by Democratic election headquarters, where the winners were marking individual victories but not celebrating. Debra made the briefest remarks possible.

Liza told her there would be a mandatory recount. "Anything could happen," she said.

"Yes, but let's be realistic. 'Anything' just did happen." Debra turned to Howard. "Tomorrow, not tonight. We will have a postmortem tomorrow. Right now I just want to go home."

— CHAPTER 10 —

The new term commenced July 1. Debra did not attend the swearing-in ceremony because, for the first time in decades, she had nothing to be sworn in for. Liza called her afterward and told her the ceremony had been blessedly petite, and that Wendell's speech was all about his margin of victory.

"Debra, he said he won by eleven votes. Honest to God."

"Liza," said Debra, "it's a lie. He won by six votes."

"I know, we all know," answered Liza. "I'm sure by next week it will grow to fourteen votes."

It did, and by the time Wendell gaveled in his first Board of Selectmen meeting the following Wednesday, he had already told a half dozen people that in an imaginary recount he personally supervised, his margin of victory had grown to seventeen votes.

Debra decided to watch Wendell's first meeting as first selectman on cable access. After all, she told herself, it had been a number of weeks since Election Day, she was a fully grounded and secure individual, and she had accepted the loss. Nevertheless, she poured a large glass of wine and brought the bottle with her to the couch.

Her husband told her she was an idiot to watch the meeting.

The cable access cameras were always poorly angled, so the selectmen always looked tiny at the big table, and the public or empty chairs, as applicable, in the opposite shot looked oversize. Nothing had changed there. Tiny Wendell called the meeting to order. No "good evening" or introductory remarks, just a rustle of the script the executive assistant had prepared for him.

"Uh, Agenda Item Num—uh, 1, the first thing on this piece of paper. Uh, Public, uh, Comment."

The camera switched to the chairs set up for the public. Given that the election was over, the seemingly oversize chairs were unoccupied.

"Okay, good, all good. Next thing, two, on this agenda thing. Um, school superintendent."

Debra had never known Wendell to stay for the full balance of any Board of Selectmen meeting, ever, and no script, no matter how fulsome, can make you sound like you know what you're talking about. Now, sitting at the wide selectmen table and in charge, no less, and on camera for the entirety of the meeting, he had no choice but to stay, listen, and participate. But it was obvious to Debra—and the cable access audience and his fellow newly sworn-in selectmen—that he had no interest, none whatsoever. He yawned. He rolled his eyes. While the superintendent babbled on about summer school and union contracts, Wendell took his pen apart and put it back together, took it apart again, dropping a half dozen pieces to the floor, all of which scattered beneath the wheeled executive chair he occupied. He vacantly called for Agenda Item No. 3, a report from the human services director, shuffling his papers and looking under the table for the broken pen. He pulled a bag of M&M's out of his pocket and poured all the candies out onto the table and ate them, color by color, starting with the green ones. He then took a different pen apart, leaving his agenda and hands covered in ink splotches. Agenda Item Nos. 4, 5, 6, 10, 12, and so on. While other selectmen asked questions and attempted to engage in governance, the camera stayed focused on Wendell while he doodled, ate M&M's, and ran out of pens.

Debra had used some of the time since her election loss to twice decalcify her coffee maker, rearrange her cookie sheets, and pretend to exercise. But the defeat and hiatus had also conferred a jaundiced eye, and now, watching him chair the Board of Selectmen meeting, as per Granny Charter's rules, she was newly riveted and revolted by Wendell's performance. She watched Wendell that first night on cable access the way she imagined a hawk might watch a cockatoo, if a hawk had nothing but disdain and dislike for the cockatoo. As a barfy divorced guy, or gadfly, or a political opponent, Wendell had been annoying, but Debra had long ago acknowledged that he had no responsibility to behave otherwise. But now he was first selectman, and it mattered for all purposes, in person and on camera, how he conducted himself, in public and on behalf of the town. At least Debra thought so. But to her eye, Wendell was detached and indifferent. He was not substantively rising to the occasion. He liked the gavel, no question, but he did not like the meeting.

It didn't help that his hand was again, always, in his front pocket, not inappropriately exactly, but not entirely suitable for a public official in the course of a televised meeting. It was difficult to watch and impossible to look away.

He dodged all substance and contributed nothing.

But when Peter Reilly, the finance director, mentioned Somerville Woods, Wendell perked right up and made a big deal out of shushing the side conversation between Caroline and Henry. Peter, surprised that Wendell was now paying attention, informed the selectmen that he needed BOS authorization to auction off as an entire lot all The Club maintenance equipment, which would generate a few thousand for the municipal kitty.

"All of the maintenance equipment? Everything?" asked Wendell.

"Uh, yeah," answered Peter, "everything."

"The backhoes? You're auctioning off the backhoes? No way, we shouldn't auction them off. It's important to have multiple backhoes. Backhoes are incredibly important."

"Uh, Wendell," responded Peter, "we already have multiple backhoes at Public Works and we've sold three out of the four that were at The Club. There's only one left in The Club maintenance barn. We don't need it, and we'll do better auctioning if off with the mowers and everything else that's in the garage."

Wendell leaned in and was suddenly very serious. "Which one is still in The Club garage?" Wendell asked.

"Which backhoe? I have no idea. It's a backhoe," said Peter.

Henry interrupted with an appropriate motion, which Liza loudly seconded.

"Wendell," said Henry, "you have to call for discussion."

"I don't want to call for discussion," said Wendell. "We should not get rid of this, uh, very important backhoe."

Henry called the question, forcing a vote. Everyone voted in favor of the motion except Wendell, who refused to vote, or even countenance that a vote was taking place. "This is a complete hoax," shouted Wendell, but after some procedural shoving, Wendell moved on to the next agenda item.

Debra, still watching on cable access, was mildly satisfied that Wendell looked like an ass, but something niggled, and inexplicably van Gogh came to mind. Peter must have thought it wiser to wait until after the election before seeking authority to get rid of all the equipment, but neither his timeline of choice nor a possible van Gogh painting explained why Wendell cared about keeping a backhoe or why he needed to characterize a backhoe as important. All selectmen over the centuries could agree that education is important. Health and safety are important. Taxes and social justice are important. Backhoes are expensive and necessary.

But why did it ring a bell? Debra asked herself.

Wendell was pouting and perfunctorily got to the last item.

"Agenda Item No. 22. Liaisons." Wendell both mispronounced and misread "liaisons" so it came out "liar-sons." No one corrected him. "Whatever. Um, Brendan, you should take, will take, the 'liar-son' positions that Debra had, Debra who I beat by twenty-two votes . . ."

Debra, sitting at home and watching, growled at the television.

". . . I want the ones that have something to do with things I care about, or at least say I care about, yes, care about, so I will take those from Henry. Henry, you will take the Police Commission. I guess everyone else stays where they are."

"Wait a second," interrupted Henry. "Why do I have to take the Police Commission all of a sudden? The first selectman always takes the Police Commission." Debra could see that Henry had made a quick on-camera political calculation, adding up in his possible future favor. "Okay, fine, I'll take the Police Commission."

Liza called Debra the next morning and gave her the behind-the-scenes update.

"Well, Debra, the liaison appointments were pretty much the last agenda item, and after we adjourned Wendell cornered Peter Reilly in the hallway and insisted that the list of equipment to be auctioned off be altered to exclude the backhoe."

"What do you mean 'insisted'? How can he insist? The board voted."

"I know, I know, but Wendell was practically shouting at him. I don't think we have room in the Public Works garage for another backhoe."

"Is that the point?"

"No, of course not, and you don't really have to keep it in a garage, do you? I guess it needs to be covered, somehow. Don't we have a covered vehicle area at Public Works? Not that that's the point either, but, well, I'm not sure what is the point."

"Why is Wendell so insistent about it?"

"No idea, but I thought Henry was going to punch him. Honestly, he was being such a jerk about this ancient piece of equipment. And Peter was just trying to keep the peace."

"How did it end?"

"Well," said Liza, "Peter agreed to conduct a tour for the Board of Selectmen to view all of the equipment that was on the list."

"Lucky you."

Non-backhoe-related gossip was abundant. Town Hall staff was not happy to have Wendell in their daily midst erratically telling them what to do and how to do it, or in his office doing Lord knows what with the door closed. He was first selectman, true, but it's not as if he ran the town in any meaningful way. Everyone knew that was Peter Reilly's remit as finance director, the municipal equivalent of the Deep State. He wore every hat and actually did the work.

Wendell's only talent in evidence was his seeming ability to be the most disruptive force at every meeting and, at the same time, run the meeting. Wendell barely followed procedure, erratically veering off into Wendell-land.

He made a motion to change the name of Somerville Woods, upsetting both the agenda and the other selectmen. "As a result of the idiocy of prior and current selectmen, who have voted the wrong way for a very long time, I move that we rename the property the Beautiful, Really Beautiful Acreage and not use any words that say 'golf course' or 'Somerville Woods.'" The motion died for lack of a second, and Wendell and Henry nearly came to blows during the cookie break.

At the next meeting, he brought it up again, and it was clear he had no intention of letting anyone harness him. He coupled that disorder with a motion to create a Public Works commission and further moved that he be appointed the chair of the Public Works commission. Somehow, Somerville had survived for more than two hundred years without a Public Works commission, but Wendell wanted one.

"Wendell," said Caroline, "Public Works does not need civil oversight. When it snows, they plow. When the road crumbles, they pave. When a tree needs to be removed, they remove it. Why would you want to bureaucratize it?" Wendell made a piteous argument aggrandizing construction equipment, but it fell short, as did his other wacky efforts.

His antics took up time at meetings that were already too long. Wendell was doing little to endear himself to anyone who actually performed a municipal service. No question, the tension on the BOS was palpable. It was about to get worse.

•••

A month and a half into Wendell's term, George Goldsmith's bladder couldn't take it anymore, and rather than disrupt the on-camera meetings with his bathroom needs, he resigned from the Board of Selectmen. Filling the vacancy was wholly within the remit of the Democratic Town Committee. Naturally, they asked Debra to rejoin the BOS. Naturally, she said no. Naturally, they asked her again. Naturally, she said yes.

A different sort of leader might have called to congratulate Debra on rejoining the Board of Selectmen, or reached out to set a tone. Wendell was a different sort of leader, no question, but not the right sort of different. Not even close.

Debra called Wendell. Twice. He did not take or return her calls.

The meeting packet for Debra's first return meeting was waiting in her mailbox, and as she opened the bulky envelope, she briefly regretted saying yes to rejoining the BOS. The one-page agenda served as a wily dodge for the multitude of detailed reports covering everything from assessor to zoning, pages of data from the state, from the regional this and that, from the finance director, the human services coordinator, the fire chief, the town clerk, just endless hard copy of everything municipally imaginable.

But Debra read everything. She followed the rules. And the procedures, practices, customs, and rituals. At bottom, she loved all this stuff, adherence to standards and civic engagement. She was home again.

On the day of her first meeting, Debra arrived early to get sworn in. The town clerk administered the oath of office, and when he finished, he grinned at Debra. "This should be interesting."

It was. Debra's name placard had been placed in her old spot, just to the left of the first selectman's seat, so that's where she sat. But as soon as Wendell sat down, he passed her a note in his familiar spiky cursive. The note noted: "Debra, you are sitting too close to me. Move."

Debra didn't move. Wendell had no choice but to rustle his papers and recognize that the cable access cameras were on. "Okay," he said, "I'm starting now. Public Comment." Dr. Holzer was there again, and while he talked about basal cell carcinoma, Debra wrote back to Wendell: "Why?"

Wendell scrawled back: "Because you are the newest so you should be the furthest away from the most important person."

Debra wrote back: "Who is the most important person?"

Dr. Holzer finished. Instead of moving to Agenda Item No. 2, Wendell went off script. "I need to point out that Debra Wolfson is not sitting at the correct place. She should be in that old guy's spot, whatever his name was, George something, his old spot on the end, far end, very far end of the table. The name signs are incorrect, not correct, not at all correct, and she should not be this close to where I am sitting. You all need to move around to fix this."

Liza caught Debra's eye and subtly indicated that she should stay put. Debra had no intention of moving in any event, but she appreciated the solidarity. A long five minutes went by.

Caroline was not having it. "Wendell, for crying out loud. We're not here to play musical chairs. Get on with the meeting."

"Fine. But this needs to be straightened out. Agenda item whatever."

Wendell pouted. Ninety minutes later, he announced a short break. When the cameras stopped, he turned to Debra and loudly insisted that she move her seat, but Debra's fellow selectmen, both Rs and Ds, told Wendell to shut up. Wendell got through the rest of the agenda, but he was fuming.

The meeting adjourned. Henry and Caroline followed Wendell to his office, and Henry's shouting followed everyone all the way down the hall and out the door.

Wendell was, evidently, persuaded to drop the seating arrangement controversy, but now, because of the controversy, Debra was stuck. As a matter of principle, she couldn't move her seat whether she wanted to or not. She hated sitting next to Wendell for the simple reason that she hated Wendell. He doodled endlessly, and Debra could not help but see his scribbles, all over his papers, circles within circles, like tires and bagels, and the initials BG, over and over. Debra couldn't remember the name of his six-day spouse or whether her initials were BG, but there was no other explanation. She must have been BG. *Maybe her name was Betty Grable,* thought Debra.

If he wasn't doodling, he was shredding meeting procedure into his own personal confetti. Then, one evening, for just the briefest of moments, he became a sort of on-camera first selectman.

"Okay, everyone," said Wendell, "I am happy to announce that the tour of the old maintenance garage at The Club has grown bigger so that you can all learn about the property from me. And good news, excellent news, we have removed from the auction list the old backhoe that was on the list, and we have removed it so it isn't on the list anymore. The town owns the backhoe anyway because we, I, own everything, so after the tour we are going to move it to the Public Works garage and use it for town stuff, like whenever we need a backhoe."

He had gotten something he wanted, and in return, he agreed to back off from the Somerville Woods name change and the Public Works commission setup. At least that's what Caroline told Liza and Debra when they were all in the ladies' room later that night.

"Look, he was making us all look bad, so finally Anthony screamed at him and told him to stop fucking around and get serious," said Caroline. "He said he would, but only if he led the tour and only if the backhoe in The Club garage got transferred to the town garage.

Anthony spoke with Peter, and Peter spoke with the director of Public Works, who of course said yes to another piece of equipment, even an ancient piece of equipment, so there you have it."

"Don't we have to vote on it?" asked Liza.

"Probably," said Caroline, "but don't hold your breath. It's not worth the fuss. It seems that it only makes a difference to Wendell."

Debra felt that familiar pinch of memory, just a sting at the edge. Only this time, her thoughts of van Gogh were accompanied by banjo music in her head.

By the next meeting, Wendell had reverted to his old ways. He bypassed the agenda, insisting that the public water connection at Somerville Woods was crushingly expensive and should be disconnected. "No water, revert to Open Space, no digging, ever," stated First Selectman Wendell.

"Uh, Wendell," said Peter, "I've explained this a dozen times. Our insurance requires the water to stay connected because it serves the sprinkler fire alarm system in the old clubhouse building and locker room complex."

"Screw that," Wendell yelled. "The complex is way too complexicated. We should tear it down."

Silent astonishment carried the moment, but Peter pressed on. "Uh, as I've explained to everyone," said Peter, "the water cost is insignificant. By contrast, demolition is in the high six figures, and the only way to make it affordable is to bury tons of noncontaminated demolition debris on the site." Peter was in his administrative glory as he took this deep dive into civic specificity. "Burial would have to be alongside the old eleventh and twelfth fairways because of access and neighbors' wells. All of this would require state involvement and permitting, not to mention individual homeowner complications."

"God, no," shouted Wendell, pounding the table as he did so, knocking to the floor the pile of cookies he had stacked on his meeting packet. He was very red in the face, and he stammered to find his voice. "Oh, damn, uh, yes, complicated, so complicated, no one's ever seen anything, uh, like it, stay connected, we should all stay connected." Wendell turned to face the cable access camera, way in the back of the room, and repeated his "no digging" mantra, adding, "and no estimates, very bad idea, very sad."

During the break, Debra told Liza that Wendell's antics amounted to a complete waste of perfectly good cookies. "And," she went on, "I can't believe he backed off. Wendell only backs off if he gets something."

"I know," replied Liza. "There is no way he cares about the water cost. As it is, from what I can tell, he only cares about that backhoe. Oh well, of course he cares about his NUDE movement. Sort of. I think. You know, Debra, I think Wendell might be a little, uh, unbalanced."

"A little unbalanced?" Debra hissed. "Are you kidding? He's completely off his rocker. Who knows what he cares about? I doubt he cares about anything. He never played golf, but he wanted a golf course, in perpetuity. He has no known commitment to environmental issues, but he wants open space, or Open Space. He cares not a whit for, nor gives a shit about, governance, but he ran for office. He had not one volunteer hour to his credit toward any Somerville imperative, but he believes that he is the oracle. He's got his hand in his pocket and his head up his ass."

Liza was agape. "That was quite a speech, Debra. Maybe you haven't fully accepted—"

"No. I mean yes. I have accepted the loss, definitely. I don't mean to rant." Debra took a deep breath. "But Wendell is not just odd, he's destructive. And sneaky. It's driving me nuts." Debra was reluctant to tell Liza, or anyone for that matter, how cockatoos and van Gogh kept each other company in her head. *Talk about being off one's rocker*, she thought.

The meeting came back to order, or what passed for order in the Wendell regime, but Debra was still agitated. *There is no way van Gogh played the banjo*, Debra thought. *It's an upside-down thought in an upside-down Wendell world.* Debra was a divorce mediator and a lawyer. She lived in the rational, problem-solving world. She lived in the government-has-a-role world. She lived in the rules-and-standards-matter world.

And Wendell kept popping up in her world.

•••

Setting up the tour was a logistics nightmare, and Granny Charter was nervous because, technically, the tour constituted a public meeting, but the first selectman's executive assistant wrestled the challenges to the ground and got it set up, weather permitting, and when weather did not permit, she wrestled it to the ground again. At the last moment, Wendell insisted that the members of the Board of Finance, the Conservation Commission, and the Recreation Commission be included on the tour. He wanted a big audience, no question.

The day turned out to be sunny, but cold. Everyone huddled together at the clubhouse entrance. Wendell had brought a bullhorn. "Hello, hello," he blared. "The focus of this tour is my vast knowledge of the property and stuff. First the clubhouse."

The clubhouse, gracious in its day, took only twenty minutes to walk through because Wendell practically jogged through the Grille Room, the kitchens, the bar, the banquet facilities, the locker rooms, and the adjacent pro shop. No furniture, furnishings, fittings, or fixtures, just memories and days gone by. The group briefly lingered at the huge windows that overlooked the property and the patio, the very patio where Wendell had gotten married.

"Nothing important to look at here, moving on," he said.

The group made their way to the dilapidated pro shop, where a herd of decrepit, newly charged, and barely cleaned golf carts gathered like old horses at a sagging hitching post.

After much discussion about how to drive a golf cart, and who should drive a golf cart, and the town's liability if something should happen while they were in or driving a golf cart, everyone got in the golf carts and miraculously got them driven. Wendell made sure he was in Golf Cart No. 1, labeled by him as such, and everyone was meant to follow him.

Wendell carted to this spot or that, hopped out, and blared loudly through the bullhorn, nonstop, causing birds to flee the treetops. He stopped at random shrubs and old water hazards, sans coherence. He zipped past the frail and crumbly snack bar and up the back nine.

Wendell offered very little substance ("That tree is a, uh, very tall tree"), but Peter cleared up any doubts, if any there were, that what the town owned was an enormous piece of property with nearly nothing to look at, just acres of neglected trees, neglected woodland, and neglected buildings and a mélange of topographical features, all man-made and sculpted, disheveled and desolate. The tour achieved its desired goal of common terms so that going forward, all references to the southwest corner, or the hill where the fourth fairway used to undulate, or the pile of boulders near the swinging gate, would be understood by all.

The caravan stopped somewhere along the old eleventh fairway, and Wendell used his bullhorn to encourage everyone to get out of the carts and wander about to take in the vista and the vast proportions of the acreage. The wind was howling on the rise, but Wendell gravitated toward a dimple on the gentle hill, and the group followed, as they were meant to. It looked like every other dimple, a slight swale full of leaves and debris, perhaps a little deeper on one end but in no other way remarkable. By dribs and drabs, there were a few comments about the old days, many of the town leaders having been members of The Club themselves back when, and then there were a few questions and comments that Wendell glommed onto. It was stand and listen to Wendell or get back in the cart.

"It used to be beautiful," said Wendell, "and now it's still beautiful and also a mess, very, very big, huge mess. Where we're standing now, right here, this is my favorite spot, my absolute favorite spot." *Oh Bunker Girl,* he thought, *look at all the people listening to me!*

"Wendell, let me ask you something," said Doug Giordano, a longtime member of the Board of Finance who had no filter whatsoever. "I remember the old days very well. My wife and I were members here for a few years, and when it was a good club, it was great, always looked good, always in great shape, but they screwed it up, didn't they? Right? They screwed it up."

"Well, that wasn't, isn't—"

"I know, but I remember hearing, somebody told me, in fact I heard it from a few people, four or five people, that towards the end, even when things were starting to go bad, they would spend a ton of money on bad decisions, like thousands of sets of new barware glasses or new pool chairs or sod, just to cover up some brown grass. People can live with brown grass, you know what I mean?"

Wendell didn't answer right away. "Uh, it wasn't my fault, never my fault, no fault. I mean, I didn't screw it up, I wasn't management. I was, well, you know, I was grounds. I was the best backhoe guy they had. I was, really, an excellent backhoe guy." Wendell twinkled.

"Ah, okay, fair enough. And, yes, you were an excellent backhoe guy. I remember you always saying that. I heard it from you. I think you even said it at your wedding. I remember that wedding."

There were murmured admonishments and everyone squirmed.

Doug realized the gaffe. "Oops, hey, sorry, Wendell, sorry, didn't mean to drag up an old skeleton. Sorry, old-timers like me, well, we know where all the bodies are buried. Hah!"

Wendell quickly turned away, so no one heard his sharp intake of breath, but Debra, who had listened to the exchange, heard something else.

The wind, the echo, the sound rustling in the disheveled trees, here on this slope, this day, softened and shaped the words mumbled by a sappy and intoxicated Wendell on his divorce day. *Oh my God,* realized Debra, *Wendell wasn't a van Gogh Guy or a Banjo Guy, he was a Backhoe Guy. An excellent Backhoe Guy. That's what BG stands for. That's why he doodles it all over the agenda and meeting packet inserts. Not Betty Grable. Not Banjo Guy. Backhoe Guy.* Yes, she joyfully reckoned, Backhoe Guy!

Wendell abruptly turned toward Golf Cart No. 1. "On to the

maintenance garage," he blared through the bullhorn.

Everyone carted to the maintenance garage. In the heyday of The Club, it was well hidden by stone walls and foliage so as not to intrude on the gaiety of the golf experience, but now it was fully exposed, ugly, and heavily padlocked.

Wendell got to the big garage doors first, and the civic gaggle all straggled up to him. "Peter," he boomed through the bullhorn, "I should have a key to this garage."

"Why?" asked Peter, covering his ears. "I have a key, and our Public Works director has a key. That seems to work out just fine."

Wendell frowned and stood there, just like everyone else, while Peter fiddled with an enormous bunch of keys and the three huge padlocks.

When the doors finally swung wide, the assemblage was greeted by darkness and the musty smells of nature too long enclosed. Peter got the overhead lights on, and hoses, plow attachments, a half dozen riding mowers, stacks of barely used pool chairs, rakes, trowels, pallets, and, not too far from the entrance, an older dilapidated backhoe all came into view. Debra didn't want to think about how many litters of creatures had safely been birthed in this rodent haven, and given that she didn't really care too much about used mowers, she held back.

Most of the group had gathered around Peter. "Yes, well, you can all see that this used equipment is more saleable . . . " and he went on about auctions and how it's all set up. But Debra's eye followed Wendell, who had made straight for the backhoe.

Of course, Backhoe Guy!

Liza had also held back. "For God's sake, Debra, don't ask a lot of questions. I have a nail appointment, and I want this tour to be over." The maintenance garage was disgusting, but Debra's reluctance to enter the building was overcome by her new realization about Wendell. She watched as he climbed up into the backhoe cab. "Liza, look at Wendell."

Wendell was spinning in the backhoe seat, first facing one end, then, like a happy child, spinning the seat around to face the other end. He did it a few times, then looked in and around the visors, evidently encountering several insects, because he was shooing. Debra tried not to breathe as she walked purposefully over to the backhoe, and whether Liza wanted to or not, she followed.

Peter moved the group over to the backhoe as well, so now all were gathered round. "This is the backhoe we are going to keep, I guess." Peter shrugged.

Wendell had stopped shooing insects, but he did not climb down. He was still seated and seemed to be searching for something under or near the seat. Even though the group was moving toward the wide-open doors and oxygen, Wendell made no move to dismount. Debra remained where she was, watching him.

Debra had never paid any attention to any backhoe, ever. She looked at this one, dusty and rusty, with new eyes, eager to learn something, but all she saw was Wendell gazing intently inside the opening of the vertical turret that held the gear sticks. He was using a small flashlight to gaze into the channel. He saw her looking at him looking for something. Debra heard Wendell swear under his breath as he opened the right-side cab door to jump down. With the door open, she could just make out the letters BG scraped on the inside edge of the door panel, barely concealed by a sad tatter of duct tape. To Debra's eye, it all made pathetic sense. He was indeed Backhoe Guy. Wendell clambered down, and after giving Debra a dirty look, he moved to join the group. Debra kept pace and decided then and there to fully embrace her older-lady-pain-in-the-assdom.

"Wendell," she said, "what were you looking for?"

His face went ashen. "Nothing, absolutely nothing. Not looking for anything, ever. I've never looked for anything, ever, in a backhoe. Why would I? Nothing to look for in a backhoe." He stumbled around, not sure where to look, but it was clear he had no intention of looking Debra in the eye, absolute well-established-in-divorce-mediator-world proof he was lying about something.

"Really? Seemed like you were looking for something."

"No. Leave me alone." He strode over to where Peter was standing and blared, "That concludes the tour. There is nothing else to see here, nothing. Drive your carts back, now, and go home."

Debra decided that one way or another, she was going to get into that backhoe.

•••

By the next week, the auction for the equipment had been set up, and the bedraggled backhoe had been driven from The Club maintenance garage to the Public Works facility. It would now have to live out of doors, poor thing.

Wendell insisted on meeting with the Public Works guy who had driven the backhoe the short mile from The Club over sidewalk-less town roads to Public Works. He couched it as a great congratulatory moment that the Republicans could use for his reelection, telling Anthony that the messaging was about saving money and valuing the workingman, but when all was said and done, Wendell had second thoughts about drawing attention to the backhoe that nobody cared about except him, so he just summoned the Public Works guy to his office, sans fanfare.

"Hello, uh, nice job driving the backhoe," said Wendell.

"It's a backhoe. But, okay, thanks, I guess."

"No problem with the gears?" asked Wendell.

"Nope. No problem."

"No problem with anything else on the backhoe?" asked Wendell.

"Nope. No problem."

That was the extent of the interview.

From his office window in Town Hall, Wendell could see the Public Works garage, the maintenance bays, and, on the edge of the parking area, his backhoe. He was delighted. The bucket end was in full view, and memories of Bunker Girl dropping from the bucket's full height made him smile. He could visit Bunker Girl, he could see his backhoe, and when he was home, with the single earring in his pocket and whiskey on the table, he could write notes about them both.

The backhoe had been on-site for a couple of weeks, and mostly it was ignored. But on a rainy afternoon, the Public Works guy Wendell had interviewed pulled up to the building and saw that the right-hand door panel was open. He hustled over to the backhoe to shut the panel and keep the rain from pouring in. He was shocked to find Wendell draped across the seat with his eyes closed shut and his mouth wide open. But then he saw the whiskey bottle. He retrieved his supervisor, and they stood there in the pouring rain, looking up through the right-side open cab door at Wendell snoring with his head thrown back. They stared. Wendell stirred.

"Oh, ooh, fuck," yawned Wendell. "I fell asleep. I mean, I took a, uh, nap, or something." Wendell quickly reached into his pocket. *Whew*, he thought, *my earring, Bunker Girl's earring, is safe*. "Uh, guys, no big deal, right? I mean, it's just a nap."

"I thought you were dead," smirked the Public Works guy.

"No," said Wendell, yawning, "just a nap."

But it wasn't just a nap. It was either an incipient Republican scandal, a municipal taxpayer outrage, a full-on delicious humiliation for Wendell or leverage for Public Works come budget time.

Anthony was furious, and at the premeeting ahead of the Republican Town Committee meeting, which would likely be attended only by the attendees of the premeeting, he raged at Wendell.

"Fuck, Wendell, you're a screwup. On what planet was your 'nap' a good idea? It was the middle of the day, for crying out loud. And the backhoe? I don't get it. You're going to ruin this for the Republicans for a decade. You're making us all look bad, following your stupid open space or Open Space crap. Look, if you want to stay in politics, you have to stand for something, and you have to be nimble, all at the same time. Stand still and move."

Wendell did not care about staying in politics as such. He only cared about smoke and mirrors. Outrage worked for him. He didn't even bother to look up, concentrating instead on drawing circles within circles all over his napkin. "Anthony, fuck you. It was a nap, good nap, very good."

"Wendell," said Caroline, "even a maverick has to follow the norms."

"Who's Norm?"

"Not Norm. Norms."

"There's more than one? Do they know each other?"

"No, Wendell, norms, as in norms of behavior."

"Norms of behavior? There are two guys named Norms from the same place?"

Anthony had had enough. "Wendell, grow up. If you want to take a nap, go home."

Wendell turned to Caroline. "You think I'm a maverick?"

Henry slammed the table. "Wendell," he growled, "you're not a maverick. You're an idiot. And an ass. And stop telling everyone that the disposition of the damn golf course is your destiny,'" he said, using ugly, exaggerated, and derisive air quotes. "Let's be clear. You wouldn't have run at all if we hadn't asked you. You were living in mommy's house, just making a whole lot of noise about open space until this committee came along, so show some respect."

Wendell got in Henry's face. "That's right, you asked me to run and I got elected. That means the people are listening to me, not you, to me, got it? Tremendous listening. I'm practically in charge of everything now. I won. And I am doing a great job of running the town."

"Shit," mumbled Anthony. "This guy's a fucking whack job." Anthony made eye contact with Henry, and they stared at each other like two cranky mountain goats. Anthony and Henry had always had a difficult time with each other, always doubting the other's judgment and vying for control over the last word at Republican Town Committee meetings. Now, as they stared and glared, they both saw it. They were now bedfellows, nestled together against Wendell.

"Shit," said Henry.

Wendell got up to leave. "You can't leave, Wendell," said Caroline. "This is the RTC premeeting. You're the Republican first selectman.

You have to stay for the full meeting and then stay for the postmeeting meeting."

"Well, I'm leaving anyway. I'm going home to take a nap."

He smiled to himself as he left the premeeting, satisfied that on the one hand, the first selectman hand, he had launched dizzying disorder and chaos, and on the other hand, the Murdering Wendell hand, he had everything well-ordered and organized.

It was a lively teeter-totter, and he was the fulcrum.

His notes were still key to his routine, and he had briefly created a separate notebook, calling it TBS, which stood for The Bitch Stella, hoping to segregate his thoughts of her from his thoughts about Bunker Girl, but it messed with his sequential system and confused him no end. He abandoned the topic-driven system and continued with the daily, in-order, inserted notes so he could keep all his stories straight and threads secured.

I took a nap and I am an excellent First, always First, Selectman.

I might be a fraud and a liar. But, no one has ever asked me if I am a murderer, so I've never denied it. So I'm not a liar. Besides, if I admit to myself that I am a fraud, then I am being truthful, and I am not lying and, ERGO, or EGGO (not sure which is witch) not fraudulent.

These are excellent notes, perfect notes.

And he was consistent. If things got too quiet, even for a day or two, he would start a rumor, disrupt a meeting, or insult a volunteer, and he did not let up, not with other Republicans or members of his base, or at preservationists' kitchen table meetings, where his base and the politically minded Republicans were melded, or during televised meetings, and not in his liaison role with other commissions. He grandly latched onto the idea that the politically minded Republicans were beholden to him and that in the next election cycle—which began in less than a year—they would have to join him, along with his base, his message, his momentum, not because they thought doing nothing on or for the property was right but because it worked for their political ambitions to take over the town and have a majority on all boards and commissions.

Reluctant or not, second thoughts or not, remorse or not, they chose him as their comrade. He owned them.

• • •

Wendell could now wave at familiar faces at the little food shop and while tramping the golf course property. He went to the elementary school book fair and lingered at the transfer station on Garbage

Saturdays. He attended events for the seniors at The Center at The Center and happily cut a ribbon for the occasional new merchant. He now knew how to pronounce "liaisons." He was everywhere, waving, smiling, smoothing his hair, and not working.

Mostly, though, and on any given day, when Wendell should have been reviewing a meeting packet or learning something about how to run a municipality, he would sit in the library, pretend to read the books he carried around so he looked smart and really, very really, intelligent, doodle circles within circles or the letters BG, and scan obituaries, hoping to find his mother's former and scattered Connecticut friends amongst the dead. Rumor had it that the library staff was never happy when Wendell was in the building. He lingered, his hand was in his pocket, and he strutted around like he owned the place. If there were people waiting to use the public computers, he honored the time limits, but he idly meandered around the shelving until a terminal became free to use.

On one such occasion, while settled at one of the public computers, he clicked on a random Rockmore death notice. His heart nearly leapt out of his chest.

> ROBERT DALES, longtime owner and operator of the Triple B in Rockmore, passed away on November 5 following a long illness. He is survived by his two sons and five grandchildren. He was the beloved husband of Greta Dales, who predeceased him. Mr. Dales was a lifelong resident of Rockmore. He was known to the entire community as Bob-Behind-the-Bar, which gave his well-known enterprise the name, the Triple B, which will continue in operation under the ownership and management of the deceased's sons and daughters-in-law. The funeral will be at St. Matthew's Church in Rockmore, following a wake at the O'Brien Mortuary. Donations in his memory may be made to Rockmore Tee-Ball and Little League.

Wendell was so pleased that he briefly thought about going to church, but the obituary so bolstered his spirits that he decided instead to research a topic he had been avoiding for a very long time.

He took a deep breath and removed his NUDE cap. He pulled up a search engine and typed, "how long does it take for a body to decompose."

He clicked. He skimmed, taking in what seemed to be good news. He had decomposition, dirt, worms, moisture, decay, and time. He figured tatters and teeth, total. He deleted the search history, mindful that servers don't decompose, or have dirt, worms, moisture, or decay but, from Wendell's point of view, better a public computer than his own computer. He was always so careful.

He clicked out and got on a different search engine. He typed "DNA stuff."

He girded himself for the worst, because just the week before, there had been a big hoo-ha on television about how the FBI or the police in some big state somewhere out west solved a cold case using a DNA match for the very first time. He had listened to these new reports, increasingly unnerved by the prospect of discovery, flexing and rubbing his hands, his heart beating faster as the reporter kept using the word "incredible" to describe the emerging forensic techniques, the new evidentiary possibilities, the size and scope of worldwide data banks yet to come. It's not like a cop show, folks, it's not television magic, it's a slow slog for the police, but cold cases will be solved, you can't hide, the fact that they are coming to get you, now, whoever you are or whoever you might be, they will, count on it, find the bad guys because of up-to-the-minute DNA science.

He quickly perused the hoo-ha and the information, all of which was inconclusive, and clicked out, but he couldn't leave the library because it was pouring outside, a real torrent, and he had spent a lot of time that morning getting his hair the way he liked it. Besides, if his hair got even a little wet, he would be able to smell the hairspray he had applied. He considered going back to the terminal and printing out his search results, but he thought better of it.

When the rain stopped, he went home and wrote several notes.

DNA match, whatever, depends on death, life, a match, match to what, match the body, the bones, the hair, the toothbrush, death, it depends, is contingent on, forensic, varies, suspends. It depends on a lot of things.

But they have to find her. And then find the other one.

I left no clues. I am CLUELESS.

Wendell reviewed his notes, inserted them into one of the many three-ring binders he had pilfered from the town finance department, and declared himself thoroughly satisfied. He poured himself a whiskey and got comfortable in front of the television. First Selectman Wendell Williams was settling into his new role, having greatly expanded the plain sight in which he hid.

He was finally the success his mother wanted him to be.

— CHAPTER 11 —

Vinnie was a natural.

He was well-liked by his fellow Democrats and respected by his Republican colleagues. Leadership pegged him as a rising star.

With fundraising for an excuse, Vinnie and Debra met for coffee at the Starbucks on the edge of Somerville's sidewalk-less commercial hodgepodge area. They chatted briefly about the legislative calendar and Vinnie's reelection chances.

"You know, in a way, the next election cycle is a long way off," said Vinnie, "but I know it comes around fast. I don't want to spook this thing, but I'm feeling pretty good about it, mostly because I don't see any signs of an aggressive effort by the Rs in the district." He paused again. "I shouldn't say that, though. It will come back to haunt me."

Debra laughed. "Well, you're only saying it to me, and I'm really glad to hear it. But in politics, even when it's easy, it's not easy."

"No, not easy, but still, sometimes I can't believe how quickly I went from being a cop to being a prosecutor to being a legislator. It has all just zoomed by."

They gossiped a bit, touching on the stupidity and complexity of Somerville elections coming up immediately after the statewide elections.

"Are the Republicans going to run Wendell again for first selectman?" asked Vinnie.

"No idea, and it makes me a little sick to think about it. One thing is certain, though. Wendell and the Republicans have one of the most perverse political relationships I have ever seen."

"Hah, I imagine you've seen your share of perverse relationships." Vinnie grinned, then paused, as if taking a mental measurement of Debra's tolerance. "You know, Debra, he called me."

"Who called you?"

"Wendell. Wendell called me."

"Wendell called you? Good heavens. If it were anyone else, it would be so, you know, normal, but Wendell?"

"I know, weird, huh? It shouldn't be that weird, but it is weird. And, duh, he is so weird. I mean, he's the first selectman in a town in my district, but he's never called or reached out in any way, even though I've tried to connect with him a dozen times since he, uh, you know, got elected."

"Vinnie, you don't have to tiptoe around it."

"I know, but, well, he's such an ass. When he called me, the first thing he said is that he beat you by twenty-seven votes. It must drive him crazy that you got back on the Board of Selectmen."

"It does. I confess, I love that it drives him nuts." She waited a moment. "He beat me by six votes. Not twenty-seven."

"I know. We all know."

"So," she sighed, "why'd he call you?"

Vinnie took a deep breath. "He had a question about state funding for construction projects, or grants, or something about getting the state to pay for a project he has in mind."

"That's it?" Debra was briefly disappointed. It sounded so normal, so appropriate. After all, that's what a real first selectman would do. But her disappointment quickly switched to suspicion. "What project?"

"He wants to build a wall."

"A wall?" Debra racked her brain for any town building where a wall was needed, but as far as she knew, all the buildings had perfectly good walls.

"And he wants the state to pay for it."

"He wants the state to pay for it? For a wall? What wall?"

Vinnie had been looking down at his shoes. When he raised his eyes to look directly at Debra, he was grinning. "He wants to build a wall around the former golf course."

Debra's horrified gasp was all Vinnie could have hoped for. "It's not funny, Vinnie," she protested. "Not funny."

"No," said Vinnie, laughing out loud, "not funny, not funny at all."

"Good grief. Was he serious? I mean, what?"

"I have no idea if he was serious," said Vinnie. "But for whatever reason, he wants this piece of land fenced, or walled, or something. I sent him an official letter with official information, and he scribbled all over it, and sent it back to me. Look."

Vinnie pulled from his briefcase a single sheet of Connecticut General Assembly letterhead. The typewritten content was largely obliterated by Wendell's scribbles.

"Bottom line," said Vinnie, "he loves that property."

"Better he should love punctuation," said Debra, trying to decipher Wendell's scrawls. She handed the letter back to Vinnie. "It's unbelievable. I mean, we all know he is totally fixated on that property. But still, a wall?"

"And," added Vinnie, "he told me it's a secret and I shouldn't say anything to anyone because it will ruin the surprise."

"What does that mean?"

"I have no idea. I told him he's a public official and I'm a public official and he's asking me stuff in that capacity, so what's the secret?"

"So it's a secret or not a secret? Which?"

"I don't know or care. I just gave him basic information about state grants, and you're the only one I'm telling, not because it's a secret but because the whole conversation wasn't really about anything."

"You're telling me because you know it will aggravate me."

Vinnie busted out laughing again. "Look," said Vinnie when he stopped his guffaw, "I know this might not be the right question, but it's just the two of us here. Why not give this Wendell character what he wants and let it go as Dedicated Open Space? It would take it off the political table and shut him up, no?"

"Shut him up? Weren't you at our debate? Nothing shuts him up."

"True," said Vinnie.

"And," continued Debra, "why would you empower a schmuck like him? It's bad enough that during the last election cycle he turned Public Comment into a circus, wearing his stupid NUDE hat all the time. I get that he has no use for the Dems, but he doesn't have any use for the Rs either. I think he enjoys embarrassing them."

"True," laughed Vinnie. "It's like his very own guilty political pleasure or something."

Vinnie was still talking, but Debra had stopped listening.

He looked at his coffee, then at the barista, then at Debra's face. "No, Debra, no, I was just kidding around. I didn't mean it like a cop, or a prosecutor. Don't go all sixth sense on me about this."

"But Vinnie, you're right. Guilt. I hadn't thought of it quite that way before, but whoa, it's so obvious. It explains a lot." Vinnie was about to interject, but she put her hand up. "And it's not just cops and prosecutors, you know. It's also a divorce mediator thing. No question about it. He did something, something bad. He's jumpy, like he's about to get caught—"

"No, c'mon, he's an oddball, nothing more. True, he's an oddball who got elected, but really, Debra, there's no bigger meaning here."

Vinnie grinned. "Now if we had a body or something—oh, look, there's Sam Michaelson."

A body.

Of course, Debra thought, *a body*. She cringed at her own naivety. It was unthinkable, so she hadn't thought it.

A body.

A golf course, a backhoe. Burial.

Not piles of money, or classified information, or international security threats, or blackmail capacities. No. A body. Of course.

But Senator Sam Michaelson was upon them. Debra wanted to shout about the body, but instead she had to do the kiss-kiss-face-face with this old man who had been in the state senate way too long. Vinnie and Sam were laughing at the coincidence of running into each other at Starbucks, as if running into someone, anyone, you know at a Starbucks was still a coincidence.

"Yes, Debra, of course," said Senator Michaelson, "good to see you again. I think the last time I saw you was at a fundraiser for this guy," giving Vinnie a mock punch in the shoulder. "By the way, Vinnie," he continued, "speaking of fundraisers, I assume you've been contacted already by the Rockmore Dems. Hard to believe that they're already planning the big fall fundraiser at the Triple B. Highlight of the season, absolutely."

"Of course," said Vinnie. "No question, it's already on my calendar." A moment more of small talk, trailing off with the usual, yes, better-get-goings, there's a premeeting for the meeting, yes, okay, good Vinnie, good Sam, nice to see you, Debra.

"I have to run. Sorry, Debra. We'll talk soon. Gotta go." Vinnie threw Debra an apologetic look, but she could hardly tell him to stay and talk cockatoos.

"Yes, of course, go." They left her there with her coffee and turmoil about the guilty barfy divorced guy who probably slashes tires and thinks bagels are a divorce ritual and, most importantly, had a body or hid a body or, *Oh my God*, thought Debra, *buried a body*. At Somerville Woods.

No question, thought Debra, *this calls for a cinnamon bun*.

• • •

"We have to run Wendell again," said Anthony at an RTC premeeting. "It kills me to say this, but I think we have to have him on the slate at the top of the ticket."

"Absolutely not. I cannot spend another two years with this guy as first selectman." Henry was flexing his own political muscle, wondering how to best parlay this dilemma to his own political benefit.

"Just think this through for a minute." Anthony was frustrated. He looked around the group sitting at Tim's kitchen table, but no one sitting there had an answer. "We don't put him up for first selectman. Do you think he's just going to go home and be quiet for the next two years? Or four years? He thinks this base of his will follow him anywhere. What if he's right? What if he really has political traction with this base?"

"You think he might run as an Independent?" asked Caroline, maybe a bit hopeful.

"How do I know? But I do know it's better for us to keep him tethered to the RTC than let him run around without a leash all by himself. And we have to make a decision soon."

Everyone was unhappy, but that did not prevent the jibber jabber from continuing for another hour.

Finally, there was consensus. "Okay, we're agreed," said Anthony. "We won't make a decision tonight."

"That's the agreement?" said Henry. "Not to make a decision tonight?"

"Correct," said Anthony. He sagged. "We are fucked."

•••

The executive committee of the Democratic Town Committee gathered at Liza's house. No baked goods, just a bowl of nuts, sat on the table.

"We have got to make something out of this golf course property issue that has something that will work for everyone," Howard said, picking through the fistful in his hand, isolating the cashews. "We need to consider whether we should be thinking about different uses for this property, uses that will address all of the crap we have had to listen to all this time, and I am including the possibility that some portion of the property, not all but some, be considered Dedicated Open Space."

If Debra had a hammer, she would have hammered herself senseless with it right there next to the bowl of mixed nuts.

"We were never against having a portion of the property be Dedicated Open Space," said Liza. "It's this all-or-nothing crap of Wendell's that got everybody's back up."

"Nevertheless," said Howard. "I think we can beat him if we run Debra again, but we will get more votes with a decent proposal and outcome for the property than we will with no solution and him on the ballot."

"That makes no sense," said Liza.

"You know what I mean," said Howard. "Whether Wendell is on the Republican slate or not, we still have to have something to say."

There was another hour of jibber jabber.

Finally, there was consensus. "Okay, then we're agreed," said Howard. "We have to have something to say."

"That's our agreement?" said Liza. "We have to have something to say?"

It was as good an agreement as any.

•••

Betty Halloran loved being part of the political whirlwind in Somerville. She was oblivious to her spiritual alignment with the Democrats because she had strong feelings about Open Space and the RTC had opened that door to power. She happily doddered through that door, leaning on Wendell's strong young arm, confident that if Wendell would just listen to her and follow her lead, he would be a meaningful political force.

Two of her fellow preservationists, many decades her junior, had set up a primitive website, posting blogs about open space, Open Space, preservation, conservation, and, occasionally, town politics of a Republican bent. Betty dubbed the group COOP, Conserve Our Open Properties, but Betty was not in any way tech savvy, nor a careful proofreader, so just before it all went live, she decided at the last minute to use the name she liked much better, Preserve Our Open Properties. There was nothing to be done. They were POOP, and it stuck.

Betty innocently morphed into a rather destructive Wendell groupie. She repeated any number of Wendell's lies during the Public Comment portion of the Conservation Commission meetings, all while Wendell sat there in his liaison or ex officio capacity, grinning, smoothing his hair, and rubbing his aching, murderous hands, all of which resulted in a significant spat one evening amidst an otherwise ordinary agenda.

Betty rose at Public Comment to say she was against the pig-butchering facility that the Conservation Commission was supporting as the best use for the golf course property.

"Betty," said Mrs. Kebel, chair of the Conservation Commission, "where the hell did you get that ridiculous rumor?"

"It's not a rumor. At least I'm pretty sure it's true. Wendell told me that the pig-butchering plant is the plan. I'm against it."

"Betty, there is no such proposal by anyone, anywhere to convert this property into a pig-butchering plant."

"But Wendell is the first selectman, and he knows what's what, and

I'm against what's what. It should not be a pig-butchering facility."

Mrs. Kebel turned to Wendell. "Wendell, did you tell Betty this nonsense?"

Wendell slowly turned his head toward Mrs. Kebel but turned it back to face the camera before he spoke. "I said no such thing, I said it would be a shame if it became a pig, or chicken, or cattle facility of any kind, particularly if it involved digging or turning over soil to build a methane lagoon. That's all I said. A shame, yes, I did, it would." He was smiling and taking his time.

"Wendell," said Betty, "I'm sure you told me that it was a done deal and that I should be against it."

Wendell stood up, faced the camera, and completely hijacked the meeting. He told the camera about the number of votes he received when he ran for first selectman and that he had saved Somerville from Debocracy. As it was, Mrs. Kebel had little use for COOP, or POOP, or whatever they called themselves because, in her opinion, their belligerence about the golf course property and solidarity with Wendell repelled any thoughtful concern about the broader issues of acquisition, management, and sanctioned use of open space or Open Space. Now, having lost control over her agenda and her meeting, she ran out of patience.

"Wendell, honest to God, that is the biggest load of crap I have ever heard. You're a liar. Betty, if you repeat anything he says, you're a liar too. Get out of my meeting."

"I'm the first selectman. You can't throw me out. I have every right to say what I want. Particularly if there's a camera."

"I can throw you out. Particularly if you lie and make crap up. Get out." She looked around the table for support from her fellow commissioners, one of whom was sharp enough to loudly make a motion to adjourn, triggering an immediate unanimous vote to get the hell out of there.

•••

Debra hadn't mentioned the slashed tire of long ago to anyone except her husband, and at the time, he was of the opinion that the tire had not been purposefully slashed by Wendell or anyone else, but that it was much more likely she had caught a sharp edge in a construction zone somewhere. Debra was of the opinion that it was no coincidence that both Miss Marple and Hercule Poirot were single and unmarried.

But now she had the possibility of a body to worry about. She decided to keep her speculation to herself. Even she thought it was irrational, and she was the one who thought it.

Debra was in Town Hall for a quick ordinance committee meeting, and on her way out she poked her head into the tax collector's office. She did not have a plan. The assistant tax collector was not there. Only Sylvia Purdue.

"Good morning, Debra," said Sylvia. "What's up?"

Debra wished she knew. "Sylvia, I have a question."

She lobbed a few generic questions about the tax implications of home offices and car leases, but Debra already knew the answers and Sylvia knew that Debra knew the answers. Debra swung in a different direction.

"Any projections about the upcoming budget cycle?"

Sylvia eyed her suspiciously. "Debra, you're not subtle. You're asking about Somerville Woods."

"Well, yes. I know it's not a new problem but just wondered if there's an update."

"No update, no, Debra, of course not, and given how much Wendell pushes for open space and Open Space, there might never be an update." Sylvia laughed, but Debra heard a mental door creak open.

"Does Wendell ever talk to you about the tax implications of Somerville Woods, I mean as first selectman?"

"Oh, heavens no, and you know as well as I do that even if taxes did drive his obsession about that property, he would hardly talk to me about it. Even in the old days, when he used to come and pay his property taxes in person, he never engaged in chitchat. He would say hello, I would say hello, he paid his taxes, I would ask about his mother, you know, nothing beyond that."

The door opened just a little bit wider.

"You know Wendell's mother?"

Sylvia looked at Debra, assessing, as only a tax collector can. "Well," she began slowly, "we aren't, weren't, friends or anything. I remember her mostly from the days when she played bridge because I knew some of the women she played with at the country club, the other country club, the one that still exists. And of course she stopped into Town Hall every so often and we would say hello, but I didn't really know her." Debra said nothing, hoping Sylvia would keep talking. She did. "Still, it's just terrible that her mind is completely gone. I wouldn't wish that on anyone."

"No, no, of course not. Do your friends, the women who played bridge with her I mean, ever mention her, how she's doing, or anything?"

"No," said Sylvia, shaking her head, "I haven't heard anything about

Stella Williams for quite a while. I'm pretty sure that all of those connections are long gone." She paused and then quietly laughed. "She had a reputation, though, as kind of a, well, I don't want to speak ill of her, what with her dementia and everything, but I don't think anyone really liked her. She was known for being something of a pain as I recall."

"Well, that would certainly explain Wendell." Debra giggled, hoping Sylvia would too.

She did, but only briefly. "Still, I have to say that Wendell is incredibly polite, at least to me. But yes, I guess he's also a pain."

Great, thought Debra, *I got confirmation that Wendell is a pain and that he possibly inherited that trait from his mother, who is doolally*. She said goodbye and clambered down the ancient back stairway to the Town Hall lower level, where the town clerk's office was. With a quick wave to the assistant clerk, Debra made her way into the vault.

Debra loved the vault. The long shelves held logs and records dating back to the adoption of The Charter of 1784, and every recorded document told a Somerville story of birth, death, marriage, war, peace, good and evil, and what property was transferred and to whom. But on this visit, she didn't linger.

She did a quick title search on Wendell's house. It was public record and told an entirely straightforward story. Nearly forty years earlier, Cecil and Stella Williams had purchased a building lot. They both signed mortgage and construction documents. Many decades later, Cecil's estate conveyed the house free and clear to Stella, and shortly after that, Stella conveyed the unencumbered house to Wendell. Debra made and paid for photocopies of the documents.

It all added up to nothing.

She tramped back up the stairs and down the long hallway to the finance department. Without waiting for an invitation, she walked into Peter's office.

"Peter, I need to speak with you."

He looked up expectantly, but his eyes told Debra he was getting sick and tired of crazy selectmen in his face. "Sure," he sighed. "What's up?"

"I want to inspect the backhoe. Wendell's backhoe."

With neither questions nor fanfare, Peter picked up the phone. "Uh, Alan, hi, it's Peter," he said to the Public Works director. "Yeah, uh, Debra Wolfson and I have a few questions about the new backhoe, I mean the old backhoe that we just got from The Club garage. Right, new to us, but old. Right. Great, we'll meet you down there in a couple of minutes."

Alan evidently thought it was an opportune moment. He gave Debra the history of backhoes and front loaders, throwing in tidbits about compactors and excavators, telling her more about big and medium-size construction equipment than she ever could have cared about.

"Alan, all good. Can I get in the backhoe? I want to look around."

They indulged her, and she offered no explanation.

It was disgusting. Dirt, dead bugs, and windows nearly obscured with dust and cobwebs. But Debra looked where she had seen Wendell look. The visors, the thing that holds the gears, behind the pedals, under the rubber mat. She even sat in and spun the seat, the way she had seen Wendell do it on the tour. To her exasperation, she gleaned neither insight nor discovery.

Alan and Peter helped her down from the cab. She looked up and saw Wendell watching them from his office window.

— CHAPTER 12 —

In her four decades as a lawyer, Debra had never once stepped foot in a criminal courtroom. There is a good chance that most of what she knew about solving crimes and proving guilt came from watching PBS whodunits. All of the intrigue and none of the gristle. Ah, Morse, you solved another one!

But she knew whodunit. Wendell dunit. The question was whadiddydo.

She had only one certainty. Wendell was a genuine charlatan, a moron as well as an oxymoron.

She had little else that could be called absolute.

Debra was at her office, where she should have been calculating someone's child support obligations or drafting language for a separation agreement that needed to last longer than the busted marriage for which it served, but instead she studied the photocopies of the documents she had gotten from the vault in the town clerk's office. Whatever needed to match up did so, and the documents conformed to the rules for property conveyances. The conveyance to Wendell from his mother was totally within the bounds of what people did for a whole host of estate planning reasons, particularly if geography and dementia were about to complicate things. Debra supposed it was possible that Wendell had forged the deed and all the signatures, but premature ownership of a house he would likely inherit anyway did not seem to have anything to do with the golf course property. *It's not as if he stole the title, sold the house, and ran away with the money,* thought Debra. *No, he lives in the house and pays the taxes.*

Debra stared at her Mediator of the Year award hanging on the far side of her office and collected her nebulous thoughts of cockatoos, Liza's concern over Wendell's threatening visage, slashed tires, misunderstood bagels, and Wendell's wall. She added to the list Vinnie's offhand laughter about guilt and a body.

A body. That nebulous thought trumped all the other nebulous thoughts.

Debra's desk was a mess, a complete jumble of files, papers, and books. She looked under a pile of documents, hoping for insight about a missing body. But no, just a few paper clips. She heard steps coming down the long hall. The paralegal who worked for the other lawyers on her floor popped in.

"Hi. Haven't seen you in a while," said Jen, plopping into a chair at Debra's conference table. "You must be busy with all your municipal stuff." Debra welcomed the distraction, and they chatted easily, as they always did, touching on Jen's book club selection, her elderly parents, and some juicy gossip about one of the receptionists who worked for yet a different firm in the building.

But Debra could be distracted for only so long. "Hey, can I ask you something?"

"Okay, but not if it's about that Wendell guy you're always complaining about."

"Uh, no. Do I complain about him that much? Sorry, but well, I guess maybe I do. But not Wendell exactly."

"What is it?"

"Well, has your office ever dealt with a case where someone is missing but there's no body or person or, well, anything?"

"So, it is about Wendell."

"Why would you say that?"

"Not a big leap. Unlike you, we actually practice criminal law. Your clients just *want* to kill each other but mediate instead. Our clients actually *do* kill each other. In fact, as we speak, my boss is in trial, defending a murderer. Oh, wait a sec," said Jen, "an alleged murderer."

"Okay, fine," said Debra. "Whatever. It's a question about a body."

"Who are we looking for?"

"I have no idea. I'm not even sure we are looking for someone. It's something someone said, kiddingly, of course, about a body, but I can't stop thinking about it."

Jen considered. "Well, based on what you've told me about Wendell, I would go with a girl, a girl he raped or got pregnant. Possibly his sister, or a cousin, maybe a classmate. Does he have a sister? Oh, how about a guy? You know, Wendell is gay and can't accept it so he killed and buried his homosexual lover. A random robbery victim—yes, that's how he supports himself. Does he have a job? I thought you told me he landscapes, so maybe he doesn't need to rob to support himself. He just likes strewing bodies all over your golf course."

Jen was chuckling.

But Debra had never been more serious. "You think there could be more than one body?" she asked.

Jen sat up straighter at the prospect of multiple bodies all over the golf course. "Didn't you tell me that his father died on a golf course?"

"Not *a* golf course. *The* golf course. The one that makes my life a misery."

Jen considered. "Well, there you go. He might be working through grief over his father's death on *the* golf course by forcing old men to reenact the death of his father. And then he buries them, one each year to mark the anniversary of his dad's funeral."

"Ah," whispered Debra, "a yahrzeit gone wrong."

"What's a yahrzeit?"

"A Jewish thing."

"I didn't know Wendell was Jewish," said Jen.

"He's not, but that has nothing to do with anything. Or at least I don't think it does. More to the point, as far as I know no one is looking for a passel of old men."

"No. As far as you know no one is looking for anyone."

"True," said Debra. "That's what makes this so tricky."

"What about his mother?" asked Jen.

"No, his mother is still alive, in Florida, so it can't be her. She's totally out of it, but I think someone, somewhere would notice if she were dead. I mean, she used to play bridge."

"Did she play mah-jongg?"

"I have no idea. What does that have to do with anything?"

Jen shrugged. "Just wondering. You know, if you're going to imagine a victim, a body, go all in. That's all I got. Is that my phone?" And with that, Jen ran down the long office hall to catch the call.

Jen hadn't taken the conversation seriously, but Debra couldn't help but think that Jen's jocular speculation might explain Wendell's obsessive need to protect the property from development. But how could it be that Wendell had buried a body—or buried more than one body, or buried something—and no one knew? And just as confounding, when did this, whatever this was, happen? There were no answers, and in fact all this reflection only generated more questions. *What about dogs?* she wondered. Wouldn't a dog, even a yappy, obnoxious purse dog, be intrigued by the scent of a newly decomposing body or, possibly, an already fully decomposed body? They didn't teach decomposing body science in law school.

Debra snuck a peek under a different pile of books, looking for further inspiration. All she found was a candy wrapper. She checked the candy dish on her shelf, which was supposed to be full of endorphin-boosting chocolate maintained for the benefit of tense and tearful mediation clients. The candy dish was empty. *Jen has been at it, no question*, thought Debra. Fortunately, her stash was well hidden. She refilled the candy dish, took a chocolate, took another, and thought about Wendell's stupid backhoe.

How long had it been locked up in the maintenance garage? She had to acknowledge that if he used the backhoe to bury all the old men, or his boyfriend, or a girl he raped, he would have had to have been working at The Club because that is when he had access to the backhoe. But he could have easily dug a grave and buried someone using just a shovel or, like the ancient peoples of the Neolithic era, a simple ox scapula. Debra doubted that a golf club would be an effective digging tool, and she was close to certain Wendell did not have access to an ox scapula. But neither access to the backhoe nor the backhoe itself seemed determinative of anything.

Debra doubted she was going to discover anything from the comfort of her desk, but what the hell? She took another chocolate and tried this newish Google thing. She searched "Missing Persons in CT." If only a link would appear to take her to "Wendell killed his Somerville lover," but no such luck or link. Somerville was not even mentioned, which, on reflection, was a good thing, good for Somerville's municipal crime stats, good for housing values, good for the "Best Places to Live in CT" placement, but not good for Debra's hunch.

•••

Wendell called Finance Director Peter Reilly into his office.

"Peter, I want you to see what you can do about getting the state to pay for the wall I want. The state rep guy, Vinnie whatever, was not helpful. And remember, it's a secret."

Peter knew that Wendell had mentioned the wall to State Representative Vinnie Hamlin, but Peter was now used to Wendell's ways. "Sure, I'll get right on it," he said, but he didn't. He had a town to manage. He was not going to waste time chasing down one of Wendell's goofy impulses, secret or otherwise.

Wendell called Betty.

"Wendell, what a nice surprise. We hardly ever chat anymore. The meetings are always so long and so late."

"Betty, I'd like to come over and talk about my latest idea. It's a great idea. Maybe you could have a few of the committed POOP people be there as well. At the moment, it's a secret."

"Wendell, do you want to preview something with me?"

"No, not now. Can we say Sunday morning? I'll bring the bagels."

"Fine, Wendell, fine. I'll just call Kate. Oh, and Lionel. Yes, he's new to POOP. Cares about open space. No, no, don't get coffee. I'll make it here."

Betty called Kate. "Kate, I don't know what he wants to talk about, but he offered to bring the bagels. I know, I know, he's never brought the bagels before. It's a huge shift. What could that be about? I mean, he as much as said he didn't want the Republican Town Committee people to know about the meeting and that it should be just us, just POOP, not RTC people. I thought we were all on the same page here, right? And not only that," she added, lowering her voice to a whisper, "he said it's a secret."

"Betty," Kate asked, "did you tell him to bring cream cheese?"

On Sunday, the coffee was poured, bagels were toasted, and Betty had bought backup cream cheese, but Wendell came through not only with cream cheese but doughnut holes as well.

They settled in, and Wendell launched. "We should get a state grant of some kind for open space or Open Space construction money. We'll build a wall or a fence of some kind around the golf course property. We'll use state grant money to pay for it. The state grant will pay for construction of the wall. Or fence. Or whatever."

It landed like a mattress thrown out of a twelfth-story window.

"What?" asked Lionel.

Wendell repeated it, adding that it was the ultimate protection for the property. "You know what I mean, right?" he asked. "We can just wall it up."

"Wendell," said Betty, "no one is more passionate than the four of us about that property, and we have all worked very hard, very hard, to make sure that it stays as it is, even though I think we can all agree that the town is not taking care of the property, no offense, and it is a complete mess, no offense, so no matter what happens, some kind of mapping or trails or trash cans or maintenance will still be appropriate. And I'll give you that passive recreational use might have some, ooh—what do they call it?—oh yes, open-space-grant-money potential." She meandered back to her original point. "But still, even I have to acknowledge that walled-in open space or Open Space is a little, well, out there."

"Why do we need a wall?" asked Kate.

"We need the wall," said Wendell, "to, uh, keep things in and to keep things out."

"What am I trying to keep in? Or out?" asked Lionel.

"I was hoping that we could have a robust discussion with the four of us first, on a completely secret basis, and figure that out, secretly, so that we can then go to the RTC and see if they'll buy the idea."

"Wendell," said Kate, who was hoping to run on Wendell's slate again in the next election cycle, "let me get this straight. You think we can build a wall and get the state to pay for it, all before the next town election?"

"No, of course not. That's ridiculous," answered Wendell. Wendell had no idea if that was ridiculous or not, because, as he wrote to himself later that night, even he had to admit that he had no idea what he was talking about. "But we could put the idea out there, start talking about it, make it a platform. The RTC would be forced to accept it. We could manage the whole slate, get rid of Henry, even Caroline, and instead of the RTC controlling the Board of Selectmen, the POOP people and I, me, we would, I would, really, we all would control the BOS. Even if it takes five years to get the grant or the state money, or whatever, nothing will happen on the property in the meantime. We buy time, we get a fence. We tie up the Democrats, we get time. We tie up the impossible Republicans, we get open space, maybe even Open Space. We have a demonstration here and there, very noisy, very big, lots of big marches, but no marches on the property, just, you know, maybe in front of The Center at The Center or the library. Many marches. Or parades. We make sure that every developer comes to understand that Somerville is a little 'out there,' just as Betty said, and who would ever want to do business with us? God, these bagels are pretty good."

• • •

They swore each other to absolute secrecy, so it took a full forty-five minutes for everyone to hear about Wendell's plan.

It was "out there," and there was no way to put the seeds back in the tomato. With Kate's help, Betty posted something on the POOP website:

> Finally, one of the Somerville elected leaders is using his imagination and urging us to think about the former golf course property in a new and exciting way. Our champion, Wendell, has met with state and local officials to initiate discussions and an application for a state grant to construct a boundary wall or fence around the former golf course. POOP is excited and we are on the move! Hedge the Edge! Talk to your friends, fellow POOPers, and your elected leaders about this thought-provoking proposal!

Anthony heard about the post from Tim. He was apoplectic. He had no choice. He set up a meeting.

Henry, Caroline, Betty, and Wendell traipsed into his kitchen. There were no bagels, no coffee, no doughnut holes.

"What the fuck, Wendell," Anthony began, forgoing any introductory thoughts. "You've only been in office since last July. It's not even a full year yet. We haven't even come up with a strategy for next year's election, and you go off on your own and create chaos with this fringe group, this so-called base of yours, your POOP people, and you don't consult with or think about the political consequences for the party that is making this all possible for you?" He pointed angrily at Betty. "Who the hell do you think you are, anyway?"

Betty did not get a chance to answer.

"Hey, I thought we were supposed to be creative," puffed Wendell. "I'm being creative. The POOP people like the idea, and let's face it, they, no we, no I am the difference between all of you winning and the Democrats winning. Without the POOP people, you got nothing. All these people are talking about me, not the Dems, us. Me."

"Wendell, do you have any idea how stupid this is? You really think we can credibly promote walled-in open space paid for with a state grant?"

"Can I ask," interrupted Caroline, "what the wall is for?"

"Who the fuck cares what the wall is for?" seethed Henry. "It's for nothing. Nothing at all. His personal satisfaction, that's what the wall is for."

Now that the idea was out there, now that it was on the POOP website, now that his choices had been circumscribed by the blabbermouths, now that he had taken all the risk, Wendell figured he might as well just go all in and claim his reward.

"The wall," he said simply, "is for winning." *And protecting my Bunker Girl.*

Only Betty was nodding.

"You can dump me if you want, dump POOP if you want, but without my base and my brain, you have no chance of grabbing the first selectman spot next time around or getting a majority on the BOS."

The faces staring back at him were grim. No one said anything.

"You know I'm right," said Wendell.

•••

Betty was in overdrive. She wasn't entirely clear why a wall was a good idea or why it would be needed for the protection of open space. *After all,* she thought, *isn't open space supposed to be open?* She wasn't even clear that a wall was even in her interest, or the interest of POOP, or of Somerville, but let's go, Wendell! Anything that prevented developers and the town from even thinking about that property was a positive direction, and she wasn't going to let facts or reality impact that trend.

Kate helped her with an hour of online research, and she now considered herself the most well-informed POOP group member. Most of that hour was a frustrating loop as "open space with wall" searches took her to home improvement and remodeling websites that featured sprawling open-concept kitchen designs, probably for people who never cook, but she finally got to something that explained Dedicated Open Space. She knew the term of course, but only in its magic, abracadabra aspect, invoked as needed during Public Comment. Now she knew it was a boring and complicated legal term. She felt wholly emboldened.

She set up a meeting with Wendell and the POOP inner circle, some of whom were on the RTC but none of whom were in the RTC inner circle.

"This is so exciting," began Betty. "I'm kind of getting used to this boundary idea, and I can now see the potential. I think. Maybe. I thought we should spend some time brainstorming on different things to think about wallwise. Yes!"

"What kind of things?" replied Wendell, suddenly very wary of Betty's enthusiasm.

"Well," she said, lowering her voice to her favored conspiratorial level, "what should the wall look like, and things like that, because, you know, it wouldn't make sense to have this lovely open space, albeit unkempt open space, surrounded by an ugly fence or an unattractive border of some kind. I thought it might be the kind of wall where seasonal growth could attach, you know, like clematis or morning glory or, well, yes, even some of the nicer climbing ivy plants, yes, on both sides of the wall, so it would look spectacular in the spring for those driving by and those inside walking . . ." She paused, as Wendell was now staring at her, looking unhappy, pulling on the edges of his bushy mustache.

"Why," he asked, "would anyone be inside walking?"

Lionel was startled. "Wendell, you know, the walking trails, well, the old golf cart paths, would still be there. This would become like a walking park—"

"No, you're missing the point—"

"—and benches would be nice, maybe a drinking fountain here and there, the water and sewer are already there—"

"—not the purpose—"

"—and bathroom facilities, no porta-potties, so ugly, plus path markings of some kind—"

Everyone was speaking at once, pouncing on ideas for the interior of heavily bordered passive-use plumbed Open Space, with Wendell trying and failing to lasso the gusto and lead it back to his murderous needs. He calculated what he needed to say, mindful that each person who asked about the purpose of the wall needed their own calibrated response so they could put their arms around the idea and feel like it was theirs to own and enjoy. "The point," Wendell shouted above the other voices, "is to keep things in, like open space, AND keep things out, like people."

The group broke into garbled protest.

"You mean," Lionel hissed, not caring that Betty was trying to shush him, "that the wall is to prevent people, the community, people outside the community, POOPers, walkers, strollers, whatever, from having any access to the property? That can't be right, can it?"

"Yes, of course," replied Wendell. "That's what walls do. Keep things in, keep things out. We could fully isolate the Dedicated Open Space."

Lionel was incredulous. Kate was confused. Betty was beside herself.

"Calm down, everyone, calm down," said Betty. "I'm sure Wendell doesn't mean that the way it sounded, do you, Wendell? You don't really want to prohibit or prevent complete access, do you? That would be like, I don't know exactly, but that would be like having an enormous box of land. That can't be what you meant. The barrier is such an, uh, exciting idea, maybe, such a great way to make sure that the land is protected forever, but even a wall has a gate, or an entrance, or an opening of some kind," she continued, using her hands to indicate swinging doors, "for some kind of human access, and animals need to be able to get in and out. Well, birds wouldn't have a problem, I suppose, or squirrels—they can leap branch to branch, dear things— but even I would have a problem justifying a fully enclosed piece of land with no access whatsoever. I mean, what would be the point . . .?" She suddenly escalated, getting upset that Wendell's idea might be bad even for POOP. "I mean, we want to keep housing for old people OUT. But we, I mean us, I mean people who are like us and who care about Dedicated Open Space or people who are not like us but who just want to take a walk, we want IN."

He had miscalculated.

It didn't matter in the long term, because the wall was never the point to begin with, but in the short term he had wagered that this group would follow him to the ends of the earth. He told himself that to protect his bunker, his sand trap, his dark and beloved secret, and, oh yeah, the pile of rocks too, he would foment an insurrection if he had to. But he had overplayed his hand.

He looked around the table at the gaping faces. "I just feel so strongly—"

"We all feel strongly, Wendell," interrupted Lionel.

"Okay, okay. A few openings for walking access. Fine. The cart paths can be trails. But nothing with plumbing. Plumbing is a bad idea." He turned to Betty, his inadvertent helpmate in all things messy and confusing. "Clematis, morning glories, whatever, okay. A hedge would work, but that needs a lot of maintenance, so maybe not, still, maybe a hedge. Hedge the Edge. And I'm a champion. Good. Money, no problem. The state is paying for all of it."

•••

Debra briefly worried she was becoming obsessed with Wendell's secrets, and her concern was particularly troublesome to her because she had thus far made the whole thing up. *But I know there's something not right*, she mused. No digging, No Upsetting Development Ever, and let's plant a hedge. *The whole thing is so obnoxious and not at all in the spirit of open space or Open Space or, for that matter, Somerville,* thought Debra, *but crazy Wendell wants that golf course property packed up tight. He might as well ask for duct tape and bubble wrap.*

She had mediated all week and was grateful that no one needed her to figure out custody of a reptile, or an armoire, just everyday destabilized soon-to-be neurotic children. No problem, divorce world has answers for that! She left her office and entered the elevator, where she ran into the criminal defense lawyer Jen worked for. Serendipity! By the time the elevator got to the lobby, Debra had what she wanted. "No problem, Debra. I'll email the contact info to you. He's probably the best guy they have in the state police K-9 unit. He's a straight shooter for sure." That might or might not be the best way to describe a cop, but Debra knew what he meant.

The chance encounter was Debra's excuse for not reaching out to Vinnie, who, as a former prosecutor, would have been a resource for this type of referral, but Debra didn't want Vinnie to intercede. She just wanted to ask a few questions without an editor looking over her shoulder.

The next morning, Debra got right through to Sgt. Jeffrey Birmingham.

"Yes, Mrs. Wolfson, how can I help you?"

"Thank you, Sergeant, and I hope this isn't an imposition, but I need some basic information."

"Sure, whatever you need. Go." Go, sit, stay, heel. She was definitely talking to the right guy.

"How long does a scent last?"

"Human? You mean at what point is it not trackable by a trained dog?" It was clear that Sgt. Jeff Birmingham had one prism through which he saw the world, and at the particular moment, Debra was grateful that his single-mindedness brought clarity to the issue.

"Yes. How long?"

Debra assumed that the extended silence meant he was thinking.

"You still there, Sergeant? You thinking?" she asked.

"Yeah, I want to get this right," he answered.

Finally, he spoke. "In my experience, not that long. Maybe a few weeks, maybe a month or so under perfect conditions—wet, moist, no wind."

"Okay, Sergeant, one more question. How deep can scent be detected?"

"You mean deep in the ground? Well, that could change everything because decomposition—I assume we're talking about a body here—well, anyway, decomposition changes the odor of the soil, and over time . . . well, it's pretty dynamic and different in every circumstance."

"Thank you, Sergeant. That helps."

"No problem, Mrs. Wolfson. Any time."

Debra didn't think it helped at all, but given that she still couldn't define a problem, at least she had eliminated a solution. She went to the library and found a book about ways to locate buried objects. She read about ground-penetrating radar, detectorists, the Roman ruins in the British Isles, and tunnels beneath apartment buildings. Her chat with Sgt. Birmingham confirmed the obvious. She was barking up the wrong tree.

—CHAPTER 13—

Betty couldn't shake the feeling that Wendell was no longer a steady advocate for Dedicated Open Space. The grant-and-wall thing was nutty even when it was a secret, and she knew that, but on the off chance that Wendell was successful in getting the state to pay for an enclosure, her aspirational Dedicated Open Space could end up being surrounded by an ugly industrial fence. That would be worse than nothing, and she had heard as much from several of her fellow POOPers. And for all that Wendell had relented on access for walkers, she got an earful from the POOP inner circle and some of her friends at church who were part of the RTC inner circle that a wall, even a beautiful wall, even an elegant brick structure covered with clematis and morning glory, even an enormous hedge would still block their view of the landscape, whether that landscape was called a golf course, a former golf course, open space in limbo, or Dedicated Open Space. And if she were being completely honest with herself, she still wasn't sure if a boundary hedge really accomplished anything or met any of the goals of POOP. She thought, somewhat embarrassedly, that this barricade idea of Wendell's amounted to a solution without a problem. She resolved to tell him of her concerns.

She busied herself with thoughts about who should join her in confronting Wendell. No Democrats, but only because Wendell would have a fit. *Wendell hates Debra for some reason,* thought Betty, *but it makes no sense, Debra is a lovely person.* Other POOPers, for sure. But which Republicans? That was the question. Henry? No, he was hostile. Caroline? Maybe. Anthony? Yes, of course Anthony. Of everyone, he was the one most likely to understand that the boundary idea might need to remain intact at the same time that it might need to be fully undermined.

Betty called Wendell and told him she had pulled another meeting together.

He resisted. "Betty, no way. Why did you do this? Bad idea. Very bad. No Rs, not good. Cancel the meeting. I won't show up, no way." Betty waited for Wendell to complete his self-negotiations. "Okay, I'll be there," he growled, "but I will not bring bagels."

They met the following Sunday.

"Thanks, Betty, thanks. Where's the sugar?" Anthony asked, settling in. "Look, I'm not sure why we're meeting. What are we doing here?"

"I want to talk about the wall," said Betty, looking directly at Wendell. "I don't want any of us to get caught up in something that has no chance of getting real traction."

Anthony turned toward her. "Well, from what I can see, only you, a few POOP people, and Wendell are caught up in the so-called wall issue. Believe me, no one else is buying it."

Caroline, whom Betty had included at the last minute, said, "Betty, it sounds like you have doubts about this."

Wendell said nothing.

"Well," said Betty, "I'm not sure I would use the word 'doubts.' But, well, the idea is really a metaphor, right? To protect the open space, right?" She looked directly at Wendell, again.

"No, it's not a whatever you said. It's a wall."

"Wendell, well, okay, in that case, call them doubts. I just don't see how this will work. What about openness and what we stand for?" Anthony rolled his eyes, but Betty forged ahead, a little faster. "And it's town property, and what if the town doesn't want the wall?" It all came tumbling out. "And not for nothing, I'm a taxpayer in the state. I'm not sure it's a good use of taxpayer dollars. It's one thing to purchase property as open space with state funds. It's another thing to use state funds to fulfill a, uh, questionable campaign slogan."

She had spoken directly to Wendell, but it was Caroline and Anthony who were agape. Caroline reached out and grabbed her hand. "Betty," she said, "I had no idea you had these concerns." She turned to Wendell. "But like it or not, Wendell, they are the right concerns."

Anthony threw up his hands and covered his eyes. "What's going on here? If I remember correctly, Betty, you're the one who came up with the 'Hedge the Edge' chant to begin with. Are we changing armies here? Just let me know. I mean after all, we're trying to consolidate our political gains, and you want us all to stand for this hedge thing." A pause. "More or less."

Wendell's face had gone ugly. "Nothing has changed. NUDE."

"Wendell," Betty replied, "everything has changed. You're first selectman—"

"Barely—" interrupted Anthony.

"—but the POOP agenda has come to be, well, defined by the wall thing. Dedicated Open Space is the point. No development is the point. The wall has taken on a life of its own."

Wendell was about to retort that the wall had taken on a death of its own, but he resisted. Confusion, yes, distortions and lies, yes. Jokes that provoke questions, no. If it weren't for the entombments, he might have thought Betty had a point, but he was sure that idiotic consistency served his criminal purpose more than any rational parsing, as it were.

Anthony was pissed off, but it felt like Betty had thrown him a life preserver, even if she hadn't meant to.

"Betty," he sighed, "help me understand what POOP really wants."

Betty let her gaze include Anthony and Caroline, but her comments were fully directed at Wendell. "The goal of POOP is to keep the property from being developed for any kind of housing or, God forbid, commercial use. The goal is to keep it undeveloped. Period."

Wendell recalibrated. "This is kind of a hoax and not nice. But I get it. You're telling me the Democrats on the BOS won't support my wall. The vote is rigged, completely rigged, and the Democrat people do not want to, uh, preserve and, uh, protect open space the way we do. It's a shame, really a shame. Very sad."

"Wendell, don't assume that you have the Republican votes," said Anthony. "This wall thing is not a good idea. It's stupid. The Republicans do not want to look stupid. Let it go."

He looked directly at Anthony. "No, no, I don't want anyone to look stupid, certainly not me. I mean, I'm not stupid, so how could I look stupid?"

The tension did not abate, because Betty, Anthony, and Caroline all knew a "but" was on the way.

"But," continued Wendell, "we, okay, I, have made a promise to POOP, and I don't want to back down on that. I need to keep talking about the wall, the state grant, and all my promises to everybody. If I break a promise, it would be really bad for my political career. So I'm just going to keep talking about, you know, my promises. And stuff."

"Wendell, what are you talking about?" said Anthony. "You don't have a political career!"

"Of course I do," huffed Wendell, flexing his tingling hands. "I'm first selectman for the rest of my term. And my slogan is incredibly adjustable. I can be against all kinds of projects for many years, many, many levels and years. Instead of No Upsetting Development Ever next time I'll make it No Unwanted Development Ever, then No

Unwarranted Development Ever, then No Ugly Development Ever. I won't even need to buy new hats. Undesirable. Underhanded. And I know I can come up with more, so my career is long-term. As long as I have a hat, I have a political career. And who knows, I might run for even higher, way higher, office."

Anthony was quiet and resolute. He spoke slowly. "You need me and my support and our Republican committee to make your so-called political career happen, and you are never, ever going to get that. Ever. And we are NOT running you for first selectman again. Ever."

"—can you believe this guy—"
"—I don't see how this helps—"
"—again, it's all about Wendell—"
"—we're losing sight of the goal—"
"—POOP will back me up—"
"—the arrogance—"

And so on.

The shouting stopped of its own accord.

"I have to leave," grumped Wendell. He got up, did not say goodbye or thank you to Betty for hosting the meeting, and walked out.

The three of them sat there, momentarily muddled.

Finally, it was sweet, ditzy Betty who said, "Anthony, we have to shut this guy down."

•••

Wendell went home. He clipped Bunker Girl's earring to his belt where he could see it and reached up to the top shelf of his closet, pulling down the box with the never-used gun he had purchased for his long-ago murderous rehearsal. Figures one through five in the instructions told him how to load the bullets, and there it was, a loaded gun, happy in his shaking and painful hand. He unloaded it, loaded it, then unloaded it again. He nervously returned the gun and the bullets to the top of the closet.

It was early afternoon, but he poured himself a whiskey and took out his note-preparation materials, usually reserved for late in the evening. He had a lot to say and considered going beyond the six-to-an-insert-sheet limit.

Next step, sincerity. Or, possibly, shoot them.
Leave gun in closet too messy in Betty's kitchen blood yuck.
No digging or equipment of any kind, very bad, very dangerous.
If they find Bunker Girl, no connection to me.
But Fucking Stella. Again. Always. She still controls my life. Shit.

Keep talking in circles.

• • •

Debra invited an old mediation colleague to meet up for a glass of wine. She recalled little about the colleague's circumstances, only that she had been one of the earliest first-wave mediators in the area, that she had referred lots of cases to Debra, that she and her husband had a second home at the far end of Cape Cod, and that she had been an avid golfer during The Club's halcyon days. Debra was honest with her to a point, telling her that she was active in Somerville municipal governance and that any recollections about The Club-now-Somerville-Woods would be oh so helpful. Whether the colleague believed the ploy was questionable and irrelevant.

Debra had a glass of Sancerre, and her colleague ordered a pinot noir. They gossiped for an hour about all the mediators they had in common, and just as Debra had wrung all the water out of that laundry, she switched loads.

"So, do you still play golf?"

"Oh no, we gave it up some time ago. Once it was clear that The Club was in trouble, we joined the other country club and played there for a few years, but then grandchildren happily got in the way." She laughed, and Debra made all the required inquiries about children and grandchildren, geography, and employment.

"Do you miss golf?"

"No. Not even a little bit." She hesitated. "Let's face it, it lost some of its allure for us after that man died on the golf course, just dropped dead on the sixteenth fairway at The Club. Horrible business."

Debra signaled to the waiter to bring another pinot.

"Really, a man dropped dead? On the sixteenth fairway? Did you or your husband know him?"

"Yes, yes, of course, you know, my husband knew him, I mean they weren't best friends by any means, but over the years they had played golf together at one course or another. My husband was actually at The Club the day the man dropped dead. He was with a foursome, and they were on the green of the twelfth hole when they heard sirens and saw an ambulance come barreling down the fairway. He often told the story that after the ambulance got that dead man off the course, everyone just kept playing as if nothing had happened, and someone, I don't know who, complained about the delay of play. My husband never really enjoyed golf after that." She chuckled.

"I have a vague recollection of that story. What was the man's name who died?"

"Cecil. Cecil, let me think . . . oh, of course, Cecil Williams." She paused. "I knew his wife, but only a little."

"Oh? What was she like?"

"I barely knew her, but you know, you see people on the course or the clubhouse and you say hello. Funny, I can't think of her name. Terrible way to lose a husband, like that. Well, not that there's a good way for someone to drop dead, but you know what I mean. Why?"

Debra was sitting in a bar speaking with someone she hadn't seen in a decade about someone she had never met. "Well, uh, just wondering, you know, I mean, well, it was just such a different era in Somerville. I wouldn't expect you to have kept up with Somerville and its small-town struggles given that you live in Elmstown, but those old days of golf glory loom large in our, uh, municipal conversations these days."

"Yes, indeed, a very different era." The colleague was close to seventy, and she had aged since Debra had last seen her, but evidently, even with nostalgia tugging at her, she had not lost her edge. "Oh, I just remembered her name. Stella. Stella Williams. I think she had a reputation as kind of a bossy golfer. I do recall one time I was in the pro shop and Stella Williams was there having an argument with her golf partner about Stella's belief that no matter what, tollbooth workers on the parkway should not be entitled to a pension at the state's expense. Strange that I would remember that."

"Do you know the name of the golf partner?"

"Yes I do, but she's been dead a long time, I think."

Debra gulped the rest of the Sancerre and signaled to the bartender for the check. Her colleague suddenly looked up from her pinot. "Funny how you remember things once you start thinking about them. We didn't go to Cecil's funeral or anything, I mean, it's not like we were friends, but The Club, or Stella, or someone had a reception of sorts where the members could pay their respects, sort of a membership tradition, I think. Nothing fancy, just a receiving line. I remember that Stella's son was there. Well, of course he would be there—it was his father who died. He must have been in his midtwenties or so, and he had a huge mustache. He shook everyone's hand, I guess, but it was so odd because he wasn't standing next to his mother. He was standing off to the side, away from her, and glaring at her the whole time. Kind of sad, really."

Kind of familiar too.

—CHAPTER 14—

Debra had little choice but to put the whadiddydo on the back burner. The Board of Selectmen had plenty of work to do even without the golf course property opera, and the statewide election season was heating up, which would involve a brunch one weekend, a wine and cheese the next, pols rubbing elbows, and nonstop vying for vote-getting attention.

Vinnie and the Rockmore cohort would be the focus of the fundraiser at the Triple B, and Rockmore did it up big, cashing in on the old-boy network, twisting all available arms to get a huge swath of local, regional, and statewide bigwigs to show up. It had been that way for years, and everyone knew that headcount was nearly as important as dollar count. No excuse was good enough, so a good Democrat gets her ass to the Triple B seasonal event.

The coatroom queue at the Triple B was long, so Debra skipped it and kept her lightweight fall jacket on as she and her husband made their way through the noisy bar. After a half hour or so, the music was turned down and the Connecticut muckety-mucks were recognized, applause, applause, and finally the speeches began, applause, applause. Vinnie was the last to speak, an insider acknowledgment that he was the local draw and a golden boy on the rise.

"Thank you, thank you everyone," he began. "When I got elected to my first term . . ." and off he went, elegantly acknowledging supporters, sharing an anecdote, poking fun at himself, a serious, and blessedly brief, nod to statewide and local issues, then bringing it in close, sharing a personal connection "Yeah, the Triple B, it's always very emotional for me, no doubt for many of us, because we all knew Bob-Behind-the-Bar, may he rest in peace." Vinnie smiled mischievously. "I have no doubt that many of us learned one or two life lessons from Bob in this very room." The locals ate it up, and when the applause finally died down, Vinnie went on. "There was this one time, well, I was a new cop, and

I had to ask Bob a few questions about, well, it doesn't matter what it was about, but whether he remembered two particular patrons on a certain evening. He had no reason to remember either one of them, but he not only remembered them and what they looked like, he even remembered what they drank. At the time, what did I know? It didn't seem like a big deal, but as I've made my way forward in politics, there is no question that it has proven to be the most valuable lesson of all time. Never forget a face and remember everyone you meet. Thank you all very much for being here, and don't forget to vote!"

Applause and more applause. The crowd thinned out, leaving clutches of stalwarts who would, themselves, thin out, but only after one or two more rounds of drinks.

Vinnie worked the room and made his way over to the Somerville group.

"Very nice," Debra said to Vinnie, "but just wait a few years. You'll forget every face you see and you won't remember anyone you meet." They all laughed, and just as that propitious moment for a graceful exit was upon them, a youngish man came up behind Vinnie and enveloped him in a boisterous hug.

"Hey, Vinnie, so good to see you," he said. Debra thought he should have looked familiar to her, but she had just made the relevant point. "It's been too long, way too long."

"Patrick, this is great, wow, great to see you. And thank you so much to you and your whole family for stepping up, again." Vinnie was grinning ear to ear, happy to be with people who knew him when. "Patrick, I think you've met all these good people from Somerville." Vinnie went through the introductions.

Smiles all around. "Hey, listen, man," enthused Patrick, "that was a great story you told about my dad. I remember that whole thing."

"What whole thing?"

"The thing about those two customers you asked my dad about."

Vinnie cocked his head and looked at Patrick curiously. "No way," said Vinnie. "Why would you remember me asking your dad a few questions about, well, it turned out to be about nothing as far as I know?"

"Because you questioned me too. It was about a missing girl."

At that moment the music got very loud, and Debra had to lean in to hear what he was saying. " . . . and I was underage, but my dad had me at the cash register," shouted Patrick. "You talked to me sort of off-the-record. I was what, only sixteen or seventeen, and I guess I was an idiot, you know, but I thought it was so cool. Vinnie the cop interviewing me about a missing girl in Rockmore."

Debra felt a light ruffle in her mental filing cabinet. The music was turned down, but Debra leaned in even further.

" . . . and nobody seemed to know anything or what was going on," continued Patrick, in a normal speaking voice. "You asked me if I knew who the supposed guy was with the supposed missing girl, supposedly here at the Triple B. Believe me, I remember that you asked me a bunch of questions."

Debra didn't know if she was meant to be a part of the conversation, but Vinnie wasn't saying anything. "So, Patrick," she jumped in, "did you?"

"Did I what?"

"Did you know who the supposed guy was with the supposed girl, supposedly at the Triple B?"

"No, not at all," Patrick answered, "but I told Vinnie at the time, I know I told him, that I would recognize the guy if I ever saw him again. Turns out I have my dad's talent for faces."

Vinnie briefly seemed burdened, and his golden boy visage evaporated. He was socially forced to turn toward a clump of Democrats who wanted to shake his hand, say thank you, and go home. "Yes, thank you for coming, good night. Yes, of course, remember to vote." He turned back to Patrick, puzzled by the turn of conversation. Debra jumped in again.

"So, Patrick," she said, vaguely aware she was clenching a single glove in her jacket pocket, "have you?"

"Have I what?" said Patrick.

"Have you seen him again?"

"Yes. I mean yes sort of. I saw the guy like maybe a year ago, but something was different, maybe a mustache or no mustache, I'm still not sure, but no question, I knew I had seen him before. At the time, I couldn't figure out why he looked familiar or why I recognized his face. I just couldn't place it, and I sort of forgot about it, I guess, until just now when Vinnie told that story about questioning my dad. That's when I made the connection. Bingo! The guy, the one in the bar, he was on a billboard, the one near the dry cleaners in Somerville. It was an election billboard, and this guy was running for first selectman."

•••

Debra was up all night.

The phony barfy divorced cockatoo selectman had a drink in a bar a number of years ago with a girl who was not missing and who no one was looking for.

Sometimes people do just disappear, Debra considered, or at least they do on the BBC mysteries shown on her beloved PBS station. And if they do just disappear and are accidentally discovered years, decades, or centuries later, those discoveries invariably involve a safari or a bear or a priest's hole in an old castle. None of that applied here, or at least she didn't think so, but it had already been a long evening.

Debra's husband shouted from upstairs that she should come up and go to sleep. Yeah, right. She had a clue now, an actual clue, a witness statement of sorts, a connection to the past, a lineup, a perp walk. Yes, something happened, and now something was going to be done about it.

There was a box of campaign materials in the closet of her upstairs laundry room, and given that she had lost to Wendell barely eighteen months prior, the box was easily retrievable. She found a huge envelope of both formal and informal photos, many of which Debra was now looking at for the first time. She wasn't interested in a general stroll down campaign memory lane, and she didn't even bother to feel bad as she glanced at the photo of the Democratic billboard with her and the slate assembled and smiling, entreating all who saw it to vote for Debra and the Democrats. She just plowed through, and finally she found it, a photo of the Republican billboard with Wendell and his slate, not as assembled and certainly not smiling, entreating all who saw it to vote for Wendell. There was mustache-less Wendell on the billboard Patrick had seen, standing off to the side, neither photographically nor, it seemed to Debra, connected in any other way to any of the other Republicans on the billboard. He stood apart, no question, but Debra hadn't realized how the distance diminished him.

Debra put the photo off to the side and returned downstairs. She could have gotten involved in a movie or, even better, a PBS mystery, but instead she opened the refrigerator. She found cream cheese, which necessitated a search for a bagel. While the bagel toasted, she sat at her kitchen table and noticed that the light fall jacket she had worn to the Triple B event had slipped off the hallway hook and was on the floor. She opened the closet door to get a hanger, and there on the floor of the closet was the right-hand glove mate that matched the one in the pocket of the jacket she had worn that evening. Debra remembered clutching the single glove in the pocket during all the speeches.

Funny, she thought, *I hadn't looked for the other glove because I hadn't realized it was missing, but it was missing, whether I looked for it or not.*

Something niggled, something about a lost glove and Rockmore, but synaptic pruning was in full swing. And she was tired. She took her bagel to the couch, brought along a cookie just in case, turned on PBS, and found an old Miss Marple, the one with the body in the library. *God*, thought Debra, *I love PBS*.

•••

Debra was briefly fired up by Patrick's revelation, but no matter which prism she viewed the revelation through—criminal culpability, partisan politics, intense dislike of Wendell—she had nowhere to go with it. She knew she had to be careful. Wendell was first selectman, at least in name. Any accusation would generate controversy, local press, and partisan how dare yous. And if she was the source of an accusation, sour grapes would be on the menu. Moreover, she still didn't know what to accuse him of. Looking familiar to Patrick? Having a relationship with a backhoe? She was going in circles.

She wasn't the only one. The Democratic Town Committee inner-inner circle met several times for the sole purpose, it seemed, of also going in circles. Circles within circles, just like Wendell's doodles.

The Republicans got wind of the DTC inner-inner circle meetings in no small part because everyone was everyone's neighbor, and while the bulk of folks in Somerville paid no attention whatsoever, the partisans on both sides were inordinately attentive, noting whose car was in whose driveway and for how long. They rarely leapt to the illicit-schtupping conclusion, because no one was all that attractive to begin with, and if there was schtupping going on, the schtuppers wouldn't park right in the driveway. But the cars told the story, so everyone knew who was meeting and where.

Debra had just completed a short morning at her office, and on her way home she pulled into the little food shop, where she saw Howard's car in the parking lot. When she walked in, he had just ordered a tuna on rye with lettuce and tomato. No, not toasted. The little food shop was famous for its tuna salad, which you could get on a sandwich or in a container. No one in Somerville even made tuna salad anymore.

Debra said a quick hello and walked to the other end of the store to get the attention of the butcher behind the meat counter. When she glanced up from the vast display of meat behind the glass case, she saw Anthony come in and surprise Howard. He also ordered a tuna sandwich and, from what Debra could see, paid for them both.

Anthony led Howard to one of the tables in the tiny and completely empty table area. He had not noticed Debra, and she could hardly chase after them given that she was involved in a tri-tip steak trimming discussion with the butcher. Howard's face was just visible to Debra, and she could see he was smiling and nodding, signifying a chatty lunch, no doubt about spouses, kids, college applications, and kitchen remodels, all so Somerville.

Debra moved down the counter to the deli goods, where she could order a container of tuna salad and, possibly, overhear a smidgen of Anthony and Howard's conversation. She distractedly asked about a container of cucumber salad, which triggered a providential delay, as the deli guy had removed the entire tray of cucumber salad over to his workspace, igniting a minor to-do between the deli guy and the butcher, giving Debra the perfect excuse to loiter at the counter and listen.

"How'd you know I was here, by the way?" she heard Howard ask.

"I saw your car in the parking lot," answered Anthony. They kept up a steady stream of yackety-yak about sports and gutters, leaving Debra briefly disappointed that their conversation was not eavesdrop worthy.

She was about to turn to leave, cucumber salad now in hand, but she saw Anthony lean in. He seemed to be doing most of the talking, but they had lowered their voices. She could hear whispers, but no words. *That could mean only one thing*, thought Debra. In an older-lady flash, Debra made her way to the table area, nearly dropping her beautifully trimmed tri-tip, and without waiting for an invitation, she plopped down next to Anthony.

"Well," she said, laughing, "this looks like trouble." Howard and Anthony were surprised, but they grinned like a couple of teenage boys caught buying condoms. "I don't want to interrupt," she lied. "I had to stop in to get something for dinner. And tuna, of course."

The ensuing pause was awkward, and Anthony scraped his chair back as if to leave, but Debra wasn't about to let that happen. "So," she artfully asked, "what are we talking about?"

Anthony turned and looked Debra right in the eye. Over the years, he had quietly referred three of his cousins to her for divorce mediation. She had thanked him for the referrals but had never otherwise spoken a word to him about any member of his family or their marriage troubles. Partisanship notwithstanding, they held each other in grudging regard.

"Well, Debra," said Anthony, "if you must know, Howard and I are talking local politics."

"Anything in particular?" asked Debra, as ingeniously as she could muster.

"No, nothing in particular," said Howard.

"Bullshit," said Debra. "You're talking about Wendell."

No one spoke. Anthony studied the sandwich crust on his paper plate. Howard shrugged as Debra looked from one to the other. "Let me guess. Anthony, you're mad at Wendell. Or Wendell told you to drop dead. Or you told Wendell to drop dead. Or maybe, just maybe, you're getting as frustrated as we are, as the Dems are, but you don't know what to do about it. Which is it? Am I right?"

It took a moment, but finally Anthony looked up, now resigned to the fact that Debra was fully part of the conversation. "Okay, look, we've all known each other a very long time, right?" Howard and Debra nodded noncommittally. "You both know me well enough to know that I would never, and I mean never, ever bad-mouth another Republican to anyone other than another Republican, right?" They nodded again.

Anthony stumbled and struggled to find the right tone, but once he got going, it was a full-blown Wendell dump, both cathartic and remarkable. "And now, Wendell's wall, or medieval rampart or whatever he's calling it now, is just a pain in my ass. I mean, people on the RTC are getting pissed off with this guy. You both know that I've been a Wendell skeptic from day one, but this goes beyond everyday political aggravation." Anthony took a sip from the Diet Coke can. "There, I've said it. And Debra is right. I am frustrated."

Howard leaned in. "Anthony, no surprise, we've all known since the beginning that you don't like the guy. The only question is why you're bringing it up now."

"I'll bet I know why," said Debra.

"Why?" challenged Anthony.

"Yeah, why?" asked Howard.

"Because you're worried. You think he might be dangerous."

Anthony and Howard looked up at the exact same moment to see if she was joking.

Debra went on. "Anthony, far be it from me to tell you how to run your party, but Wendell is, well, he's everything bad I can think of for a selectman. It sounds like you now agree, right?"

"Well, uh—"

"And you think he's crossed a line somewhere, right?"

"It's complicated—"

"And you're not sure what to do about it, right?" She took a moment to collect herself and smiled. "Anthony, if I didn't know better, I'd say you're looking out for the common good. Wow."

"Debra," said Howard, "your sarcasm is entirely unnecessary."

"But accurate. So shut up."

"Well," said Anthony, "I hadn't thought of it quite that way, but the way Debra is saying it sounds a lot better than 'the chair of the local Republicans is throwing their own first selectman under the bus.'"

"He didn't hesitate to throw you under the bus," Debra pointed out.

Howard had hunched over a bit and his forearm was scrunched against the edge of the table. It must have hurt, because when he sat back, he rubbed the compressed spot.

"Anthony, for crying out loud." Howard was quietly ticked off. "Look you two, maybe he's dangerous, maybe he's just everyday ordinary corrupt, but either way, Anthony, you launched this idiot. We've been trying to clean up this mess for nearly a year. You sold your political soul, if you ever had one, no offense, for six votes and a campaign slogan. He was a bumper-sticker huckster, and now you want me to hand you a hanky?"

"Yes."

"Yes? That's it? Yes?"

"Yes."

"Are you telling me that if somehow Wendell was the top of the ticket again, you wouldn't vote for him?"

"I would not vote for him," said Anthony.

Howard was appropriately dumbfounded. "But Anthony," teased Debra, "the real question is whether you would vote for the Democrat."

"I can't believe I'm saying this," said Anthony, shaking his head, "but under the present circumstances, I think I would have to. For the good of the town."

Now Debra was dumbfounded. She would have bet her tri-tip steak that he would have said he just wouldn't vote. She put off wondering what she would do if the tables were turned. "You're more worried than you're admitting, aren't you?" asked Debra, but before Anthony could answer, Howard jumped in. "Anthony, do the Rs want to solve the golf course problem or do the Rs want to get rid of Wendell?"

"Both. Yes. I think getting rid of Wendell would be the first step to getting the town back on the right track."

Anthony leaned in, so Howard and Debra had to lean in again, but Howard protected his arm. They were all nearly head-to-head over the paper plates. "There are two things you can take away from this," said Anthony, "and if you want, we don't ever have to speak about it again. First, the Somerville RTC will never support Wendell for any higher office. Ever."

"Duh. What's the second thing?" Debra finally asked.

"The RTC is breaking ties with POOP."

Howard raised an eyebrow at that. "How so?"

"I have the RTC votes. If you're part of POOP, gave them money, helped build the website, wrote a letter in support of their agenda, or hang out with Betty, you're off the RTC unless you publicly renounce them."

Debra was stunned. "Renounce POOP? It's like the Inquisition."

"Maybe so," sighed Anthony. "But the problem has been their blind faithfulness to Wendell. And just because I'm a nice guy, I'll give you another tidbit. That faithfulness to Wendell and the wall is on the wane."

So there it was, all the rumors were now fully confirmed and no longer speculation. The Rs were split, and still splitting, and POOP was now a divergence. "Well, okay," sighed Howard, "I've got the two things, plus the tidbit. But Anthony, what do you want me, or us, to do with this?"

Anthony threw up his hands. "I have no idea at the moment," he said, "but can we keep this just between us? I mean really keep it between us?" Howard and Debra nodded, happy with the intel but bummed with the burden. "Hey, I'm glad we all had this conversation."

"Yeah, me too. And thanks for the sandwich."

"You got a sandwich out of this? Anthony, you owe me a sandwich."

"Debra, anytime. It would be my pleasure."

•••

Howard and Debra arranged to have a face-to-face postmortem the next morning on the Anthony-ambush meeting. It had to be at Debra's house because it couldn't be in public, and it couldn't be at Howard's because, well, they never met at Howard's.

In the meantime, Debra got a call from Betty. Debra was not surprised. Betty was her neighbor. They used the same snowplow guy, and during the winter months and electrical power outages, they always checked on each other. It's what one did. But this was late summer, and at the moment, only political power outages were at issue.

"Hi Debra, it's Betty. I'm glad I caught you at home. I want to talk about Wendell and the golf course. Do you have a minute?"

Betty and Debra had never had a single conversation about Wendell because the footing was just too treacherous, but Debra loved that Betty was direct. "Of course. I'm leaving for the office in about a half hour. You want to come over now?"

"No, someone will see my car."

"Okay, when do you want to connect?"

"Can I come to your office, maybe tomorrow morning?"

Debra was floored. She had mediated the divorces of dozens of

Somerville couples, but none of them knew about the others, at least not from her, and she had always regarded her office as wholly separate from her Somerville political nuttiness. Her office was her well-ordered sanctuary, where process was put to good use, where tangles were disentangled, one knot at a time, in an orderly and deliberative fashion. Debra had her mediator hat and her community political hat, and wearing two hats at the same time for no good reason was just silly. She needed her boundary.

"Uh, Betty, that's not a great idea. I'm jammed up tomorrow, but I have a DTC meeting at my house tonight around six, so let's meet at the library around four o'clock and we can talk in one of the study rooms." Betty agreed, and Debra's worlds retreated to their respective galaxies.

When they finally did connect later that day, Betty was in her most conspiratorial mode. The study rooms at the library were full of high school students who, remarkably, were studying. "Ooh, that's not good," said Betty. "I don't think we should be seen speaking together. Wendell wouldn't like it." Debra was about to protest, but Betty went on. "Let's separately walk across the parking lot and pretend to bump into each other in front of The Center at The Center."

"Betty," Debra pointed out, "this is absurd." But Betty turned and purposefully walked out of the library, signaling Debra with her eyebrows that she should hold off for a moment and then follow. Debra had little choice. She walked out of the library and crossed the parking lot to where Betty was waiting for her, just in front of the gym and under the portico.

"Oh, Debra," Betty exclaimed. "What a surprise!"

"Betty, hello. Yes, uh-huh, what a surprise."

Debra waited.

Betty lowered her chin and her voice, forcing Debra to contort to hear her. "POOP is breaking up with Wendell."

Memories of sixth-grade crushes and passing notes under the desk came to mind. "You're breaking up? Wow, uh, this is huge." Debra could hardly tell Betty that she already knew this and that Anthony was the source of her information.

"I know."

Debra waited, again. "Betty," she finally said, "this is all a little too special ops for me. What is it you're telling me?"

"Okay, Debra. Here it is. I can't deal with Wendell anymore. His ideas are not good for POOP, and I think he's mad that I'm pulling away from him, politically. I thought you should know."

"Well, thank you, I think, but Betty, what do you want me to do with this information?"

"I haven't told anyone, not even Wendell, so don't tell anyone what I've told you. I mean anyone."

"Why not?"

"Well, I'm not sure, but I'm fairly certain that POOP's agenda is not Wendell's agenda, and if the truth be told, he's starting to scare me a little bit, so until we know what Wendell is really all about . . ."

Debra stopped listening. Wendell scares Betty. Wendell tries to scare Debra. Patrick recognized Wendell from the billboard. Some, but possibly not all, of the RTC inner-inner circle think Wendell is bad for the town. Debra wondered how Betty felt about large crested birds.

". . . so that is why I don't want to make a public fuss just yet by letting everyone know why we are breaking ties with Wendell."

Debra wanted to tell Betty that a public fuss was unlikely and that, apparently, everyone was getting more curious and concerned about Wendell's agenda, although as far as Debra knew, she was the only one who imagined human remains under each and every abandoned tee box. But Debra didn't tell her any of that. *It seems an unnecessary detail for Betty,* thought Debra, *and she is clearly more worried than anyone had realized.*

"Okay, Betty, no problem. Your secret is safe with me, and I won't say anything, but trust me, people will not be surprised when your breakup with Wendell becomes public."

Later on, the DTC inner-inner circle showed up at Debra's house. The wine came out, and the pizza delivery was expected shortly. "Sorry, guys, I didn't have time to cook. I had back-to-back mediations all day and a meeting with—" She caught herself, in fulfillment of her promise to Betty. She started to offer excuses for not cooking dinner, but instead tried very hard to remember the last time anyone had cooked her dinner. Her husband was on one of the zoning boards and wouldn't be home for at least an hour.

Debra caught Howard's eye, and he nodded, signifying that they were still on for the next morning. First, they had to get through tonight.

The pizza performed its role in furtherance of governance and the wine lubricated the chatter, but even as they finished eating, they did not finish drinking. Apropos of nothing, Howard said, "I think we should embrace the ultimate capitulation. Long-range planning." They all stared at him. He went on. "We've allowed Wendell to distract us. Forget Wendell. Forget all or nothing."

He paused, for effect. "We do it all."

"Howard," snapped Liza, "we've had this long-range planning conversation a dozen times. We rejected it. It won't work."

"No, Liza," he said, "you're wrong. The moment is exactly right. Wendell has been the moving force behind all-or-nothing thinking, and now, politically, he's cooked." Howard looked directly at Debra. "Don't ask me how I know. I just know. We should capitalize on the moment and become the moving force behind something-for-everybody thinking, spread it out over ten years, marginalize the naysayers and layer out the political ownership so no one party has to own all of the crap."

Debra brought out a bottle of Scotch. She heard distant strains of celebratory music in her head.

David, ever the cynic, was gearing up to complain or leave. Howard was writing something down. Liza was gulping Scotch. "Well," Debra said, "this is what happens in mediation."

"Fuck mediation," said David.

"Yes, thank you, David," she answered, "but I simply mean that you can go in circles forever, talk, more talk, lost in the fog, on the edge of the forest, lost in the trees, and then, one day, you trip over a log and it all becomes clear."

"Fuck mediation," repeated David. Debra laughed.

Howard waved a piece of paper. "I wrote it down. Long-range planning that includes all of it. A great big Wendell-less plan."

"I don't think—" started David.

"—go ten or fifteen years out—" said Liza.

"—encompass all of these goals or only some of these goals—" said Howard.

"—upcoming election cycle—"

"—create priorities—"

"—diversify housing—"

"—two years to draft, engineer—"

"—generate tax revenue—"

"—fundraising—"

Howard was taking notes, trying to keep up.

"It's a little, well, out of the box, I suppose, but we could go long," Debra said, mixing her metaphors as usual. "Fewer age-restricted units—"

"—water and sewer to our advantage—"

"—convert the building—"

"—new police station—"

"—The Center at The Center at the Clubhouse—"

"—ice-skating rink—"

This rat-a-tat-tat continued, and they finally quieted, collectively embarrassed that they had gotten carried away. Debra was sure that by the next morning, someone would figure out that this was all nonsense and impossible, but Liza, of all people, tentatively asked, "So you think we should go from doing nothing to doing everything?"

"I don't know," said Howard, "but it can't make it any worse than it already is." He looked at David, who was sulky. "Some future board of selectmen is going to have to figure out how to make this all happen and how to pay for it. But," he added, "it completely changes the conversation, and we all desperately need to change that conversation."

It was daft, but the celebratory music in Debra's head swelled, evoking triumph, epiphany, and patriotism. She brought out a box of chocolates.

They rat-a-tat-tatted all over again at full volume, building toward a mighty mental musical crescendo.

Applause! Bravo! Unfurl the flag!

Howard banged the table. "Enough, enough. We aren't going to do ten years of planning tonight."

The music in Debra's head died down. "And don't forget," Howard said thoughtfully, "this completely, and I mean thoroughly, neutralizes Wendell, the motherfucker. What's he going to say? The whole damn acreage has to be open space with a conservation easement? He'll look and sound ridiculous. He's going to be against a community park, a playground, walking trails? He'll get boxed out, and he'll have nowhere to go, period."

"What about the Republicans?" asked Liza. "I mean, they don't have the votes to stop this, whatever this is, but it would be great if they could get on board with some of this, right?"

On that note, the meeting ended, and everyone went home.

The next morning, Howard showed up at Debra's right on time. She made coffee. They sat in the kitchen.

"Okay, Debra, I think we should be happy about that crazy meeting with Anthony, but it was completely bizarre."

"I know."

They rehashed the entire conversation, draped it with any number of interpretations, projected pernicious motives onto Anthony and the Republicans, and concluded that Anthony had been completely sincere and was genuinely worried.

"He's not the only one who's worried," Debra said, thinking of Betty but committed to the confidentiality she had promised. "I'm worried too. I not only think Wendell is dangerous, I think he's covering something up."

"Yeah, nothing new there, Debra. You've implied that before."

Debra wasn't sure how far to reveal her speculative thinking with Howard. He didn't do speculation, as a rule. "You know, Howard, there is a lot you can hide on a golf course."

He looked at her. "Don't say it, Debra."

"A body. There, I said it. Yes, you can hide a body on a golf course."

"No, you can't. Impossible. People don't just disappear, and even if they do, God forbid, eventually they get found. Mostly, most of the time, I think. People look for missing people."

Debra had nothing concrete to offer to the contrary, but it was obvious to her that Howard did not watch a lot of PBS mysteries.

•••

The members of the Board of Finance were appointed, not elected, and were thus unsullied by campaign promises and untethered from political calculation, resulting in an abundance of inappropriate on-camera statements about nearly everything. They were rarely, if ever, impressed with spontaneous and imaginative long-range planning, but they loved any idea that suggested future revenue.

In her capacity as liaison to the Board of Finance, Debra emphasized the future revenue possibilities and, with Peter's help, got the finance folks to pony up a big chunk of contingency dollars for planning and preliminary engineering services.

Wendell got his meeting packet. He glanced at the agenda.

"Item No. 6: Approval of Long-Range/Ten-Year Planning Project, including design and concept, with appropriate funding as per Finance Director's Transfer Request, per attachments 1-17, below . . ."

He couldn't believe his eyes! How happy was he! Ten years! But who put this on the agenda? Whose idea was this? He didn't care about an answer to that question. He was just delighted that his pressure regarding open space or Open Space had resulted in a decade of no worries. But of course, as always, he had not read the full proposal.

As it happened, very few people showed up for Public Comment, possibly because it was pouring rain, possibly because it was a nonelection year, or possibly because Wendell had ruined Public Comment for just about everyone. When Agenda Item No. 6 came up, Wendell turned to Peter and said, "I love this long, very long, plan, but what is this all about?"

Peter explained the whole thing, doing an excellent job of covering for Wendell's ignorance. He emphasized that there was support for a whole new way of thinking about the golf course property that, for the moment, did not involve a sale of the property to a developer, although that was possible down the road for a smallish portion of the property, that he hoped the BOS would consider multiple uses of the property, including a portion to be dedicated for open space and a conservation easement, that a wish list would set out broad outlines of guiding principles and uses for the property, that there would be lots of opportunity for community input, and that nothing would happen without appropriate notices and transparency.

Peter was an excellent explainer.

He concluded noting that "the only thing on the agenda tonight that requires a vote is the question of funding to undertake survey, engineering, and preliminary long-range planning studies."

Liza immediately made the motion, and Caroline, who had cleared it with Anthony, seconded Liza's motion. The bipartisan plan would pass.

But Wendell was red in the face. "Wait, is this for surveys? I thought this was for a ten-year do-nothing plan."

Peter explained, again. Wendell did not care.

"We should not be spending money on engineers, or surveyors," said Wendell, looking at the camera. "It's bad. I've always said it's very bad, and no good can come of this. It's sad, very hoaxful. I'm against this. No transparency. The public does not know what this money is being spent on, and here we are in a budget cycle when everyone, including me, is planning on complaining about spending. We have to build the wall or plant the hedge, or do both, and make the state pay for it before we do anything else, because we have to keep things from getting out and keep things from getting in. And—"

Henry loudly called the question, which forced the vote.

Only Wendell voted no. In a matter of six agenda items, he had gone from content and secure to deeply shaken.

●●●

Wendell went home, and even though it was nearly nine o'clock and he hadn't had his dinner, he called Anthony. Anthony had watched the meeting on cable access, and when he answered the phone, he told Wendell he was already up-to-date.

"Fuck, Anthony, why didn't Caroline and Henry vote with me? Why didn't we stick together on this? You keep telling me we have to stick together. The Dems got what they wanted, for chrissake, and I'm the only one who's out there on this. I know you're behind this. I can tell."

"Wendell, suddenly you're about the team? I did not tell Caroline or Henry how to vote on this, and it would never occur to me to tell you how to vote on anything," he lied. "Let's face it, you are kind of getting what you want here, aren't you? It's a long-term plan that will likely include a conservation easement for a significant part of the property. What more do you want to make out of this?"

"I made a promise, a campaign promise. We have an emergency now. I'm going to have to declare this an emergency and—"

Anthony interrupted Wendell. "Look, your so-called campaign promise was idiotic, and you barely squeaked by. NUDE was dumb. The state was never going to pay for a wall or a flower bed or whatever you're calling it, and your so-called base did not propel us, us, Wendell, the party, to a lasting victory."

Wendell did not respond.

After several uncomfortable moments, Anthony spoke again. "What do you mean, 'emergency?'"

On the other end of the line Wendell sat, the phone at his ear, his head in his hand, his shoulders slumped. His hands ached. He hung up, leaving the question unanswered.

He was so disheartened that he wrote only one note.

I can't leave Bunker Girl. I can't.

He filed the note in its insert, pulled it out, kissed it, and refiled it. He pondered and wandered for the rest of the evening, his robe flopping about, Bunker Girl's earring clipped to his ear, restless, watching TV, then not watching TV. At least it was getting chilly. The town had to get engineering proposals and price it out and decide who to work with, and winter would have to come and go, freeze and thaw. He had a couple of months to figure this out.

•••

The feedback from those who gave feedback was mostly upbeat. "A refreshing reset," said one email; "good to move forward," said another. The incipient social media mavens were all over the map, more interested in being heard and read than in actually saying anything worth hearing or reading, but amidst the negative and hateful, there were some very positive posts and considered viewpoints.

Mostly this is great, thought Howard, delighted that the focus was not on the failures of this Board of Selectmen but rather on the possibilities of success or failure for future Boards of Selectmen. *We had a problem, not a real problem*, he thought, *like crumbling schools or a wasting urban tax base, but a Somerville-type problem. We sidelined Wendell and are doing the right thing. Doubts, yes, but this moment*, he thought, *was a good moment.*

By early December, proposals and bids had all been processed, and the BOS had approved a contract for survey, engineering, and design work. All the dips, vales, swales, and swaths would be redrawn and depicted for multiple municipal imperatives.

Wendell loudly argued against the contract, changing up his quarrels on an hourly basis with the hope that one of his pretexts would stick. When he argued that the survey work would likely be substandard, he got an earful from the president of the survey firm and a lawyer letter threatening a defamation lawsuit. Wendell backed away from that tack.

But he took every opportunity to push back against every element, feature, schedule, cost estimate, and next step. He showed up at both relevant and inapplicable board and commission meetings and insisted on speaking. If it was clear that a first selectman's report was neither welcome nor on any agenda, he used Public Comment. He was out four nights a week just so he could Publicly Comment everywhere and as often as possible. His message never varied. "We should not be touching the golf course for any reason. Any reason is a hoax. We have an open space emergency. We are ruining the emergency with all this survey and engineering work. Very bad, very bad things are going to happen. Very bad and very hocus pocus for all of us. The property should have a wall, and the state should pay for it. And no hoaxes. Thank you." He became a Public Comment junkie, manically traipsing across Meetinghouse Lane every evening in search of any Public Comment fix he could wrangle. But even the chatty Recreation Commission stopped engaging with him. They let him have his say, and then, to everyone's shock, they actually followed their agenda.

The Fire Commission pushed back. There, the volunteer firefighters, some still burly and big, others gone a bit slack, responded to Wendell on the record, telling him to stop wasting everyone's time with this wall thing and to stop calling it an emergency. "Wendell," said the fire chief, "if you don't have flames and sirens, it's not an emergency. We know what an emergency is, and this is not an emergency."

Wendell did not attend the Police Commission meetings. *Not a good use of my valuable time* he told himself. Instead, he went to the library and borrowed *The Great Escape, The True Story of the Great Escape, The Count of Monte Cristo*, and *The Secret Life of Harry Houdini*. He caressed the earring in his pocket. His hands ached nearly all of the time now.

∴

Howard called Debra and told her his plan.

"I'm going to call Anthony and suggest—what should I call it?—a bipartisan fuck-you meeting with Wendell."

"Oh, that should go over really well," Debra said. "Let me know what Liza and Brendan say when you ask them."

"I already asked them. They said great."

"How come you're asking me last? You're going to do it no matter what I say."

"True, but I made the calls alphabetically. You're last-name last." Debra was all set to argue, but she had given up litigation a long time ago, and since Brendan had joined the BOS, she could no longer make the case that she was first-name first. "Fine. Let me know how it goes."

When Howard suggested the meeting to Anthony, Anthony feigned reluctance, but he was actually thrilled because he could use the bipartisan momentum to shove Wendell off the slate for the upcoming odd-year election cycle. Had Anthony and Howard known that the other was aglow with bipartisan fervor, they would have been suspicious, sensing that somehow a bipartisan effort against Wendell would benefit the other in unanticipated ways, but as it was, they were separately just delighted. These were uncharted waters, they each told themselves, and we are explorers, about to embark on a journey not seen in this town, this state, this nation for well nigh . . . ever! Nautical theme music, without a doubt.

On the spectrum of town gossip, the arrangement of the meeting fell somewhere between responsible discretion and juicy fair game. All the selectmen were in the know.

"I would give anything to be a fly on that wall," Debra told Howard. "But I get it. No way, I can't be there. None of the BOS can be there."

"Correct. But you could hide in the closet." Howard grinned.

God, thought Debra, *I really want to hide in the closet.*

The Center, not the Senior Center now known as The Center at The Center but The Center building itself, had rooms that could be and were used for Boy Scouts, yoga classes, and community groups. It wasn't private, but it was neutral, and to Debra's frustration, every room had a perfectly good closet. Anthony did not give Wendell a choice whether to attend, but he didn't need to. "You're all trying to shut me up, right? You want me to stop declaring my emergency, right?" Anthony was not surprised that Wendell thought it was about him because Wendell thought everything was about him, and Anthony leveraged Wendell's narcissism to secure Wendell's commitment to show up. "Yes," Anthony told Wendell, "we want to talk this through and get your input on the BOS reset. By all means, bring Betty."

Everyone was on time and a little bit nervous. The old schoolroom had a bunch of folding chairs, a long rectangular table off to the side, and old blackboards with chalk still in the grooved sills. Anthony and Howard had arranged six chairs in a circle so as to dissipate any perception of power or control. Anthony would speak first because, no matter what, Wendell still belonged to him.

"Uh, good, glad we're all here," began Anthony, "and be assured that Howard and I recognize and appreciate the effort at municipal comity."

"Municipal comedy?" interrupted Wendell. "Was I supposed to bring a joke?"

You are a joke, thought Howard, but he kept silent. "Wendell," said Anthony, "not comedy. Comity."

"I know, I heard you. Comedy. We're planning a comedy night? Will there be a microphone? We could make it a part of Public Comment. I could emcee—"

Howard was jumping out of his skin. "No. Not comedy. Comity. Anthony, go on, for crying out loud."

"Uh, yes, Howard is right," mumbled Anthony, a little shaken that Wendell had derailed things from the start. "Yes. Okay, first, I think no matter what, we should be able to rely on each other's discretion and keep the contents of this meeting private amongst the six of us."

Lots of nodding, but everyone knew that everyone knew that secrecy was mere whimsy.

"Second," he continued. "I think at this point we should recognize that a slogan, even a catchy slogan that fits on a hat, is not the same as governance, or policy, or law." Anthony looked directly at Wendell. "It's just a hat." No one said a word.

"And third," he went on, "I'm sure we can all agree, well, I hope all of us agree, that our public meetings have become abusive and uncivil, to the point that governance itself has been undermined." Anthony looked at Howard. "So, Howard and I, and a few others, are promoting a bipartisan effort to curb the abuse and elevate, if you will, the level of discourse and Public Comment that will no doubt be part of all our lives for the next several years."

Betty, seemingly oblivious to the tension in the room, broke in. "What does that mean, exactly, a bipartisan effort?"

"Howard," said Anthony, "why don't you jump in?"

Howard did not want to jump in, but he did want to make Wendell look like an ass. "Bottom line, Betty," he began, "is we can have chaos or we can have a functioning and principled town." Nobody bit. He could have gone on about societal values, volunteerism, and tolerance, but Wendell was ripping his backpack apart, zipping and unzipping every pouch. "Wendell, did you lose something, or what?" said Howard.

"No, I just forgot my . . ." Wendell looked up to see everyone staring at him. "Never mind. Whatever."

"Uh, Wendell," said Anthony, "I am going to recommend to the RTC that we should support the reset that the Dems have come up with. It should be a group effort. Can we count on you to be a part of this, not for the Rs, not for the Ds, but for the town?"

Wendell said nothing and did not look up at the direct question.

Betty broke in again. "Uh, Anthony, I think I have this right, but I just want to make sure. There will definitely be Dedicated Open Space with a conservation easement on Somerville Woods, correct?"

Anthony and Howard answered at the same time. "Yes."

"Any idea how much land will be devoted to the easement or the location?" Wendell whipped around to look at Betty, suddenly very interested.

"No, uh, Betty, no one knows yet, but from what I've heard so far, it's a good-size piece of the pie, likely to be over on the old back-nine side," said Howard.

Betty wanted to flex her newfound political muscle, and she turned to Wendell. "Wendell, that sounds like a plan we should go with. This reset thing that Anthony is talking about makes sense, don't you think?"

Wendell took his time, his aching hands grasping the backpack on his knees, barely raising his eyes from the floor as he answered. "Well, Betty, I will continue to call for the, uh, entire property to be Dedicated Open Space, protected from development in perpetuity." Wendell glared at Anthony. "First base, NUDE. Second base, POOP. Practically, a home run. No development, ever. That's what I promised my base, big promise, big base, big, very big, and that's what I will keep doing."

"But Wendell," said Betty, barely aware that her moment had been eclipsed, "if your base thinks some is not as good as all but is better than none, you should too."

Wendell grabbed his backpack and stomped out of the room.

Perfect, thought Anthony. *He's now on his own. I don't care what he does. The Republicans don't owe him a thing.*

Perfect, thought Howard. *He's pissed off his base. The Democrats don't have to worry that he controls any votes.*

Perfect, thought the two vice chairs. *If this bipartisan thing works, we all look good. If it doesn't, we're next in line to be Chair.*

Imperfect, thought Betty, *but good enough.*

The meeting was over.

— CHAPTER 15 —

Howard wasted no time. By the next day, everyone knew everything there was to know about the marginalization of Wendell and the fact that he now carried a seemingly empty backpack.

"Was it a new backpack?" asked Liza.

"No idea, and what difference does that make?" Howard answered.

"I just can't picture Wendell shopping, that's all."

At the next BOS meeting, Wendell zoomed through the agenda. Debra was, of course, seated next to Wendell, but he no longer wrote her notes. He alternately rubbed and flexed his fingers, fondled his pocketed lucky charm, and used several different colored Sharpies to doodle. He was no longer casual about his doodles, covering his scribbles up with loose papers.

Wendell winced when he got to Agenda Item No. 12 and desultorily continued to doodle, forcing Peter to explain and put the content on the record.

"There is an explanation in your packet," started Peter, "but for those watching on cable access, we want to create a planning group for Somerville Woods." Peter did not take the time to enlighten the cable access audience on the behind-the-scenes tussle over how best to title this group because, in the end, all demands found accommodation. "The Ad Hoc Committee on Concept, Harmony, and Use will be charged with the Somerville Woods preliminary siting and design issues going forward. AHCCHU will be populated by representatives of all the stakeholder boards and commissions. You need to vote on this."

There was the anticipated bureaucratic scuffle because Wendell did not want any of it, but the selectmen procedurally overcame his resistance, voted to create AHCCHU, then voted to defeat Wendell's motion to appoint himself to sit on AHCCHU, and instead voted on Liza's motion to appoint Debra to AHCCHU.

"This is completely rigged, illegal, completely rigged," complained Wendell. "Not fair." It *was* rigged. All the selectmen had agreed ahead of time how to block Wendell's resistance.

The cameras recorded Wendell's pout. When Wendell eventually gaveled in a ten-minute break, he practically ran out of the room. Debra quickly moved Wendell's papers around to expose his agenda, and she used her flip phone to take a half dozen photos of the scribbles and scrawls that covered the sheet of paper. She got his stuff back in order. He came back into the room, lingered at the cookie table, and shouted at the cable access person to restart the cameras.

Debra didn't care that she was on camera or seated next to Wendell. She wanted to see what was in those photos. She removed her glasses and tilted her phone to avoid glare and Wendell. She could see that next to "Agenda Item No. 7, Finance Director's Report," there were rows of dollar signs, but everyone doodled dollar signs next to the finance director's report. And there were circles all around the margins, circles within circles. But the lower right corner had the initials BG scribbled over and over, big and bold. Backhoe Guy was still the top contender, but absent confirmation, Debra felt compelled to keep Banjo Guy in the running. The doodle in the lower left was nearly impossible for her to read. She really had to squint. Although the writing was blurry, the message was clear. In teeny-tiny letters, Wendell had scrawled: Hi Debra. I know you're watching me. Be careful.

•••

As happens every January, Debra's mediation practice shifted into high gear. No one wants to start divorce mediation as the winter holidays gear up, so everyone waits until January 2. Fresh start, turn the corner, clean slate, start anew.

But it brought full days at the office. All of Debra's volunteer efforts were getting in the way of actually working, and the newest horizon, AHCCHU, had no pattern or habits to ease the way. She was fully squeezed, and she begged off the liaison meetings. It was just too much.

Still, Debra had made plenty of time to pester Vinnie about Patrick's recollection of Wendell on the billboard, telling Vinnie they needed to go to the Rockmore or Woodbridge police, the FBI, the State Criminal Investigations Unit, any TV show that solved cold cases anywhere, but Vinnie had become circumspect. True, it had been a number of years, so urgency did not loom large, and true, Wendell wasn't going anywhere, and true, for at least part of the time that Debra nagged Vinnie he was busily running for office, but still, Debra argued, let's arrest Wendell or interrogate him or slap him around or something.

"Debra, no," he said. "I thought it meant something, but it doesn't. Patrick is probably correct that Wendell was at the Triple B, but so what? We don't have much else. We need to be thoughtful about this. It was a long time ago, and it is all just too random. No."

It occurred to Debra that Vinnie had bungled an investigation. But when she asked him about those early days, he was pretty clear that he had followed up all the possible leads and there was, simply, neither a formal report of an actual missing person nor evidence in furtherance of an investigation.

It also occurred to Debra that she had become the crazy old lady in the small town who sees a weekly murder in the vicarage garden, but she had to acknowledge that even if Patrick proved to be correct, what crime had Wendell committed? There was no body, no DNA evidence, no crime scene, no grieving family, and no one complaining that the police were doing nothing. Vinnie had Florence Nuffield's peeved employer statement, but that was it. On the one hand Debra had a cockatoo, and on the other hand, well, she had a cockatoo who doodled vaguely threatening miniature missives. She had no other hands.

Another BOS meeting had just ended. Wendell was gathering up the library books he had brought with him, all to impress the cable access audience. Debra went up to him, well within earshot of everyone.

Debra looked him right in the eye. "Hey, Wendell, what are you reading?" she asked.

He glared at her, and she could see the wheels spinning beneath his coiffed crest. "Not much, just a couple of books about something."

"You know," said Debra, "I just finished a terrific book, nonfiction, about a volcano, total eruption, very orange, out of control, hugely destructive. Do you know it?" Wendell was doing his best to ignore her, but Debra took a step toward him and continued. "I'm pretty sure the title is *Kaboom!!*, by, uh, Colmeister, Lucas Colmeister, but I'll look it up and get it for you." Instead of provoking Wendell, as she had intended, she was providing outstanding reading material. "You always have so many books with you. I just couldn't resist asking you about it again."

Wendell contemptuously looked Debra up and down. "Yeah, Debra, you don't look like you resist much."

Did he just call her fat? "Did you just call me, well, fat?"

"Yeah, Debra, so what?"

This was new, and her cohort, all of them, who had listened with one ear, were not sure what to do. If truth were a defense, well, there wasn't one. But if courtesy is a required standard in civic discourse, no question, he had fallen well short of the standard. Debra stepped back.

David came to the rescue-ish. "Wendell, that's enough. Debra, c'mon, we'll all walk you out."

That was that, and except for the fat part, Debra was delighted. He had lashed out. He was incapable of adult discourse. He was a verbal klutz who could only shoot a cheap, trashy, crass shot.

So many adjectives, so little time, thought Debra.

She ordered a copy of *Kaboom!!*

A few nights later, there was a Fire Commission meeting. If she was going to poke again, she thought the time had come when she should do it where emergency medical equipment and skilled ambulance guys would be present.

Debra got there early, but Wendell was earlier, glum and already busy with his pocket. The room was otherwise empty but Debra could hear voices down the hall where the pizza was set out. "Wendell," she said, "here, I got you a copy of the book I was telling you about." He was suspicious. She was suspicious.

Wendell abruptly stood up, possibly to walk away, possibly to cosh Debra on the head. His foot caught around the base of the folding chair, forcing him to bend awkwardly to keep from falling, and the hand in his pocket came free a moment earlier than it should have, releasing something that skittered across the hard floor and seemingly disappeared. He was horrified. Wendell lurched, bent, squatted, and searched.

Debra cocked her head at the familiar scene.

"Wendell, what are we looking for?" she said, peering around chairs and wastebaskets.

"No, don't look. No, I'll find it, just stop looking. I will find it."

"Okay, okay, Wendell, I'm just trying to help."

"No," he said, on his knees, scanning the floor, "no, don't help. I do not want you, you of all people, to help. No."

"Fine, I'll just look at you while you look for whatever it is." *And don't barf*, she thought, *whatever you do*.

The chair of the Fire Commission came in, as did a quorum of commissioners, all of whom had been enjoying the pizza. "Uh, I need to get this meeting started. Why are you on the floor, Wendell?"

"I dropped it. I need to find it."

"I'm starting this meeting. Now. You can look for whatever it is after the meeting." Wendell had no choice but to take a seat. He was so agitated that he waved away the invitation to speak during Public Comment, seemingly desperate for the meeting to be over.

The chair got through the first few agenda items and looked up. "Well," he continued, "we have two selectmen here tonight, neither of whom are actually our liaison, but do either of you want to give a liaison report?"

"Uh, no, uh, there is nothing to report." Wendell barely looked up except to give the chair a dirty look. Debra shook her head, subtly scanning the floorboards for Wendell's object, quietly relieved to know she was, evidently, not the only liaison who skipped meetings. Wendell made no move to leave, and if Wendell was staying, Debra was staying.

But sitting next to Wendell was like sitting next to an eggbeater. He fidgeted and spun about, his eyes searching the floor, under chairs, behind the blinds. It was thoroughly disruptive. The cable access camera recorded both jittery Wendell and pissed-off commission chair, but finally, after an eternity, there was a motion to adjourn. Everyone filed out, except the fire chief, Wendell, and Debra, and although Wendell continued his search, he could not locate his precious whatever-it-was. A half hour later, with impatience and keys in hand, the fire chief escorted Wendell out of the building. "Wendell," said the fire chief, "come by at 9:00 a.m. I'll have the room open for you, and you can search all morning if you want. Unless there's a fire."

The fire chief locked up and walked Debra to her car, as was his habit with the last to leave.

"What was all that about?" he asked.

"No idea, but will you open the room first for me at seven thirty?"

"Debra, you're up to something. Don't be stupid."

"I won't. I just want first crack."

Bright and early, the fire chief let Debra into the meeting room. He went off on his own business down the hall, clearly annoyed that he now had not one but two dotty selectmen in his face. Like most women of a certain age, Debra was an excellent finder, so it did not take long. There it was, behind a cabinet, well hidden by a large trash can. It was an earring. She was gobsmacked. For years, she had done all she could do to not imagine what Wendell was fondling in his pocket, but the last thing she expected to discover was that it was an earring. *Was it his mother's earring?* she wondered. *That's not sweet, it's disgusting. Was it someone else's earring, maybe his fart of a wife? Less disgusting, but incredibly pathetic. Was it his earring? Paradigm shift.*

It was a clip-on, a round, flattened disk with a center cutout, with a little orb dangling in the opening. Cheap, not gold, at best a department store costume nothing. Not the earring of a mature woman nor the earring of a woman of style. It was junk. It was a junky circle within a circle. It was his doodle.

Debra had no idea what to do. Leave it for Wendell to find, take multiple pictures of it on her phone, give it to the fire chief to give to Wendell, take it and let Wendell flounder, call her husband, call Vinnie, call David, call Liza, have a pecan sticky bun all sounded like good options. Maybe she should call the police. I found an earring! Alert the media, send out an APB, issue an Amber Alert, attach an ankle alarm! No, don't call the police. It was ridiculous. Debra saw Vinnie's point.

She took multiple photos of the earring, front, back, dangling, and flat and rubbed off her fingerprints because that's what they do on TV. She started to replace the earring where she found it but instead wrapped it in a tissue and stuck it in her purse. She took herself to the station coffee room and helped herself to a croissant and the newspaper. After about an hour, she heard the buzzer, and she knew the fire chief was letting Wendell into the station and escorting him to the meeting room. She got up and walked the maze of hallways to the meeting room, where the fire chief was watching Wendell move every chair, table, trash bin, cabinet, and hose hook looking for his whatever-it-was. He was red in the face, and angry.

"It has to be here. I heard it drop. I saw where it went. It has to be here."

"Wendell," said the fire chief, "is it valuable or something?"

"What the fuck difference does that make?" screamed Wendell. "And it's none of your fucking business anyway. Get outta here and let me look."

"Now just a goddamn minute, this is my station—"

"No, it's my station. I'm the first selectman, I'm in charge. It's my station, mine, and you can't tell me what to do. I can do what I want—"

They finally noticed Debra, who had been watching the testosterone combat. "Can I help?" she asked sweetly, certain Wendell would explode. But the fire chief quelled the blaze and intervened.

"Look, you two, stop. Whatever this is has gotten out of hand. Wendell, go to your office and cool off. You can come back later. Debra, I say this with all due respect, but mind your own business. Go to work or whatever you do when you're not doing whatever it is you do here in town. Go. Leave the station."

Wendell was desperate and nearly tearful. "No, I can't."

"Go. Now."

Wendell pulled himself up off the floor and sulked his way out the door, brushing dust bunnies off his knees. "I'll be back," he told the fire chief. "In an hour." Debra hung back as the fire chief escorted the crumpled Wendell out the door. She quickly pulled the earring out of her purse, unwrapped the tissue, and tucked the earring behind a gap in a cabinet, letting it peek out from behind the slight opening. *If he didn't find it this time, well, that's his problem,* thought Debra, *but what a tantrum!* The earring is the key! But what did it unlock? Door Number One revealed an unhinged first selectman and an unhinged encounter. Door Number Two?

Debra made her way to the exit, and the fire chief silently walked her out to her car. He had questions, Debra knew, but she waved goodbye and offered no explanation. She drove straight to her office.

She was supposed to be drafting a separation agreement for a nice middle-aged couple who had no idea what they wanted in life, only that they did not want each other. But Debra was distracted by Wendell and that deranged wrangle involving the fire chief.

So instead of doing what she was supposed to do, she flipped through the photos of the earring on her phone. She logged onto the newly launched and technically glitchy judicial website. "I can't believe I'm wasting time with this," she mumbled to herself as she searched for and found Wendell's divorce filing, indexed under his name. There it was. He was the plaintiff, his wife did not participate in any actual or legal way, and judgment entered, signed by Judge Marlene Hamlin. He divorced the girl he married, and aliases, if any, were not at issue.

With all the work Debra had to do and all the meetings she had to attend, with all the documents she had to draft and emails she had to answer, here she was, in her office, traversing her self-imposed inviolate boundaries, wearing different hats, wondering about a young woman from a long time ago whose name she had never bothered to learn who married a political and likely illiterate fraud. She couldn't stop herself. She Googled the wife's name as it appeared in the divorce file on the judicial website.

It took several tries, but a well-buried newspaper reference caught her eye. Debra clicked, and there it was, an old article from a Maine newspaper with the story of a young woman with multiple aliases, none of which had the initials "BG," who had been arrested for a number of crimes, including theft by deception and receiving stolen property, and who was also the subject of outstanding warrants in Vermont and Connecticut. This was her, no question. Wendell married a thief, and then Wendell divorced a thief, a New England small-time grifter. There was no mention in the article about whether she wore cheap earrings.

Debra deleted the search, got up, paced around her office, and moved papers around. She made a note of the name, got a cookie out of the office cookie jar, then got another cookie. She was restless, and after one more cookie she knew she wasn't going to draft that separation agreement. Debra got in her car and drove back to Somerville.

•••

On the morning of April 1, Wendell looked out his front window and saw yellow daffodils and fluorescent vests all over his golf course property.

On the evening of April 1, Wendell wrote notes to himself.

This is very bad very not good. Too many tripods and the other things I don't know what they're called.

Dumpy Debra made me drop the earring, my Bunker Girl. It is totally her fault.

Bang.

Oh, Bunker Girl, I found our Earring!!

New professor person, very bad, sad, should be me.

She has too many rules, like Stella.

The Board of Selectmen, over Wendell's objection, asked Faith Cooper to be the chair of AHCCHU. She was a retired professor of forestry from the prestigious university just down the road in Elmstown. She was and had always been a registered Independent, no doubt facilitating her service in a high-level capacity with the Environmental Protection Agency in Washington, DC, under both Democratic and Republican administrations. She had always held herself aloof from local tussles, and she was one tough and very smart woman. No one called her Faith. Everyone called her Professor Cooper.

Professor Cooper insisted on a daily check-in with Peter Reilly, wearing his clerk-of-the-works hat, and Dan Solomon, the no-nonsense director of the survey team. They always met at Town Hall, as there was nowhere to meet at the golf course property given that the parking lot was heaved and broken, vermin had taken up residence in the clubhouse, and, although no one gave voice to it, meeting in the former men's or women's locker rooms was just way too creepy. Dan invariably reported that no, no real surprises yet, and yes, we're moving right along.

At one of the early meetings, Debra referred to Somerville Woods as the town's Opportunity Real Estate, or ORE for short. *It's no RALLYS*, she thought, but it stuck, as did her suggestion that the engineering firm entitle its presentations and exhibit slides as an OREport.

And when Debra started referring to any potential property outcome as an Opportunity Real Estate Option, or OREO, even Professor Cooper smiled. Who doesn't love an OREO? everyone joked, and goodness, isn't Debra clever! After that coinage, Oreo cookies showed up at every meeting, and the work of AHCCHU, which would have been impossible only a few months earlier, generated some excitement. Wendell was furious—clever Debra, AHCCHU progress, Oreo cookies at every meeting—but he did not attend AHCCHU meetings, seemingly because there were neither cameras nor Public Comment. He was also likely afraid of Professor Cooper.

AHCCHU stood as the perfect intersection of responsive governance, adherence to procedures, and snacks. Debra loved this intersection. She hated that Wendell jaywalked all over this intersection, ensuring only gridlock. She hated Wendell. Period.

Whatever speckle of empathy she had briefly imagined for Wendell had scattered. She had photos of an earring and doodles on her phone. She clicked through them way too often, looking for meaning or a thread. She found neither. Only the itsy-bitsy message stood out, and only because Liza's months-ago comment about Wendell's threatening demeanor still echoed in Debra's head. When she was home or at work, she let it go, reasoning that Wendell was a creep, a noncriminal creep. But when she was engaged in governance, it was hard to ignore the fact that the elected first selectman acted like a bully and, for some reason, more of a bully toward her than anyone else. He was untethered, more irrational than ever, wearing his NUDE hat and spreading falsehoods all over the place.

It was a lot to take and a lot to handle, but Debra was more certain every day. All of it—his quickie marriage, his so-called base, the mysterious earring, all his lies, and especially his election to the Board of Selectmen—was tied up in the golf course.

•••

AHCCHU had turned into a group of eleven people, and a core group of eight or nine, including Debra, managed to show up at every meeting. They generally met in the morning and were always joined by Buzz Hawthorne, one of the senior consulting engineers, who was blessed with infinite patience. Occasionally, David Silver showed up, but only if there was a legal question that needed to be addressed.

Finally, the design firm announced that it had come up with seven possible layouts, and AHCCHU convened to begin the vetting. There was a premeeting, of course, attended by Debra, Professor Cooper, Buzz, David, and, most importantly, Granny Charter. David and Granny Charter were jittery and unhappy. "Look, I don't know what Charter section applies if you want to have a full-blown town meeting for everyone to see all of the options," he told Professor Cooper. "It's going to be like asking for the entire town to design this, whatever it is. Just approve a plan, and then we'll worry about the public later."

"No, that's not how we're going to do this," said Professor Cooper. She was not overly fond of David Silver. "We're going to start this vetting work, eliminate and narrow, then have one or more information forums and get public feedback. At this point, the last thing we should do is shut out the public." Granny Charter was not her problem, and she was not going to spend her precious weekly meeting talking about it.

"I know, I know," said David. "But there are still a few crazies out there who will make everyone miserable."

"At the moment," said Professor Cooper, "the crazies are greatly diminished in number and are there only to give this Wendell character some kind of cover. I don't see how they can hold this up at this point. This new direction, at least so far, has been unbelievably positive, don't you think?"

Buzz interrupted. "Oh, speaking of Wendell, I need to tell you that he's at the property all the time."

"Yes," said Professor Cooper. "We know all about that."

"Well, it's gotten a bit intense."

"Is he interfering with your work?" Debra asked, hopefully.

"No, not as such, but he's been spotted by our guys all over the property at different times of day, just about every day. I finally caught up with him about a week ago, way too close to The Turn, that snack bar structure that's about to collapse. By the way," Buzz said, turning to David, "I've got those demolition bids for you all to look at today, because that has to come down no matter what you all decide to do with the OREOs. Demolition is outside the scope of our services, but we obtained a few prices, and we can call it a change order under our contract."

"What happened when you caught up with him?" asked Debra.

"Well, I explained about all of the safety concerns, what with our trucks and guys out there and whatnot, and I asked him if there was something specific he wanted to speak with me about, stuff like that."

"And . . ."

"And, well, I don't want to sound unprofessional, but he told me to, well, drop dead. But he used the f-word."

"He told you to fuck off?"

"Well, I'm glad you said it, David, and not me, but, yes, that's exactly what he said to me. I didn't want to escalate the situation, so I just walked back to the trailer and made a note about it, knowing I would see all of you today to bring it up. I have to say, he was pretty belligerent. He kept telling me to stay the F away from his property."

"His property?"

"That's what he said. He was, well, really red in the face too, if you know what I mean."

David promised to have a word with Wendell. "I'll couch it in terms of his personal liability if he causes an injury," said David, knowing full well it would make no difference to Wendell. David left, grabbing the demolition bids, and as the AHCCHU members were dribbling in and the Oreo cookies were already being passed around, Professor Cooper signaled that the meeting would begin.

Lots of papers fluttered, and big maps were unfurled.

"We'll never get through all of this if we jump around," directed Professor Cooper. "Let's look at everything Buzz wants to show us, in the order he presents it. Hold your questions."

Buzz began. He showed how OREOs 1, 2, and 3 each used a hub-and-spoke design concept, each showing a ten-acre vaguely circular hub in the center of the property and acreage roughly emanating from the hub to the border of the parcel, each chunk varying in size and use depending on the OREO. It was all very conceptual with dimensions and notes and provided a dizzying array of options. OREO 1 showed the hub as a dog park, a playground, and a botanical garden, all with shaded seating. One spoke on the far side consisted of forty-five units of active-adult-over-fifty-five housing and a community room, another showed a greatly expanded pool with a water playground and a remodeled clubhouse for either The Center at The Center or the police station, a third spoke showed forty acres of Dedicated Open Space over by the swinging gate, and a smaller spoke on the side next to the main road showed an amphitheater and gazebo designed, said the notes on the OREO, for little concerts, perhaps, or a dance pavilion or possibly an outdoor skating park and hockey rink. OREOs 2 and 3 showed a similar layout, but with five and six spokes, respectively, adding rental units and a driving range and everything else shrunk accordingly.

OREOs 4 and 5 abandoned the hub-and-spoke layout and instead arranged everything as if it were a quilt, rectangles of different sizes, incorporating all the same uses, adapting the sizes of the uses to the number of patches on the quilts.

It was like porn for zoning geeks. Debra was in blueprint heaven.

Buzz buzzed through OREOs 6 and 7 because the group had now grasped the basic idea, and whether they quilted or hubbed, Somerville would have OREO platters filled with choices and parking, roads and trails, community and connectivity. "And finally," noted Buzz, "I just want to make sure you all understand that each OREO impacts the entire property, no matter which arrangement you opt for or what uses you choose. For planning purposes, the location or designation of a given use is interchangeable with another use. Our choices were somewhat arbitrary."

It was a lot to take in.

"Well," began Professor Cooper, "there is a great deal here that we need to understand and get through, but let's just begin with general or initial responses. We might have to think about how to schedule our meetings to tackle these specifics. Debra, why don't you start?"

Ugh, thought Debra. She was obsessing about Wendell telling Buzz to fuck off while acting in his first selectman capacity. But Professor Cooper wanted a positive statement, and Debra could hardly refuse. "This is all great, just great. It's clear a huge amount of work and imagination went into this. I love the concept and allocation choices . . ." Debra blathered on for a few minutes, very upbeat. She heard a marching band in her head, a resounding cascade of musical accompaniment fitted to this uplifting moment. Professor Cooper wanted a tone, and Debra provided it. ". . . and I love both concepts, as they afford flexibility today and for the future."

"Yes, good," said Professor Cooper, who then went one by one around the table for individual comments. Debra barely listened. She could not concentrate on hubs and spokes, quilts and skate parks, rentals, diversified housing, and open space. Or Open Space. She was still flabbergasted at the fact that Wendell called Somerville Woods his property. *Does he really believe that?* wondered Debra. When everyone had an uninterrupted say, the back-and-forth began, and Debra had to engage, in no small part because her mediation skills kept everyone on a productive path. After two hours of a robust exchange, everyone was exhausted. But it had been a positive discussion, and no one had gotten positional. It was agreed that OREOs 1, 4, and 6 should be refined for a second look by AHCCHU.

As the meeting concluded and everyone filed out, Debra pulled Buzz and Professor Cooper aside. "Look, I think this wandering Wendell thing needs to be nipped in the bud. It's one thing to take a walk on a

Saturday, even if he gets too close to where Buzz's people are working. It's another to be aggressive and nasty."

They agreed, but it was also clear there wasn't much to be done about it. Yes, Wendell is difficult, but anyone can take a walk on the cart paths any time. Yes, certain areas can be isolated from the public for safety reasons, but it's a fluid situation as no two days are the same. Yes, he's a horrible person, but there is no law against being a horrible person. Debra apologized to Buzz on the town's behalf and made noises about trying to keep Wendell under control.

Dammit, he was on a billboard! He carries around an earring!

•••

The BOS needed to authorize and fund the destruction of The Turn, and Wendell, who was doodling, did not hear Liza's motion, Henry's second, or Peter's explanation.

Wendell snapped. "Further and additional destruction. Very sad. I vote no."

The motion passed, and Peter arranged for Dan to meet with the building official to organize the raze.

Wendell bolted out of Town Hall as soon as the meeting adjourned. Debra grabbed David's arm and said, "Let's go," which, given their ages, meant ambling down the long hallway, slowly crossing the parking area, unlocking the car, getting in, and buckling up, but mentally Debra was at full throttle. She could see Wendell pulling out just ahead of them. "What are we doing?" asked David.

"We're going to follow him. I am telling you, he is not happy about this demolition."

"What if he just goes home?"

"Fine, I'll bring you back to your car here at Town Hall. Big deal, it's a mile out of your way. I just want to see what he does."

They could see him up ahead. It was easy to hang back. Wendell made a turn.

"See, he's going home. That's the way to his house."

"Maybe. But it's also the way to the back corner of the golf course, where The Turn is."

"What if he sees you?"

"So he sees me, so what? There are only so many roads in this goofy town, and we all have to drive on them, right?"

Wendell pulled into his driveway.

"See, I told you. He just went home."

"Hang on, let's just see what we can see."

Debra drove past Wendell's house and used a driveway about a half mile down to turn around and head back the way they had come. It was still light out, and they could see Wendell donning his yellow fluorescent vest and hard hat as he walked toward the swinging gate. If he heard Debra's car, he did not turn around. He climbed over the gate and walked all around the crumbling snack bar, poking the ground with a long walking stick, muttering to himself, dipping his head like a frightened bird as he walked around the crumbling building's perimeter.

"What the hell is he doing?" mumbled David, not expecting an answer. They sat there watching, not saying anything.

Finally, Debra spoke. "We should not get out of the car. Agreed?"

"Agreed. But I don't get it."

Wendell drifted away from the teetering snack bar toward a group of clumsily stacked boulders clumped together under a branchy and lethargic copse of trees.

"What's he doing now?"

"I have no clue."

"He's just poking around all those boulders."

"Weird, huh."

"Very weird. What a creep."

"What a weirdo creep."

They had naturally lowered their voices. There was no reason to whisper, as Wendell was distant, but given his threatening doodle-ette, Debra could not assume they went unnoticed.

David spoke so quietly that he was nearly inaudible. "I think Vinnie should run for governor."

"Me too."

They continued to watch Wendell, who had perched atop the boulders, bobbing his head up and down.

David lowered the window and leaned his head toward the open air. "He's singing."

"What? He's singing? No way. What's he singing?"

David strained to hear Wendell.

"I think it's 'New York, New York.'"

They drove back to Town Hall.

— CHAPTER 16 —

It rained for the next several days, one of those summer storms that augur a hurricane in the Northeast but blow out to sea just as all the Public Works overtime has been incurred but not used. Somerville continued to be Somerville, and for Wendell, the rain was a reprieve. It gave him time to consider running away and starting a new life somewhere, anywhere, where he could disappear and not be burdened with the prospect of having his secrets unearthed. But the thought of leaving Bunker Girl left him bereft, and the thought of forsaking the spotlight afforded by the gavel, the cable access camera, and of course Public Comment left him devastated.

He was certain his only option was to be even more visible, to fully embrace his obnoxiousness and become an even greater pain in the ass. Who knew better than he did how to disrupt, deflect, and distract?

Sure enough, on the day the rain abated, opportunity presented itself. Wendell got confirmation from Peter that the demolition of The Turn would take place at the end of the week and that a little ceremony was being planned to mark the event.

It was to be called The Turn of The Turn.

Liza took credit for the name, the selectmen loved it, and even Professor Cooper thought it sent the right message. But when the engineering firm offered to have Wendell ride in the excavator for the first crunch against the building for photo opportunities, Wendell called Peter into his office. "Peter, I heard that the engineering people want me for a photo shoot. Not good enough, no, not enough. Instead, I think we should use the old backhoe from The Club for the first crunch against the building."

"Why?"

"Good photos and, uh, full-circle things, you know, whatever that thing is about stuff comes full circle, and stuff like that."

"Uh, I'm not sure we can do that, but—"

"And . . ." Wendell paused for effect and puffed himself up like a cockatoo, "I want to be the one to do it. I will operate the backhoe to flatten the building."

"Well, that could be a problem because—"

"You know I'm an excellent backhoe guy. You know that, right? Make it happen."

Peter reluctantly made inquiries, but the engineering firm was not happy because it meant having to take a back seat to Wendell and his ancient piece of equipment. Peter was not happy because the town's insurance carrier insisted on an expensive policy rider to cover Somerville in the event that the first selectman caused an accident or injury. The Republicans weren't sure if they were happy or unhappy. Professor Cooper was neutral. Debra was miserable because it was not a terrible idea and she did not want Wendell to get credit for any idea whatsoever.

But Wendell kept up the pressure, so with the assistance of the Public Works guys who drove the backhoe from Public Works to The Turn, Wendell and his creaky cruncher would have the first whack at the crumbling building.

On the day before the ceremony, Wendell looked out his living room window. He saw the open swinging gate and all the big machines belonging to the demolition contractor being maneuvered onto the property, having been off-loaded from the flatbed transports they were on. He saw his backhoe. He grabbed his vest and hard hat, snuck under the fence opposite his house, and walked over, sticking to the boundary, blending in as he approached the ceremony location. The demolition guys didn't know Wendell and likely assumed he was with the engineering team, so when Wendell picked up a spool of yellow caution tape and joined another guy threading the posts in the dirt, no one noticed or said anything. It was like the old days when he worked at the golf course, when he had tools in his hands, when he could caress his backhoe, and when he nurtured and took care of his own private cemetery.

"Hey, Wendell. What're you doing, man?"

Wendell whipped around and faced the town building official. Wendell never liked when he was around, and the building official never liked when Wendell was around. Neither of them spent a second analyzing this dynamic.

This guy hates me, thought Wendell.

I hate this guy, thought the building official.

"Nothing, uh, nothing," said Wendell, not looking the building official in the eye. "Just came over to, uh, see how it was going."

"In a vest and a hard hat? You're not supposed to be here until tomorrow for the ceremony. This is a demolition site. Go home."

Wendell would have loved to fire the guy on the spot, but he was pretty sure that was impossible. He left the site and spent the afternoon desultorily staring out his window, flexing and rubbing his aching hands. At least his backhoe was visible and onsite, ready to go. He could also see yellow caution tape here and there and a little ceremony space on the dirt driveway. The gate itself was closed and likely locked. His copse of trees and pile of boulders were a fair distance from where the ceremony and the demolition would take place. He breathed a little easier.

By 8:45 the next morning, about thirty people were milling around, having parked their cars on the bigger road, way off to the side to allow traffic to pass. The cop had blue lights flashing to alert traffic, such as it was, to the abnormal appearance of pedestrians on the big road and, with the help of the flagmen who were present for the equipment movement, was able to herd the few ceremony attendees toward the dirt area where it would all take place.

Professor Cooper was given a bullhorn. "Thank you all for coming to The Turn of The Turn, marking the first step on the new path we are forging." Thank you to this one and that one and so on and so forth, all congratulatory and upbeat. Wendell had been standing off to the side, holding a huge bunch of celebratory balloons. He was led over to his backhoe, and before he entered the cab, he tied the balloons to the backhoe. He grabbed the bullhorn. "I am totally against a lot of this, and I can't believe you would plan a ceremony without balloons. Very sad and not festive." He easily climbed into the high cab from the right side and waved for the cameras, then literally shifted gears so that the backhoe lurched forward. He skillfully nudged the bucket toward the side of one of the stilts, and just like a puppy using its nose to wiggle under any nearby hand to be petted, he maneuvered the bucket just under the lazy stilt and barely knocked it to the side. He really was an excellent backhoe guy. Everyone sort of applauded. Wendell liberated himself from the backhoe, and the entire ceremony was over. He leapt out, casting himself as the hero of the day.

The town's communications director, who was also the website manager and the assistant assessor, herded the selectmen together and took multiple photos, first in front of the backhoe, then in front of the swinging gate, and, finally, down along the fence, with the copse of trees in the background.

Wendell chose to be in the photos even though he supported none of this, but he refused to remove his NUDE hat. He pushed Caroline aside to be in front of her, and then when the communications director said that the tall people had to be in the back, he insisted that the important people had to be in the front.

"Wendell," she said, "could you please cooperate? Get in the back and take your hat off. This is not a campaign event."

"It's always a campaign event," he replied.

"Take the damn hat off, Wendell," snapped Caroline. "This is not about you. Or better yet, get out of the picture altogether."

Wendell took the hat off, stood in the back of the group, just a little too close to Debra's right shoulder, and a minute later the photo opportunity was completed. Debra turned to Wendell, hovering over her as he was. It was as good a moment as any to have a go at him.

"So, Wendell, I hear you play the banjo." He was in Debra's space, but she was in Wendell's face.

He backed up a bit. "No, Debra," he started slowly, "I do not play the banjo."

Debra knew that of course, but he didn't know that she knew or that she even suspected, or had concluded, that BG was likely Backhoe Guy, not Banjo Guy. And how could she expect him to know what was in her head, particularly since it wasn't even clear to her? But he, Wendell, was in her head, all the time, and she couldn't evict him. Only a few nights earlier, she had had a nightmare with Wendell's face captured on hundreds of small screens all flying about on colorful wings in a dark sky, and all of Wendell's thoughts, random, rehearsed, and revolting, popped up on the screens in little cheeps, peeps, chirrups, and squeaks. She couldn't make it stop, and it was deafening. Dreadful nightmare.

Wendell cocked his head and smiled at Debra, the old twinkle and a bit of new evil showing itself. He was thinking, thinking hard. "No, I don't play the banjo, Debra." He took his time. "I play the bass guitar."

Bass Guitar.

Shit, thought Debra, *Wendell plays the bass guitar?* No way. It just didn't fit. *But if he did play bass guitar,* she thought, *it would explain why he was always rubbing and flexing his fingers.* He has carpal tunnel syndrome, or tendonitis, or trigger finger.

But no way. He was toying with her. He knew that Debra knew about the BG doodles. He was watching her watch him. BG. Bass Guitar.

Score one for Wendell.

She stood there, somewhat dumbfounded that Wendell had hit a high lob that she could not chase. Bass Guitar didn't rhyme with the sloppy divorce day "bottom sex element banjo guy," which for Debra's money still had to mean "but I'm an excellent backhoe guy." *That's the only explanation*, she told herself. But she now had to acknowledge that she had been stuck in a rhyme rut, mentally insisting on a connection between the doodle BG and the drunken mumble. This was not a clean parrot-carrot rhyme, or an antelope-cantaloupe ear rhyme, or even a bury-jury eye rhyme. BG might not have anything to do with an ear rhyme or an eye rhyme. *Damn, it might be something else altogether. Or,* she scowled, *nothing whatsoever.*

Debra was rarely confused, and she did not like it. And it did not suit her.

She needed to go back to the beginning. She briefly wondered where that might be.

The only thing now clear to her was that she wasn't going to be able to figure this out as the gathering shuffled in front of the copse of trees and pile of boulders. Wendell had walked off, and as he passed his old backhoe, he gave it an affectionate pat on its back end, or what Debra imagined was the back end. He turned back to look at her and smirked, kicking the tire of her parked car as he strutted past it. All doubt about the slashed tire was swept aside. She resolved then and there that the copy of *Kaboom!!* she had been carrying around for Wendell would be donated to the library auxiliary.

With Wendell gone, Debra turned and stared at his backhoe. It was parked, if parked is what a stationery piece of machinery is when it is not moving. Debra hadn't noticed before that a person can enter the cab of the backhoe from either side. It had two door panels. But on both occasions when she had seen Wendell in the backhoe, he had entered and exited the door frame on the right, as had the Public Works guy who moved it from the crunch site to its parking place here on the road. When Debra inspected it with Alan and Peter, she had also used the right-hand door. But here was the backhoe, parked on the road, and someone had left the left cab door wide open.

Debra wandered over to the open left side of the cab. At her eye level, the door-frame edge and its jumble of metal bars and glass panels offered a view of a dead mouse nestled against something small and metallic, just beyond the edge where the rusty seat mechanism met the filthy floor. It was too far for her to lean in and retrieve whatever it was, and the dead mouse was a full stop, but she was sure that whatever she saw was visible only from the left, not the right, and not from the seat. Debra did not want to be seen or caught mucking about in the cab, but she had little doubt that the mouse's bier, whatever it was, was what Wendell had been looking for on that day of the Somerville

Woods tour.

Debra decided to keep the mouse intel to herself.

The Public Works guy came over.

"Excuse me, Debra. I have to drive this back." He closed the left side panel, walked around, and started to enter the cab from the right.

"Hey, can I ask you something?" she said, as she followed him around to the right side. "Is there a reason why you guys always enter the backhoe cab from the right?"

It was a stupid question, and his look confirmed that he thought so. "Yeah."

"Yes? There's a reason? What's the reason?"

"Habit." He climbed up, waved with a smile, and off he went, down the road, back to the Public Works garage.

Within an hour, the photo of Wendell in the backhoe cab with the balloons was on the town website, captioned "The Turn for the Better at The Turn." Liza called Debra, very upset that the communications director had mangled her slogan. Nevertheless, everyone spent that afternoon sending and forwarding positive and congratulatory emails and phone messages.

It's not like we've achieved peace in the Middle East, thought Debra. *It's a former golf course that might now be something else.* But she was relieved that for the first time in a long time there was something positive to say about that damned acreage.

•••

Even the most cynical citizen had to acknowledge that the following weeks saw enormous strides. The design people were in the intermediate-advanced stages of producing site plans for AHCCHU, and Mrs. Devlin, a homeowner who had been a naysayer from day one, now stepped forward to spearhead fundraising for all those elements of the plan still being planned that needed fundraising. Mrs. Devlin had been a golfer herself and a board member of The Club, and while she had been furious about devoting the property to 125 units of active-adult-over-fifty-five-age-restricted-high-end housing, she had been equally furious about devoting the whole of it to Dedicated Open Space and even more furious about a boundary wall encircling the property paid for by the state. She was delighted when the Board of Selectmen hit upon productive long-range planning. She pressured her social group to join her in support of the new efforts, and they called themselves Friends of Opportunity Real Estate, or FORE. The handful of golfers who were still pissed off wrote nasty letters to the local paper about the name, believing that it was intentionally disrespectful to the golf community, using a golf term to rub the golf failure in the faces of golfers, but given her former position on the board of The Club, her letter to the local paper in response was taken as sincere and at face value when she claimed that the name was fitting and appropriate and that no offense was intended.

She reached out to former golfers, former members of The Club, and former Somerville residents asking for photographs of The Club when it really was a club, in the sunny days of white shoes and plaid pants, and she soon had access to hundreds of photographs, formal, candid, black-and-white and color, all showing off The Club, the clubhouse and banquets, the weddings, bar mitzvahs, and sweet sixteen parties, the pool parties, bridge tournaments and golf outings, the foursomes, the ladies' days, and The Turn, all depicting the heyday of that life and that place.

Mrs. Devlin was friendly with Anthony Delgado, and when she suggested that the photographs be archived and possibly used in a celebratory or fundraising way, he was all for it. He brought in Howard and the communications director for ideas about how to work with the town on this aspect of ORE.

She thought the campaign could be called Before and BeFORE. Mrs. Devlin and Liza bonded over clever acronyms. Professor Cooper invited her to be a community member of AHCCHU, which upset Betty, but Betty was wholly out of the loop. Mrs. Devlin got the web design and tech class at the high school to help her create a website, and she set up an intergenerational scanning club with the old people at The Center at The Center, formerly known as the Senior Center, and the junior high school technology club, who, together, the old and the young, scanned hundreds of photos to create a digital archive.

Everyone was sleeping really well. Even Debra. She now drifted off after getting only to Louisiana in her alphabetical state-naming exercise.

Mrs. Devlin treasured the archive that was coming together, and she brought a handful of photos to every AHCCHU meeting just for the fun of it. "These are really special," she would say. Not everyone thought they were special, and there were those on the committee, including the survey and engineering people, who had no interest in the old days and old ways, but Professor Cooper and Debra always stayed after the meetings to take a look at what Mrs. Devlin had dug up.

They were poring over the two dozen photos Mrs. Devlin had brought that very afternoon, all in color, the styles and sideburns signifying the era.

"You are not going to believe what I have here. This is gold, photo gold!" said Mrs. Devlin. She pulled out a stack of photos showing the swinging gate and The Turn, both festooned with colorful balloons.

"What is this?" asked Professor Cooper. "It looks so familiar."

"It's the dedication!" exclaimed Mrs. Devlin, opening her arms wide. "The first one, the original one, I mean. When The Turn was built! And dedicated!"

"Oh my god. This is quite something." Faith Cooper was uncharacteristically impressed.

"I know! This one shows a group from the board of The Club back then. Oh, look, I think that's old Eric Simsky. Look how young he is. And this is the Board of Selectmen, all men, too funny, right? It's the same angle as the photo that's on the town's website from just a few weeks ago when they knocked the snack bar down. Can you believe this, how perfectly parallel this is? And there are balloons! The BOS then and the BOS now, both shots in front of all these trees, right?"

It was clearly the same fence, the same angle, the same trees, younger, shorter, and in better kept. And without a doubt, the same copse. But something was off and different. Mrs. Devlin and Professor Cooper had moved on, marveling at other photos, but Debra was quite still. She removed her glasses to get a better look, peered closely, and put her glasses back on. She removed them again. And then she saw it. In the old photo, the boulders were broadly scattered about, under the trees, against the fence, and embedded in the soil, but none of them were near each other. The boulders were not stacked up against each other in a rock pile.

Someone had moved the boulders.

•••

One of the first things a first selectman does upon taking office is appoint a deputy first selectman from his or her partisan cohort on the board. Wendell had refused to do so, and it hadn't much mattered at first, but now, with a big public meeting looming, the BOS had a problem. No one doubted that if Wendell ran the meeting, he would do everything possible to blow it up. It should have been, could have been, the deputy first selectman, but they didn't have one, and Granny Charter made it clear that only the first selectman could appoint the deputy.

The Rs and Ds circled the wagons, got Granny Charter in a good mood, and voted to have Professor Cooper run the meeting.

Wendell was furious.

"I'll speak at Public Comment," he said. "You can't shut me up."

"Wendell," said Henry. "That's true. Lord knows we've tried."

The Board of Selectmen, sans Wendell, and AHCCHU engaged the gears for the public presentation of OREOs 1, 4, and 6, dissing the gym in favor of the high school auditorium, supposedly for the improved sound and visual technology. That was an excuse of course, which David gave voice to when he told Liza and Debra that the vibes in the gym were just too negative and the walls had witnessed too much civil abuse.

The script for the public presentation was straightforward and intensive, meant to encompass the history of Somerville Woods and depict the reset process and options in the best possible colors. Public Comment would be put off for ten days, during which, it was hoped, the public would study the options and email and call with questions and concerns. The presentation would be recorded and posted on the town website, and if Mrs. Devlin took it upon herself to also post the presentation on the FORE website, well, it was against the rules but so much the better. All of the presentation slides had been produced as posters and would be set up on easels throughout the library and in the gym, where they could be studied until they had to be moved for basketball.

Everything would be part of the public record. David didn't care. "You can hope all you want that this gap in the meeting is a good idea," he told Professor Cooper one evening shortly after an AHCCHU meeting, "but I am telling you it's a disaster waiting to happen. Everyone will go bonkers if you don't offer Public Comment right then and there. It will look like a shutout."

On the night of the public presentation, the auditorium was packed and vibrating with chatter. The gap format had been announced well in advance, so no one questioned why there was no microphone set up in the middle of the room. Professor Cooper and the chief planner each presented their respective parts. Professor Cooper then announced that the meeting was suspended and encouraged everyone in town to use the ten-day gap to study all that had been presented.

There was a smattering of clapping, no, more than a smattering, a genuine moment of applause, and the chief planner and Professor Cooper shook hands, and Liza and Debra smiled at each other, and Caroline waved to the crowd, and David shrugged in acceptance. Wendell got up to speak, to use this opportunity to shame the BOS for shutting out the public or to take credit for the public's satisfaction, whichever or both, but by the time he got down off the stage and centered himself in the auditorium, the aisles were filled with chattering townsfolk, some upbeat, some still a bit anxious, some enthused, some shaking their heads, but all heading toward the exits.

There he was, angry and flushed, in the middle of the room, standing where the Public Comment microphone would have been, his arm raised as if to offer a toast, or a protest. He opened his mouth to speak, but nothing came out. *Finally*, thought Debra, *maybe, just maybe, he is finally irrelevant*.

•••

Wendell went home. He was so agitated that he filled up two sides of the photo insert sheets with notes.

First, good news The Turn, knocked down by me, nothing found, all good, great.

Tremendous demolition, excellent boulders on top of Stella. Good balloons.

Second, bad news Big meeting, camera, big, but Cooper crap Very sad.

I don't even know what we're deciding, something about hubs and wheels, maybe a blanket, but I am voting against it whatever it is.

The AHCCHU people with the OREOs, the Sneeze People AHCCHUOREO, gesundheit, well except for the R, nobody sneezes with an R and No Unhappy Development Ever.

That Mrs Devlin is a pain, like Dumpy Debra and Cut-Up-Caroline except for the Oreo cookies.

I do like an Oreo. And tuna.

I'm hungry right now. I don't care, just don't hurt my Bunker Stella, I mean my Bunker Girl, or Stella, or me, or my hat.

No Public Comment, no Public Comment, terrible, no transparency, against the law and its rigged.

No rigging. No digging.

•••

Debra used the ten-day interregnum to set up an appointment with the Rockmore chief of police. She had pressed Vinnie to smooth her way, but he dragged his feet. In the end, Debra was just as glad. She showed up at the Rockmore Police Department on her own terms, with her phone fully charged.

Chief Telford was younger than Debra thought she would be, and short, which surprised her. They quickly dispensed with preliminary chitchat and got to the reason for Debra's visit.

"Chief Telford, there's some history here, but I'll try and keep it brief." She laid it all out, Vinnie, the Triple B, Wendell, Patrick, the missing girl who didn't exist, a golf course, a mustache, an earring, as much as she knew and some of which she only supposed. To her credit, Chief Telford nodded and listened. *She would have made a good mediator*, thought Debra.

"Who did you say called in the disappearance of the girl?"

"I didn't say. I don't know. I assume it's in your file, or closed file, or open file, whatever it's called."

"Does Mrs. Nuffield ring a bell?"

"No."

Neither of them had a choice. They both stared meaningfully out the window.

Chief Telford turned to her keyboard and clicked away for a few moments.

"Mrs. Wolfson, I know Patrick of course and I know Vinnie, mostly by reputation, but neither the billboard nor the earring means very much." She turned to her keyboard and resumed clicking for several prolonged minutes. Debra figured that was that, so she got up to leave.

"But a missing girl . . ."

Debra sat back down.

". . . rings an uncomfortable bell."

Debra had stopped breathing. "We are such a small town," continued Chief Telford, "even smaller than Somerville. We have very few open files, and according to what my screen tells me, only one that involves an old report about a female, possibly missing, but never actually reported as such. It's not digitized, so we need to actually bring in the old file, which is in our storage facility. It will take a day or so to get it and bring it here to Rockmore. I'll circle back as soon as I know something."

Debra was enormously pleased that she had been taken seriously. She was halfway home before she realized she hadn't asked who Mrs. Nuffield was.

•••

Mrs. Devlin was in high gear. She set up baskets at the Town Hall reception area and at the library circulation desk, where, in exchange for any spare change, you got a packet of Oreo cookies. She hit up everyone she knew to throw in twenty dollars to buy the cookies in bulk, "just to see what happens." She put a little sign next to the baskets that read "Let change bring change!" Cookies and goodwill, no information, no pamphlets, just a little note next to the baskets that explained that the money would go toward one of the revenue-neutral options in OREO 1, 4, or 6. She continued to post old photos on the FORE website and encouraged people to comment on the photos and on the people they recognized. She set up a series of coffee meetings in her kitchen, or any kitchen she could recruit, to spread a positive word, and she had her fourteen-year-old granddaughter teach her about embryonic social media to get the word out to the PTA, the T-ball parents, the library auxiliary, the land conservancy, former POOP people, and the historical society.

As it turned out, Mrs. Partridge, a longtime Somerville resident who was active in the historical society, found a photo in the historical society archive of the old Appleby Farm, and she suggested that if and when OREO 1, 4, or 6 ever became a reality, there should be a commemorative plaque that told the story of Old Man Appleby and the farm, deemphasizing the Jewish controversy of the day. The historical society threw itself into a separate fundraising and design effort, all subject of course to Board of Selectmen approval.

Town Hall was inundated with mail, email, and phone messages, particularly in the first week after the presentation. The comments were running mostly curious and neutral, but very few were miserable and negative. There was a steady stream of folks in the gym and the library, sometimes as many as seven or eight at a time, taking the occasion to look at the informational posters. The entire presentation was online, and the answers to the frequently asked questions were frequently updated.

Downhill was easily just one meeting away. The positive impetus could be diverted by disinformation, by one or more effective lies or gadflies, by reasonable concern over money, by the erratic comments of any member of the Board of Finance or Wendell or any taxpayer with a microphone. Ten days between presentation and Public Comment. Ten opportunities to torpedo the entire long-range plan.

Wendell's tirade continued unabated, unchanged, and untrue, just an unsteady thump, thump, thump of his voice blaring through a bullhorn or a cable access camera. He frantically tried to organize something resembling a boisterous demonstration, but his base, whatever it was to begin with, now consisted of just two disgruntled and very confused old men. "We will never reach those people," said Professor Cooper.

•••

The public meeting reconvened after the ten-day suspension.

They had relocated back to the gym. The communications director had retrieved the posters and easels from the library and set them up in the gym along one side and arrayed the posters and easels that had been in the gym all along on the other side. She printed up and set out for the taking one hundred updated-to-the-last-minute copies of the FAQs, and the custodial staff set up 250 chairs. The Board of Selectmen would face the crowd seated at long, end-to-end rectangular tables. A standing microphone had been placed in the middle of the room.

People wandered in and took seats.

Wendell did not wear a tie. Professor Cooper had begged off the Public Comment portion, so the Board of Selectmen, without Wendell's concurrence but with Granny Charter's grudging approval, had appointed young Brendan as a temporary town moderator.

At exactly 7:00 p.m., Brendan took the lectern. "Good evening, everyone," he began. He introduced Peter, who took ten minutes, eight minutes too long, to summarize all of the communications that had been received during the ten-day gap. Brendan then announced that "the only thing on tonight's agenda is Public Comment. Please line up behind the microphone and state your name and address, as always."

There were no more than a hundred people in the gym, much fewer than had been anticipated. Some were viewing the posters, some were seated waiting for something to happen, perhaps, and some were waving to the neighbor they had just spotted. But not a single person lined up behind the microphone. No one stood up to rant or praise, or holler, condemn, or commend.

Brendan tapped the microphone. "I guess now *this* microphone isn't working. Hah. We are going to commence with Public Comment. Can you all hear me?" There was nodding. "Anyone for Public Comment?" he asked again. He waited. Finally, old Eric Simsky stood up and ambled up to the microphone.

"Eric Simsky, Parsonage Road. My preference is OREO 1. Thank you." Old Eric sat down. A half dozen people tentatively followed, mostly positive and with reasonable concerns about money and timing. Momentum started to build, and there were now three and four people in line at a time, all with constructive concerns and reasonable questions, nearly all of which were about what process would mesh the best of OREOs 1, 4, and 6. Mr. Bevington, who rarely missed a big Public Comment opportunity, approached the microphone, and the room silently groaned because everyone knew he loved the sound of his own voice. He summarized all that had been presented at the meeting ten days earlier, then summarized the controversies, then finally got to his question about housing diversity and concluded, as he always did, with a poem.

Oh, Oreo, my Oreo
Wherefore art the milk?
We're taking a sow's ear
And we're making silk.
I hope it all happens as we speak with one voice,
In support of an Oreo, the cookie of choice.

He earned a ripple of applause.

Mrs. Devlin got up and looked around. She had a big, positive finish and wanted to go last, but there was no way to ensure that, so she launched into lauding the long-range planning and options, the wisdom of the reset, the consequences of doing nothing, or the same thing over and over, and when she finished, there was more applause, and in fact no one else was in line to speak.

Brendan leaned into the microphone. "Is there anyone else for Public Comment?" he asked as he, the selectmen, the townspeople, and the cameras all turned to look at Wendell, seated at the long selectmen table. Wendell sat there, eyes forward, clasping and unclasping his hands on the table surface. Brendan waited a further and notable moment. "Okay, thank you all for coming. This public information meeting is closed and adjourned." People surged forward to chat with the selectmen, now in a neighborly way, sharing doubts and concerns, but laudatory about the process and possibilities for the property. "No, no point in prolonging the meeting. My questions were answered at the library" and "Well, I'm not a fan of the dog park, but I love the idea of the community pool and diversifying our housing" and "I was encouraged by the presentation and the posters." "Seventy-Six Trombones" provided Debra's mental musical accompaniment, and if she had a baton, she likely would have twirled it.

Afterward, back at Debra's house, David was practically jumping up and down. "That could not have gone better. A home run. Totally fantastic. This is a great result." Everyone concurred and babbled for longer than was completely necessary, wine in hand.

No one would sleep that night. Emails were exchanged late into the evening between everyone on the BOS and AHCCHU, marveling at the success of the evening and the reset. The planners and engineers saw before them a decade of projects and billable hours, and the feathers in their caps got in the way of their pillows. Mrs. Devlin was already considering a gala as the next fundraising step, and her mind was spinning over how best to plan that event.

• • •

Wendell left the meeting, went home, and poured a huge glass of whiskey. He wrote:

This is bad not nice very bad. Need to undo the vote on the cookie.

Spinning plates not working anymore, it's like I'm completely out of plates.

Oh, Bunker Girl. Big Dedicated Open Space size is so important. I'll get a new hat and a new Sharpie I am rich but I'm worried.

I need concepts for my plans, excellent plans, best plans, ever, no one has ever seen anything like my concept plans.

It's Stella's fault, and Debra, Dumpy Debra. I think she knows about you, Bunker Girl.

—CHAPTER 17—

Chief Telford called Debra the next afternoon.

"Mrs. Wolfson, I have some remarkable information."

Debra was in her car in ten minutes, turning off her oven and leaving the pumpkin bread batter she had just assembled in an unbaked glop.

She got to the Rockmore Police Station and was quickly shown to the chief's office.

"Mrs. Wolfson, look at this."

There was a file carton, and it contained a folder with a brief report. There were some stray items of clothing, all bagged in plastic. There was a photo of a teenage girl clipped to the report.

Debra saw it immediately.

She was wearing earrings. There was no question. The stray of the pair lived in Wendell's pocket, and the image of the stray lived on Debra's flip phone.

"Oh my god." She sat, shocked. "Chief, I think I need a glass of water."

"Yes, of course. Are you all right?"

"Yes, just, well, this is quite something." She sipped, caught her breath, and looked from the window to the photo to Chief Telford. "Chief Telford," she said, "I know this might not be the most obvious question, but who is Mrs. Nuffield?"

"Mrs. Nuffield was my mother."

"Your mother?"

"Yes. She briefly employed the girl in her shop, and it's her report of the girl's no show at work that more or less started all of this. I grew up listening to the story—the girl who didn't come to work, who no one could really look for because, well, she didn't seem to exist. The story became the proverbial cautionary tale. Never go out alone, always be with friends, make sure someone knows where you are, you know, what mothers have been telling daughters since time began. It's probably the reason I became a cop."

"Your mother is Florence?" Debra was stunned.

"How on earth did you know my mother?"

"Wait, no, really, your mother is Florence? From the little shop in Rockmore?"

"Yes, well, she *was* Florence," said Chief Telford. "She's no longer with us."

Debra murmured appropriate, albeit distracted, condolences, and then told the chief what she remembered about the shop, a vague recollection of lost gloves, possibly an attractive poncho, and a fuzzy conversation about an employee who had not shown up for work, causing a delay of the fall sale.

"You married and took your husband's name?"

"Yes," said Chief Telford. She stared at the small filing cabinet in her office. "It's remarkable how this has come full circle."

Debra wanted to say it had come full circle within a circle, but she restrained herself. "Can we go arrest Wendell now?" She was half laughing, but Chief Telford did not join in.

"No, but we'll ask questions, and I'll coordinate with the Somerville police." She got suddenly serious. "I'm a little worried because we've been trying to rent radio tower space from Somerville. Wendell is first selectman, right? If we start an investigation, will this jinx the radio tower negotiations?"

Debra was not surprised that Chief Telford had an angle, but given her involvement in all things municipal, she was surprised Somerville had radio tower space available to rent.

•••

Debra drove by Wendell's house on her way home from Chief Telford's office and again the next morning. Her meeting with Chief Telford had validated her suspicions about Wendell, but while there were now more threads than ever, she still had no loom on which to weave them all together. She had no doubt Wendell had harmed the young woman with the ugly earrings, but that was hardly proof of anything.

A body would help, thought Debra.

She drove by Wendell's house again, this time parking about a quarter mile up the road. She could see Wendell's mailbox at the end of his driveway, but she was certain Wendell could not see her car. She hoped for inspiration, but if the young woman was going to speak to Debra from the great beyond and tell her how Wendell killed her, she could easily find Debra in her parked car.

Nothing happened, and Debra did not have a visit from beyond the copse.

From where she sat in her parked car, the boulders took on a different shape. She normally saw them facing the other way, because in all of her drive-bys, Wendell's house was on her right. But she had turned and parked facing the other way, with Wendell's house down on the left side of the road. The stack of boulders looked higher from this side and sloped dramatically away from the road. The boulders had been moved, as confirmed by the photo Mrs. Devlin had shown her, so perhaps, she now thought, Wendell had moved the boulders! But perhaps not. She had no idea when, why, or how the boulders had been moved, and for all she knew, it could be for any ordinary golf course maintenance reason having nothing to do with the Wendell turmoil she was obsessed with.

Still, she could call Public Works and get the tree warden to come out and look at the unkempt trees that were practically draped over the pile of boulders. She could come up with selectman-ish outrage about the trees, which were dangerously rotted and should be removed before they fell over in a storm and knocked out a power line. After all, it was town property, and if the copse presented a public peril, the tree warden had authority to hack those trees down to the stump.

But, Debra realized, the tree warden had made his annual report to the Board of Selectmen at the beginning of the summer, nominating a list of offending trees on town property his guys had slated for removal or to be cut back from power lines or just tagged for the following year. Of course, Mother Nature had a way of reorganizing the nominations, but until she stormed in, the list was the list. Besides, the bedraggled trees were no longer tall enough to interfere with a power line, and the tree guys wouldn't move the boulders just to chop the trees down. Debra had to hope Chief Telford would do her job sooner rather than later.

Debra drove home and called Vinnie. She asked him when he would have time for a coffee. He suggested a glass of wine at the end of the day, and since she already had food to cook for dinner, she offered to feed him. She wanted to call David to join them, but she waffled because David could be prickly. After fussing for a half hour, she called him, and he said he would stop by but not eat.

She grilled a beautifully cut-up chicken and a pile of root vegetables, all servable at room temperature, and threw together a green salad. Dinner was out and available. Whoever wanted it could have it, and whoever wanted to pretend they didn't want it didn't have to eat. Her husband would be home late because he had a faculty meeting, so room-temperature grazing worked all the way around.

Vinnie got there just as Debra had plattered it all, wondering as she did when had "platter" become a verb. No rush, Debra said to Vinnie, have a glass of wine to decompress, no? Yes, he replied gratefully. Hartford shenanigans are making me crazy, he said. They moved into the living room.

Debra was jumping out of her skin. They heard David coming through the back door, and Debra yelled to come through to the living room. Hellos and how are yous, and the conversation turned, as Debra knew it would, to Vinnie's thoughts about running for governor. Debra had to give David the space for this topic—he had been on the inside and early track for two of the last three Democratic governors in the state, little Connecticut being what it is, so he had credibility and credentials to add weight to any idea that got floated, but this early in the state election cycle, it was just an easy-breezy conversation. Vinnie knew the steps to this dance, and, although he was not quite as adept as David, he kept time and did not miss a beat, even when a dip and a spin were called for. There was a moment, a pause, and Debra poured Vinnie more wine. They moved to the kitchen with the usual murmurs about Debra's cooking and Vinnie's appetite. To her surprise, David made himself a plate, and they all sat down at the kitchen table.

Debra cleared her throat by way of introduction. "I need to tell you two what Chief Telford found. What I found. What we connected."

"I know," said Vinnie. He smiled. "Back channels." Vinnie lightly trampled on Debra's big moment, revealing that he had heard from the former, now-retired chief about the meeting with the new chief and the archived file. "You know, the old chief still takes credit for my career. I love that guy."

"Great."

"But that's all I know," said Vinnie. "So was the new chief helpful?"

They took a moment to chew. "Did you know that Chief Telford is Mrs. Nuffield's daughter?" Debra trampled back.

"What?" Vinnie was genuinely surprised. "You're kidding. I had no idea. Wow."

"Hah. So much for your back channels."

"Who is Mrs. Nuffield?" asked David.

Just then, Debra's husband came home, ate chicken, and caught up on the alcohol consumption. Debra caught everyone up on absolutely everything else.

"Okay, Debra, this is now a criminal matter, and the police are involved. I think you should back off," said her husband. Vinnie and David agreed. "No," said her husband, "I think all of you characters should back off. This isn't a game."

Vinnie was about to protest that he was part of the police effort, but he came to his political senses. "Yeah, you're right. I don't even want to be part of this."

"So," said David, "when are they going to question Wendell?"

"Soon," said Debra. "I got a courtesy call from Chief Telford. A Rockmore cop and a Somerville cop are going to stop by his house."

"This is huge."

"I know."

"Totally."

Debra poured more wine, and even David agreed to half a glass.

It was quiet for a few moments.

"I fear the worst," said Debra.

"Me too." It was David, rational, practical David.

The evening was over.

•••

Debra didn't know if radio tower negotiations had slowed things down or if the two chiefs had suddenly locked horns or were inundated with small- and smaller-town criminal matters beyond their respective capacities, but no one appeared to be racing to Wendell's house to ask him about jewelry.

In the meantime, the property continued to buzz with fluorescent vests, hard hats, equipment, supervisors, trucks, backhoes, and lots of pencils behind lots of ears. Debra wanted to conduct surveillance so that Wendell would be under constant watch, but she had no idea how to conduct surveillance in any circumstance, let alone the present circumstance, covering an individual on foot over one hundred and fifty acres with no way of knowing when she was supposed to find Wendell wandering the property and no way to hide once she got on the property. She abandoned the idea of round-the-clock surveillance. *Besides, it's not like I don't have an office to go to.*

Small-town governance was moving at record speed, and a likely murder investigation had come to a standstill. The world was upside down.

On a whim, she contacted the lead environmental engineer on the ORE project.

"Hello, is this Dr. Stephanie Jordan? Yes, hello. This is Debra Wolfson, on the Somerville Board of Selectmen." They engaged in the usual preliminaries. "Yes, you are all doing a great job and I do not mean to do an end run with you, but I thought I should be in touch about something which has come to my attention."

"Oh, of course, Mrs. Wolfson."

"Call me Debra."

"Yes, Debra. What can I do for you?"

"Well, I heard from a few people that before Somerville bought the property, there was a terrible chemical spill over by the boulders, near that group of dead trees on Appleby Road. I thought you should know." Details were sketchy, because Debra was inventing them.

"Debra, well, this is the first I'm hearing of this, but we can always track these things down through required records. I'll get in touch with Dan."

Debra stopped at the little food shop and ran into a half dozen familiar faces, employing verbal acrobatics to mention a chemical spill on Appleby Road to anyone who said hello. The rumor was off and running and briefly got traction, but the required records yielded nothing because there were none. Debra had to start another rumor, this one suggesting that, possibly, asbestos had been buried near the old swinging gate where the now-dilapidated copse of trees stood adjacent to the stack of boulders. But that rumor was even less credible than the first. It was two to zero, boulders against rumors.

That week's BOS meeting, remarkably unremarkable for a welcome change, had just finished. It was still light out, so one more time Debra drove by the copse of trees, hoping for drive-by inspiration. She assumed Wendell would be home because he had scampered out of the meeting. Sure enough, when she made her way past his house toward the skinny two-lane road, his car was in his driveway and his silhouette was in the window. She followed the road all the way around once and did the circle again, finally pulling over and stopping at the boulders.

Debra got out of the car, more worried about mosquitoes than anything else, reasonably certain she was just going to stand there. After all, she was not going to climb the fence—she didn't think she was capable of hopping it—and while the slats were big enough for her to slip through, it would still involve a high step in and over and a moment of straddling. A lot could go wrong, and if she did end up on her ass on the muddy, tick-infested grass, she couldn't be sure how she would explain her conduct to an ambulance driver or her husband.

Oh, screw it.

A moment later, she happily found herself standing on the inside side of the post-and-slat fence right next to the pile of boulders. She was surprised that the boulders were dirty and covered in lichen, but her surprise was a surprise, as she really had no idea what she should have expected. But standing there, with the boulders dramatically sloped on one side, she pictured that poor dead girl eternally doomed to hold the boulders up, to keep them from crashing down, down, through and to the bottom of the earth.

She gingerly made her way over to a spot where she could lean and almost sit. Debra thought about the girl in the photo, her pathetic earrings, her seeming disconnection from any human being who might have cared enough to look for her. Poor girl, buried under these boulders.

Poor boulder girl. Boulder Girl. BG.

•••

A week later, yes, incredibly, the BOS had another meeting, mostly dedicated to reports from the environmental consultant, the chief engineer, the chair of AHCCHU, and Mrs. Partridge from the historical society. Given the expected length of the meeting, Public Comment was eliminated from the agenda, and the starting time was moved up to 5:00 p.m. Inexplicably, Vinnie wandered in at some point, stayed for a half hour or so, and left. Dinner was provided to the members of the Board of Selectmen, a selection of sandwiches from the little food shop together with chips and of course Oreo cookies.

Debra had remained circumspect about BG and kept her conclusions to herself.

Wendell came to the meeting completely intoxicated. He was silent and glum. Ninety minutes later, he perked up when the environmental consultant stepped up to deliver the results of the environmental investigation.

"Good evening, everyone. My name is Stephanie Jordan. You have my credentials in front of you as part of the packet of information we have submitted. As you know, our firm has been working very hard on this project, but there are a few limitations." Dr. Jordan, young and enthusiastic, articulated all the usual caveats about random and targeted soil sampling. She went on. "We also followed up on a couple of rumors, but that's what they were, just rumors, nothing credible to follow up on. You have our written report. Briefly, there were no surprises, and the chemical composition of the soils is what we would expect to find given the use of the property over the past forty years or so. Some monitoring is called for going forward, as this is not a pristine parcel, and there is always going to be exposure to corruptive influences and polluting events. I encourage you all to read the report, but I think the takeaway here is that while the evidence of actionable contamination is limited, we cannot—nor could anyone, really—fully exonerate, if you will, or guarantee that this property is without contamination. I am happy to answer whatever questions you have at this point."

There were questions, all perfunctory. Wendell had his chin in his hand, barely awake, and Debra was slouched and unhappy. The balance of the meeting was full of facts, options, Gantt charts, and planning challenges. But such is actual governance.

By 8:45, everyone had had enough, but the historical society had yet to make a presentation, and there were still a few scheduling matters that had to be voted on. Wendell was practically snoring, and the cable access camera operator was having a field day with closeups of his gaping mouth. Debra was thoroughly miffed over her ineffective rumors, but she knew it was unrealistic to expect Dr. Jordan to show up with an on-camera dramatic reveal about bodies and so-so jewelry.

But BG was not a coincidence. The Rockmore girl was Boulder Girl. Debra had it in hand. She was certain.

Wendell was halfheartedly running the meeting, but it was Henry who goosed the agenda. "Okay, Agenda Item No. 14, Mrs. Partridge, on behalf of the historical society." At the mention of Mrs. Partridge, Debra briefly wondered about the long-ago mediated fate of the cockatoo.

Mrs. Partridge could have been irked at having to wait so long, but she had her knitting with her and had seemed very content to wait through the bulk of the meeting. "Good evening, everyone," she started, "as you know, I'm Patty Partridge, Parade Drive, and I am a member of the historical society. As part of ORE, which we think is an excellent step in the right direction, by the way, we think the Appleby Farm should be part of the conversation, so to speak."

Mrs. Partridge went into way too much detail about the farm and the Appleby family and why the historical society thought there should be recognition, but finally, after an eon, she distributed to the selectmen a mock-up of the hoped-for plaque. The design showed an angled view of the entire property as it existed back in the 1880s, with the old farmhouse, the barn and stable, even some livestock, and the fields, marked with stone walls and some fencing. The plan was to have it rendered as a laser engraved etching on stainless steel for durability, using the original road onto the property as the perspective.

"It's the kind of thing you see at some of the national parks, you know, as if the entire vista stretches in front of you in a three-dimensional sort of way, with little explanations and descriptions all over the plaque pointing to things and telling you what you're looking at. It has to be installed on a stone wall, and it sits at an angle of course.

Yes, it is quite large, and a post in the dirt to hold it up will never work. It's a big piece of property, a big plaque, and it needs a big support. We like this perspective, because it's what the archive material shows and we can save a bit of money just cribbing off what we have."

"And where do you want to locate this?" asked Brendan.

"Oh, I thought I was clear about that, sorry. So the perspective of the plaque only works if it is placed at the point of perspective, you see? The plaque exactly lines up with the location where that bunch of dilapidated trees are now, you know, the ones with the pile of boulders, just on the inside of the fence right on the road there."

Wendell sat up. Debra sat up. Mrs. Partridge could not help but notice she suddenly had two very attentive selectmen. She looked directly at Wendell. "The installation has to be where the boulders are, right behind all of you in that photo that is on the town website."

— CHAPTER 18 —

The very next morning, Debra told Somerville Police Chief Tom Drummond about Boulder Girl.

Chief Drummond was, perhaps understandably, reluctant to investigate the first selectman in his town for a possible crime that might have been committed, or not, years earlier in another town, or not, based on accusations chucked about by the first selectman's political opponent. Debra offered truth without proof, which was not the same as evidence.

"Debra, somehow you have become a fact witness to something, whatever this is, involving an earring, no less, not to mention that our state representative was the original cop, and the source of the missing person information is the mother of the chief of police in a town where something is alleged to have happened. I'm not sure any of this constitutes probable cause, but I'm sure all of it is lunacy."

"Tom, you know Wendell is weird."

"Weird is not a crime."

"Besides, I thought Chief Telford was ready to go."

"She was. Is, in fact, but she has spoken with the police commission in Rockmore, and they don't want to do anything to mess with the rental negotiations on the radio tower. As it is, they and we are all dropping emergency calls all over the place. They need the tower space, and we could use the rental revenue."

"Why do you need the rental revenue?"

"To pay for overtime."

"Why do you suddenly have overtime?"

"To pay for foolhardy criminal investigations like this one."

"Tom, it's worth a few questions. You know it, and I know it."

"Yes, I know it." His office did not have a window, so he meaningfully stared at the door. He sighed. "I'll check with David." Debra knew that was nonsense. Tom hated David. "But it is going to be informal and a little bit off the record. You understand."

Debra didn't understand, but she didn't care. "Just do it already," she said.

Chief Drummond called First Selectman Wendell Williams and invited him into the chief's office for an ostensible discussion about public safety at the old golf course property. The chief offered coffee and then suggested that they move to the interrogation room.

"Why?"

"Well," said the chief, "as you know, I wanted to go over some public safety issues at the golf course property, and all the maps are laid out there on the big table."

They settled into the interrogation room, and Wendell was briefly awed. "It's just like on TV."

"Well, Wendell, we like to think the interrogation rooms on TV are just like the ones in real life."

The huge maps were laid out, and the chief conversationally drew Wendell in, seductively acknowledging that Wendell knew the property better than any of the other selectmen, that he probably knew it better than anyone in town, so the police, for public safety purposes, really valued Wendell's input.

"Well, yes, it's true, I know more than anybody. But the property should be open space or Open Space, in perpetuity . . ." Chief Drummond let Wendell have his say, and when it was over, he noted that reasonable minds would always differ, but for now, while studies were being conducted, and for the future, in the event of development, what did Wendell think?

Wendell blathered about his time working at the old golf course, how he understood equipment and irrigation, vulnerable property elements, and sturdy golf course components. The chief let Wendell go on. And on.

"I just want to show you one more thing." The chief moved all the big maps off to one side of the long table and pulled a thin folder from the top of the cabinet that was against the huge mirror that lined the wall Wendell was facing. He pulled out a little photograph.

"Do you know this young woman?"

Wendell's past rear-ended his present. He visibly stiffened. He pretended to study the photo. Finally, after many minutes, he spoke. "Uh, shit, no, I don't think so. Why, who is she?" Wendell adopted nonchalance, but he overacted, like a ham in a community theater production.

"Look again, Wendell. Do you know her name?"

"No, I don't know her name." He told the truth.
"Do you recognize the jewelry, the earrings, she has on?"
"No," he lied.
"I hear you have an earring like the one the girl is wearing, that you keep it in your pocket. Isn't that true?"

Wendell now took time to collect himself. He smiled at Chief Drummond and faced the mirror, smoothing his hair. He must have assumed the mirror was a two-way mirror, just like on TV, and that cops were on the other side of that mirror, listening and watching, but that wasn't the case, because the Board of Finance had never funded a two-way mirror in the police department budget despite the annual request for one. But he smiled at his image and cocked his head for effect, just like a cockatoo in front of a mirror. "I found an old earring a long time ago in a, uh, parking lot, yeah, a parking lot, when I had to reattach my license plate, which fell off my car. I've had it ever since. Maybe a bunch, yes, a whole bunch of years ago. I keep it as a good luck charm. It's always in my pocket or, uh, somewhere, whatever. It could be the same earring as in the picture, but I don't know or, uh, care."

Neither the chief nor Wendell smiled, frowned, grimaced, or harrumphed.

"Okay, Wendell, all set."

"Whatever."

•••

Somerville was still Somerville, raspy, cranky, entitled, and self-impressed, but the vast majority of folks were now AHCCHU friendly and no longer angry and exhausted from the community's tortured time in land-use hell.

Meetings continued because that is what meetings do, but Wendell, who had started to fray at the edges long before his chat with Chief Drummond, was now fully unraveled. His distress was unruly, and his votes, when he voted at all, were meant to undermine governance at every juncture. He flounced in and out of the Board of Selectmen meetings, making a perfect ass of himself on camera and in person.

There was never a question whether Mrs. Partridge's plaque would be approved, but of course Wendell voted against it. The plan was to prepare the site immediately with a festooned ceremony and, ultimately, installation and a big reveal in the spring. Mrs. Partridge was delighted, but she had expected nothing less.

AHCCHU revved up, and with Public Comment under its belt,

made its formal recommendation to the Board of Selectmen, which in turn put the matter before the voters at a referendum-style election, which in turn met with overwhelming success, which in turn resulted in the drafting of a conservation easement protecting forty-seven acres along Appleby Road as Dedicated Open Space, to be recorded at some future point, eventually, on the land records.

The big picture was taking shape. A survey yielded acreage to sell to a developer for a much reduced active-adult-over-fifty-five-age-restricted-housing community over by the skinny two-lane road and the old eleventh fairway, and proposals started to roll in for the purchase of that chunk at prices higher than could have been imagined. A developer who had originally offered an option on the property was now just one of several suitors sniffing around, and there was flabbergasted talk of competitive bidding.

Wendell briefly imagined he could buy the property himself, but when that particular alcoholic haze lifted, he grimly realized that one of the first inquiries would be into his financial bona fides. *Not good*, he thought. All of "his" money still, legally, belonged to Stella.

Mrs. Devlin rejected the gala idea and opted instead for a square dance. The recreation department, dog owners, and moms all started planning how best to ensure that their ORE priorities were moving up in the world.

Still, every positive step created new challenges. "This is progress, sure," Liza said to Professor Cooper, "but the devil is in those details, right? Now that we have the Dedicated Open Space figured out, people are talking about parking. Do we really need to provide parking?"

"Look," said Professor Cooper. "Let's not forget the concept component of AHCCHU. We got the concept across the finish line. I'm done. You now have a chunk of open space. Let the Conservation Commission manage the details. Isn't that their remit? Let them figure it out."

The Conservation Commission was delighted to have input on how best to integrate this newfound parcel of Dedicated Open Space into the community. The parking issue was placed on the upcoming agenda. Mrs. Kebel, who was still chair, expected it to be a slow-moving discussion about possible ideas, but Betty showed up at the meeting and, in the course of Public Comment, shared a number of incredibly constructive and helpful suggestions about parking, signage, safety, trash, and trails. Wendell also showed up at the Conservation Committee meeting, glaring at Betty and voting against the ultimate recommendation.

"Wendell," said Mrs. Kebel, "you don't vote on this commission, remember?"

Wendell railed and voted against all of it even though he had no authority to vote. He should have been thrilled. It was not public safety or national ideologies or tenets or patriotism or war. It was a piece of property that had been a farm and then a golf course. It was practical, pragmatic, political decision-making at its most elementary and satisfying.

But Wendell went on as if it were a matter of life and death.

He was being driven to distraction with an onslaught of minutiae, intrusive process, and dreams, all these fucking dreams, for his Dedicated Open Space, *his* space. The community idea-a-thon was relentless. Each chirp of inspiration from the Bettys of Somerville pulled a thread from the snarl he had fostered, then another thread, and the growing pile of threads made him crazy.

He was briefly heartened when he succeeded in getting a few abutting property owners to cause a ruckus. They were thrilled when the chunk of Dedicated Open Space had been carved out under OREO 1 but confusedly unhappy when Wendell told them about the Conservation Commission-approved parking just across the road from their houses. Mrs. Carmichael, an otherwise lovely woman, wrote not one but two letters to the paper, protesting even the point that she favored. Wendell claimed them as part of his shrunken base, but when Mrs. Carmichael sincerely acknowledged that parking was a welcome addition to the site, Wendell condemned the small group as enemies of the town.

But a kvetch here and there could not sustain Wendell or the many deflections he launched. His momentum was nearly depleted, and with nothing else to offer, he got drunk, then sobered up, then got drunk again. No amount of alcohol satisfied or changed anything. He could only briefly dismiss the interview with Chief Drummond, particularly when he came to grips with the fact that no matter how much he might ultimately practice with the unshot gun in his closet, the chief would know how to shoot back.

He longed for the foot-dragging he had so successfully put in place, the distracted votes and diversionary resets and tactics that popped up and got smacked down like an accelerated game of Whac-A-Mole. It had not really occurred to him that municipal governance was capable of getting something done, and now all this hub-and-quilt shit was relentless. No hurdle would be the last hurdle, but stakeholders and volunteers leapt and cleared, enthusiastically embracing the how-to of, oh, so many challenges.

By this point, Wendell barely bothered to pretend to be first selectman-ish. He couldn't remember if the Conservation Commission or the Board of Selectmen had voted to move forward with the parking lot recommendation, but somebody must have voted on something, he thought, because it was all happening.

Early one morning, Wendell looked out his window to see the Public Works guys clearing an area on the edge of the proposed Dedicated Open Space.

He watched them from his front yard, standing at the bottom of his driveway in a heavy jacket with a coffee cup in his hand. He paced. The Public Works guys cleared along Appleby Road near the swinging gate and made room for ten or so vehicles. *Don't panic*, he told himself, *don't lose it, after all this time.* The work area amounted to a large patch of dirt at a bit of an angle and a footpath that would lead to the forthcoming trails to be marked and blazed, probably by some future Eagle Scout. For Wendell, all the planning and paperwork had been unnerving, but the rock-and-soil reality was terrifying.

He returned to his house, checked all of his mother's accounts, consolidated as much cash as he could into the checking account, and started to pack a suitcase. He got only as far as his socks, most of which were in the dirty-laundry basket. He sagged under the varying weights of desperation and belligerence. He wrote a note telling himself that no matter what, he was a visionary champion of something. He had little choice but to wander around his house, his mother's house, and watch television. He could not leave his Bunker Girl.

That same morning, Debra got a call from Betty.

"Debra," she said, "let's go watch Public Works prepare the parking area. You know I had a lot to do with it, and I want to be there. I am so excited."

"Betty, I can't. I really don't think there's any reason for us to be there. The Public Works guys are just going to clear a small area. We'll be in the way, believe me."

"Okay, Debra, but I'm going to go anyway. You know it's right across from Wendell's house, and I'll bet you anything he's going to be watching."

That did it. Debra picked up Betty and drove down the hill to the drive-through window at the Dunkin' Donuts, just over the Somerville boundary with Elmstown. "Why are we getting doughnuts?" asked Betty.

"Trust me, Betty, just trust me." They drove the mile back up the hill to where the Public Works guys were working. Betty could not contain herself.

"This is so thrilling," she said.

It was not thrilling, but Betty was correct about Wendell. They could watch him watch the Public Works guys. Wendell was pacing, drifting back up his driveway to his front door, then returning to pace and sip coffee at the bottom of the driveway. Betty and Debra parked a little way down. They waved to the supervisor, who waved back, even as he shook his head in disbelief that he suddenly had an audience.

Ten minutes later, Patty Partridge pulled up behind Debra's car.

"Hi, Patty."

"Hi Debra, hi, Betty."

"Let me guess," said Debra.

Patty laughed. "You don't have to guess. I figured that if the Public Works guys are going to prepare this area where my plaque is ultimately going to be located, I should be here in case they need me or if there are any questions."

The Public Works guys were clearing the area, and there were big rail ties and an old bicycle rack off to the side. Betty was telling Debra more than she really wanted to know. ". . . no pavement, because we still want it to look like it belongs here, so just the illusion of a parking lot, parking area, really, with a bike rack and possibly a water fountain and a nonintrusive . . ."

Debra pretended to listen.

The work had come to an abrupt standstill. It was time for a coffee break. Debra grabbed the box of doughnuts and walked over to where the supervisor and a couple of the guys were drinking coffee.

"Good morning. We knew you'd be here doing this work today, and we just want to thank you for all that you do." She opened the box of doughnuts, passed it around to a few of the guys, and then set it down on the hood of one of the smaller trucks and told everyone to help themselves.

There were a few mumbled thank-yous and some eye rolling. She gave the illusion that she was there in her selectman capacity, but she didn't care whether they bought it. Debra could see that Wendell was watching her, Betty, and Patty get chatty with the Public Works guys.

"So, it looks like it's going well," Debra said to the Public Works supervisor. "No problems?"

"There're always problems. Nature of what we do."

"Really? Looks very straightforward."

"No, never is. Always something. Those boulders caused quite a problem."

Debra had forgotten to look at the boulders. She was so busy giving out doughnuts, not listening to Betty, and watching Wendell watch her that she hadn't even thought about how different the site seemed, but now she looked. The Public Works guys had relocated the boulders away from the copse and had created a stone boundary for one side of the parking area.

The supervisor warmed to her seemingly sympathetic ear. "We hadn't even considered how much work that would be, because so much of the stack was hidden under that mess of old trees, but once we moved the first few, the rest was easy. I think they look pretty good along the edge there . . ."

Betty had walked over to the new stone wall, but Debra kept the supervisor chatting. "Oh yes, looks good, who would have thought, big rocks, and now what about the trees, what a mess."

"Yeah, well, that's what I'm saying. It's always something. We're going to clear those trees as soon as we're done with our coffee. Oh, and thanks for the doughnuts."

And with that, he walked off toward the port-o-potty that had been set up for the day's work.

Betty came back over to Debra, and together they walked to Debra's car.

"Well, we hadn't planned on that stone wall thing," said Betty. "It kind of just sticks out, sort of haphazard, but I guess they had to do something, and it could be a lot worse. It's low enough to be a bench, although it might get buggy, but I'm sure there's something we could make out of it. Well, anyway, I guess we can leave now."

"No. I want to watch them remove the trees."

"Me too," said Patty.

"Oh, I hate to watch trees get destroyed," said Betty, "even dead trees, even messy trees. So sad."

"Betty, we're not leaving. Have a doughnut."

The guys with the chainsaws moved into position, as did the cop who showed up to direct the nearly nonexistent traffic on sleepy Appleby Road. The chainsaws were incredibly noisy, and for safety reasons, they had to stop every few branches so that the guys without chainsaws could get in there and incrementally clear out the bigger branches. Wendell was riveted.

Twenty minutes later, most of the copse had been leveled, and there was enough room for a small backhoe to approach the area to clear out what was now a considerable pile of debris. But the small backhoe got no nearer than the edge before its front track started to sink into the ground.

"Shit, we got some kind of sinkhole here. Quick, turn off that equipment," yelled the guy closest to the backhoe, desperately signaling the operator to turn off his engine before he and the equipment went deeper and the big machine tipped over. "Stop!"

The backhoe operator stopped and jumped out. All the Public Works guys gathered around the angled backhoe and offered opinions and anecdotes, all meant as solutions. The supervisor finally concluded they needed a truck with a winch, but that it was a funny place for a sinkhole to appear, he said, if that's what it was.

There was a lot of looking and pointing, and finally a truck with a winch showed up and gently helped the backhoe operator move out of the depression in the earth. Not a big deal, said the operator, happens all the time. The backhoe got clear of the area, leaving scattered earth and a rather large depression in its wake. Betty had stopped talking. Debra was riveted and distractedly chewed on a doughnut, watching both Wendell and the Public Works guys. Wendell stood at the bottom of his driveway, his head lowered, no fluorescent vest, no hat, an empty coffee mug dangling from his finger, his other hand busy in his front pocket.

One of the Public Works guys was poking at the area, using a shovel to move tablespoons of dirt around. He stopped, kicking at the soil, as if testing for solid footing. He dropped his shovel off to the side and picked up one of the big rakes leaning against the foreman's truck. He stood well off what he thought was the edge of the dip and began raking the earth, which sloped decisively toward the hole. Wendell had turned away.

But Debra watched as the guy's rake got caught on something and wouldn't yield. He lifted the rake horizontally to his body and a shoe appeared, hanging off one of the tines.

The Public Works guy did not move. Debra did not move. Betty and Patty kept chewing, but they did not move. Wendell turned back around. After a long moment, the Public Works guy shook the rake off to the side and dislodged the shoe. He leaned in with only his eyes to look down into the swale, the rest of his body reluctant to participate. All the other Public Works guys were still over by the road, unwinching, backing up, driving forward, doing all the things Public Works guys do when there are big machines to maneuver. The Public Works guy with the rake tentatively began raking again, sort of shrugging at the same time, as if to ask himself what a shoe, a woman's shoe, would be doing buried three or four feet down under a bunch of old trees.

He continued to tentatively scrape around. He lifted his rake and produced a second shoe out of the hole.

He called his buddy over, and they conferred. His buddy called the supervisor over, and now the three of them conferred. They called over the cop who had been leaning against his cop car checking his phone, directing the dribble of cars that traveled these Somerville roads. The cop came over, squatted down, and used his hand to brush away some soil. He stumbled back and fell on his ass.

There was complete pandemonium.

All the Public Works guys were now waving each other over to look, and the cop was on his radio, trying to wave the Public Works guys away from the hole, and then there were phone calls and sirens, yellow tape, and blue lights. All the big machines were driven away, back to the Public Works department behind Town Hall, and Peter Reilly, who always monitored the police scanner from his desk, ran across Meetinghouse Lane to find Chief Drummond, and together they drove over to the edge of the incipient Dedicated Open Space parking area on Appleby Road.

•••

The cops asked the three do-gooders to leave, and when they dawdled, the cops told them to leave. On the way to her car, Patty casually mentioned that she thought the shoes pulled up by the rake were not at all stylish.

Debra drove Betty home. She was thoroughly ticked off that she had to get to her office where she had back-to-back mediations scheduled, one of which was particularly brutal—third marriage for him, first for her, stillborn child, don't even ask—but when the mediations concluded, she postponed all the remaining mediation sessions she had set up for the rest of the week.

She raced back to Somerville, mindful that her presence was of no significance whatsoever, but no matter what, she thought, people still need to eat. Debra stopped at the little food shop, stocked up on sandwich stuff, got a to-go tuna sandwich for herself, and hustled over to the cashier, who asked her what's with the dead body in Somerville. Before she could find her voice, David came in.

"I saw your car in the lot. Quick." They took his car, and within a few minutes pulled up and parked on the main road behind all the flashing lights. They exchanged versions of events. Debra told him what had occurred early that morning. Nothing was happening.

"Maybe it's just an animal," said David. "It was a farm, you know."

"And which farm animal wears women's shoes?"

"Peter made it sound like all hell had broken loose, but everyone is standing around. Do you see him? He said he was here with the chief."

"I think everyone is just standing around," Debra whispered, "because they are waiting for the state police. And if they are waiting for the state police, it means they found a body."

"Why are you whispering?" asked David.

"I don't know."

"We can't leave."

"I know. You want half a tuna sandwich?"

"Okay."

An hour later, they were still sitting there, speaking in whispers, watching all of their worst fears come to death.

•••

Debra had opened a third bottle of wine. Her house had become an anxiety portal, people popping in all evening, staying, not staying, eating, looking for any update or shred of information. They had neither, but that did not stop Debra from nearly tearing her meniscus jumping to her conclusion.

"It's the girl from Rockmore. I just know it," she said. "And Wendell killed her."

Well, why not. It was as good as proven as far as Debra was concerned. The body was Boulder Girl.

"Don't you think you're getting a little ahead of the facts?" asked her husband.

"Yes, possibly, but that doesn't mean I'm not correct."

But, damn, she was not correct.

Chief Drummond told Peter, and Peter confidentially told David, and David told Debra that the forensics guys had not found a body, a whole body, but rather some random foot bones, a single intact human fibula, and a skeletal hand apparently sporting a rather large and expensive diamond ring.

"No way," said Debra. "It's not a large and expensive diamond ring. It's a cheap earring, a single earring."

She called Chief Drummond. "Tom, what's this about a ring?"

"How did you hear about that?"

"Never mind. Did the earring show up?"

Tom sighed. "All right, Debra, here's what we know. The fibula likely belonged to a postmenopausal female. It is not the girl from Rockmore. The facts don't line up."

It's not Boulder Girl, Debra realized. *Shit.*

"Tom, do you know who it is?"

"No."

Big diamond ring. Postmenopausal female.

Debra tripped over a log, and it all became clear, nearly tearing her other meniscus on this leap, but she knew she was right, really right, this time. "I know who it is, Tom."

"It's not the girl—"

"I know. It's Wendell's mother. It's Stella Williams."

•••

They cordoned off a large area around the copse, but the bulk of the property was still accessible, so Wendell went to visit Bunker Girl. It was cold, and Wendell wore his fluorescent jacket over his fluorescent vest and then a big coat over that and a cap beneath the hardhat with a scarf, so he appeared to have doubled in size, and he clumsily plodded along like a yeti on the hunt. He wished there was snow on the ground, snow that covered everything that should be covered and hid all that needed to be hidden, but it was not yet winter, just nasty and raw, so there was not a snowflake anywhere. The ground was brown, exposed, and bare, but still diggable. Wendell had a feeling that the cops would figure it out. *As long as I am free, though*, he told himself, *I will use every hour to work even harder to pretend to care about Dedicated Open Space so that I can protect you, Bunker Girl, and keep our secrets buried, I promise.* It was a load of crap, like all his other loads of crap, just an ongoing burden as heavy and clumsy as the extra coat he wore over his fluorescent jacket and vest.

He returned to his house. No cops, no questions. He wrote several notes for his notebook.

Somerville cops no good. They should be asking me questions.

Should de-fund. Wonder if de-fund is like re-fund.

Fucking Stella. Obvious, so annoying.

Somehow, an emergency meeting of the Board of Selectmen got scheduled for that night.

A meeting? That's ridiculous. Sad.

He was early for the meeting, but as it turned out, so was everyone else. Both Chief Drummond and David Silver were present.

It was tense. Granny Charter was front and center. It was an Emergency Meeting, with its own rules, and the hastily conceived agenda simply called for an Executive Session, which also had its own rules. It all meant that the BOS could and should exclude everyone from the room except anyone they invited to stay. Anything said in Executive Session was by law highly confidential. There was no Public Comment.

Wendell was distracted. Peter had to prompt him to read the script.

"Uh, call meeting to order. Uh, Executive Session, I guess. Everyone leave, everyone except, uh, town counsel and Chief Drummond." Debra was of course next to Wendell, and she could see his hands trembling. "Uh, Chief, yes, whatever. Go ahead. I guess. Whatever."

The chief eased his way into a summary of the events. "We found human remains. Older, female. We do not yet know who she is, but we will." The chief had begged Debra to keep her conclusions to herself so as not to spook Wendell, so everyone accepted that the body was a mystery. "At the moment," continued the chief, "we are operating on the premise that this is a homicide. We do not know if she had any connection to Somerville."

There were a thousand questions, but no one asked any.

The chief was excused. He and one of his officers lingered in the hallway, visible to the BOS through the windowed wall. "Are we done or what?" asked Wendell.

Henry jumped in. "Look, I think we should discuss how best to proceed or not proceed with the parking area, the Appleby plaque, and the Dedicated Open Space conservation easement in light of this criminal turn of events."

Wendell was now alert and silent. He was not doodling. He did not stop rubbing and flexing his hands. It was Executive Session, so they were off camera.

Everyone babbled some version of the same thing, that it was a crime scene, that once that onus was lifted OREO 1 should proceed, that a garden should be planted at the spot, which would nicely showcase the Appleby plaque, and that the area was probably not hallowed ground.

Wendell said he didn't see what the big deal was, just dedicate the damned Open Space.

"Wendell, you live across the street from all this. Do you think you and your neighbors will be comfortable just moving on, as you say, once it is no longer a crime scene?" asked Caroline. "I mean, we, the town, have put so much work into this. None of us want to see it stopped, but after all, we have a likely murder, right?"

"I have no idea what my neighbors want. I only know what I want. No digging."

The meeting uncomfortably concluded with concurrence that they would meet again in emergency session the following evening and that Public Comment would be on the agenda. The police gratuitously walked everyone out to their cars.

At the next night's meeting, Wendell was jumpy. He tapped his pen impatiently and got up and wandered behind Debra's chair. He managed to gavel in Executive Session, where the chief reported that a skull and additional bones had been dug up, that on-site forensic investigation was ongoing, and that the area would continue to be designated a crime scene. The chief emphasized the importance of keeping all of this preliminary information absolutely confidential.

When Executive Session ended, the cameras were turned on, and Wendell feebly called for Public Comment. Only Freida Goodman, the president of the garden club, came forward, confirming the garden club's commitment to design and plant the garden in the upcoming spring to beautify the plaque placement but informing the BOS that the entire garden club membership refused to do any digging "because," said Mrs. Goodman, "it is way too creepy. But, yes, if someone else does the digging, it will be a riot of color in the spring, and we promise to stop calling the area the 'corpse' of trees."

•••

Debra was completely flummoxed.

Okay, she thought, maybe it would have been silly to question Wendell about an earring or a billboard or a slashed tire or a property conveyance, but now there was a body.

They were governing with a murderer at the table. A murderer who did not care about procedure or municipal administration.

And they were talking about gardens and plaques.

The expectation was that the BOS was going to keep meeting and governing, and Wendell was going to be at the table. It was lunacy. Nothing had yet been firmly established, despite Debra's certainty, but still, no one wanted anything to do with Wendell, and no one wanted him on the BOS or as a liaison to their commissions or as a partner at next month's square dance or anything, but there was nothing to be done about it.

No one talked about anything else, as an unsolved murder proved to be considerably more compelling than planning for a gazebo. Caroline thought the Board of Selectmen should express the town's condolences to someone, but the bones, such as they were, had still not been officially identified. Mrs. Partridge was in a complete frenzy, as her beloved signage had to be placed right where the shoes were found. Historical society, hysterical society. Tomato, tomahto.

Two days passed. All was nebulous. David spent a moment reviewing the Charter for any reference to impeachment proceedings, but even if there was something to go on procedurally, being a gross, distasteful, and suspicious person did not amount to grounds for impeachment. Vinnie discreetly spoke with some of his former colleagues at the state prosecutor's office but learned little.

Wendell remained an active member of the Board of Selectmen, using his visibility not to further the mutual goals the community had embraced, but to criticize, belittle, and castigate any and all legitimate governing efforts and the people who participated in those efforts. He was unleashed, and it no longer mattered whether his comments were tethered to Dedicated Open Space, reality, or common decency.

Debra was furious, but she should have had more faith. The Somerville cops and the state police, it seemed, had the matter well in hand. They had quickly and quietly conducted a dozen interviews and had spoken with anyone who had anything to do with Wendell or the management of The Club and Somerville Woods. They interviewed Wendell's ex-wife at the Connecticut prison where she was incarcerated, discovering that Wendell had told her he was rich, that his wealth was, indeed, the only reason she married him, that no, she never met or heard him speak of his mother, yeah, what the fuck, he was an idiot, but he was a rich idiot. They went through the Social Security Administration and both Connecticut and Florida Medicare Services. They looked at whatever finances they could access in the name of Stella Williams. They contacted all the people whose names appeared on The Club's payroll records back in the day, particularly the guys who operated the big machines.

The state investigators showed up at Wendell's door "just to ask a few questions, about, well, you know, sir. We're speaking with everyone of course."

Wendell's answers to the investigators' questions neither contradicted anything the investigators had learned from the other guys nor confirmed anything. Yes, I care, still care, about that property, he told the investigators. Well, sometimes one can have a deep and meaningful connection to the land, you know, like Theodore Roosevelt or Daniel Boone. No, I didn't sing to the land, how silly, who said that, oh, maybe when I was working on it, you know, just to pass the time.

The cops did not yet have forensic confirmation, but still, they were certain whose fibula it was, and they had Wendell under surveillance pending laboratory confirmation. Debra didn't tell the chief that she was also watching Wendell, but she didn't have to because Chief Drummond saw her parked on the skinny two-lane road. The chief pulled his car up next to Debra's, like cops do when they want to talk to each other in the Dunkin' Donuts parking lot.

"Hi Debra. What are you doing?"

"Hi Tom. Just sitting here."

"You're watching Wendell, right?"

"Uh, right. Well, yes."

"You don't have to."

She got huffy. "Tom, somebody has to. I know what I know."

The chief put his hand up. "Debra, we know what you know too. And you're right, it's Stella Williams, you've been right, mostly right, all along. But go home. We've got this. He's not going anywhere. He's walking the course right now, and we've got our eyes on him. Trust me."

At that moment, Debra did trust him and was relieved she didn't have to watch Wendell anymore, because she really had to pee. She rolled up her window, and Tom, the chief of police, gave her a wave and a droll smile. "America the Beautiful" wafted through her head.

She started to pull away, and as she glanced out the window of her car, sure enough, there was Wendell, some distance off but visible with his hard hat and fluorescent vest, purposefully walking up the back nine. He stopped at a dip, the same dip where he had held forth on the day of the tour when he and the Board of Finance chair talked about sod and brown grass, the same dip where one could enjoy an excellent vista across the acreage. That dip must have been a sand trap at some point, she thought, although, inexplicably, she recalled a long-ago Golf Commission kerfuffle over whether those course hazards should properly be referred to as sand traps or bunkers. Bunkers. Wendell is standing at the edge of a bunker right now. Bunker, clunker, dunk, drunk, drunker, too drunk to hurl, ear rhyme, not too drunk to hurl, barf, bunker, bunker girl, Bunker Girl. BG.

It smacked her like a golf ball to the forehead.

Debra knew that BG was Bunker Girl and that Wendell did not play the bass guitar. She knew that Bunker Girl had worked at Florence Nuffield's shop and that her absence had delayed the fall sale. She knew that Bunker Girl had had a drink at the Triple B with a mustached Wendell and that Wendell had murdered her. She knew that Wendell had buried Bunker Girl at The Club, when it was The Club, and that he had buried her in a bunker, branding her, in perpetuity. She knew that Wendell had hijacked municipal governance and Public Comment to keep his murderous secrets buried. She knew that Bunker Girl was in a bunker.

And she knew which bunker.

Debra jumped out of the car and hustled back to where the chief was parked, still watching Wendell. He rolled down his window. She could see he was annoyed, but that was not her problem. She explained as much of it as she could, mindful that he was still watching Wendell and that she still had to pee, but he heard it, heard her, heard the whole painful conclusion, and nodded, already drafting a search warrant in his head, weighing the sufficiency or insufficiency of the probable cause she had provided for judicial scrutiny.

"Tom, you don't need a search warrant to dig up the bunker. It's town property. You just need consent. And it's an emergency."

He was nodding again. "Debra, okay, yes, but I want to get a search warrant for Wendell's house. We've started the process for an arrest warrant for Wendell based on the body under the boulders. I'll get someone to take my place here to keep Wendell under surveillance. Meet me at Town Hall in ten minutes. But keep it quiet. I do not want to spook Wendell."

"I know, oh my God." She turned to go back to her car but then turned back toward Tom. "No, Tom. Meet me at Wendell's backhoe at Public Works. And bring latex gloves and an evidence bag."

Behind the scenes, the gears were quickly engaged, but Public Works and the police could not begin digging up the bunker on the eleventh fairway without alerting Wendell, so those in the dead-body-in-a-bunker loop had the excruciating task of behaving normally, as if they had only a fibula buried under boulders to worry about. Another Emergency Meeting was called for that evening, and Public Comment was on the agenda. They did not go into Executive Session, but stayed on camera. The chief was there with one of his newer recruits, a cop so young that Debra worried his mother might be worried. The chief provided a purposefully mushy update, and although he and the young cop left the meeting room, they remained a presence, loitering in the windowed hallway, visible to all. The meeting forced Wendell into public view, as it were, and everyone was meant to behave as if this were normal, that governance was churning away, that the town was stable, that the institutions would survive, that this was just another day in Somerville.

Wendell read from the script and called for Public Comment. Jim Haggarty was there, complaining about his neighbor's garbage cans and about the news of a body at the golf course, stating that the town never should have bought the property in the first place, as if the correlation amounted to causation. He left.

"Anyone else for Public Comment?" Wendell recited. No one else was present. But instead of moving on, Wendell stood up and moved to the little Public Comment table. He sat down. He shakily moved the microphone toward him. He reached into his pocket and pulled out the earring. He clumsily clipped the earring to his ear, his hands twitchy. He pulled a gun from the backpack he carried and placed it on the table.

•••

Just as people often describe these moments, it happened both quickly and in slow motion. When Debra saw the earring on Wendell's ear, she knew they were in trouble, but within seconds the gun was on the table, and there was no time to share her concerns about costume jewelry. The selectmen all ducked, gasped, and scrambled. The cable access camera operator screamed and leapt to hide behind the bulky cable access gear, sending expensive pieces of town-owned equipment hurtling to the floor, tripping as she did over the heavy extension cord and disconnecting all cable access and recording equipment. The chief and the young cop reached for their weapons and the door. Wendell precariously went for the gun to do they knew not what.

But he never got a grasp on it, and instead he clumsily knocked it off the front of the little table. Wendell lurched over the table as if to grasp it in midair, but that never works, so of course the gun hit the floor and went off, sending an errant bullet underneath the table, shooting Wendell in the foot. He collapsed in agony, screaming in pain, but managed somehow to grab the gun off the floor, so he was now armed, bleeding, screaming, and accessorized.

He flailed only briefly as the young cop easily kicked the gun out of his hand, keeping his own weapon drawn and ready. The chief was doing his best to call for the ambulance, but the Somerville ambulance was, at that very moment, on an ambulance-town-sharing emergency in Rockmore, which did not have an ambulance. Although only a few minutes elapsed, there was just too much blood, and Wendell went into shock, vomiting, repeatedly.

It all looked too familiar to Debra. Except for the blood. The blood was new.

An ambulance finally arrived and drove off with Wendell, the siren screaming like an enraged cockatoo.

No one watching cable access at home knew what had happened because Wendell's ultimate and ugly use of Public Comment was a private screech, performed, as it turned out, for a select audience, and for the inadvertent heroism of the three-pronged plug, the community did not witness what he wanted them to see. But it took only a few minutes, and the rumors and reports were quickly circulating, pinging from one house to the next, confirming, thankfully, that only Wendell was injured and that everyone else was safe.

The next few hours were surreal, blurring statements, crime scene stuff, little evidence cones, paper bags for hyperventilating selectmen, phone calls to families, and tears and fears, but the Somerville police drove everyone to their homes with the understanding that additional witness statements might need to be taken.

Wendell survived shooting himself in the foot, but his attempted murder of the Board of Selectmen, or his attempted suicide, whichever it was, was a complete shambles.

He should have rehearsed.

By eight o'clock the next morning, David, Liza, Caroline, Brendan, Anthony, Howard, Henry, and Debra met in the first selectman's office, well segregated from the meeting room, which was still a crime scene. No one was going to go to work, but that didn't mean they were going to stay home. Peter was trying to shoo everyone out.

"Peter, I don't care if you have work to do. We're not budging until we find out what the hell is going on," said Liza. No one spent a moment worrying about Wendell's fate, but everyone wanted to know whatever could be known.

"No one knows anything yet," said Peter. "But no matter what, this looks like an illegal meeting, with no proper public notice. At least sit in separate rooms."

David rolled his eyes. "Really, Peter? A selectman is under arrest, a search warrant or a consent form to dig up town land is on the way, there are human remains found on the town-owned golf course property, and all of this is attributable to the first selectman, who shot himself in the foot, accidentally or on purpose, during Public Comment, thank God not on camera, and nearly killed all of us and you're worried about whether we have an illegal, unnoticed meeting to answer for?"

That settled it. They all hunkered down in the little conference room with Town Hall staff, and no one got anything done. Everyone wandered the halls, checking, listening in Peter's office to the police scanner. Selectmen and staff hugged each other all day, grateful that only Wendell had suffered damage.

Late in the day, the chief showed up. He reported that at Debra's urging, they had forensically searched Wendell's backhoe and found a dead mouse rotting away on a corroded earring that matched the photo of the earring on Debra's phone, which was a photo of the earring in Wendell's pocket. They had little trouble excavating the dimple near the old eleventh fairway and found Bunker Girl's bones, her broken neck, her compressed and crushed skeletal remains, all of which would prove to be of the right height and heft, buried deep inside the sand trap.

The chief sang Debra's praises and told everyone that had it not been for her hunches, her perseverance, and her intuition, they likely never would have looked for nor found Bunker Girl.

He was correct.

•••

Two nights later, there was another Emergency Executive Session. Nothing was as it should have been. All was tumult.

"Well," said Caroline, now the de facto emergency acting deputy first selectman. "We now have two crime scenes, or graves, or whatever. Unless we are advised to the contrary, we have no choice but to suspend discussions with developers. I think we have to advise Mrs. Partridge that her plaque is going to have to wait. We have to give Mrs. Devlin a heads-up that the square dance will have to be indefinitely postponed, and I think we have to assume that OREO 1 has no future until we are sure that there are no more bodies!" Caroline took a moment to gather herself. "Okay, I think we should go back on the record and vote that all activity associated with OREO 1 be indefinitely suspended. Can I assume that you will all support that?" There were nods and concurring murmurs. Wendell was not there to vote one way or the other, so the vote was unanimous in favor.

Twenty-four hours later, they had another Emergency Meeting, but not an Executive Session, so Public Comment was on the agenda. The selectmen sat there, governing more or less, and the seven or eight people who showed up at Public Comment wanted to know how they could be assured that there were no more bodies. It was an impossible question to answer, but no one could argue that it was an unreasonable question.

The next morning, Caroline and Brendan convened a meeting with the Catholic priest, the Congregational minister, and the Jewish rabbi ("What is this, a joke?" asked the rabbi) to see if Somerville Woods was now hallowed ground or a cemetery, or was there a special cleansing, or purgative, or something? "Caroline, you're clearly stressed," said Father George, but after a subdued chat, it seemed to all of them that a community interfaith prayer meeting might go a long way to calm everyone down, and although it could not provide answers, it might help put it all in perspective.

The emergency interfaith service was held. All plaques and dances were on hold.

Finally, the chief got a call from the state forensics unit. "Yep," he reported to the BOS in yet another Executive Session, "we got a match, a probable match, through a new DNA data bank. Abusive father situation, mother dead, so from what we can tell, the father never reported her missing. No, not in the missing persons system. No, he's long gone too, but he had a criminal record in Minnesota, nothing big, but the DNA match is confirmed. Distant relative backs it all up, including her photo. She left Minnesota right after high school, probably five or six years ago. And then it's almost as if she never existed after that, but now we know her real name."

•••

Stella's murder was straightforward. Money and matricide, a story as old as time.

Bunker Girl was circumstantial, but it did not take long for the investigators to weave all the threads provided by Debra into a sturdy fabric. Wendell's old driver's license was pulled up, showing his huge mustache. Debra produced the original group photograph from Wendell's campaign billboard and Patrick, Bob-Behind-the-Bar's son, confirmed the match. Chief Telford's recollections of Florence's shop and the delayed fall sale were made part of the official report. Vinnie had no firsthand knowledge, but he was the investigating cop, as it were, so his report was put in the mix. Mrs. Duncan was long gone, and her boarding house was now a Krispy Kreme. The payroll records of The Club and the interviews with all the maintenance guys were stirred into the pot. One of the investigators located the old GM, now an active adult living in over-fifty-five, age-restricted, high-end housing in another state, and he remembered the entire bunker remodel, in part because Wendell had changed so much after that day. He was pretty sure Wendell had a mustache the day before the bunker was completed. No, to his knowledge the trap was never touched again. Wendell's odd and obsessive behavior, his lies about playing football in high school or working in Florida on a golf course or taking classes in creative writing were all easily established as lies. His shifting positions about continuity of golf, or Dedicated Open Space, and the statements from the guys at The Club about his relationship to the bunker—all of it was circumstantial, but no one doubted for a moment that he had killed that girl and that he killed his mother, killed them, buried them, and then skulked behind land use policy and municipal governance and procedure to conceal his crimes.

He used his ill-gotten wealth to secure the services of defense counsel who, by sheer coincidence, was the very same attorney who had given Debra the name of K-9 Unit Sgt. Jeffrey Birmingham. The case was assigned to Judge Marlene Hamlin, who immediately and correctly recused herself from the proceedings. A different judge was assigned, and Wendell entered a plea of not guilty to both counts of murder. Wendell insisted on representing himself. Counsel did everything possible to withdraw from the case as soon as he had entered his appearance because Wendell was abusive, dismissive, and contemptuous of his recommendation that Wendell not testify in his own defense.

Ultimately, Wendell was permitted to represent himself, but counsel was not permitted to withdraw, as the seriousness of the charges warranted his ongoing participation. But once Wendell got the bullhorn, so to speak, he as much as ensured his own conviction. He insisted on a full trial, then insisted the trial was rigged, then insisted he be allowed to wear his NUDE hat during the trial, then insisted that a flurry of defense motions be considered and ruled on.

As incompetent as he was to defend himself, he was found competent to stand trial.

Most folks were only too happy to follow these events from the distance the local newspaper provided, but Debra was served with a subpoena to appear in court as a defense witness on Wendell's behalf. It was ridiculous. Defense witnesses offer alibis or forensic impossibilities or factual statements against a given prosecution. Debra had none of that, but a subpoena is a subpoena, so she showed up. She took the stand, was sworn in, and immediately informed the judge that she had no testimony to offer in Wendell's defense. But Wendell wanted to argue with the judge, or with Debra, and on a very legal and technical basis, the judge ordered Debra to step down and allowed Wendell to take the stand instead to testify as to why Debra should be compelled to testify.

They were trapped in an ouroboric circuit, a legal circle within a circle. Debra was forced to spend the day in court with barfy divorced guy. Again. No surprise, though, she was not forced to testify, because she had nothing to offer in Wendell's defense.

But she had a front-row seat. She learned everything about everything, why he did what he did, whom he blamed for it, his thoughts before, during, and after their meetings, Debra's tire, his love of tuna, the reason he had the earring, everything. She learned that "reversal fling" was "rehearsal thing" and that Bunker Girl's murder was just that, a rehearsal. His lawyer was correct of course. He opened his mouth and a polluted stream flowed forth, ultimately convicting him of two murders. No amount of guidance from counsel or admonishments from the judge caged his utterances, and he blathered on about his mother and her faults and her money and how much he loved Bunker Girl and his pocket and that it was just a rehearsal but it captured his heart, that none of it was his fault, that Debra Wolfson was to blame, that she had promised him a copy of *Kaboom!!* but had not delivered it, that he didn't even know anyone named Patrick, that the Republicans didn't stick with him, that the Democrats never believed he was elected in the first place, that he should be allowed to stay on the Board of Selectmen no matter what, that he just wanted to be on camera, in the spotlight, hide his secrets, and get all of the glamor and attention that was his due.

His testimony revealed it all, and if it was incredibly revolting, it was at least a relief.

Somerville had truth. Somerville had proof.

—EPILOGUE—

Immediately upon Wendell's arrest, Granny Charter revealed a well-buried provision about removal of a selectman for "inappropriate conduct," and the vote was unanimous to that effect. Caroline continued as emergency acting deputy first selectman, and when the election cycle came round, she chose not to run. Instead, young Brendan was elected by a wide margin as the new first selectman. The interfaith service had given solace to only a few, but all of the therapists in town reported a huge surge of people looking for appointments. The crime scene designations were finally lifted, and the golf course property was liberated. Mrs. Partridge's Appleby plaque was erected right where the boulders had been stacked. All of the ceremony photos were on the town website, but it was difficult for Debra to derive carefree joy from the photos, the plaque, or the ceremony. She favored a hiatus, but she was the only one, and her motion for a stabilizing period lost in a four-to-one vote. She was not ashamed of her tentative impulse.

Wendell's property taxes on his house, or legally, possibly, his mother's house, or possibly his mother's estate's house, fell fully delinquent, and the tax collector was able to force a foreclosure, by which process the town got title to the house. The BOS voted to demolish the house, thrilling the neighbors who did not want a murderer's abode impacting their property values, as it most surely would have. The Board of Selectmen, exhausted as they were by the long battle over the golf course property, did not want to have to figure out a use for the lot, so they unanimously voted that the lot become Dedicated Open Space, protected by a conservation easement, duly recorded on the land records.

Given the size of the Wendell/Stella pile of dough, he was ordered to reimburse the state for the costs of his trial and the associated investigations. No one knew what the balance of the fortune was or whether it would be subject to further court orders under receivership, but only a month after he began his prison term, Debra got a letter from Wendell.

> Dear DD (Dumpy Debra) Hah!
> We have our differences, I know (and you still owe me a copy of the volcano book), Hah again, but I still have money, though after I pay my lawyer who did nothing and was useless, I might have enough to pull together a production company for television. I am contacting writers and people to help me tell the story (no one can tell it the way I can tell it and of course I am the whole story), but I will surround myself with only the best people, the very best, exclusively the best, to write a five or six part mini-series about my experience as a murderer and a selectman. I enclose a draft of a script or treatment they call it that I have written. You were there at the beginning sort of so I have instructed my attorney to make sure that you are given all of my notes and notebooks (except the ones the cops are keeping). I am looking for investors and thought you might want to invest. I can make you look good (even thin!) or I can make you look bad. Your choice. Let me know if you want to support this artistic great thing. Wendell

This "artistic great thing" was all in Wendell's head, and there it would remain. Debra turned the letter over to Chief Drummond because she didn't want to keep it, she didn't want to throw it away, and it was vaguely extortionate.

All the yellow tape disappeared, and red tape took its place, generating new requests for proposals for the development of active-adult-over-fifty-five-age-restricted housing for the designated fifty acres that had been allotted under OREO 1. All the amenities were in the planning stages and got real traction, or as much as they could get given that there was no money in any near-term budget for the construction of any of these amenities, but at least the planning and priorities were going forward. The dog park people had a joint fundraiser, the water playground and public pool people began a clean-water initiative, and the fire department association adopted the hockey rink as its baby.

The much delayed square dance was a huge and cathartic success. The fire marshal would not permit it to take place in the gym (too many people), nor would he permit bales of hay to be used as benches or decoration (fire hazard), but he was seen doing the do-si-do with Mrs. Devlin during the high point of the evening, which ultimately took place in the much larger and newer high school gym, sans hay.

The DTC and the RTC established an annual joint picnic, where a vigorous just-for-fun tug-of-war would be the featured activity.

Stella Williams' remains were ritually interred next to her husband, and as per a court order, Wendell's funds were used to pay for the marker and clergy. The Board of Selectmen, the chief of police, and Sylvia Purdue attended the interment.

They all moved on, painfully at first, but then life took over, making room for joy and normalcy.

Vinnie quietly fell in love with Dr. Stephanie Jordan, the environmental consultant, and happily she fell in love with him too. They married, and Judge Marlene Hamlin officiated at the wedding. Vinnie is running for governor, and all the polls are predicting an easy win.

Rockmore rented space on the Somerville radio tower, and at Somerville's urging, Rockmore purchased its own ambulance.

The young woman's remains were unclaimed because there was no one to claim them. The BOS started a fundraiser—not a fundraiser exactly, more like hitting up individuals they knew and trusted for funds—to bury the poor girl in the Somerville cemetery with a proper marker and all that should go with it. The money flowed in, well beyond the funeral and marker costs, so the BOS voted to designate the additional funds as a special fund in her name for humane and humanitarian needs, managed by Peter, and to be disbursed only by a unanimous vote of a future Board of Selectmen.

Her remains were interred, and two hundred people showed up at the graveside, Somerville residents, Patrick, Vinnie, Chief Telford, Somerville cops, the Public Works guys, the state investigators, the entire Conservation Commission, Mrs. Devlin, Betty, Sgt. Birmingham, the fire chief, Professor Cooper, Peter Reilly, and many more, and there were guitars, some singing, and a few statements, but it was not a town event or a religious service or a family funeral, so there were no big speeches or formal eulogies. The young woman was left, finally, to rest in peace. A good number of folks came back to Debra's house, and her table overflowed with homemade baked goods from dozens of generous Somerville kitchens. It was, at one and the same time, a weepy and light occasion, involving, as the day moved toward evening, wine and pizza, many tears, hugs, and a good deal of laughter.

Public Comment returned to its civil, civic, cranky, and constructive place in Somerville life. For those who carp, for those who praise, for those who show up only once in a while, Public Comment is there, the way it once was and always should be.

–ABOUT THE AUTHOR–

S.L. Jacobs has spent most of her adult life at the intersection of law and politics and, even with that, she still manages to find hope and humor in the world. Although she hails from Los Angeles, she is a long-time resident of Connecticut, with residential stints in Washington DC, France, and England. She is a loud and long-standing participant in any choir that will have her, and she has performed in and written for dozens of community theater productions (if the show calls for a bossy woman, she gets the part). *Public Comment* is her debut novel.

– ACKNOWLEDGEMENTS –

We write alone, but we rewrite, edit, cut, angst, shred, query, and publish with others by our side.

I am deeply grateful for early reads and critiques by authors, educators, and mavens Erika Krouse, Rachel Weaver, Michaela Papa, Ron Blumenfeld, Tina C. Weiner, and Colleen J. Shogan.

Many thanks to Jericho Writers in the UK and to the Washington Writers Conference for all the lessons learned and, especially, to Killer Nashville 2023, where *Public Comment* was named a Claymore Award Finalist.

I owe David Duhr and his team at Write By Night LLC more than I can say. Their services, support, and friendship have proven invaluable.

I am indebted to David Bushman, whose early and ongoing enthusiasm for *Public Comment* gave me hope and heart, leading, ultimately, to publication with Fayetteville Mafia Press/Tucker DS. David Bushman and Scott Ryan at FMP have been generous and supportive, and I am proud to be an FMP author.

A special thank-you to Parker Keirn, who kept a straight face when I asked him if I could climb into and explore his golf course backhoe/front loader. He answered all my backhoe questions and even showed me how to spin the seat!

To my husband, Stephen, I owe everything.

MORE TO READ AT TUCKERDSPRESS.COM

www.ingramcontent.com/pod-product-compliance
Lightning Source LLC
LaVergne TN
LVHW012040070526
838202LV00056B/5547